THE TEMPLE LEGACY

(The Temple - Book 1)

As an author, D. C. Macey has always been fascinated by the conflict between good and evil that seems to have dogged the footsteps of man throughout the ages. In this novel, good and evil once again come together as the worst vices of bad men seek to overwhelm the innate goodness of ordinary human nature.

Set in the present day, this first novel in The Temple series introduces young church minister Helen Johnson and archaeologist Sam Cameron as they struggle to find their feet in the face of evil's unexpected assault.

Also by D. C. Macey

The Temple Scroll - Published August 2016
The Temple Covenant - Published April 2018
The Temple Deliverance – Published April 2019

THE TEMPLE

LEGACY

(The Temple - Book 1)

Butcher & Cameron

D. C. MACEY

Published by Butcher & Cameron

ISBN: 9780993345821

Prologue

COAST OF LOTHIAN, 1308

All afternoon the old man stood staring across the broad waters of the Firth of Forth. He saw high tide come in around two. Later, as it turned to ebb, he dispatched four ships to the north. One after the other they slowly tacked away, struggling out into the worsening weather.

He watched the winter afternoon darken away into evening and witnessed the sea grow ever wilder, driven by the strengthening wind. Time and the growing distance shrank the ships to bobbing flecks. And one by one, they were hidden from his sight. His worry grew with the fading light; here the water was angry, but this was just a fraction of what his men faced as they sailed out beyond the firth and into the open sea.

They had set off in good spirits but even as the first of the ships pulled away from shore, that wind had started to freshen. In less fevered times he would have called a halt, waited another day, but theirs was an important task that could not be delayed. There was as much danger here on the land as there was at sea, perhaps more. He would trust in his men and thank God that the four ships he sent south the day before were already beyond the storm's reach.

The cold of the evening suddenly struck him as a shiver went to the marrow of his ageing bones. Henri de Bello turned his back on the sea and pulled his cloak around him; it was emblazoned with the distinctive Templar cross, now suddenly picked out by the flickering light of two torches. The torchbearers had been standing well back but quickly closed ranks with the old man as he turned. They were fitter and stronger, but there was no doubt authority sat on the older man's shoulders. The wind tore at the torchlight, throwing shadows that danced around the men as they moved steadily towards the shelter of a low building behind the headland.

He would pray for the crews. They are in God's hands now, he thought. And he must hurry; the task was not yet complete. There were plans still to execute and arrangements to make, while he was still able.

• • •

The storm had driven the ships apart, and in the darkness each now fought its own desperate battle for survival. The last of the four ships to leave had fared worst, a later start into the ever-worsening conditions had handicapped its progress more, and now it laboured alone as the wind screamed threats through the near empty rigging. A solitary patch of sail was up, trying to maintain some vestige of control, though the master and his crew had long since surrendered any attempt to hold the original course.

Spray flew through the dark, soaking those trying to find some shelter around the deck while the remorseless roll and pitch of the ship synchronised with each wave as it surged beneath.

It was miserable. The crew understood the circumstances and muttered quiet prayers for their lives. Meanwhile, the passengers, four Templar Knights and their sergeants, all crouched low, held tight where they could. Beneath them, in the hold, horses were crying. Earlier, while still in the firth, one horse had broken a leg, caught unawares and stumbling as the ship lurched violently in the growing seas.

The horse had been quickly dispatched, its throat opened by a sergeant's blade, but in the fermenting sea it had not been possible to put the carcass overboard. The ship's master had insisted the hatch be closed and sealed at once. The remaining horses were distressed by the sudden flood of equine blood as it flowed to and fro with the roll of the ship. The blood was now slowly congealing around their hooves and their dead stablemate's body.

They were frightened. They had good reason.

Impassive, crouched near the deck's stern shelter, the senior Templar Knight kept a firm grip on the bulwark while he watched the shipmaster's frantic exchange with his mate. Waving hands sometimes pointed south, other times westward towards distant lights on the shoreline of Fife; the men's shouted words were lost to the wind. Finally, they nodded in agreement. The master turned and struggled across the heaving deck towards the watching Templar Knight. The master's world was his ship, on board his word was law, yet he still felt slightly uneasy as he approached this man of God and war.

The master crouched down beside the Templar. 'My lord, we must make for shelter or we will all be lost,' he shouted and pointed towards the twinkling lights on the shoreline that called them to safety. 'A fishing village. We can shelter there and move on when the storm is past.'

For just a moment, Francis de Bresse held the master's gaze. Seeing fear in the man's eyes, he recognised it for what it was: truth. He had seen it before in other eyes: in battle, in execution, in many forms of death. In his experience, the eyes of men did not lie as they explored their own fate. He nodded, leaning forward to shout his words into the master's ear. 'Move quickly then. Is it a safe coast?'

'Safer than here,' screamed the master. Momentary relief propelled him up, shouting orders to his crew. Their responses quickened as they realised the ship was to head for land and safety.

De Bresse signalled the change in plan to his huddled knights and he saw their relief, shared it too and then wondered at more screaming from the hold. Another leg broken? He hoped it was not his own favourite, but whichever one, it would have to suffer unattended until they reached the haven. The crew were too busy saving the ship to open the hold now, even if they dared.

The combining wind and tide carried them towards land surprisingly quickly. The little cluster of distant lights had now opened into a wider arc, signalling the presence of fishermen's homes and a place of safety.

The master was peering ahead as the ship surged landward, his eyes searching for the breakwater, some feature that he would need to guide his ship past to reach safety, but he could not see it. He searched and searched again. Suddenly uneasy, he cast about. Where was it? All he could see was the string of lights flickering behind and above the surf as the great breakers rolled and foamed across the beach. A sudden fear struck him. A beach! Lights set in the dunes above! No lee, no safe haven. His stomach tightened into a knot and he turned to everyone and no one at once. 'Wreckers! Wreckers! We are lost!'

De Bresse looked on in horror. His task! God's task! Was it to fail even before the first day had passed? Now he could see the danger clearly, the ring of torches above the beach, bait luring them in and they were caught, carried forward by the driving force of combined wind and tide. There was neither time nor way to turn the ship around. Now he could hear the surf roaring, he could feel the keel grounding in the troughs between waves, then lifting again only to ground harder again and again as the ship was carried closer to shore on successive waves. The end seemed imminent and inevitable.

Bracing himself against the bulwark De Bresse signalled his knights, not even trying to speak over the roaring wind and surf. He looked each in the eye, and then took the heavy purse of gold from his waist and threw it far back out to sea. The wreckers would not have the Templars' gold, God's gold! The other knights recognised his purpose and each stood in turn, bracing themselves against the storm to hurl similar purses overboard. The funds for their mission, the labours of perhaps a thousand lifetimes, lost to the deep in just an instant.

The Templars edged forward along the ship, the sooner to meet their foe. Around them crewmen knelt down and cried or mouthed silent prayers while others milled about cursing the wreckers. They cursed the Templars too, for their pig-headed determination to set sail in such conditions. Others went overboard, hoping to swim through the huge waves and beyond the arc of torches. Futile. All knew they were already dead men.

Suddenly, as the ship ground on to the beach with a final backbreaking lurch, a rain of arrows showered down. Men fell, some pierced by arrows, some thrown by the force of the boat's impact. The mast groaned and broke loose; it fell, crushing others. Screams and cries and blood mixed with the howling wind and whipping spray.

De Bresse leapt ashore, followed by his two surviving knights. Together they charged up the beach towards the torches that burned in the dunes. The open beach was a killing ground; any man left there was dead or waiting for death, from an arrow or a cutthroat's blade.

'Beauseant!' Now De Bresse was shouting as he ran up the beach, the battle cry of the Templars, *Be Glorious.* 'Beauseant!' The knights to either side of him picked up the cry too, screaming for blood and vengeance. For De Bresse, events seemed to play through in slow motion. He had expected to die in God's service, probably violently, but here? On a dark nowhere beach? To die for no reason save the greed of local brigands? No honour here, it was not how he had imagined so many years of loyal service to God would end. But the task: he must get the box safely away from these attackers. Somehow, get it back to the master, back to Henri de Bello so he might start the mission again.

Without their shields, helmets or chainmail the three surviving Templars were vulnerable to the arrows that traced their path up the beach. The knight to De Bresse's left fell with a gasp and two arrows through his chest. Reaching the top of the dunes, the two remaining knights were met by a surge of attackers. Amidst swinging sword blows, the two parties were past each other in a moment. Four wreckers were down, chopped, cut, butchered in the flashing of the great Templar swords, but De Bresse was wounded too. A sword cut through his left arm, hard into bone.

The wreckers paused for a moment, suddenly shocked by what they had brought ashore. This was no soft touch merchant ship. The unharmed Templar turned to face them, shouting that De Bresse should go and see to their task. De Bresse hesitated, he was not afraid to stand and fight, to die, but there was still work to be done, and to do anything of use he would first need to tend to his wounded arm, to stop the flow of blood. He turned towards the darkness, moved beyond the torches and struggled away into the dunes as the remaining knight fought a short and futile rearguard.

The knight sliced open a wrecker, splitting his side and belly with such force that his blade lodged in the man's spine and as the body collapsed it momentarily trapped the knight's sword. In a flash, the wreckers took their chance, slicing at the Templar's hamstrings, bringing him down to his knees. From that angle, he could never free his blade; suddenly he was defenceless. The wreckers closed in and the Templar suffered a flurry of wounding blows. He was chopped and slashed and made to feel pain as the assailants sought to exact a bloody and protracted vengeance for their own dead.

Cheering in triumph, their leader made a fatal error, getting too close too soon; he stood over the dying Templar and prepared to deliver the killing stroke. In his death throes the Templar stretched up and with the iron grip of his warrior's sword hand grasped the leader's genitals through the thin cloth of his trousers. In one fluid motion the knight's fingertips probed and positioned, sliding in behind the testicles while thumb wrapped tight round the penis, encircling all, then tightened hard and ripped everything down and off. For a moment the leader froze in silent shock, then, suddenly a woman, he collapsed squealing in a castration flood of blood and urine and pain. The Templar died a much faster, easier death.

De Bresse hurried away towards the darkness; he was followed by a final hopeful arrow. It plunged into his back, knocking him forward and down. He rolled into the darkness, over and down between the dunes. The arrow's shaft snapped and each roll pressed the head deeper into his body. Finally, he came to rest at the dune's base. He was still, staring up at the dark and angry clouds, watching bright starlit gaps that opened and closed at the whim of the driving wind. He felt everything was becoming distant, knew he was fading, dying.

He experienced a passing pang of distress at not completing his task: that faded as he anticipated death and thirsted for life eternal. His hand still kept tight hold of his sword and his body felt the comforting pressure of a slim lead box, his task, pressed into his waistline. He was aware of sand from the disturbed dune trickling slowly down to cover him, hiding him from view. De Bresse faded, the task faded: slipping under the sand, buried, it was as though they never were.

Chapter 1

WEDNESDAY 1st MAY

Cassiter sat at the desk in his private office. His firm occupied the whole self-contained top floor of a building on Edinburgh's Princes Street. The floors beneath his office were occupied by a department store. Set high above the capital's most famous thoroughfare, the office suite had wonderful panoramic views. His private office looked south, towards the Old Town and the castle, which together combined to form an almost Disneyesque backdrop.

Between his office window and the fantasy scene were the Princes Street Gardens, creating space to offset the theatrical skyline. Looking down into the gardens Cassiter could see the warm midmorning sun had already attracted some eager early season sun worshipers to the benches.

There was no obvious public access point to his office, a private lift carried staff and invited visitors directly up from the car parking bay in the building's basement. On exiting the lift, visitors immediately encountered a sour faced woman sat behind a reception desk; she seemed slightly out of place in the exclusive environment. Running off to left and right, a broad and bright corridor fed into the office spaces from which a tight little team ran a thriving international trading business, buying commodities and products in transit and selling them on for a modest return long before they reached their destinations. No products to handle or warehousing to secure, just money to move and records to keep. Other work was planned here too, but that sat off the public record: Cassiter's world.

Far below, the basement parking was accessed from a lane at the rear of the building. A lane that sat in near permanent shadow save for a few days at the height of summer.

During working hours, the lane was frequented by delivery vehicles and department store staff slipping out for a quick smoke. By night, the lane was the preserve of the carnal, courting couples who could not wait to get home or those who had someone else waiting at home. No office signs and no welcome mat; his was an invisible business. Most people working in the department store below were oblivious to its presence and those few that were aware had no idea what it did: some IT stuff probably.

Cassiter spun his chair away from the window and back to his desk, he read and reread the newspaper article in front of him. A sense of anticipation prickled his spine. Could this be it? After searching for so long, a genuine breakthrough? He carefully folded the newspaper so just the relevant article was visible, framed the paper in his phone's view screen and photographed it. This might be big news and he must get it to Eugene Parsol as soon as possible. Before sending it, he expanded the picture, checking the text was clear and legible. Satisfied, he sent it off. Then he turned his attention to other things while waiting for events to unfold.

His was a challenging role. Often the silent observer, the monitor and reporter of events. Yet, as and when occasion demanded, he and his team could and would rearrange the pieces: a cruel tool of swift response. Few ordinary people could sustain such a conflicted mix of attributes without becoming blunted. But Cassiter was not ordinary; he relished the contrast and thrived on his work, loving both the still and the storm.

He returned to the article. Could this old church minister really hold the key? Had this old man in an unguarded reminiscence let slip the clue they needed? His team had conducted endless searches, silently scouring the country, trawling through church records and academic libraries, checking and rechecking. Now, here at last was a possible reference, just popping up in a local newspaper's profile page.

It was one passing and slightly ambiguous reference, perhaps just an old man's ramble, mentioning some old blade, a Christian dagger, a relic of sorts. It did not sound very holy, not for modern Christians anyway. The local journalist had not picked up or developed the line, just used the quote and left it unexplored, had probably only included it to boost his word count while privately dismissing it as the babbling of old age. It was almost certain that amongst the whole readership only Cassiter had given the comment a single thought. It was his job to give things thought.

From here, his team and their contacts stretched out around the world. Unseen, unknown: as anonymous as the office they reported to. The team worked hard, sliding around life's edges, finding, fixing, finalising.

Most of Cassiter's people were based abroad and he had been a little reluctant to take on a job so close to home; never foul your own doorstep was a useful maxim. However, it had come in as a simple but confidential research job, highly paid and no hassle, and Eugene Parsol was one of his longest standing clients, so he had taken it on. For nearly three years, his people had been working on the job without success. But the contract and generous fees continued unabated.

Now this, not much to go on, but warmer than anything that had been unearthed before. What did the old man mean or was it really just ranting senility? Cassiter's deliberations were interrupted as the phone in his hand started to ring. He checked the caller. It was Eugene Parsol. Cassiter answered it quickly. 'Hello, Cassiter speaking.'

'Cassiter, this is interesting. We need to know more as soon as possible. Whatever else you have on now, please stop it and focus on this alone,' said Parsol, his perfect English not quite masking a very slight hint of France.

'Cassiter, I want to be sure that no one else can follow the same trail, it must run cold behind you.' Only those few who really knew the man could fully appreciate the darker meaning in the things he often left unsaid.

'Yes, I understand.' Cassiter knew Parsol, appreciated the unspoken. He was already considering his approach. 'I know where the old man is, this will be straightforward.'

'Good, be sure to keep me fully informed of your progress, this may well be what we want. If so, I don't want anything getting in our way, do you understand? If you need more resources just use what you need. Money is no object. No object at all. You must act at once. Grasp the initiative while you can.'

'Yes, I...'

The phone went dead. Cassiter looked at it and shrugged. Parsol had made clear what was required, now it was up to him to deliver. It should not be difficult; the article had been published in a local newspaper whose distribution area included Dunbar, a small coastal town in East Lothian. Helpfully, the article had identified the sheltered housing complex where the old man lived. Time for action and he would need no extra help with this little job.

Cassiter's small but trusted team spent the afternoon harvesting information from both publicly available sources and from the apparently secure. He prepared a plan of action.

• • •

It was just after seven in the evening when Cassiter set off along the A1, the main east coast route out of Edinburgh. Locally the road is a commuter corridor to and from the city, but it stretches much further; follow it far enough and it eventually links Edinburgh with London. He reached the turning for Dunbar well before eight.

An inconspicuous parking spot off the high street met his needs. He waited for just a moment then got out to pursue his business. Short brown hair, a medium build and a face that was quite unremarkable; he could have been any age between thirty and forty-five. His appearance was exactly what anyone would aspire to if aiming to blend in anonymously, and behind the bland façade, he was sharp, hard and physically strong.

Midweek evenings in country towns are normally quiet affairs and Dunbar proved no exception. He would have preferred a Friday night, busier, some noise and more people to blend amongst. A Wednesday evening in May would not have been his chosen time for a job like this; it was still daylight, the northern evenings' long stretch into summer now well underway, and a handful of locals dotted here and there, going about their business.

He set an unhurried paced up to the High Street, a ribbon of confident two, three and four storey stone built buildings that had provided successive generations with shelter and prosperity. Cassiter's team had general, albeit unauthorised, access to most CCTV feeds, enabling him to identify camera blind spots. Without hesitation, he used that knowledge to proceed unrecorded.

Crossing over the High Street he walked on a little way and then turned into a quiet lane. Beyond the far end of the lane, he could just make out a splash of calm water, the Firth of Forth, but he was not interested in the view. He walked calmly down the lane. At the end, he turned the corner into a mainly residential street and walked a little further before ducking in behind the houses to reach a cluster of little homes; tranquil sheltered housing, a true haven for the old folk. But tonight evil was calling. It smiled contentedly and rang the first cottage's doorbell.

Archibald Buchan stirred at the sound of his doorbell. Confused for a moment, he struggled to think who would be at his door, wondered if he really wanted to bother answering it. A retired church minister, Archie to his friends, he had always taken care of himself, and now well into his eighties he was still doing pretty well, but time slows even the fittest. Archie's care worker had left half an hour earlier after helping him into his pyjamas and giving him some toast and tea. Archie was not expecting anybody else tonight.

The doorbell rang again. He turned down the television volume and pulled himself up. With a quiet grumble, he shuffled his slippers over the carpet as he journeyed slowly towards the door.

Cassiter smiled as the door opened. 'Good evening, sir, I'm so sorry to disturb you, Mr Buchan isn't it? I wondered, might I have a minute of your time please?'

'Ooh, I don't think so laddie, it's a bit late. Morning's best for me. Can you come back then?' Archie looked more closely at the man. He wasn't a carer, didn't wear a council ID card either. 'What's it about anyway?'

Cassiter smiled again. 'I'm only passing through this evening Mr Buchan, I've been visiting relatives up the road in Haddington and they showed me the local paper with the profile article on you. It's fascinating and I really had to speak with you about it, just for a few minutes please?' Cassiter smiled again and gave a slightly sheepish shrug. 'I'm an academic and I've been working up a paper on how time has changed the nature of Christian ministry in our parishes. Your experience seems so relevant, a real window on the subject.'

'I don't know. It's far too late for that sort of thing now. Come back sometime during the day when I can think and we can make an arrangement.' Archie started to close the door. He didn't like being disturbed and something made him a little uneasy about this man, but in the daytime with care workers around he'd be more than happy to help him.

Cassiter leant forward, resting his forearm against the closing door, stopping its motion abruptly and bringing himself face to face with the old man whose body was now partly tucked behind the door. 'Please, it won't take long,' said Cassiter.

Archie's unease was growing into real concern. He could not close his door with this man leaning on it. The home next door was clearly empty for all to see, the resident having died recently, and he knew the next neighbour along the row was stone deaf; shouting for help would do no good. Worse still, the care alarm that could immediately summon a support worker was not hanging around his neck, as it should be. It was sitting on the table beside his TV chair. Archie was stuck.

'Go away, I've nothing to say to you, leave or I'll call the police,' he said. His once deep and powerful voice had faded in recent years and now it was thin, reedy, and suddenly it wavered slightly, betraying his concern.

Sensing the weakness, Cassiter could almost smell the rising fear. He smiled benignly. 'I'm so, so, sorry, I didn't mean to worry you. Look, I'll go away now, but maybe I could write and make an appointment? We could speak on easier terms. Perhaps when your carer's around?' he said. His voice oozed concerned sincerity and his arm eased back a little, releasing the pressure on the front door.

Feeling the door go slack a sense of relief washed over Archie. He nodded agreement. 'Yes, we can do that, but only during the day.' He flexed the door slightly, moving back half a pace and sidestepping from behind it, better to bid his unwelcome visitor goodnight.

Cassiter smiled at him and nodded in seeming agreement. He was calm, but with the slightly detached sense of pleasure he always found when things worked out as planned and a victim succumbed. Archie Buchan had made a mistake, a big mistake. His half step back into the hallway of his little home was all that was required to guarantee Cassiter's seamless entry. In a sudden movement Cassiter pressed forward again, he pushed the door hard and fast, it swung wide open, brushing Archie backwards and leaving him completely exposed.

One step forward and Cassiter had the old man on the floor. He swung out a foot and kicked the front door closed as he passed. Now he could begin work properly. Standing just inside the door he paused and from his shoulder bag pulled out a disposable forensic suit, complete with cap and shoe covers.

He put them on as Archie Buchan stared up in stunned amazement. Then Cassiter grabbed the old man by the collar of his pyjamas and pulling him to his feet, he propelled him backwards into the lounge.

Cassiter spoke calmly as he pushed the old man down into his armchair, but his tone made clear who was in charge. 'Now Mr Buchan, I'm interested in your newspaper article. I want you to tell me simply and clearly what I need to know and then things won't be so unpleasant for you. Okay?'

Archie sat in silence. He was frightened and did not know what to do. He nodded his understanding even though he didn't actually have the slightest idea what this madman wanted.

'Good, it's so much easier when people co-operate,' said Cassiter. He smiled warmly. Crouching down beside the armchair, he produced a copy of the newspaper article and scanned it for a moment, allowing Archie's sense of confusion and tension to rise. Then he suddenly looked into the old man's eyes and stretched out his left hand to grip the old man's right hand, forcing their fingers to slide together, interlocking in what appeared a perverse gesture of affection. 'Tell me about the blade, Mr Buchan, I need to know.'

'I don't know what you are talking about,' said Archie. Fear coursed through his body, matched by despair. He knew no one would be coming to his aid.

Cassiter's voice remained calm. 'Archibald, Archibald, you do know. You know you do. You must tell me at once...' He paused and smiled. He held up the article with his free hand and read out the dagger quote, then fell silent and looked steadily into Archie's eyes, waiting for an answer. After a moment of silence, he shook his head and tutted quietly.

'You told the journalist you had taken care of an old Christian artefact, a medieval dagger. You told the newspaper, why won't you tell me too?' Then in a suddenly hard voice, he shouted into Archie's face. 'The dagger. Tell me now!'

At last Archie understood exactly what Cassiter wanted. He had guarded the secret for so many years, how could he have been so stupid as to mention it to that journalist? In fact, he could hardly remember what had been said; perhaps he had just got too tired and let his guard down. His mind whirred, could he resist this man? Maybe in the past, but he wasn't so strong anymore. He didn't think he could hold out for long, but he would try. Hunching his shoulders a little, he shook his head in defiance, and averted his gaze. 'No!'

Cassiter felt a thrill inside at this blunt rejection, his victim presenting him with an invitation to apply some pressure. He would oblige. His fingers were still tightly interlocked with Archie's. With a strong hand and steady pressure, he very slowly bent back the fingers of Archie Buchan's right hand. The old man was helpless to resist as one by one his old finger joints began to snap.

Cassiter watched the old man's face, heard the moans grow into howling screams. He felt the old man's squirming, sensed the intense pulses of suffering, so strong they almost seemed to transfer through to his own hand. He thrilled at the electric tension and savoured the cracking and grinding of each old finger until they were all reduced to useless jelly sticks. He rolled them gently between his own strong fingers for a little while longer, relishing the cries and gasps of pain as each movement ground shattered bone ends against each other; triggering fresh waves of agony that fired contorted ripples across Archie Buchan's tear streaked face. Then, satisfied with his work, he let go and looked carefully at the old man.

Archie's screaming finally subsided, but his continuing distress was signalled by the heavy rhythmic groans that accompanied his every breath. Tears continued to flow down his cheeks as his left hand struggled to support the right. It was no use, wherever he touched caused more pain, eventually he just settled on supporting the wrist and avoiding any movement in the broken bones. It took many minutes for his distress to settle into a frightened and sullen silence, broken only by occasional little whimpers and rapid but shallow breathing.

Cassiter had remained crouching in front of the old man, now he smiled. 'Now then, I'm sure you understand I need to know about the dagger. Do you want to tell me now?' The inflection in his voice mimicked concern. 'Let's put this pain behind you, hey? We can make it stop, just tell me what I need to know.' Cassiter leant forward. He carefully wiped the tears from Archie Buchan's face and stroked his hair back into place.

'I don't want to hurt you. You know that, don't you? Help me, please, hmmm? Just tell me what I need to know.' He cupped the old man's chin and pulled his face up so their eyes could meet. He drank in the pain, the weakness and the fear in the old man's eyes.

Archie so wanted to tell, to give this monster exactly what he was asking for, but he could not get the words to flow properly, his brain seemed to be repeatedly stalling, tripping the words off his tongue before he could say them.

Archie looked down at his broken, twisted hand. Even while he was consumed by the pain and fear of the moment, he was acutely aware of the monster watching him. He had to tell him what he wanted, to make him stop, make him go away. He just needed to be alone with his pain. Then, something strange started to happen. Suddenly he could not feel the pain in his hand, his body started tiny convulsions, almost imperceptible twitching, shaking, and then he slumped forward, sliding off the chair.

His attacker made no attempt to break the fall, watching dispassionately as Archie slumped to the floor and slid onto his back. Archie Buchan mumbled and shook and could not speak for trying. His stroke was massive. Now he was still, lying prone on the floor, his head twisted to one side, cheek resting on the carpet. Only his eyes moved, they watched his tormentor. Frightened, bitter, silent eyes.

Cassiter realised what had happened at once, was suddenly concerned, he had not yet gathered the necessary information. This man must not die until he had the required answers. Leaving his victim in silent suffering, he started a careful search.

It took less than fifteen minutes to search the tiny home. Nothing. Now, considering the repercussions of failing to gather the information, Cassiter returned to his victim.

Trapped, frozen tight in a broken body, Archie Buchan understood his own predicament, knew it was all over for him now. Yet behind a wall of frustration and fear, he felt a growing sense of triumph. Triumph that he had managed to keep the secret. This monster had got nothing from him, his friends would remain safe and he could face God with a clear conscience.

His eyes rolled off to one side, seeing the television and beside it the photo of himself with his friend, John Dearly, his protégé. It had been taken outside the parish church just before Archie's retirement. His eyes smiled, suddenly content. A happy vision to leave the world with, he was ready to meet his maker and this monster could do no more damage.

In need of inspiration, Cassiter glared at his victim. There must be a way to get information from him, but how? How? He was about to kick the old man when he noticed his gaze and traced it to the photo. With a cry of triumph Cassiter crossed the room and picked up the picture, instantly recognising it for what it was; the lead he needed.

Archie saw Cassiter pick up the picture, saw the monster's elation and realised that he had just betrayed his closest friend and the secret they shared. His little moment of triumph and consolation evaporated, lapsing into dark, bitter despair. His spirit finally withered, he was beaten. He watched Cassiter's look of growing pleasure. Oh God. What hell had he unleashed on his friend?

From his place on the floor all Archie could see was carpet, a sideways angle of the television and Cassiter moving behind it. In a detached way he wondered what Cassiter was doing with the television, but he didn't really care, nothing mattered now, he had betrayed everything, everyone. Then Cassiter was gone from his view and the front door banged shut. Just the television and carpet left in his life. Could he last until his morning carer arrived? He did not think so.

Slowly, almost imperceptibly, little wafts of smoke started to drift from the television. Then flames, small at first but growing: smoke began to curl up above the television and roll overhead as it expanded to fill the room. He realised it was going to end badly for him. Very badly.

Chapter 2

THURSDAY 2nd MAY

Old Edinburgh grew up packed tight along the ridge that joined castle and royal palace. Expansion to the north was barred by the ridge's sheer drop down to the Nor Loch, now drained to create Princes Street Gardens. To the south, the city spread down the ridge and up the next, filling much of the trough between. Properties built across successive ages crowded in on top of each other as they jostled for space; sometimes stretching down to fill the trough below, sometimes just hiding it from view.

Right in the heart stands the National Library of Scotland, a big stone-built building. From its main street level on George IV Bridge, it rises up four or five solid but unremarkable storeys. However, below street level the building drops away unseen, down into the trough beneath; a reflection of the city itself, passers-by see what they see, but there is always more, the unseen, the unknown.

From the library's understated doorway leading out onto George IV Bridge Helen Johnson emerged into the street, pausing for a moment to let the afternoon sun caress and warm her face.

In her thirties, and loving life, she was exploiting every opportunity her church exchange had brought. Over from

America, she had landed lucky with the opportunity to develop her experience in Scotland. She loved her work and thrived on the proximity of so much learning, art and the sometimes controversial culture too. As a twenty-first century female and a church minister too, she considered herself both liberated and enlightened: able to make up her own mind and to make her own way in life.

Natural confidence and poise complemented her red hair and pretty face as she stepped out along the pavement, heading south for the short walk home. Home was a neat flat in one of the sandstone tenements that lined many of the inner-city's streets. A church property that came with her job, it was situated in Causewayside, part of the university district and just outside her parish's boundary. A familiar face emerged from a newsagent's store and Helen waved, calling out a greeting. 'Hi Grace! How are you doing?'

Grace McPhee was nearly twenty and blessed with a real sense of fun. She smiled and paused to chat.

'Helen, have you been in that library again?' said Grace, teasing with what was only a half-mocking reprimand. Grace loved life today and she could not help but view books as a barrier to living rather than a bridge to a richer life. School had not been a high point for Grace, though she had recently resolved to go to college after the summer. 'Aren't you meant to be going away on holiday today, Helen? You should be at home packing and getting ready.'

The two women had met through Grace's mother, a senior elder at the church Helen was working with. While Grace was not particularly committed to religion, she did help out at the church, partly to keep her mother happy, partly from habit. It seemed to Grace that she had been helping at the church all her life. She would set up chairs for church meetings, sort flowers, and do a bit of cleaning or whatever else might be needed.

Grace had now reached the point in life where she needed to spread her wings and her zest for living was constantly challenged by her mother's strict views. She did still try to please her mother, and certainly tried to shield her from some aspects of how modern girls lived their lives. The pair would bump along, grating, sparking and having the occasional flare up, but love and family, and mothers and daughters always brought them back into some sort of harmony, until the next time.

Helen smiled. 'I'm heading home right now. It won't take me long to get things together. Sam's picking me up about six.' Helen had met Sam Cameron a few months before, soon after she arrived in Edinburgh. He was an archaeology lecturer at the university. They were from very different backgrounds and both had been a little surprised to realise how much they enjoyed each other's company. They even found it easy to disagree without falling out.

Today he was taking a group of students away on a field trip, and Helen had signed up to do the catering. It was an opportunity for the two of them to spend some time together away from the bustle of the city.

'Well, have a good time,' said Grace. Smiling, she leant forward a fraction to rest her hand gently on Helen's forearm. 'Though I'm not sure digging holes is my idea of a great holiday. I'll take the Costas any day.'

Helen grinned back. 'I'm not doing any of the hole digging. I'll just be sitting out soaking up some sun, cooking barbeques, and watching the world go by for two weeks. Just like Spain!'

'That sounds more like it, great. You have a good time then and I'll see you when you get back,' said Grace.

Grace disappeared into the pavement crowd and Helen set off for home. Living in the university district made for a lively atmosphere and was convenient for just about everything. The great thing about this old city, she thought, was that everything was close by, one thing layered on another.

Helen crossed Lothian Street and moved into the heart of university land. She paced quickly across Bristo Square; the pedestrianised space that spread between the university's imposing McEwan Hall and the Potter Row Student Union. She spotted John Dearly, the church minister. He was standing on the far side of the square, deep in conversation with Elaine McPhee, Grace's mother.

Elaine had dark brown hair cut short in a practical style, with no attempt made to mask the streaks of grey that had begun their steady spread. A neat but plainly dressed woman of around fifty, her tweed skirt and jacket made no concessions to the imminent arrival of summer. Helen smiled and waved to them as she passed; they acknowledged her wave warmly but without breaking their conversation.

John Dearly was a worried man. Tall and slim, with cropped grey hair, John was a confirmed bachelor. Now in his sixties, he had devoted more than thirty years' service to his parish. All those years ago, he had arrived as Archie Buchan's assistant and following Archie's retirement he had been selected and called by the parishioners to fill Archie's place.

John planned to retire in three or four years himself and he had harboured thoughts of joining his old mentor at the retirement complex in Dunbar. Based on today's news that plan was lost.

Reports had spoken of a dreadful fire, but the church's bush telegraph was working overtime and throughout the day, darker and darker reports had been seeping out. Elaine had just shocked him with the latest word, and he was struggling to come to terms with it.

'Are you sure about this? Who could possibly have wanted to hurt the old boy like that? And why? Why?' he demanded, not expecting a rational answer.

Elaine nodded. 'No doubt about it, John. The fire investigators haven't finished yet, but the word is pretty clear. Somebody tampered with his television. Officially, the police want to wait for an autopsy report, but you know we have plenty of members over in Dunbar and the word is filtering out. It's not been announced yet but it seems like he had some pretty nasty stuff done to him before he died.' Her normally gruff tone wavered slightly as she grimaced and momentarily averted her gaze.

'He was such a good man, God rest his soul,' said John.

'Amen to that,' said Elaine.

'When will the autopsy report be done?'

'Tomorrow, I think. We'll need to make arrangements to attend the funeral in Dunbar too, but who knows when that'll take place? It depends on when the authorities release his body. I'll keep you posted and we'll probably need to run a minibus down there for it. I know many of the older parishioners will want to go from here.' Elaine's blunt speech pattern had reasserted itself, composed again to mask the pained emotions she was feeling at the loss of an old friend and spiritual guide.

John nodded agreement. 'I think Archie always wanted me to officiate at his funeral. We'll need to liaise with the minister in Dunbar about that. I'll give him a call and talk it through with him.'

'Right, I'll leave that to you. I'll make a start on our own arrangements in the meantime. But John,' the elder hesitated and looked around, almost conspiratorially or perhaps she really was just a little nervous. Taking the minister by the arm, she turned so they were close together with nobody able to cross their line of speech. 'I have to say it again; we do need to resolve the parish's succession issue. You have been putting it off for too long.'

Elaine was concerned about the parish's future and right now felt John was not addressing it as he should. The Church of Scotland comprises a host of individual parishes. Each has a degree of autonomy and selects its own minister. The minister is in turn supported by the parish's own administrative court of elders, the Kirk Session. From amongst the elders emerges the session clerk, Elaine, the elder who guides and organises the others, ensuring the parish keeps the records and the rules.

Wider Church rules stress that retiring ministers should never influence the selection of their successors. However, by informal custom long since lost in the church's past, St Bernard's operated at slight variance from the rule. It bothered nobody, caused no harm.

At St Bernard's, the incoming minister served first as an assistant in the parish, building relationships and becoming familiar with those little quirks of parish life that set St Bernard's apart. As the parish was blessed with a generous trust income, it could afford the cost of an assistant without reference to others and the procedure had just rolled along forever. It seemed an innocent tradition, but a very important one to all John's predecessors, a process they had maintained and defended with a quiet unswerving determination. Now the responsibility, the burden, all rested on John's shoulders.

As one of the many local parishes that made up the Edinburgh Presbytery, St Bernard's was subject to the rulings of the presbytery, and on a day-to-day basis, the scrutiny of the presbytery clerk.

It seemed the newly appointed presbytery clerk wanted to make his mark. Elaine had got wind that making his mark meant ensuring John's parish abandoned its somewhat idiosyncratic local traditions and fell into line with the rest. He viewed their quirks as aberrations blotting his presbytery's jotter and he intended to bring the parish into line. That was something she could not allow to happen and she needed John to step up.

John sighed. 'I know, I know, but is this really the moment to be thinking about it? It's waited this long, I'm sure it can wait a little longer, can't it? We have an old friend to bury, let's at least do that first. Please?'

Elaine was not deflected by his response. 'The truth is I don't know how long we can wait. Do you? With Archie gone only you have a full understanding. If you get hit by a bus, we're sunk. The parish tradition, your tradition, it will all be lost forever.'

On the rare occasions that she made an effort to sound warm it never really worked. Today, she was pained by the loss of Archie Buchan and faced again with John's seemingly endless procrastination over selection of his successor. She was doubly unhappy and she was making no effort to soften her style.

In spite of her gruffness, John knew her, liked her and depended on her. When a much younger Elaine McPhee had found herself suddenly widowed, with a baby daughter to support, all three had seemed to grow naturally into each other's lives. John trusted her and understood her, though they did not always see eye to eye.

'You know this can't wait any longer,' she said. 'We're not like an ordinary parish. We can't just wait for one minister to go and then appoint another. Succession needs to be assured, needs to be prepared for. Needs to be sorted.'

'Yes, yes. We… I have responsibilities to fulfil. As soon as we've buried Archie we'll make a start, okay?' John's tone sought some reconciliation.

'I suppose that will have to do,' grumbled Elaine. She fixed the minister with a stern eye. 'But we really need somebody strong, with a good sense of place and history. Our history. Somebody rooted here,' she pointed forcefully down towards their feet. 'That American girl won't do. Not at all.' As she spoke, she jerked her thumb in a short, swift upward hook that could only be seen by the two of them, but clearly pointed in the direction of the now vanished Helen.

John Dearly grimaced. 'I never thought of her for a moment, she's only here for a year. It's our little bit to bolster goodwill and the Church's international relations.' He remembered his own exchange more than thirty years before. A planned year assisting abroad that had expanded into two of the happiest years of his life while assisting at a small church in New England. During that time he had made firm friends with another young minister, Peter Johnson. When his old friend had called the previous winter, looking for help with his daughter, he was never going to refuse.

Peter Johnson and his wife were worried about their daughter Helen, the youngest of five. Her brothers and sisters had all gone into high earning business and professional posts and were successfully making their way in a material world. Helen, probably the brightest of the brood, had become a nurse, because she wanted to help people and do some good in the world. Having completed her training and built up her practical experience in hospitals near home, she set off to be a volunteer nurse in West Africa. Then, after three years of intense effort, she returned home to announce the best way she could help people was through the ministry.

John knew his old friend had been delighted that one of his children would follow him into the Church. However, following study and her ordination, Helen's short spells spent assisting at various churches had not gone quite to plan. It became clear to all concerned that she was just too independently minded for an apple pie parish. So John Dearly had been only too happy to offer her a placement where she could experience the challenges and rewards of an urban Christian parish.

Sensing that John Dearly's thoughts had wandered a little, Elaine sought to drag him back by pushing home her point. 'She's not suitable; far too modern in her ways. She's just not right. Our Kirk Session would never approve of her.' Elaine certainly did not approve of Helen and was confident of the other elders' views. With the exception of one or two of the older lady elders, she pretty well knew the St Bernard's Kirk Session would vote with her if she expressed a public view, which she would if push came to shove.

In spite of her reservations, Elaine did actually admire much of Helen's work, though she secretly felt she was a bit on the young side to be a minister. Truth was, the girl worked really hard, seemed popular in the parish and had managed to forge links with hard to reach parts of the community in ways that were very impressive, creative even. But that brought Elaine back to the nub of the problem; she simply disapproved of Helen. The girl was just too liberal in her approach to life. Elaine strived for inconspicuous stability. And Helen, well, Helen was Helen.

John Dearly frowned slightly. 'She's clever and has an open mind. Giving her an assistant's post for a year was meant to help her find her way, to develop as a minister. Surely you can see how she's blossomed?' He had no intention of letting Helen anywhere near a permanent position in the parish. Not because she would not make a good parish minister, he knew she would, but because he did not want to think of his burden landing on the shoulders of an innocent young woman. It would compromise the duty of care he felt towards her, a trust placed in him by his old friend Peter Johnson.

'Well, she can blossom all she likes, just so long as it's not here,' Elaine remained intractable, without realizing there was no case to argue against. John Dearly agreed with her, albeit for different reasons.

• • •

Helen had received Sam's text message and was already waiting on the pavement when the university minibus rolled into sight. She stepped forward, waving a hand in response to the flashing headlights and Sam's cheery wave from behind the wheel. The minibus pulled to a halt, the side panel door slid open and a young man jumped out.

Willing hands took Helen's rucksack and pointed her up to the front passenger's door. Her rucksack was stowed securely in the trailer while she climbed into the front passenger seat and leant straight across to share just a fleeting kiss of greeting with Sam, the warmth in his smile showing the real feelings of affection.

'Welcome aboard, Helen,' he shouted, half turning his head to project her name into the rear of the minibus. It was both a personal greeting and a public introduction to the first year students sprawled in informal comfort across the rear seating. Someone dropped the volume of the music playing in the back of the minibus as attention focused on the newcomer.

A mixed bag of voices fired out the friendly and confident greetings that youth and close-knit groups so easily generate.

'Hi H.'

'Run while you still can!'

'Hope you can cook!'

'Hi there.'

Helen half turned in her seat to get a better look into the rear of the minibus. She smiled and shouted a general greeting. 'Hi everyone!'

Her rich but gentle American accent registered at once, sparking general interest and producing a mock groan too. 'Oh no, the cook's American, it's going to be hotdogs and hamburgers for every meal!'

'You better believe it, baby!' Helen responded, shaking a finger at the joker, Davy. 'And your name's down for double helpings: breakfast, lunch and tea.'

The students cheered and someone ruffled Davy's hair, then the banter died away quickly as somewhere in the back a volume control turned up and music again filled the rear.

'That went well,' said Sam, 'though no cooking tonight. By the time we get there and get the tents up it will be well after eight. I propose fish and chips and a visit to the local pub.'

The mention of pub filtered through the music wall and brought a ragged cheer from the rear.

Helen settled back to enjoy the ride. Sam had planned the journey so they would be setting off as the evening rush hour subsided. The drive out of Edinburgh was easy and the minibus busied northwards in a gentle traffic flow. She had been across the River Forth several times now, but still looked forward to the journey, which gave her a thrill every time. Spanning the river were three impossibly long constructions, each one an awesome testament to man's evolving technological ability and an inspiration to successive generations.

They were crossing by the middle strand, the original road bridge. Immediately downstream, she had a spectacular view of the great old rail bridge: the Forth Bridge. Acclaimed as a wonder of the industrial age when it was first built, it still inspired today. The scale and vision of its construction had not diminished with time, just as its iron red colouring had been maintained by generations of painters.

Turning to look upstream, she took in the third strand, the newest road bridge, now emerging like a shining serrated blade cutting across the river. Beyond that, she could just make out the bluish grey of a warship berthed in the Rosyth Dockyard. From the corner of her eye, Helen noted several of the students had unintentionally allowed their façade of cool disinterest to slip as they too peered through the windows to take in the spectacle.

The bridges behind them, it took just twenty minutes to reach their motorway exit and they were suddenly driving through rural Scotland. Beneath bare green hilltops was a tightly packed jigsaw of woodland patches, hard worked fields of crops, and paddocks populated with grazing livestock. Villages slipped by, seen and gone almost before they registered. Little country towns passed in a flash, Auchtermuchty then Cupar.

Then the minibus was turning, taking a yet quieter route north, leaving the main road just before it reached St Andrews, the home of golf. In what seemed just a few moments, the country road was channelled between high razor wire fences that split the landscape and defined the area. To her right, Helen could see a tall functional cylinder jutting into the sky - Leuchars air traffic control tower. She couldn't see the runways but Sam assured her they were still there, though the base had been transferred to the army as budgets shrank and troops pulled out of Germany as part of the defence cuts.

As they neared the main gates, she could see they were guarded by camouflage clad servicemen. They watched the minibus with unthreatening but inquisitive eyes as it drove by.

Helen glanced at Sam; she sensed he had suddenly become a little pensive. He had told her something of his service as a junior officer. An exciting time, following which he had left the army, apparently without any regrets, returning to university to continue his studies and that had culminated in his PhD, and now here they were. She smiled and turned her attention back to the passing views, attributing his thoughtful face to a bout of nostalgia, triggered by the sight of the young soldiers.

The minibus left the base's perimeter fence behind. A little further along the narrowing road, Sam steered the minibus off on to what was little more than a track that wound through thicker and thicker woodland. Occasional glimpses of wire fencing and the odd camouflaged building could be seen on the right hand side, but for the most part the landscape had become dense impenetrable woodland.

The students had fallen silent as they craned to see where they were heading. Eventually a cheer arose as the woods opened up to show sky, then dunes, and as Sam cut the engine they all heard the sound of surf rolling up a beach just beyond the dunes. They had arrived.

• • •

The evening had finally darkened to night as the last of the students bundled across the sand and headed for their tents. Shrieks and laughter broke the silence as one or two stumbled en route and the clink of bottles indicated that at least one tent had bought extra drink in the pub to ensure they could carry on the party under canvas. Sam kept the minibus lights on until the students had all meandered to their tents and switched on their various electric lanterns and torches.

As the dunes finally cleared of students, Sam killed the lights and engine. The dunes were dark and still. He and Helen got out of the minibus and moved a little away from the encampment into the darkness. They wandered into the dunes and sat facing across the sands to the sea. As their eyes slowly adjusted to the black night sky, Sam opened bottles of beer.

Together they drank and leant back into the sand, staring up at the sky and watching as stars started to appear amidst the patchwork of night-time clouds. They marvelled at the blackness of the rural coastline and the sparkling scene above, shared more of their life stories and wondered quietly who else before them might have looked up to witness the same starlight scene.

Chapter 3

FRIDAY 3rd MAY

Cassiter's phone shrilled, pulling his attention away from the window through which he had been gazing down on the morning shoppers thronging Princes Street below. He was still relishing events in Dunbar as he answered the call.

'Cassiter speaking.' He listened intently to the voice coming down the line. It did not sound happy; in fact, having watched the media coverage mushroom over the previous 36 hours, Eugene Parsol was furious.

Finally, his rage began to lessen and the tone in the voice changed. '…and yet it looks like a good outcome in spite of the unfortunate news coverage. We have moved the trail forward another stage, from the old minister to this Edinburgh church,' said Parsol. Still annoyed, he could not quite allow his acknowledgment of Cassiter's positive result to stand without qualification. 'Perhaps the link was so logical this church should have been checked and picked up long ago.'

Cassiter did not bother interrupting to say it had been investigated more than once. If anything was there, it was well hidden. He listened in silence, knowing that no matter how angry Parsol was, he, Cassiter, was by far the best man for this work. Parsol and others like him, corporations and even some countries, did from time to time need particular types of service and Cassiter was the man who always delivered. Rather, Cassiter and his team always delivered.

Parsol appreciated Cassiter's application and dedication, admired his ability to stoically oversee the sifting of information, month after month without any deviation or flaw. It was an invaluable trait. His ability to respond with extreme prejudice when needed was also considered an essential aspect of the skillset. The only flaw, if indeed it was a flaw, was when Cassiter occasionally surrendered to his enthusiasm for the more brutal aspects of his craft.

The speed and volume of words pouring into Cassiter's ear finally subsided as the grumbling calmed and Parsol returned to business. He ran through the list of activities they had agreed the previous morning.

Cassiter mentally checked off the points. Each had already been initiated: identify which church featured in Buchan's photograph, identify the other minister in the picture, check who worked at the church, identify key members of the congregation, develop personal profiles, get some inside knowledge, note any unusual external links, and keep off the radar.

• • •

Set back from the beach, in the narrow sheltered space between dunes and woodland fringe, the campsite was a perfect spot: protected from the wind and open to the sunshine.

To the north end of the campsite were two large tents, the expedition's workshop and store. Slotted between the tents were the minibus and its trailer, now decoupled. Helen's cook zone had been established to the south end of the site. Joining the two ends was a neat row of accommodation tents.

Her first campsite evening meal ready, Helen banged a large steel ladle on the back of an aluminium folding chair. It did make a loud noise, but she was a little disappointed that it lacked the frantic chowtime ring she remembered from summer camps back home. 'Chowtime, come and get it!' she called. In any event, the banging and her shouting produced the desired outcome.

From behind the trestle table that she had set up as a servery, she watched the students emerge from their tents. Now cleaned up after a day in the dunes, the cheery babble of students approached at speed, signalling Helen's moment of culinary reckoning.

'Form a queue from that end,' she shouted, while waving them to one side. To her surprise the students obeyed, falling meekly into line, then she realised she was still holding the giant ladle, brandishing it like a weapon. She put it down.

The students' babble rose again as they waited hopefully for tea. Helen turned from the trestle table and picked up a prepared plate containing what may well have been the world's most unappetising hamburger and hotdog rolls. She had been keeping them warm on the gas griddle behind her for most of the afternoon.

'Where's Davy? He's first! Special order!' she called out to the student who had teased her cooking skills in the minibus the previous evening. 'I knew this is what you'd want,' she said, handing over the plate amidst cheers from the other students. 'Can I get you any sauce or mustard?'

He grinned sheepishly as the other students crowded round, cheering, jostling and pressing him to eat up without complaint. Helen reached across the servery table and pulled off a covering cloth. 'Self-service everyone, help yourselves.' Helen relieved Davy of his special order, waving him towards the table. He didn't need a second invitation.

Later, the meal over, Helen and Sam sat on one end of the servery table drinking coffee and soaking up the peaceful atmosphere. Four or five paces in front of them was an identical trestle table, the main dining table, currently surrounded by students. Their eating done too, the students were relaxed and a gentle murmur of contented voices covered the site.

Davy stood up and brandished Helen's giant ladle. 'Come on everyone, let's get this place cleaned up,' he said, then swung the ladle in Helen's direction, 'and you, stay where you are. We can deal with this lot.' The ladle swung round to embrace the students and the cluttered tables. 'By the way, Helen, thanks, that was really great scoff.' His words were echoed by a ripple of thanks and approval that ran around the table as the students rose and started to clear up.

Helen beamed a smile towards Davy and the whole group; elbows resting on the table she raised her coffee mug in acknowledgement and thanks. 'God bless you all,' she called back.

Sam grinned at her. 'They're right you know; the food really was great. You seem to have made some new friends for life over there,' he nodded towards the busy students.

'Hmm, cupboard love I'll bet. Anyway, I've had a lifetime of church picnics and summer camps. If I couldn't organise this little group there would be no hope for me.'

'Well, there's certainly hope for you,' said Sam, leaning forward and allowing his lips to brush her cheek. She chuckled and turned her face towards him so their lips just touched in the lingering prelude to a kiss. The moment was brought to an abrupt end by a round of raucous whistles and shouts. They separated, laughed and waved back at the students before settling down again to talk.

'What's the plan for tomorrow?' asked Helen.

'Well, today we marked out the areas we want to survey. Next, we are going to do a detailed survey and a little bit of digging. Just in a small sample area first, to give the students some practice, then we'll spread out over the coming days. That's about it, I guess. It'll keep us entertained for the next couple of weeks, that's for sure.'

Chapter 4

WEDNESDAY 15th MAY

Jim Barnett paused as he stepped out of the manse's front door and, turning back, he offered an outstretched hand to John Dearly. The minister stood in the doorway of his manse and took the tall slim man's hand, shaking it warmly, smiling in spite of his own personal sadness.

Jim Barnett had attended the previous Sunday's church service and they had chatted over coffee afterwards. He seemed enthusiastic, wanting to join in and participate as much as possible, so John had asked him to visit at the manse today, to get to know him a little and explore where Jim could be included in the work of the congregation. The visit had gone well and John was confident that Jim Barnett would make a real contribution to the church.

'You're very welcome here, Jim. I'll pass your details on to the elders to make sure they get you involved in things. A new member joining our church is always a reason to rejoice. You should settle into life here easily enough too, it's a friendly place,' said John. For just a moment his face dropped, and the morning sun instantly caught the change in his features, highlighting the depth of his inner turmoil. 'It's just a little difficult at the moment, with my predecessor passing away so unexpectedly. Everyone's a little upset, that's all.'

Jim's accent was from the west, probably Glasgow, but hard to pin down exactly. His face split into something between a sympathetic smile and a nervous grin. 'I'm sorry about all that. I've seen the papers, horrible, sick! Don't worry about me these next few days. I can see to myself,' he shrugged. 'You and the congregation must be cut up about it all, don't bother any of them over me just now. I'll just keep coming along to church on Sundays and we'll see how it goes. We can link up properly when the dust settles.'

John Dearly nodded, acknowledging the man's consideration. Jim's face seemed middle aged with its craggy lines but it could equally be younger. Perhaps the face of a man who has spent a lot of time working outdoors or drinking spirits or perhaps both. He watched as Jim Barnett walked out of the driveway and turned, disappearing along the road. Standing alone on the doorstep John quietly savoured the moment. Even in this mad cruel world there were always new people to be found, good souls to step forward: always something or someone new to help maintain his faith in humanity.

Further along the road, Jim Barnett was making a phone call and trying to maintain a steady pace as he weaved through a rabble of mothers, prams and pushchairs that were heading for the church hall and the church's regular parent and toddler group.

Barnett's phone call connected and he spoke briefly. 'I'm in, no problem at all. It'll just take a week or two to get properly embedded while they come to terms with the death of the old man in Dunbar. I'll keep you posted.' He hung up, pocketed the phone and picked up the pace, moving swiftly away from the happy family sounds that so irritated him.

• • •

In his office, Cassiter smiled. He now had someone on the inside. A little bit of patience would be needed while his man was accepted and settled in, then they would at long last be able to draw this to a conclusion. He called Parsol; this news would put the man in a better mood.

• • •

Their time in the Fife dunes had come and gone in a rush. Sam would be leading them back to Edinburgh in just a couple of days, content that the students' survey and dig had thrown up a range of readings and a few artefacts they could study and report on next term. However, it had not been one of the department's more exciting expeditions and a slight air of anti-climax hung over the camp. Sam needed another target to round off the dig, one that would keep the students busy and rekindle enthusiasm before they wrapped up for the summer.

Having looked again at the survey results, he had chosen a small target that had a slight mystery to it. This morning they would start their investigation. Too small and self-contained to represent any sort of building, it was also quite remote from most of what he considered to be the more significant readings, which they had spent the past fortnight working on. Because this was a small-scale signal, it was manageable in the little time they had left. It might prove of no interest. It might possibly be a cist, a small simple burial spot, or it could be any number of other things.

In any event, it was small enough to ensure a conclusion, giving the students an opportunity to see the process through from start to finish, and hopefully with some real questions to answer in the process.

Helen watched Sam and the students disappear from camp. A spontaneous but ragged burst of the Seven Dwarfs' marching song reached back to her from over the dunes. The students' spirits and sense of fun were clearly up. She smiled and as the sound faded, hurried to tidy the camp.

Chores done, Helen jumped into the minibus. Following her regular routine, she planned to pick up fresh provisions from St Andrews and had a list of requests from the students too; something they managed to put together for her most days. Occasionally, she also treated herself to a personal tour, exploring and sightseeing along the coast. She had felt a real and unexpected thrill on discovering Lower Largo.

The name carried a hint of mystery and she had found herself drawn down the slope into the village. A sign caught her attention, announcing the village as the birthplace of Alexander Selkirk: the Scot whose experiences had inspired Defoe's novel *Robinson Crusoe*. It was a story she had read avidly as a girl and acted out countless times with her big brothers though she had always ended up as Friday.

The isolated village sat low against the sea, its breakwater creating a little safe haven, a harbour to shield local fishing boats. Built right on the breakwater and jutting out defiantly towards the sea stood the local hotel. There she had treated herself to lunch and spent an hour just soaking in the atmosphere, allowing herself to be transported back in time. Eyes closed, she had visualised scenes from long past lives; waves breaking against the hotel walls on stormy nights, roaring fires, smuggling, Crusoe, and who knows what.

Immediately beyond the village, the coast arced away into the distance, a magnificent run of sandy beach regularly punctuated by ragged rocky outcrops. It was a place from another age, beautiful, mysterious, yet comfortably approachable.

No touring today though; just the now familiar short journey into St Andrews. She drove past the Old Course Hotel sitting proudly beside the famous golf course, the home of golf. Together with the ancient university, they defined much of the town's character. Moments later, she was in the town centre and searching for a parking space.

Today the mission was grocery shopping only. As she strolled through the town, Helen mused on the field trip and how things were developing with Sam; she felt good about both. Somehow, she felt he was a good fit for her; she hoped he felt the same, though he wasn't exactly one for baring his deepest emotions. She had to read between the lines in that department.

What did worry her were the other developments in Edinburgh and she regularly exchanged texts with Grace who was keeping her up to date with events. There had been a nasty murder just before she set off from Edinburgh; the victim, Archie Buchan, she knew of only by reputation. He had been close to both John and Elaine. Things were clearly difficult. Helen had twice phoned John, offering to return to Edinburgh. But he had insisted she finish her trip, there was nothing she could do anyway. She took his insistence at face value though had warned Sam she might need to leave early, but the days had passed and she had not been called back.

• • •

Having left the campsite behind, Sam worked his way through the dunes, leading the students towards his chosen target in the trough between two dunes. The students sectioned off the new dig site, photographed it and made a start on the digging. The rough dune grass and top layer of sand was cleared and then they began to move away the sandy material beneath, slowly, layer by layer.

'Watch every scrape, check every trowel, you never know what will turn up,' said Sam. He spoke with enthusiasm, both because he felt it and because he knew these practical experiences were the ones where enthusiasm was instilled, where the good habits of a lifetime were formed. He was not really expecting to see anything too startling, but he watched too, sharing in the experience and ensuring all the students appreciated the importance of diligent care.

Only three students were digging at a time, others sifted the sand or took breaks to relax and just watch the activity for a while. Davy had been given the job of recording events with the departmental camera. He was taking plenty of pictures, so many pictures that the camera battery had faded and he had now switched to using his phone; he could transfer the pictures later.

Many of the pictures managed to include Julie, one of the students currently digging away in the trench. She was steadily moving sandy earth when her trowel struck against a solid object. 'I've hit something, I've hit something,' she shrieked.

The initial stir of excitement grew after Sam had knelt down to examine the find. It was the top of a skull, facing up. A burial of some sort? Davy kept busy snapping away.

The rest of the day was devoted to clearing the skeleton, recording every stage and indulging in lots of speculation. By the end of the afternoon, Sam had decided it was no burial but a violent death, captured in and preserved by the dunes: a story held locked in for centuries until they had come along to find it. They had even been able to make out the hilt of a sword, still gripped in the skeleton's hand. The blade had long since transformed into a heavy bar of rough rust, but from its size there was no doubt this was a big sword, a real killing machine.

This was a man who had gone down fighting; his left humerus was chopped half through close above the elbow. Sam highlighted the now very degraded but still clearly unhealed bone edges, indicating the wound had been inflicted around the time of death. An arrowhead forced right through the shoulder blade and embedded in the rib behind showed that, whoever the man was, he had experienced a hard death.

Around the skeleton's neck ran a heavy linked gold chain that was threaded through a gold signet ring. The face of the ring was engraved with an ornate cross and had a small ruby offset to one corner. It was a stunning find topped off with a further mystery. In the sand immediately beside the skeleton was a slim lead box, around eighteen inches long, a little over six wide and perhaps one inch deep. It was closed tight and stamped with the same ornate cross marking.

Sam had the students bag the metal finds; they would be kept safe in his tent overnight. He did not want to leave them unattended, just in case. Finally, they laid a sheet of polythene to cover the trench and skeleton and weighed it down before heading back to camp, hungry for their dinner and eager to share their news with Helen.

Dinner passed in a frantic hum of excited speculation. Midway through, Sam had slipped off to make a phone call to his head of department at the university.

'You should have seen it, Helen, the skull was this big,' said Julie, as her hands described a watermelon.

'The jaw though, did you see that?' Davy leant across and squeezed the soft flesh of Julie's underarm. 'I thought it was going to grab your arm and pull you right into the sand after it!'

Julie squealed in mock fear. 'Stop that Davy,' she shrieked and allowed his arm to slide round her shoulder. 'I wonder who he was,' she looked around, eyes shining. 'He had golden jewellery and weapons and went down fighting. And then was just abandoned in the sand, it's so sad.'

'I wonder why whoever killed him didn't take the gold though, it doesn't make sense to me,' said Davy. 'I mean, looking at his wounds they put a lot of effort into killing him, why not take the reward?'

Others nodded and the speculation sparked more animated conversations. By the time Sam had finished his call and rejoined them, the mystery skeleton had lived and died a hundred different deaths. Everyone quietened as he sat down and the students looked to him for informed comment.

'The boss is coming over tomorrow with some of the department's technicians and staff. Seems you lot have caused quite a stir,' he said, grinning round at the group. Yet deep down he knew they would be feeling a sense of disappointment at the news so many seniors were coming. The first year students would be quickly relegated to messengers and helpers, and probably packed off back to Edinburgh early. Their find would not be theirs for much longer. Sam felt a little bit the same.

'Look, I'm going to take the minibus down to the village and pick up some drink. Why don't we have a bonfire and a party right here to celebrate the find and the end of our private dig? What do you say?' The offer of alcohol and a party pulled the students' spirits back up.

Davy stood up and shouted. 'A wake. Let's give our warrior a proper send off!' The others cheered and Sam quickly found himself en route to the village with a couple of helpers on board. The rest of the camp set off to gather in driftwood for the bonfire.

Under Helen's supervision, the students built up a great campfire and then carried three of the benches across from the kitchen area, arranging them into a horseshoe around the fire. Behind the middle bench was placed one of the trestle tables, stacked with beer and wine and a range of snack foods she had laid on. On the other side of the campfire was the huge driftwood stack the students had gathered, enough fuel to keep the fire burning well into the night.

• • •

The evening had gone well, plenty of drink and the excitement of their find kept everything bubbling along. Sam's identification of the cross as a Templar sign had sparked more interest. When had he died? Was he alone? What was a Templar Knight doing out here anyway? The questions kept tumbling out one after another.

Two of the students were from Hong Kong and did not know very much about the Templar Knights and a Kenyan student had heard they were racists. Sam tried to dispel the misconceptions and explain a little about their history and role and eventual betrayal. As twilight finally surrendered to night, the darkness was broken only by the leaping flames that cast a constantly changing mix of shimmering light and dark shadow across the faces of the group while they followed Sam's story.

'Of course, don't think of our knight set in the world we know today. In the ancient world there was no America, no Australia,' he paused, looked around the group, picking out eye contacts and moving on with a knowing nod. 'No,' he stamped his foot and pointed down at the ground around their feet, 'this was the end of the world. From Africa northwards, from Asia westwards, right through Europe, the ancient world ended here in the British Isles. And Scotland was the wildest, remotest part of the islands. Whatever he was doing here, our Templar really did die at the end of the World.

'This is an old place. You know from your lectures that there are buildings up at Skara Brae way older than the pyramids.' Heads nodded and a murmur of ascent rolled around the fire as Sam continued. 'Scotland has a full blown 10,000 year old stone calendar. Come on! Mesopotamia, eat your heart out. This place is old. Old places are bound to have some mysteries and secrets, and that's what we're here for, what you're learning to do: to unravel the past.'

Fuelled by the drink, the atmosphere, the excitement of the day's find and Sam's stories, several of the students shivered and imagined they could almost sense the ancients moving in the shadows beyond the campfire. Julie had been sitting close to Davy throughout the evening. As if by magic, the gap had finally vanished, their arms wrapped behind each other's backs.

Sam took another drink from his beer bottle. 'So, this was the edge of the world. Over time, things spin out from the centre. The best of peoples, the worst. The victims, those searching for refuge, those hunting the refugees, eventually this is as far as they all could come. But this was no empty land.' As he talked, he walked round the fire, picked up some driftwood from the stack and threw it on the flames, then continued his story amidst the shower of flame and sparks that soared up.

'People lived here, and this was no soft touch place. You had to be tough. Hard. You had to struggle to get established here, to make your mark, to come in and survive. And for every good that arrived an evil came too. Anyone here heard of Jekyll and Hyde? Holmes and Moriarty?'

A bunch of hands went up.

From beyond the shadowy firelight, an English accented voice called out. 'Don't tell us, you Scots really do have monsters. Come on Nessie!' This brought a round of laughs and lightened the mood that had quite unintentionally become increasingly dark as Sam told his tale. A couple took the opportunity to get fresh drinks from the table while a joker started to give a howling wolf impression.

The English accent called out again. 'So is this really all about that Dan Brown stuff? You know, the Templar Knights, Holy Grails, Jesus stuff?' The voice trailed off into a nervous laugh, waiting with the rest for Sam's pronouncement.

Sam laughed too. 'You're right, you're right, we don't have beasties anymore, well none that I have actually seen. As for Dan Brown, well he tells a really great story but we're archaeologists, so let's stick to the science please, yes?' He looked around and saw agreement in the students' eyes.

'But, you know, I'm serious about the history, the place: a melting pot of good and evil, kind and cruel. It's probably no accident that those fictional characters were conceived here, written by authors from here, and,' he paused for a long moment looking around the group, 'this country was the Templars' last real refuge. Like so many others through the ages, this is where they came, the end of the World, the end of their world. Perhaps this was their last stand?'

There was a silence for a moment, broken by Helen as she laughed. 'Sam, you really know how to kill a party.'

Davy chipped in. 'Yeah, too right. Remind me not to ask you to the class Christmas night out this year!' Others laughed, jeered their lecturer and the party atmosphere surged back, a student clicked on some music and the shadows suddenly seemed less impenetrable, the fire felt warmer.

Helen and Sam slipped off, leaving the students to their party.

CHAPTER 5

THURSDAY 16th MAY

Early in the morning, well before any of the students had emerged for breakfast, Sam guided Helen through the dunes to visit the Templar's last resting place. Once there, Sam removed the polythene coversheet and stepped back a few paces. He gave Helen space to do what she needed to do. She bowed her head and prayed for the dead Templar, commended him to God and sent her blessing after him.

Sam watched respectfully. In the past he had professed loudly that he did not believe. There was nothing after death; science had clearly proven it beyond any reasonable doubt. His was a very common stance now and he was not about to surrender it, minister girlfriend or not. In truth, despite his public stance he was not really sure what he believed. It was unsettling to think of an eternal blackness, and deep inside he did sometimes think, or at least hope, that there might be something after he died.

Something, anything rather than his consciousness simply vanishing into a void as though it had never been. But since adolescence he had increasingly struggled with so many of the strictures and apparent contradictions of Christianity; one day he found he had just left it all behind him. It had just become easier not to think about faith at all. It was just easier to be a nonbeliever.

He had finished his honours degree in modern languages, graduating as a fluent speaker of French, German and Spanish. Then Sam had joined the army on a short service commission in the Intelligence Corps. It had certainly been interesting, sometimes exhilarating, sometimes dark and quite scary. During his service he had made plenty of friends, forging bonds that he was sure would last a lifetime. But three years had been enough for him, and happily, enough time to satisfy family traditions too.

He returned to Edinburgh to do a second degree in archaeology and then rolled on to a PhD. That was followed by spells teaching at university in Bristol and then in Naples, where his knowledge of Latin did not help much in the settling in, though his aptitude for languages ensured he quickly grasped Italian. Then a vacancy back in Edinburgh had brought him full circle and home.

Once Helen's prayer for the Templar was over, they headed back to the camp. She pulled the students' breakfast together and Sam took a little time to look more closely at the artefacts. He wished he could open the sealed lead box, see what lay inside, but knew his head of department would never forgive him. It would have to wait until MacPherson arrived.

• • •

The air was still cool with its morning bite as MacPherson's convoy rolled into camp. Then things moved quickly. A large protective awning was spread over the Templar skeleton, and everywhere there was the hustle and bustle of busy people doing important things.

As anticipated, Sam's first year students were brushed aside in the rush of experts. Once the junior students had shown where the site and artefacts were, they found themselves redundant. Only Davy was kept busy, co-opted as the departmental photographer's assistant.

MacPherson had commandeered one of the camp trestle tables as an examination bench. Now, along with his team he was busy examining the finds, passing comment, seeking confirmation from colleagues and having everything photographed from a variety of angles. Sam and Helen had been allowed to observe, but their position well down the table clearly emphasised that power had shifted, showed where control now lay.

The photographer continued to dodge about as he took a steady string of pictures. Above them, standing on a bench and leaning over the crowd, was Davy. He was holding up a silvered reflector and directing sunlight down on to the artefacts on the table, providing the best possible light for the photos.

Having inspected the other artefacts, there only remained the question of what was in the lead box. MacPherson picked it up and inspected it carefully, turning it in his hands, examining the seal. 'It looks as though this top end has just been wedged on like the tight lid of a biscuit box and sealed with what might have been beeswax,' he said, to a murmured general agreement. 'It's interesting how the engraving on the ring is identical to that on the lead box. This establishes a clear link between the two. We can see there is clear symbolism in the cross with its representations of the Templars and Christianity. Anyone have anything to add before we proceed?'

One of the acolytes spoke up. 'Looking at all the artefacts and the engraving design, I'd estimate their date as being late thirteenth to early fourteenth century. Certainly well before 1350, and as you observed, it's definitely a Templar cross.'

Another colleague joined in. 'Absolutely, and remember the Templars were lost as a force during the early part of the fourteenth century.'

MacPherson beamed at his team. 'Fair enough, we are all agreed then. Let's see if this sealed lid will just slip open with a little assistance, shall we?' He looked around the table, daring anyone to challenge him. Nobody did.

Sam was not happy, believing that the box would be much better opened in the laboratory, but knew it was pointless to object. MacPherson probably had his mind set on future press conferences and the glory of potential 'action man on location pictures'. No doubt the pictures and story would be used to 'big up' the department, maximising exposure in its perpetual hunt for more research funding and bequests. MacPherson had shown himself a real expert in the money field, if somewhat less so in archaeology, and past experience told Sam that Mac-Pherson would not brook any obstruction to his plans.

With a little pressure, MacPherson managed to dislodge the top from the box and it fell onto the table. Everyone craned forward to see what was revealed through the opening. Davy brought his sunlight reflector to bear on the open box beneath him and the reflected sunlight cut through the shadow at the mouth of the lead box, illuminating something that itself shone bright like sunshine. The whole group gasped with excitement and the camera clicked away building a record. Davy was discreetly taking the opportunity offered by his vantage point above the throng to snap off a few pictures on his own phone.

MacPherson turned the box on its side and gently tilted it. Out slid a simple, beautiful, shining dagger. Made of pure silver and having been sealed in its lead box, no oxidation had occurred. It was as perfect as the day it was first placed inside.

This was clearly not a fighting weapon, silver was too soft. But the blade was sharp and MacPherson was very careful not to allow the cutting edges to run across his skin. 'Beautiful, exquisite!' he said, holding it out for all to see. 'Look at the workmanship. Fit for a king.' There was a ripple of agreement; this was a special thing. He placed it on the table for the photographer to take some detailed shots.

Sam was leaning forward, fascinated and desperate to see what his students had turned up. At the same time, he wondered if MacPherson really ought to have gloves on - to protect the blade, not his hands. He could see it was a perfectly made weapon.

The eight-inch silver blade was slim, and only an inch and a half wide for most of its length then quickly narrowing to a stabbing point. Topping the blade, the handle was of identical silver, constructed as a simple post grip, five inches long, an inch wide and perhaps half an inch deep. Protruding from either side of the handle, half an inch above where it met the blade, were silver quillons: little crossbars positioned at the base of the dagger handle to prevent an opponent's blade from sliding up and slicing into the bearer's hand. Each quillon was just two inches long, with a half-inch square cross section. The whole dagger formed a single, seamless, shining beauty.

Helen felt an odd sense of familiarity. Even though she had clearly never seen the dagger before, she somehow knew it, but could not place how or where. She dismissed the thought as fanciful, putting it to the back of her mind.

The dagger was perfectly constructed and appeared completely plain, without a mark or sign on it. The group fell silent for a moment, even the camera stopped clicking. Then MacPherson reached across the table and turned the blade over for photographs of the back. This instantly produced another round of exclamations from those at the table.

This side of the handle and quillons were as plain as the other, but the blade itself was very delicately engraved. At the top, close against the handle was the ornate Templar cross, just as on both the lead box and signet ring. Beneath it was a pattern of straight and curving lines: some solitary, others woven together, pulling apart and then converging again in an almost psychedelic pattern. None of the lines ever reached the cutting edges, which were left clear, plain and sharp. Set apart from the rest of the engraving and tight against the blade's point was the Roman numeral III.

The delicate and so purposefully engraved pattern on the blade had no apparent meaning or symbolism; while the dagger itself was of delightful construction, it had no obvious practical use. An artefact whose use or purpose was a mystery, an artefact that demanded careful study. MacPherson and his team had that under control.

A little while later, somebody, probably MacPherson, suggested that as there was nothing more for the first year students to do they should set off as soon as possible, leaving the seniors to get on with the job. The students grumbled quietly amongst themselves, but knew there was little point in challenging MacPherson. He had granted them a brief opportunity to view the blade and they were elated by the beauty of the find, but subdued too as they were effectively being pushed off site. It just seemed so unfair and it had taken the shine off the whole trip.

Sam engaged the minibus gears. With a ragged and slightly ironic cheer from the students, it slowly pulled out onto the track and they set off for home. With a clear road they would make Edinburgh before lunchtime. Behind them, the work on the dig continued and nobody waved them off. Probably nobody even noticed they had gone.

Sam and Helen tried to talk on the road south, but the loud music coming from the rear of the minibus restricted them to simple sentences. They agreed to meet that evening to go out for a meal to round off their unusual, exciting and ultimately a little frustrating trip.

• • •

John Dearly moved away from the communion table and walked slowly down the aisle towards the church doors. The Dunbar church minister matched him step for step as they proceeded past the packed pews of his church. The sun was nearly at its zenith as they stepped outside and turned together to greet and console the departing congregation. Archie's body had not yet been released for burial but in response to a groundswell of emotions, and to mark his life, the pair had agreed to hold a modest remembrance service. It had grown beyond anything they had envisaged.

The media were gathered across the road. Reporters, phot-ographers, radio and TV camera crews, drawn like sharks to blood in the water: hunting, determined to service the public's ghoulish fascination in this incomprehensible mix of savage killing and church innocence. In the absence of any police progress, speculation was rife and the media was in a feeding frenzy.

It took a little while for everyone to funnel out of the church, but finally the last of the people had left. Getting about their business, heading back to work or calling into the church hall next door to seal their celebration of Archie's life, to reminisce and share some refreshments. By prior agreement, the Dunbar minister stepped across the road to give a short public statement. The media pack rippled and swirled as he approached.

Alone now, John stood quietly at the church doorway, oblivious to the flashing lights and screeching questions on the other side of the road. He needed a quiet moment.

What had happened to his old friend was awful. He hoped it was the act of a madman, one who the police would catch quickly so local people could sleep a little easier. Yet he knew Elaine was less optimistic; she felt there might be a link with the church. Felt that he, they, should be taking action to protect themselves.

But what action? He was just the minister of a parish. What did he know about protection? Perhaps it was nothing anyway and he certainly could not think why this would blow up now of all times. He put the thought to one side. There was no threat, nothing to worry about.

He looked up and along the road towards the church hall, saw Elaine standing outside its doors, around her a cluster of their parishioners, all waiting patiently for him. John gave a wan smile and waved in their direction, acknowledging them and waving them into the hall. Reluctant but dutiful, the group allowed themselves to be herded inside under Elaine's guidance. She threw another concerned glance in his direction and was herself waved inside.

Finally alone with his thoughts, John allowed his right hand to lightly stroke the stone of the doorway, letting his palm rest gently on the cool upright. Pressing harder he felt his pulse beat against the stone, hoping that somehow the contact would link his thoughts and prayers with Archie's one more time. An observer would attribute his stance to just a steadying hand. After a final rueful glance up towards the church, he turned and walked to join the others in the church hall.

Across the street, the Dunbar minister was drawing his statement to an end. In a few moments the media would disperse to file their reports and pictures, and then move on to whatever their next brief might be.

Sat in the front passenger seat of an unmarked police car was a slightly chubby middle-aged man, his face more wrinkled than his age warranted. He was smartly dressed in a plain suit and tie, with short sandy hair that in a certain light verged on ginger. Detective Chief Inspector Robert Wallace was watching everything; he had been at the back of the church during the remembrance service and slipped out quickly as it ended to get in his photographer's car. In the driver's seat sat Stephens, the police photographer. Under DCI Wallace's watchful direction, he busily snapped everything that moved. They had pictures of everyone who had attended the service or hovered in the street outside.

DCI Wallace was not sure what his next move would be; they had exhausted all the usual channels without success. He could not admit to it publicly, but right now he was treading water while reviewing and revising his investigation strategy from the bottom up. In the meantime, as far as the world was concerned, the investigation continued apace.

He swung the passenger door open, gripped the roof edge and uttered a low unintelligible growl as he pulled himself up and out of the car. He leant down, poking his head back through the door and told the photographer to get himself back to Edinburgh when he was finished. Wallace wanted a quick wander round the church hall before heading back to Edinburgh himself.

Stephens nodded an acknowledgement, but before driving back to Edinburgh he allowed himself a minute's fun snapping the media - he could see several of his pals in the scrum.

Amongst the photographers was a petite, blonde female, constantly jostled by the larger men around her but always managing to end up at the front, best placed to get the cleanest pictures. Fiona Sharp had continued snapping away until the last of the mourners had departed, and then for appearances' sake took some shots of the Dunbar minister as he delivered his statement.

She dispersed with the rest of the media pack, jumped into her saloon car and quickly started to scan the digital photographs. She had no doubts about the picture quality; top end equipment and years of practice ensured a reliable outcome. However, now the shoot was over, her professional interest demanded she scan the material. While taking the pictures she had not concerned herself with who was framed in the viewfinder, she just took the pictures, lots and lots of them. She would now invest some time in doing a detailed review, working out who attended out of duty, who was there for friendship or love, and who was there for business - assessing the pecking order to establish who the really important people were. For those who could read the pictures, it was a bonanza of information to be exploited to the full.

After scanning through the pictures, she started the car and pulled calmly away. Her departure did not even register with the remaining journalists who were themselves packing up and leaving. She headed back to Edinburgh to prepare a comprehensive folder for delivery to her boss: Cassiter.

• • •

The church hall was thronged with people. A mixed bag of church officials had come over from Edinburgh and now they stood all clustered together in the middle of the hall; probably as interested in being seen to be there as in grieving for a man some did not even know. To one side gathered concerned local residents and active members of the local church, all those people Archie had got to know in the years since he had retired to their town. People who were fretting over his fate and what might happen next if the madman was not caught.

The parishioners from Edinburgh rallied together as though for protection while to the side of the hall a small group of his oldest and closest friends naturally gravitated towards one another.

No family had attended. Archie was the last of his generation; there were a couple of nephews and a niece somewhere. The boys had gone to Australia long ago and even the exchange of Christmas cards had finally petered out. The niece had gone to live in England, a fresh start after her marriage had ended. Archie had not seen her since christening her daughter, who would be grown up now.

The local minister, freed from his media duties, had returned to his element and now buzzed between the groups encouraging them to mix, to share stories and remember the man. Slowly, duty now seen to be done, some of the church officials were gravitating towards the exit, heading away to deal with the day's work.

John had been circulating around the hall and found himself being drawn slowly towards the refreshments. He smiled to himself. This spread would satisfy any reasonable person's expectations. Wine and sherry were available alongside the ever-popular hot tea. Archie was getting a good send off.

John hoped it would provide some closure for people worrying over events and give the media an end point to close the story on. Hoped, too, it would then allow Archie to rest and the living some space to grieve.

John spotted a familiar face ahead of him. Doing a little grazing at the food table was Francis Kegan, an old friend and ally in the perpetual struggle to keep the Church relevant in a modern world. He was the parish priest of Our Lady of Lourdes Roman Catholic Church in Edinburgh. Their overlapping parish boundaries meant they pretty well served the same community, but there was no rivalry. They were both investing time and life into combating the same problems. Working together was a more productive process than competing, and a thirty-year friendship had grown from that.

Francis turned and caught John's eye. He tilted his head a little to one side and groaned. 'Oh. This is a bad business, John. What could possess someone to be so cruel? I just don't understand.' The pair had met up almost every other evening since Archie's death. Asking the same questions again and again. They had finished off more than one bottle of Scotch while trying to reconcile events, trying to come to terms with what had happened. Why did their old friend and mentor die? They had toasted him aplenty. Neither could rationalise events yet. In private the pair were both grief stricken, though in the public eye they presented more stoic faces to provide support for others who also struggled.

John gave a wry smile and shrug. 'No sense to it, Francis,' he said, letting his arms wave a little and sighing. 'At least he's not suffering now.'

Francis nodded. 'God rest his soul.' He leant forward a little. 'In Dunbar of all places! You couldn't find a nicer little town!' He stopped to let a pensioner pass him, letting her reach the food.

DCI Wallace drifted slowly round the room, catching snatches of conversation, moving on, eyes everywhere but never consciously connecting with anyone. Having just about completed his circuit, he was nearing the exit when John Dearly spotted him across the hall and nodded a greeting, which DCI Wallace returned discreetly, and then the detective was gone. His presence had probably not registered with anyone else in the hall.

John was relieved the man had not come to speak to him. The police had visited the manse twice since Archie's death. They were searching back through the old man's life for possible motives or links, and while John wanted to help the police, he had found the interviews difficult and pointless. This had clearly been a random attack.

Another movement at the door caught both Francis and John's attention at the same moment. 'It's Xavier!' said Francis. They both hurried towards the door to greet the old Sardinian priest. 'He's made it after all. Archie would be so pleased.' Francis waved as they crossed the room.

Xavier smiled when he saw them and the old friends greeted one another with real affection. Closer to Archie's age than theirs, Xavier was well past any normal retirement age. But he still had a thirst for life that would put many younger men to shame, and clearly, he did not intend to go quietly any time soon. Behind the old priest stood his assistant, Angelo, a much younger priest. As John and Francis untangled from Xavier's Latin greetings, the younger man shook their hands and expressed condolences in broken English.

They had met the young priest several times before, both in Edinburgh and when visiting Xavier in Sardinia. Angelo felt an unspoken ranking that kept him quiet. John and Francis were not really aware of the distinction, just thought he was a quiet man.

While Angelo went to organise more refreshments, they found some seats at the side of the hall and sat Xavier between them. All three men were pleased to sit and talk, to reminisce and console one another. Both local men pressed Xavier to stay in their homes but he declined. 'We have accommodation arranged already through the local curia. Anyway, I don't want to be intruding just now,' said Xavier.

John objected. 'How could your being here intrude? Archie and you go way back. We all go way back…' his protest trailed off as Xavier's hand waved him down.

'John, John, it's been a long day. The flight from Sardinia was long, and I'm old and tired. We were late arriving in Edinburgh. The taxi driver couldn't get us out to the church in time. We missed the service. Let me get a peaceful night, hmm? Tomorrow we will meet, eat, and put the world to rights. Share our news.' Xavier had stretched out his right hand and rested it on John's forearm. 'Let's do that, what do you say?'

He turned his head and looked Francis in the eye while his left hand reached out and settled on the Scottish priest's forearm. 'Yes? Both of you? Old friends.' They placed their hands on top of his and nodded.

'Good, now, just one thing I must know at once. Tell me what caused this? Are we safe?' said Xavier.

'John and I think it might have been a random act of madness,' said Francis.

'That's right, though Elaine is not so sure,' said John.

'But you know Elaine, she always thinks the worst,' added Francis.

Xavier looked from one to the other, was silent for a moment, thinking. He leant back a little. Pulling his hands from beneath theirs, he slid them up to grip their upper arms, drawing them a little closer to him. He glanced from one to the other. 'My friends, Elaine is careful, she is always careful. Let's find out why she feels so concerned. Tomorrow, yes?'

He looked up and his eyes sparkled as he glanced around the room, speaking with genuine enthusiasm. 'Is Elaine here? Where is she? Is she hiding from me?' They all laughed and scanned the room for Elaine, spotting her in earnest conversation with the local minister and a cluster of the Dunbar elders. They would get her over soon enough.

• • •

Cassiter carefully reviewed the photographs. There was nothing remarkable in the shots, no unexpected faces that demanded further investigation. He had felt sure that if there were a chain to be followed the links would have presented at the remembrance service. This was not the outcome he had hoped for. It was always easier when the prey stepped out into the clearing, but that had not happened so he would just need to dig a little deeper.

Having a man on the inside would make things altogether easier now. It would be relatively straightforward to organise some surveillance and find out what, if anything, was going on at Dearly's church. He reached for his phone and started setting arrangements in place.

Chapter 6

FRIDAY 24th MAY

It was just over a week since Archie's memorial service and John Dearly continued to struggle over why such cruelty had been visited on the old man. DCI Wallace had visited for a third time but John did not know what to tell him. It was almost beginning to feel as though the detective was searching for inspiration.

John had engaged in some heated discussion with Xavier about what the murder might mean, if anything, and what should be done. Elaine, the senior elder and trusted confidante, had been involved, like Xavier, she too saw shadows where there were none. Eventually, John had won the arguments; the killing must be the act of a madman - and it was decided that for the time being nothing needed to be done.

They agreed to meet again in the autumn, at Xavier's, in Sardinia, to hold a proper review and then decide how to proceed. It would be something to look forward to. If nothing else, a chance to get out of Edinburgh for a few days. Placated, Xavier and Angelo had flown home.

John hoped that later in the year he might at last get his wish and persuade Xavier it was finally time to bring things to a conclusion. They were investing so much of their lives and lots of money to protect something that had no intrinsic value or relevance today. Other than a few academics and the odd history buff, it was probably of no interest to anyone in the twenty-first century, and certainly did not present any sort of threat. This autumn he would try again to move things into the open, permanently. Perhaps even start a little museum.

In the meantime, John had to focus on what often proved to be the busiest week of his year. Towards the end of May the great and the good from the Church would join the rank and file, the ministers, the elders and the foreign representatives, all coming together in a mass migration to Edinburgh; all gathering for the annual General Assembly of the Church of Scotland. Being based in an Edinburgh parish meant John was always in high demand, expected to entertain old friends and acquaintances, participate in the Assembly and be available to support every odd request from out of town visitors.

Friday was his regular day off and this Friday was the lull before the Assembly storm. He left the manse first thing, following his usual Friday morning routine, strolling along in a bubble of calm while so many other people struggled to get to work by pushing their cars and stress levels to the limit. It was a little self-indulgent, drawing pleasure in observing the efforts of others, but he just found everybody else's rushing only served to accentuate his own quiet time, and he savoured every moment.

John passed the church and the primary school to reach the local general store where he collected his newspaper and then strolled back to the manse, looking forward to a leisurely coffee and read. As he approached the manse, he felt just the slightest of irritations when he noticed somebody standing inside the driveway. Were they waiting for him on his day off? He realised it was Jim Barnett, who seemed to be making a phone call. Putting on a smile, John walked into his driveway. 'Jim, I wasn't expecting to see you today. What can I do for you?'

'Oh, John, I just thought I would come and speak to you. To see whether I could volunteer for anything,' said Barnett, clutching at straws. Trustingly, John did not recognise it as just a flimsy excuse.

'Well that's great, Jim, we'd certainly welcome your contribution. Could you give me a call at the start of the week, Monday morning? We can arrange a meeting to talk through some of the opportunities,' said John as he kept walking towards his front door.

Inside the manse's kitchen, Fiona Sharp was busy replacing the smoke detector cover. Having gained entry directly after the minister left, she had done a little work on the computer in his study and now its camera and microphone were subject to remote access and control. Then she went to the kitchen and stripped out the smoke detector's insides, repacking it with a camera and microphone. She had just started to replace the cover when her phone had rung with a warning about the minister's imminent return.

'Get out of there now. He's coming up the road,' Barnett had almost shouted into the phone.

She was furious with him. What sort of lookout was he to manage only a thirty second warning? Anyway, she could not leave the smoke detector with its cover off or that would blow the job in one. She just had to finish and hope she could get out of the kitchen before the minister got in. Barnett had better keep him talking while she wrapped things up.

John opened the front door of the manse. Jim Barnett hovered behind him, hesitated and then almost seemed to shout. 'I can visit you most times, John, would morning or afternoon suit you better?' Barnett gripped the knife in his pocket.

John turned towards him. 'Monday afternoon will be fine, but give me a call in the morning to fix the time…' he stopped in mid-sentence and turned his head, looking back into the hallway. 'Did you hear something, Jim?'

'No, I don't think so, what did you hear?' Barnett deadpanned his response while his grip on the knife handle tightened, ready for action.

'I think I heard somebody in the kitchen. Come on, let's check it out,' John headed down the hall towards the kitchen with Barnett close behind. Rushing into the kitchen John found the back window wide open. 'There! In the garden, there's someone running for the back wall. They must have done a runner as we came through the front door.'

Barnett relaxed the grip on his knife, letting it rest unseen in his pocket. 'I'll go and try to cut them off in the garden, you call the police,' he said. Then he ran back down the hall, out of the front door, round the side of the house and into the gardens, starting a thorough search while shouting up to the open kitchen window. 'No sign of anyone here, they must have got away.'

From the window, John waved acknowledgement. 'The police are on their way, I don't think the burglar had a chance to take anything. Come on in Jim. Whoever it was, they will be well away by now. We'll get a cup of tea and wait for the police.'

• • •

Cassiter was weighing up his options. He was not entirely happy with the day's activity. Yes, his team had installed a listening device in the little office behind the church vestry. That had gone according to plan but events had proven to be less satisfactory when they had gone on to the manse.

They had managed to place two information feeds, one in the kitchen and the other in the computer in the study. Those would all be very useful in evaluating the target, but he had wanted a bug in the living room too and was not best pleased that his team had failed to install it. Worse, they had nearly got themselves caught. He could not risk another incursion into the manse for now, so he would have to make do with what was in place.

Chapter 7

WEDNESDAY 29ᵗʰ MAY

Parliament Hall was filled with the universal burble of sounds heard at receptions everywhere; individual words never quite identified as hundreds of voices merged into a single living hum, underscored by the sound of clinking glasses and crockery, and all punctuated by the more distant bangs of catering staff registering restrained disquiet against trays, trolleys and servery doors. This evening's function was the Moderator's Reception, one of the key social events of General Assembly week. It was flying along nicely.

Helen did not really enjoy formal social occasions, but now she was in the hall, she was warming to it. Initially she had been reluctant to participate, agreeing only after John pressed her. On arrival, she had been a little underwhelmed by the discreet entrance. For all the world like a side door, it was almost hidden within a colonnade that traced the length of the Court of Session building. Once through the door she quickly revised her impression.

Here, just off the Royal Mile and set behind the High Kirk of St Giles, was Scotland's original Parliament Hall, pre-dating the 1707 union with England. Stone and oak and solid: history alive and working today. Lawyers still met here through the day, pacing up and down the length of the hall as they consulted under the unswerving gaze of long dead luminaries whose portraits ringed the room. The constant pacing and changes of direction ensured that listening ears could never catch anything but fragments of a conversation.

This evening there was no pacing, the hall was thronged and it took determination and focus to manoeuvre around. Guests filtered through the entrance to be greeted by the Moderator and to exchange a few words with his special guests. Then they moved on into the throng, eager to seek out old friends and colleagues, and finally put faces to new email contacts. One particular cluster of people was gathered to one side, about midway along the hall: all friends, and John Dearly was at the heart of it. They greeted one another with an easy familiarity and accepted Helen's place within the group without question. She ended up enjoying herself, for the most part.

John had moved off into a neighbouring group when, in the midst of a conversation, Helen became aware of a thin faced man in a smart but conventionally cut suit. He had seemed to drift in unnoticed and was suddenly holding onto their every word and laughing at all the right moments.

Helen assumed he was a friend of John's. He was not. James Curry smiled and nodded enthusiastically, encouraging the conversation. He had neither knowledge of nor interest in the subject. However, he was interested in Helen, or rather was interested in anything to do with John Dearly's parish, and for the moment that included her.

James Curry was a senior cleric, clerk of the Edinburgh Presbytery, and he was taking the opportunity to be seen, to mix with the elite and to observe the one parish within his domain that was a constant source of irritation to him - St Bernard's. Its financial independence and failure to observe all the rules irked him.

Since taking on his new job, he'd dug as far as he could into the parish accounts. John Dearly's St Bernard's fascinated him. They seemed to delight in breaking the rules. And he needed to know what lay behind the trust that appeared to fund its generous spending power. Here was a trust that paid for all sorts of things, not least supporting the engagement of international assistants, such as this Helen Johnson.

He had tried several different approaches to gathering information, each time he failed. He could not get access to the trust, its quirky and ancient set up in what was now a tax haven proved to be an impenetrable barrier. He could get access to only the most basic of information about it and Dearly always played the silly laddie, claiming it sat beyond the parish's influence - rubbish.

Based on the ludicrously large income transferred to the parish accounts each year, James Curry knew it was a very sub-stantial fund and he wanted access to information about it. Dearly stood in his way, blocking his every move.

Time and again his mind returned to explore, drawn like a fox to the coop. He was frustrated, he knew there was some-thing big there, something that seemed quite secret, something of interest and he could get no closer. The old urban church with its characteristically small congregation was making large donations to the Kirk's central funds every year, as well as to a host of other charities. It was a scale of giving that could not really be explained away.

In the Scottish Church, each parish is an independent entity and makes a contribution to the centre according to its means. Then the poorer parishes receive grants back, becoming net beneficiaries, in effect being supported by the richer parishes. Statistically, St Bernard's should have been one of those net beneficiaries. It wasn't.

James Curry's problem was that as the established Church in Scotland, the Kirk was trusted and empowered to self-govern. While the Kirk itself oversaw the running and accounting of every parish and was trusted to keep its own house in order, he couldn't just bully a particular parish. Well, he shouldn't. Unless there was a specific irregularity suspected, he had no legitimate grounds to snoop any further. But he wanted to know exactly what was going on.

Twice he had chanced his arm and dropped in on Dearly unannounced, tried his luck, given him a little nudge - on both occasions Dearly had been impassive, quite unperturbed, seeming not to notice the veiled pressure being applied. Frustrated, James Curry had withdrawn, unable to press harder without attracting the interest of the Church itself, which he didn't want to do, just in case there was something lurking that would reflect badly on the presbytery. He needed to know and had no intention of just letting go.

John Dearly moved back through the crowd. He returned to Helen's little cluster, nodded greetings to old friends and took James Curry by the hand. 'James, there you are, all well?' The handshake appeared a friendly gesture to the uninformed, but lacked warmth as John pumped Curry's dead fish hand up and down. 'Always on patrol, eh?' He looked at Helen and winked. His joke fell on deaf ears.

James Curry smiled thinly and let his hand drop from John's. 'It's all for the common good, John,' he said, looking round at the others, appealing for the support of reasonable people and receiving a round of nods in agreement. 'Perhaps we should get together again soon, John? You know my role, always happy to help a parish, to help the wider community. Keeping the Church safe, keeping everyone safe.'

'Always willing to have a chat about the common good, you know that, James. Give me a call sometime, let's see if we can fix up a meeting,' said John.

Helen felt the lack of sincerity, the taut atmosphere between the two men, it could be cut with a knife, but she could not understand the cause.

Helen stepped slightly across John and whispered at him. 'You're not being very friendly.' She fixed him with a short glare before turning back to the group just as James Curry wished them well and moved on round the room.

Curry made a mental note that now at last was the time to drag the covers off John Dearly and his cosy existence.

The contract photographer wandered round the edge of the hall unnoticed by the throng of buzzing, networking partygoers. Fiona Sharp snapped away, producing the publicity shots specified by the PR people at '121', the familiar name for the Church of Scotland Headquarters, based at 121 George Street - as it happened, just a stone's throw from her base in Cassiter's offices. Her zoom lens also made sure that all those engaging with John Dearly were recorded. No audio, unfortunately.

• • •

Back from the Moderator's Reception in one piece, Helen lent against the manse's kitchen worktop watching John pour coffee into two mugs. Knowing she took milk, he added it without asking and crossed the room carrying both mugs, handing her one.

'Thanks,' said Helen, taking a sip. 'I need to be heading home soon. Sam's coming over to hear all about the reception. But tell me, I don't understand what the needle was between you and James. He seemed a genuine guy. What was going on?'

John gave a wave of his hand. 'Oh, we have a bit of a problem. You know what administrators can be like. He just likes a bit of a niggle, sticks his nose where it's not welcome, nothing important.'

'It seemed like it was important to him, what did you do to upset him?' She tried to keep the tone of her voice light but was intrigued to know why John, who did not seem to have an enemy in the world, was locking horns with such a senior man.

'Curry's just being a nuisance. Thinks we've got some secret stash of money and there's something underhand going on,' he laughed as he led Helen out through the kitchen door into the hall, making for the comfort of the lounge.

'Have you got a secret stash?' asked Helen.

John laughed out loud again as she followed him.

• • •

The late news was playing on the radio as Sam and Helen slumped together on the sofa in her living room. Sam was not pleased with the broadcast. 'I knew he'd get himself some news coverage, he's such a media tart, can't help himself.'

'Isn't that what a good department head should do? Get publicity for the university, attract more money?' asked Helen, trying to find something positive in MacPherson's interview.

'Of course,' said Sam, knowing he should not let himself get riled. MacPherson had acted exactly as he had expected. 'But give credit where it's due. Let the department have the recognition. What about the students who dug up the dagger and other artefacts? They deserve some credit too. Listening to that nonsense, you'd think he found the stuff himself. In fact, you'd think it was a one-man dig. I'm surprised that idiot hasn't got a Templar outfit on for the interview. Hmm, perhaps he has.'

They both listened in silence for a moment more until Sam stretched out and switched the radio off. 'God save us from such complete idiots. How did he ever land that job?'

Helen stretched her arm round and gently poked him in the ribs with a pointy finger. 'So now you need God? I see religion's fine when it suits you. Part-timer!'

'When it comes to MacPherson, I need all the help I can get.'

They settled down again and Helen looked absently at the silent radio for a few moments, suddenly transported back to the Fife dunes. 'You know, I'm not sure what it is, but there is still something familiar about that dagger, I can't put my finger on it. Just feel as though I know it somehow, it's weird.'

Sam nodded. 'Yes, daggers can look quite alike, especially that one. It had such a simple, elegant line, sort of an *every-dagger*. I think it's probably easy for people to mix it up.'

'Hey you, how many daggers do you think I'm familiar with?' protested Helen. 'I don't know how, it's a bit weird, it just seems familiar.'

Sam thought for a moment. 'Now you mention it, remember the two students from Hong Kong? Up on the dig? Yesterday they were over visiting the National Museum of

Scotland, brushing up on local cultural stuff before their families visit them over the summer. They left me a message yesterday, convinced an identical dagger is included as part of the weapons collection at the museum. Clearly, it can't be the dunes dagger. I don't know, maybe they have just got themselves confused. That *every dagger* thing of yours, you know? But now I think about it, imagine if there was a pair. What a stir it would cause. I'll call into the museum when I'm passing, if only to rule it out.'

'Well I'm not confused.' For the second time that evening, Helen dug him in the ribs. 'Come on, let's go out for a stroll, the night-time air is lovely and warm. Maybe stop for a late drink on the way back? Where do you fancy?' They headed out into the evening while Sam began to mull over his twin dagger theory.

• • •

Cassiter switched off the radio and leant back in his chair, silently assessing the range of possibilities thrown up by the radio news broadcast. Another Templar dagger? Coincidence? It may be unconnected, or perhaps the Edinburgh parish was a red herring. Were his team following the wrong scent? There was only one way to find out for sure, he would set his team to work on it. After careful thought he reached for the phone, Parsol would want to know about this new development. It appeared that the university's archaeology department and this Professor MacPherson might be in need of some attention.

He paused to review his computer screen. A transcript of recent conversations in the manse had just been flashed across to him. Nothing of real interest. The conversations showed no guilt or knowledge on the part of either Dearly or the young woman. But what was this mystery stash of money? Cassiter wondered if it might be an indicator of something, but of what? He filed the thought for the time being.

Chapter 8

SUNDAY 2nd JUNE

Confusingly, the Department of Field Archaeology was housed within the Old Medical School. An imposing building, it linked together with the University's equally impressive McEwan Hall to dominate the south side of Teviot Place. The Old Medical School was a great rectangle of stone that hid a fully enclosed courtyard at its heart. Massive gates gave access from the main street to a deep archway that burrowed through the side of the building to open out into the courtyard.

At some point in history it had been a cutting edge building, designed to meet the needs of the best, most modern medical practitioners of the day. That time was past and some aspects of medical teaching had long since been obliged to move, following the Royal Infirmary of Edinburgh and its supply of patients out to the hospital's new buildings on the city's outskirts: leaving space behind them.

The Department of Field Archaeology, being less demanding, had found a comfortable niche in a vacated corner of the old building.

Insurance policies demanded that night security was always tight, but the strongest defence was the building itself. Intimidating scale, confusing internal architecture and few accessible external windows, it seemed a thief's worst nightmare. The security department was aware of that and so were perhaps less concerned than they ought to be. No need to worry, the building was almost certainly impenetrable once the great gates were shut. Set beside the main gate was a small pedestrian access gate; it too was securely locked at night. Nobody had tried to force entry in years.

Ali Brown was the nightshift security guard, based in the porters' office. A suite of rooms accessed through a doorway leading directly off the archway and set a few feet back from the pedestrian access gate. Like most such places, it was warm and comfortable.

Ali had just settled down to his sandwich as the electronic buzzer announced a visitor at the pedestrian gate. Slightly peeved at the unexpected disruption to his routine, he stepped out into the archway and peered through the gates into the city street beyond. A policewoman was standing looking in.

She called through the gates. 'Someone's reported seeing a man scaling the building, have you seen or heard anything? The dog handlers are on their way.'

Ali had not heard anything, but was more than happy for the police to do the checking. He hurried across and unlocked the pedestrian gate, swinging it open to allow the policewoman entry. Fiona Sharp slipped quickly through the little gate. Her perfectly fitted uniform marked her as every inch the efficient policewoman. She smiled at the guard and laughed as she entered. 'I'm not sure my partner will fit through that,' she said, 'he's a big monster.'

Ali laughed back. 'Tell him to breathe in, that'll work.'

She looked back through the gate. 'He's just coming, has to park the car properly, even we can't be too careful these days.' She turned back to Ali. 'Have you got a building plan that we can have a look at before we get started?'

Robertson, a big man in police uniform, suddenly filled the pedestrian gate. He nodded towards Ali. 'All right there? Got plans for us?'

'Come into the office, I've got plans for the whole building. Though you won't need them, I'll take you round.' He slammed shut the pedestrian gate to trigger its night latch mechanism, it instantly locked. Full of importance, he led the police to the porters' office. They looked in from the doorway, watching him pull open a drawer full of building plans. 'This is the one you'll need.'

'Great, let's have a quick look, and then we'd better make a start,' said Robertson, holding his hand out for the plan. 'You'd better stand by here; the dog handlers should be along in a while and will need you to let them in.'

Ali had been about to object at being marginalised on his own patch, but then recognised he now had a specific job to do. Now he was part of the team. Only a visit by the armed response unit could have been more prestigious, more newsworthy. 'Right, I'll wait here and let them in as soon as they arrive,' he said. Content, he looked forward to the morning shift when he would regale them all with his participation in a search with the police dog handlers. The lads would be green with envy.

The police left Ali with a final warning that the intruder could be dangerous, so he must be careful to watch his back, maybe best to keep his door locked. Turning away from the entrance to the porters' office, the visitors set off through the archway for the quadrangle. Behind them, they heard the bolts inside the porters' office door slide shut. Suddenly feeling quite alone, no longer the fit young man of yesterday, Ali had become careful.

Fiona Sharp smiled to herself. They would not be disturbed and now they were equipped with keys, plans and swipe cards. Each swipe card had its associated internal alarm code printed neatly on the back. They entered the main building from the quadrangle and pushed the heavy door tight shut behind them. There they pulled on the forensic suits, gloves and bootees that ensured they would not contaminate the crime scene.

Methodically, Robertson swept through the building, switching lights on and off in each office. If the guard did decide to venture out into the quad he could follow the switching lights to track their progress around the building. Meanwhile, Sharp concentrated on Professor MacPherson's office. Cassiter needed to know what MacPherson knew, wanted what he had.

It took a little while for her to brute force break Mac-Pherson's computer password, but she got in without any trouble and began to search his files, reviewing them, copying each one relating to the Fife dig. There was very little, nothing of much relevance, just the humdrum of administration. He had not got round to writing up a report yet, and fortunately had not put any photographs on the network drive either, otherwise she would have had to track down and break into the network backups too and that was always a nuisance. She scanned his email account and found an interesting message from the department's photographic technician; she noted his name.

Leaving MacPherson's networked files in place; she logged out from his network account and turned her attention to his computer's local hard drive. On the local desktop was a folder full of pictures that she quickly transferred to a flash drive and having carefully reviewed the computer's local document folders, started to transfer a full copy.

While the transfer was underway, she checked his drawers and files for any hard copy photo prints of the dagger. She bagged them together with a cluster of USB sticks and a camera card. Then, with the full contents of MacPherson's computer safely copied, she deleted all the files on the local hard drive and fed in a neat little virus. The virus started work, overwriting the drive with gibberish. She walked away, knowing that once the drive was full of gibberish the virus' final act was a complete disc reformat, wiping all the information stored on his local workstation.

She continued on her prowl round the offices. Once she found the photo technician's desk, she repeated the careful search and delete process.

Communicating by click code on their walkie-talkie radios, the two searchers had kept in close touch, eventually meeting in the basement, at the secure room. Here items of high value were housed temporarily while they were the subject of research and investigation. Thereafter they would be transferred back to museums, private owners or the university's own long-term secure unit. Happily, the guard's key ring included the right keys together with the alarm security code on a plastic fob.

It took little more than five minutes to establish that the dagger was not there. Taking care to leave everything as they had found it, they left the secure room, locked the door and reset the alarm.

The pair kept their forensic suits on as they left the main building. They pulled the heavy door shut behind them and locked it before heading back to the porters' office. Ali had been watching the CCTV monitor in the porters' office and spotted them crossing the quadrangle. He quickly opened the door and stepped out just in time to hear the policewoman cancelling the dog handler on her radio.

'See anything?' he asked, and then looked quizzically at their forensic suits. 'What's all the space gear about?'

Robertson shrugged. 'New directive from up high, load of mince, but hey, they pay the wages.'

Sharp chipped in. 'We just do what we're told. Apparently they lost some big case because of contamination, so now we have to protect from the outset.'

Ali looked unconvinced. 'I've never heard of that before.'

'Like I say, it's just a new thing. Costing a fortune in suits. They'll probably let it fade away in a few weeks' time,' she said.

Robertson grinned at him. 'Look, how about sticking the kettle on and we'll get a cuppa? We're due a break and you've had your work cut out too.'

'I'll get it on now,' said Ali, pleased that there was probably no intruder and he was now getting a chance to mix socially with the police. The day shift would be totally sick.

'Tell you what,' said Robertson suddenly, 'what about a quick snifter, for a job well done?'

'Great idea,' agreed Sharp, 'but just a small one for you, you're driver tonight.'

Ali looked very doubtful. 'It's against our rules,' he said. 'If I'm caught I'll be out the door.' He was struggling to come to terms with police drinking on duty.

'Come on,' urged Robertson, 'who's going to catch you? Us?' He laughed. 'Well, what are you, a whisky or a vodka man?'

'Well, I do like a wee dram,' conceded Ali.

'Good man. Come on. Have a quick one with us, hey? Teamwork! A good job done together,' said Robertson, pulling out a bottle of Scotch from inside the stab jacket that bulged beneath his white forensic suit. He paused, fixed Ali with a conspiratorial stare and waved the bottle in his direction. 'Not a word to anyone mind, this is strictly in the business, not for civilians.'

Ali nodded, guilt at breaking the rules overcome by the confidence drawn from his new-found police colleagues and the knowledge that no one would ever know. Except the lads on dayshift of course, as fellow professionals they would need to know.

Robertson poured the drinks, clicking the bottle on Ali's mug. 'Down the hatch then,' he said.

A big measure of whisky had flooded Ali's coffee and he was drinking it enthusiastically as smaller measures dripped into the other two mugs. Ali was on his second measure in moments and beginning to feel as though he had arrived in the real security world at last. He relaxed.

'Have you got that new remote store video system installed here?' asked the policewoman, as she looked at the security console standing in proud isolation in a raised section to the rear of the room.

Quickly downing his third whisky Ali rushed to explain. 'The new hardware's in but we haven't got the system hooked up to the university's main security server yet, they've had some problems with it. Off the record, it might not be sorted for a while yet,' he confided to his new-found professional friends.

Robertson snorted. 'IT guys, they never deliver a finished job.'

'That's right,' agreed Sharp. She was delighted; she would not even need to break into the university's security server to sort the cameras. This job was becoming just too easy.

Ali stepped up on to the console platform, bent down and pointed under the console. 'We have a new set of external cameras that cover the whole courtyard and archway but we are still recording onto that local hard drive. It holds about four weeks' recordings, and then we record over them again. Hey, if there is no crime noticed in a month there was no crime to start with, right?'

His new police friends both nodded. 'One for the road?' asked Robertson, while pouring the guard more whisky without waiting for an answer. 'Then we'd better get back to work.'

Ali's natural caution had long gone; he smiled and knocked back the hefty shot of spirits. Draining the mug with a theatrical groan of pleasure, he grinned at Sharp and was suddenly overcome in a single swift movement from behind. Robertson's big arms wrapped around him, pinning Ali's arms to his sides. Ali was forced to his knees and then manoeuvred onto the floor.

Ali's face rested on the stone step leading down from the console area to the main room, his body pressed flat by the weight of the giant policeman on top of him. 'What the hell are you doing? Come on, the joke's over. Let me up,' protested Ali.

With a thrusting hand, Robertson cracked Ali's skull against the step. Stunned, his resistance ended. Pinching his victim's nose Robertson emptied the whisky bottle into his mouth. That was followed by a full bottle of vodka. Finally, he pulled out a small bottle of Absinthe and poured it into the mumbling mouth.

Sharp accessed the camera system and switched off all the cameras around the building. Then she accessed the hard drive, deleted the video records and set the drive to reformat. Finally, she carefully moved around the room. She cleaned two of the mugs, wiped surfaces and the edges of the building plan Robertson had handled earlier. She rolled the now empty spirit bottles in Ali's compliant hands, fixing his fingerprints on them.

'All set?' asked Robertson.

Sharp nodded, everything was as it needed to be. She thrust her still gloved hand into Ali's pocket and pulled out his keys, then quickly stepped out through the door into the archway to unlock the pedestrian gate. Leaving it ajar, she returned to throw the keys into the office. She waited outside, enjoying the cool fresh air that funnelled through the archway. The sound of a sickening crack echoed out from the gatehouse door, then a slight gasp and a groan and then silence.

Inside, a very drunken Ali had taken a nasty tumble; perhaps he had tripped on the flagstone step leading up to the camera console area and fallen. A skull travelling downwards from nearly six feet above the ground, falling at full speed and without the protection of sober hands can receive real damage. Particularly if it cracks onto the edge of a solid stone step. This skull did just that with the extra propulsion and assistance offered by two hundred and fifty pounds of human bear. The skull broke like a dropped egg.

Outside the porters' office, the two stripped off and bagged their forensic suits and police officer uniforms, revealing smart casual wear underneath. Having checked the coast was clear, they stepped out through the pedestrian gate, pulling it shut and locked behind them. They slipped unnoticed and untraceable into the night.

CHAPTER 9

MONDAY 3ʳᵈ JUNE

Sam and Helen settled down amongst a straggle of other late afternoon visitors to the museum's brasserie. As the waitress approached with their coffee order, Sam shifted slightly in his comfortably upholstered seat and stared through the glass partition that separated them from the museum's entrance hall. A long vaulted space, it mirrored the length of the main exhibition hall on the floor above. From his vantage point, he could see the entrance hall's full length.

Immediately beyond the glass and to his left hand were the doors through which visitors channelled in and out of Chambers Street. Beyond that were public toilets and then the reception and enquiry desk, a long stretch of service counter that would not have been out of place in an airport, its sleek line both stylish and functional if slightly out of character with the environment. Behind it stood a receptionist, eager to help the public but not really needed as the museum wound down for the day. Beyond her, a little cluster of attendants stood ready to respond if called on. At the far end of the hall were the bright lights of a museum shop twinkling back at him through their own glass partition.

The whole length of the entrance hall was illuminated by soft golden uplighters that threw light across the vaulted ceiling where it bounced back down onto the dark flagstone floor. Sam felt he was looking out on to an old Edinburgh street at twilight. The impression was consolidated for just a moment as a little group of visitors emerged from the stairway to his right, pedestrian-like, they wandered across his line of vision towards the main doors and the daylight beyond. His romanticised impression fled as the group paused to examine an ancient Egyptian mummy case, a feature not normally associated with Edinburgh street furniture.

Helen and Sam considered what they had just seen in the museum's gallery and had to agree with the two Hong Kong students' view.

'You know, those boys were sharp, I don't think I'd have noticed it amongst the other blades unless I'd known to look,' said Sam, impressed by the students' observation skills. He was thrilled, almost agitated by all the possible implications, and he was desperate to start investigating.

'I know, but how do you think it got there?' Helen asked, equally excited by the puzzle.

'I don't have a clue. I need to get a closer look at that dagger, find out where it came from and get its background. That should tell us more about our dunes dagger too. If they really are the same, they will share parts of a common story.'

Helen finished her coffee. 'Come on then, who do we ask?'

'No, no, there are procedures to follow. They won't just open a display case for us,' said Sam, shaking his head a little ruefully.

'Why not? You're an archaeology lecturer at the university. Sam, you're in the business! Let's go try.'

Sam put a hand onto her arm and stopped her from rushing off to the enquiry desk. 'I'll have to go back to the office and see who's in charge of that part of the collection. Then I'll write them an e-mail and then I'll phone them. Get in touch through official channels. Then we should have no problem getting access.'

'Everything by the book, you're all drowning under your own paper mountain, no wonder you guys lost your empire.' She threw her hands up and sighed. 'Oh, for somebody's sake, we just want a quick look at the thing, Sam.' Helen was a little frustrated, not just because she wanted to make the link between the two daggers, but she had once again felt that same sense of familiarity. She felt she knew the dagger, just could not think where from.

'Well we can't just barge in and demand access to an arte-fact, and that's final. Let's get back to the university and I'll get the ball rolling from there. Then we can try to get hold of MacPherson. I want a closer look at our dunes dagger too - getting access to that should be easier. Do you want to come?' Sam rose and held an arm out to guide or perhaps more to marshal Helen towards the exit, ensuring she made no attempt to shortcut the process by engaging with the curatorial staff directly. A little reluctantly, she followed his lead and they left the museum without drawing any attention to themselves or the dagger.

• • •

Cassiter sat at his desk. On it were two computer screens, one linked to his office computer system, the other linked to another quite separate system, used for the most private of work. He could have put all his work through the private system, but he knew his team's activity at the margins of life attracted interest from all sorts of places. It made sense to let such searchers find something to fixate on. While they were busy failing to break into his apparent main system they were not searching for the real core files.

Right now Cassiter was not looking at either computer screen. Fixed to the wall beyond his desk was a large flat screen television. The picture was frozen on a local BBC news programme. It showed a triumphant looking professor and projected up behind him was an image featuring a golden chain and signet ring. The picture had remained on screen all afternoon. Cassiter glowered at the screen. The television strapline seemed to taunt him:

University finds ancient treasures in Fife dunes

On the desk, beneath Cassiter's hands, was a brief report from Fiona Sharp. They had done a good job at the Old Medical School, cleaned up, removed evidence and left no trail. By killing himself through excessive drinking on duty, the security guard had made sufficient waves that nobody on campus was even thinking about accidentally wiped hard drives or the odd missing picture. The officials were concentrating hard on explaining how their system had allowed a drunk to be placed in charge of such an important building.

Cassiter was not happy in spite of his team's efficient work. He continued to stare at the television screen. 'Where is this dagger, professor? Where have you put it?' he said to the empty room.

Eugene Parsol was intending to visit Edinburgh next week. It was unheard of for a client to encroach into his working zone, and anyone other than Parsol would have been dumped on the spot. Cassiter did not know what was so important about the dagger. He knew roughly of its time period and origins, but had not needed to know details of why the quest was being undertaken. A lost and obscure dagger might be just what a rich man would focus on. As originally instructed, Cassiter had made no effort to find out more than he was briefed. His job was just to find the artefact, not to become an expert on its history. Cassiter got big, well-paid tasks because clients could always trust him to follow their rules.

Until a day or so ago, he had imagined that Eugene Parsol was after a single dagger, which they now believed was hidden somewhere in Dearly's church, St Bernard's; it seemed now to have expanded into a multiple quest. Cassiter had forwarded the original audio news clip, wondering if it was of some passing interest, perhaps even indicating that their local church idea was wrong. Then, suddenly, the world had exploded in a fit of activity, with Parsol now demanding this dagger from the dunes of Fife be retrieved, in addition to continuing the hunt at St Bernard's. But they had not got the dunes dagger; it was nowhere to be found on campus.

For Cassiter and the world he inhabited there were no shades of grey, no partial successes. Clients wanted results. No daggers equalled no results.

Events were throwing up some issues. How many blades were there? For the first time he allowed himself to wonder about their real purpose or value, but most of all he focused on the need to take personal control of their retrieval. And there must be no trace left of either dagger by the end of the job, so the BBC archive would need to be cleaned too, at least that would be routine. Big institutions with their ponderous, ironclad security systems and multiple access points were often the easiest to work around, he'd put one of the team on that. Parsol would not expect anything else. And it would need to be done now. He reached for the phone and began making the necessary calls.

• • •

Sam drove through the Old Medical School's great archway and into the quadrangle beyond. From the front passenger seat, Helen pointed out the university's chief of security who was standing in a small doorway watching their progress. Sam steered to a halt beside the doorway. The chief stepped round to the driver's side and nodded recognition in response to Sam's half-raised hand of greeting. In a brusque voice, he told them the site was closed to all staff until the police had concluded their investigations.

On the face of it, there was little to investigate. But the guard had been known as reliable and had never drunk on duty before. Furthermore, his wife insisted he never touched vodka or Absinthe, and they didn't have a penny to spare anyway, so where would he have got money for bottles of spirits? There was something not quite right about the circumstances, and now classes had finished for the summer there was little pressure on the police to sign off quickly. They were taking the time to review things carefully and nobody was getting in the building for now.

However, the chief had always liked Sam's considerate approach to his staff, particularly that Sam took time to acknowledge the porters and guards as part of the university team; unlike some of the academics who did not seem to notice his staff were even there and certainly would not have passed the time of day with them. So the chief took the time to answer Sam's questions, assuring him that Professor MacPherson had not been on site all day. What's more, the chief would person-ally be locking the gates in a moment and, under the circum-stances, no one would now be getting in until morning at the earliest.

Then the chief leant forward a little towards Sam's open car window and tipped them off in a conspiratorial half whisper. 'There was some problem with broken CCTV.' He tapped the side of his nose with a knowing finger.

Sam did not really know what he meant by the sign but gave a sage nod in response. The chief of security was either in the know and was not saying or he did not know and was not about to let Sam realise it. Sam suspected it was the latter. The chief straightened up and waved Sam and his pretty redheaded passenger away. Helen flashed him a sympathetic smile and Sam gave a wave of thanks as he obeyed the direction to drive back out through the great archway.

• • •

An hour later, pebbles scrunched under the wheels of Sam's car as it pulled into the driveway of Professor MacPherson's house. It was an impressive old sandstone villa of the type found scattered throughout the older and more affluent suburbs. Many similar properties had now been divided to create flats: smaller, more practical spaces for modern living. MacPherson's house had not been subdivided and it retained its impressive driveway and grand façade, which presented in exactly the style conceived two-hundred years earlier. It impressed just as much today as it had done when new. This was the property of people who did not have to concern themselves with worries over balancing the monthly budget.

They were warmly welcomed at the front door by a neatly turned out woman in her early forties. Sam had spoken to Sarah MacPherson only once before, at a party to introduce MacPherson when he had been appointed as the new department head. Then they had exchanged a few words of polite conversation before she dutifully drifted away in the wake of her husband. Their paths did occasionally converge at graduation day ceremonies and such, but were only fleeting encounters, marked by just a nod and a smile. Sam had come to consider her a non-person, pretty much the self-effacing shadow of her husband.

Here at home, she was entirely different. Confident on her own territory. Sarah MacPherson greeted them with real warmth and a gushing enthusiasm. 'Sam, come on in, so good to see you again. Come in, come in. You know, we've never really talked. We can put that right today.' Catching Helen's eye as they entered she continued. 'I don't think I've seen you at the university, have I?'

Helen gave a warm smile back and stretched out her right hand. 'Helen Johnson. No, Sam doesn't let me visit very often. I think he's keeping me away from everyone at his work.'

'Oh, Sam, that just won't do,' she said, letting Helen's hand drop and shooing them through the grand entrance. 'Straight ahead now, on you go!' Directly in front of them stretched a broad hallway; coiling off it to the left was an impressive staircase leading away to the bedrooms on the upper floor.

'MacPherson's had to pop out, but he should be back in a while. He said you should wait.'

Sam was struggling to reconcile the warm and outgoing Sarah with his image of a timid mousey woman. 'I hope we're not inconveniencing you, Mrs MacPherson, we could always come back later,' he said.

'Sam, I insist you call me Sarah and it's no bother at all. You spoke to him on the phone, he knows you're coming,' she waved them into a large lounge. It was furnished and kept by the hand of somebody who clearly cared about elegant living. 'Now, the pair of you sit yourselves down while I organise us something to drink. I noticed you were driving, Sam, so you can have coffee, tea, or perhaps a fruit juice? Helen, you can have the same or perhaps a gin and tonic? A glass of rosé wine?' She gave Helen a warm smile. 'You could have a Scotch, but you don't look like a whisky drinker to me.'

Helen thought for a moment. 'Hmmm, it's very tempting. You know what? Wine sounds really nice, but not if it means opening a bottle specially.'

Sarah rested a friendly hand on Helen's forearm and squeezed gently. 'My dear, trust me, in this house there's never a special opening. Rosé's always chilled and on tap,' she laughed and Helen joined in.

'Oh well, definitely a rosé for me then,' said Helen as she sat down.

Sarah headed for the far end of the room where a discreet cocktail cabinet with integrated fridge had been blended into the general décor. 'Sam, what do you want?' she called over her shoulder.

'Mine's an orange juice please,' said Sam, still standing. He was amazed at this different Sarah. Here she was a real livewire, such fun, how on earth did MacPherson capture her? He felt a gentle kick on his calf and glanced down.

'Sit down Sam, you're staring!' Helen whispered at him as she patted the sofa beside her. While waiting for the drinks they admired a pair of beautiful bronze statuettes on a coffee table. Helen praised them when Sarah returned with the drinks. Their hostess glowed with pleasure and it was immediately clear that Helen had struck exactly the right chord.

Sarah's passion was art and they learnt all about her work as a sculptress in metals. Well over an hour had passed before

MacPherson's car finally rolled into the driveway. In that time, all three had become firm friends.

Before MacPherson had even entered the room, she had his drink ready. He took the Scotch from her hand, kissed her cheek and thanked her in a single practiced movement. Sam watched with interest. Here was the grumpiest, most self-interested man he had ever had to work with behaving like a real civilised human being, and married to such a fascinating, enthralling woman too.

'Sorry I'm so late,' said MacPherson. 'I've been along at the Tun again. You know it? The BBC's studios just up from the parliament. A chance popped up to get our find on the main Six O'Clock News. That's a real step up from the local coverage I'd already got. It all helps, but this evening was a bit of a waste. I was shunted down the running order and then right off it. Some politician with a burning topic to shout about, and I was bumped out. Still, we've been featured on the radio a couple of times and I suppose that at least I managed to get on today's lunchtime regional TV news. Did any of you see it?' He gave a shrug in response to their shaking heads and paused to take a drink from his Scotch.

'I half wonder why I bother. I took them a beautiful silver dagger and their time constraints, or more likely the world's treasure fixation, means they only wanted to feature the gold chain and ring. Media barbarians, they understand nothing. They basically ignored the really important piece, the silver dagger. It got just a few words mention on the end of their extended gold drool.'

MacPherson checked his rant, gave an exasperated sigh and looked closely at his guests. 'So what can I do for you that's so urgent it can't wait a day?'

Before they could answer, Sarah interrupted. 'Look, we'll be eating in a minute, MacPherson likes to eat early, why don't you both stay and eat, and you can tell him what you want over dinner.'

Sam and Helen started to protest, but Sarah brushed their objections aside. 'It's in the oven and I'm serving up any moment now so it would be convenient for MacPherson to listen to you over his meal.' Then she continued in a theatrical whisper that MacPherson could clearly hear. 'The old boy's got a bit set in his ways. He likes to eat dinner at *his* dinnertime. I know you haven't eaten yet, so join us, please?'

MacPherson waved his now empty glass. 'Yes, stay, I'll get us all top ups while Sarah gets the food.'

It was nearly ten by the time Sam had his car edging out of MacPherson's drive. Liberal helpings of alcohol had definitely put Helen and the MacPhersons on the merrier side of jolly. As designated driver he remained sober, but a very happy sober. Incredibly, MacPherson had the dagger and jewellery with him. They had been travelling around in his briefcase since he had returned from the dunes. It was handy if a media opportunity arose.

Over dinner, the dagger had done the rounds and Sam had completely revised his view of MacPherson. Here at home, away from the demands of leading a university department and the constant pressure to attract money and publicity, he was actually good company; they all got along famously. When Helen told MacPherson of the other dagger at the museum, he seemed as excited as they were. Better still, he was a personal friend of the relevant curator there. They had studied together years before. He would telephone the man first thing in the morning and make arrangements for Sam to get access.

The only dark spot came when MacPherson remained adamant he would not let the dunes dagger out of his possession. Once they had all admired it over the dinner table, it had been spirited away to some secret hiding spot. Sam still had a problem, no matter how helpful the museum was, they would never release an artefact to go wandering off around the city, and with MacPherson keeping tight hold of the dunes dagger it was going to make comparisons between the two difficult. Sarah had given Helen a wink as they left and told her not to worry, to leave the problem with her, promising she would see what she could do about getting them access to the dagger.

The ever-lengthening summer evenings meant that it was still twilight as Sam's car rolled through the city streets. The cityscape did not register with Sam who was thinking intensely about daggers. Helen brought him back to the present by gently running her hand down his arm and letting it slide onto his thigh, rubbing it gently. 'Well, that went well I think. What does my resident archaeologist think?'

'I think we want to know a lot more about those daggers.'

'And I think you got the MacPhersons all wrong. She's lovely, and away from the department, he's an okay guy too. Anyway, it's too late to be doing anything more tonight; I reckon it's home time.'

Sam smiled and as he drove along, he stretched his hand out to stroke her cheek. She turned her lips just in time to kiss his hand before it returned to the steering wheel.

Chapter 10

TUESDAY 4th JUNE

MacPherson had made the promised early morning phone call to his curator friend at the museum. It had triggered an almost instant response from Suzie Dignan, the curator's assistant. She had contacted Sam and readily agreed to help sort out anything possible for him. They were to meet at 10.00 inside the museum's main entrance.

It was shortly after nine in the morning when Sam drew his car to a halt in the driveway of John Dearly's manse. Helen leant over from the passenger seat to kiss him briefly. 'Have a good morning and see if you can finally solve the dagger mystery. Come back round when you've finished, I'll be here.'

'No problem and I'll keep you posted if I'm going to run beyond lunch,' Sam replied.

They both got out. Sam left his car and set off for a brisk walk to the Old Town, aiming for Chambers Street and the museum. Helen walked up to the front door, rang the manse's doorbell then pushed the door open, let herself in and made for the kitchen.

John Dearly sat in his favourite place at the manse's kitchen table. He was focusing intently on the letter in his hand. It was from the Church. From James Curry, the presbytery clerk. On the table was his copy of *The Scotsman*, trumpeting a new government drive to expose and stop people abusing charitable status for their personal benefit. Helen entered the room unacknowledged. The newspaper article did not catch her interest; however, she noted almost absently that John seemed to be cross-referring between the article and letter.

He glanced up to greet her, but his slightly preoccupied expression remained. 'Ah, there you are. Coffee's made, help yourself,' he waved towards a steaming pot before taking a final glance at the letter and folding it away carefully into its envelope. He placed it on the table beside him.

Helen poured a coffee and joined him at the table. She paused for a moment, not quite sure where to start. He seemed hesitant too. John was reluctant to break the news that she would not be given the opportunity to stay on once her exchange period was up. The commitment had only ever been for one year, but he could tell Helen had gradually come to hope for a longer stay.

Before he could deliver his news, Helen started. 'I've been speaking to my father on the phone, and you know he's really upset. Pop always enjoyed his visits to Scotland and he said Archie had always made him feel so welcome.' She searched John's eyes for a response. He nodded wistfully and then gave a thin smile, thinking fondly of his old friend Peter Johnson and of less stressed times.

'Pop sends his best wishes. They've been remembering Archie in the Sunday services back home and thinking of you as well. He's sorry he can't come over, but you know he's not so mobile anymore. Mom sends her love too.'

John shifted in his seat a little and looked out of the window. 'It seems the whole world misses Archie. I just can't come to terms with what happened to him. Why it happened to him,' he looked back across the table towards Helen. The controlled front he managed to put up to the world seemed to waver in Helen's presence. Somehow he did not feel the need to pretend in front of this young woman. 'I'm struggling to reconcile it all. It just seems so black, so evil. How could this have happened to such a good man?'

Helen tried to console him. 'It must have been the act of a madman, a psychopath. No sane person would, could, ever do such a thing.'

John Dearly looked at her, his eyes almost resigned to despair. 'Yet the police are no nearer catching the man,' he sighed. 'They have no idea who is involved. If it really were a madman, there would be a medical records trail to follow, a track record, something. They'd have him by now. I don't think they have a clue what to do. I don't think they are any nearer finding Archie's killer than the day it happened.' He paused for a moment. 'But if he's not a madman, then what is he? And why Archie?'

The conversation was moving into deep waters and Helen tried to steer it back. 'Come on John, all this stuff's beyond us. Let's leave it to the professionals, they'll get their man soon enough,' she said, then stood and picked up the now empty mugs. 'Let's get more coffee, what do you say?' John nodded absently at her as she stepped over to the pot.

'They're coming again tomorrow morning, you know?' said John.

'Who's coming?' Helen's voice tried to strike a cheery note, attempting to lift the mood.

'The police. That senior man. Wallace, DCI Wallace. We've already spoken three times. I really don't know what extra light I can shed on things for him.'

'No, but at least it shows they are being thorough. And that's good, yeah?'

'I suppose so. It would be even better if they could just track the killer down.'

Helen paused from pouring coffee to fix John with a supportive look. 'Would you like me to be here when he comes? It's no problem for me.'

John gave a weary nod. 'Would you mind? I am starting to feel a bit worn down by it all. I just can't put what was done to

Archie behind me. You won't need to say anything, your just being here would be a support.'

'No prob',' said Helen returning to the kitchen table.

He wondered again at the confusion of events. Archie's awful death, the police investigation, and now this letter from the Church had arrived. It was just about the worst possible timing, but the new presbytery clerk wanted to call in for a fact-finding meeting. The presbytery clerk suggested a meeting in the church itself so he could get a feel for the place at the same time. It was a polite request but one that could not reasonably be denied. He knew from Elaine's recent grumblings that the man had the parish in his sights, and had no interest in or respect for local difference. John's previous meetings with James Curry had been uncomfortable. It was clear he was not the type to tolerate any variation or local colour on his patch; it would not be an easy meeting. To top it all, he had to tell Helen that her stay could not be extended. And what would his old friend Peter Johnson make of that?

He should have told her before now, but other than the Moderator's Reception, they had hardly had a moment to speak together since Archie's death. And the reception had certainly not been the right occasion. He sighed again as Helen sat back down with the fresh coffees.

Biting the bullet, John broke the bad news, stressed how much good she was doing, how the congregation loved her, how he valued her good work, loved her vivacity and how it challenged so many of the old conventions. But for all that, they could not extend her stay in the parish. He was letting her know now so she had plenty of time to make other arrangements. If things were otherwise, he would have wanted her to stay, but that is how it was.

Helen was devastated by the news. She knew the post was only for a year, had no right to expect more, but she had come to harbour hopes of an extension. She felt at home here. It was just not what she had expected, though with everything else that had been happening she had really not been giving her future any thought. All she could do was lamely ask for confirmation that she could see her year out. She felt limp, deflated. In the past few months she had finally found an environment where she fitted in, mostly, and then there was Sam: this news was a disaster.

Helen looked at John, he was visibly agitated at having caused her distress; she had to accept his decision but didn't want him to suffer for it. She made an effort to change the subject. 'John, you know the strangest thing happened when we were in Fife. Sam and the students found a body.'

John looked slightly puzzled, then alarmed. 'What, another body? What happened over there?' He started to sound concerned for her.

'No, no, John, an old dead body, a skeleton, buried beneath the dunes. I don't know, hundreds of years old.' She felt flattered and a little guilty that poor John should find time to worry about her amidst his own shock and persistent grief for Archie.

He looked relieved and politely forced himself to focus on her story, to ask her for details. Helen told the story - the mystery Templar Knight, the signet ring on a golden chain, and the beautiful, inexplicable dagger. As John Dearly heard the story, his worries seemed to slide aside and he came to focus intently on her every word. He started asking questions, suddenly fully engaged, eventually leading the storytelling through ever tighter and more detailed questioning.

Helen was delighted that John was so interested, and then she became a little concerned. He was buzzing, pacing to and fro across the kitchen. His persistent questioning dragged every bit of information out of her. Finally, he needed to see the dagger. It was urgent, he must see it; could Sam let him see it? Helen told him the dagger was being kept at MacPherson's home, unofficially, but she would see what could be done. John nodded acceptance and suddenly excused himself. There were some parish papers he needed to review. Would she make sure the front door was locked on her way out? And he was gone, flying from the kitchen without a backward glance.

Having washed the coffee mugs she was about to leave when the envelope on the table caught her eye. It was the letter that had clearly been causing John so much anxiety. She threw a look up to the ceiling. 'Forgive me God, for I am sinning, again,' and she picked up the letter and quickly scanned it, scowled and read it again. James Curry, the new presbytery clerk who she had heard Elaine muttering about, was proposing to visit next afternoon. Why had it seemed to unsettle John? She would offer to attend that with him too. It seemed he was coming under extra pressure from all sides right now: police in the morning and presbytery in the afternoon.

Glancing at the newspaper article something caught in her mind and she sat to read it carefully. Then she recognised the picture, it was the Moderator, she had met him briefly at the reception the other evening. She thought back to the evening of the reception, remembered the tension between John and the presbytery clerk. She thought of John's laughing dismissal of her question about trust money, saw the political interest in old trust funds and suddenly wondered if somehow John was being put under pressure. Perhaps things were not as they might be in the parish accounts?

John was clearly a bit shaky and she would support him for the remainder of her term, regardless. She was deeply hurt by his inexplicable rejection, but she had to rise above that. She would continue to do her bit because that was her way, and just as importantly, because she knew her father would expect it of her.

• • •

Sam's watch was just reaching 10.00 as he strode along Chambers Street. The museum filled much of the south side of the street, part new sympathetic extension, part older sandstone building. Wide steps led up from pavement level. They had guided generations of visitors directly up to the original main entrance and on into the exhibition hall.

Sam ignored the steps, knowing they now served only as a rallying point for visiting tour groups or seating where friends could stop and chat when the sun shone. Just before reaching the steps, he turned and entered the museum through an unremarkable pavement level door. It led into the vaulted entrance hall where he and Helen had drunk coffee the previous afternoon.

He could see a young woman at the near end of the reception counter. She leant one elbow on the counter while chatting across it to the receptionist. At the same time her systematic scanning of those entering the museum made it clear she was waiting for somebody. Her familiarity within the environment marked her out as staff and Sam guessed this was his appointment. She was not dressed as front of house staff: an open white lab coat topped her trainers, jeans and a plain tee shirt. An ID badge clipped over her left breast confirmed Sam's guess.

Suzie Dignan was at the stage in her career where hoped for promotions and natural enthusiasm had not yet been worn down by the grind and disappointments of working life. She loved her work in the museum, was happy to help her boss, and professionally intrigued by this archaeologist's need to access one of their display cabinet artefacts in such a hurry.

Sam gave no sign of recognition as he walked over, snatching those few seconds of anonymity to consider her. She had scanned him at a distance and moved on to check others amongst the steady trickle of visitors who were entering the museum. The white lab coat was old fashioned, he was prepared to bet nobody else in the building wore one anymore, yet she was still in her twenties. Petite with short brown hair, she was what might be described as plain, not pretty, not unattractive either. A comfortable face. He wondered if she found some kind of refuge behind the traditional white coat.

As he approached, he could see that her eyes sparkled with life. Those eyes turned back to reprise him as he neared. And what had been a slightly concerned expression broke into a warm and welcoming smile. Sam just felt the day improve through her proximity; her smile was like a second sunrise. He noted that the museum receptionist was smiling too. Suzie stepped clear of the reception counter. 'Sam Cameron?' she asked.

'That's me, and you must be Suzie Dignan, who's giving up her busy morning for me.'

Suzie shook his hand and nodded. 'Great to meet you. Come on, we'll go to my office first. You can tell me what you're looking for,' she turned and led him towards a service lift, 'and I'll see what I can do to help.'

Sam kept pace with her. 'It's really good of you to see me at such short notice. I'm trying to draw together different research strands, it was a couple of my students who pointed out your artefact to me. I just need to review it and decide whether to include it or exclude it from our work.'

'Oh, how intriguing, it seems so interesting, so mysterious. I can't wait to hear more. My boss seems to be an old friend of your boss. He said I should help you in any way I can.' She paused theatrically, gave him a sideways glance and another beam of sunburst smile. 'Within the law, of course.'

Sam and MacPherson had agreed the previous evening not to mention any possible relationships between the artefacts. In fact, agreed to avoid revealing anything at all about Sam's pair theory. It would eliminate any risk of leaks before Sam had found the facts. Facts that MacPherson could then exploit to get maximum impact for the story and the department, and for the museum too. Knowing the back-story to the museum's dagger and mixing in the intrigue of the recent find in the Fife dunes would make a really good summer news story. In the meantime, hc was to proceed on a 'need to know only' basis; Sam had to stay tight-lipped wherever possible.

The need to hold back information about the dunes dagger meant Sam found the meeting quite difficult. Suzie was bubbling, enthusiastic and clever, a great combination to push at knowledge boundaries, but he had to sit on his own inform-ation. Suzie was clearly a trusting soul and did not imagine for a moment that his account was anything less than complete. She had promised him the whole day if necessary. No evening work though, her sister and baby nephew had just come to stay with her for a week or so before they all went off on a week's holiday together.

It was quickly clear that Suzie had no prior knowledge of the dagger, so she took him up to the display and Sam's eyes scanned the cabinet.

'That's the one I'd like to see.' Involuntarily, like a little boy in a sweet shop, he moved to the edge of the display cabinet and pointed through the glass. 'That's the one, please.'

Suzie dealt with the alarm then retrieved the dagger and they both returned to her office. Once she was satisfied Sam had what he wanted she left him to it, going off to start digging out background information on the dagger's story. It took Sam less than a minute to satisfy himself as to the pairing, and then he took the time to review the design, construction and perfect simplicity of the whole.

He realised there was a difference between the blades after all. The construction and materials were identical and the decorated side of the museum's dagger did have the ornate Templar cross at the top, close to the hilt. And just like the dunes dagger, the engraved pattern stayed well clear of the cutting edges. However, he felt the swirling line design was somehow different - same style but a different design nonetheless, and right at the tip, it had a different Roman numeral: IV. To make any sense of the difference demanded a comparison between the two blades and that would have to wait for another day.

Suzie returned with some preliminary findings. It seemed the dagger, together with various other items including some family papers and a generous financial bequest, had been left to the museum in the 1920s. The donor, a widow, had been the last in the line of some minor Scottish noble family. Unfortunately, the records and various artefacts seemed to have become spread around different departments over the decades and there was not much information immediately to hand.

Suzie was not content with the story as it stood and felt she could come up with more. The museum would have considered the dagger an interesting though minor artefact, it had not merited much investigation to date; she would sort that out. Sam was more than confident that she would unearth something if allowed to get on with it. Suzie intended to spend some time digging through their records to trace whatever the museum had on the dagger's history and on the widow's family too.

Having walked Sam from the office area, she left him to make his own way out of the museum and rushed back to start her search. She promised to keep him updated with any developments.

Sam decided to wander around the streets for a while, just taking time to savour the thrill of the discovery before heading back to the manse to share the news with Helen.

• • •

Grace was busy cleaning the church. She had an old bath towel and was using it as a giant duster, quickly and efficiently wiping the pews of any debris and clearing away the cobwebs that kept re-forming at this time of year. She moved steadily back and forth across the church, along one pew then forward to the next. After this, she would sweep the wooden floors and here time and labour would be saved too by the use of an exceptionally broad broom.

Grace had the cleaning down to a fine art. She worked in silence, gliding around in her trainers. If she had made a noise she would never have known - personal headphones kept her ears filled with distinctly non-Christian rock music. She was oblivious to everything but the beating music and the pew she was cleaning.

At the head of the aisle stood the communion table - imposing, expansive, stark: no artworks, no elaborate decoration. Behind it, the chancel stretched away, a deep semi-circular space. Set off to the right side was seating for the choir, to the left was the organ and at the deepest point in the chancel was a large cross of blackened wood, unadorned, fixed to the wall.

Above the cross, a great leaded window let light flood in. The mostly plain glass had at its centre a single coloured image of a burning bush; it glowed bright like fire in contrast to its plain neighbours. And spread symmetrically around the outermost edges of the sea of plain glass were eight little islands of coloured glass, each depicting a further religious scene.

Set to the left of the communion table was the great pulpit, and beyond that, the door to the vestry.

Jim Barnett hovered behind the pulpit, trapped. Earlier in the morning, he had seen Helen going into the manse to visit the minister and watched that boyfriend of hers walking off towards the city centre. He had thought he could come to the church undisturbed. Once inside, ostensibly for a quiet moment of contemplation, he had carefully, almost deferentially, walked up the aisle towards the communion table, cautious glances ensuring he was alone in the building. At the front of the church, he slipped to his left. He quickly passed the steps leading up to the great pulpit and came to the vestry door. It was unlocked and he was through it in a flash.

He commenced his search. Cemented to the ground and concealed beneath a little occasional table he found a small safe. He was not equipped to open it today so he moved on. Crossing to the back of the vestry, he made his way through another door that opened into a short corridor. Two doors led off the corridor to the left, the first to an office, the second to a toilet. Beyond, at the end of the corridor was another door, a rear exit: old, wooden, solid and alarmed. Barnett went directly to the office. He was familiar with the layout, having recently attended a meeting there with the minister, several of the elders and one or two other active church members.

He carefully and efficiently searched the office, checked cupboards, files and drawers, lifted rugs, tapped the wooden panelling right round the room while listening out for the hollow sound that would betray a secret compartment. Nothing. The desktop computer had not presented a problem as he had observed the password being used during his previous visit. In fact, the elder logging on had asked for a reminder of the password from the others and they had promptly responded, releasing the password to him in the process. Today he had a flash drive and simply copied all the documents from the computer memory.

There was no sign anywhere of any security normally associated with high value assets. In the filing cabinet, he found the parish insurance policy and photographed it. It made no reference to any special value items, though it did cover the regular things you would expect: communion set of plate, cup and cross; some candlesticks; and one or two other bits and pieces. Their total value would probably not have tempted the average burglar out of bed. There was nothing of interest here.

Jim Barnett called it a day and left the office exactly as he had found it. He returned to the vestry, but just as he was stepping back out into the church nave, he saw a moving shadow thrown across the far wall. He stopped dead and watched, then carefully edged round the pulpit to see who was there. It was the elder's daughter, Grace. He was trapped.

'Grace. Grace!' Helen stood inside the entrance to the church, calling Grace's name. She had really come for a little quiet time before Sam got back from the museum, needing to think over her future before telling Sam that she was not able to stay on in Edinburgh. But as soon as she had seen Grace, she experienced a sudden overwhelming need to speak to a friend.

'Grace!' she called again, then realised the girl had her headphones on. Deciding that John would not really want her shouting in his church, and thinking that God was probably not that keen either, she walked towards Grace who caught sight of her and straightened up with a grin.

'Helen, how are you?' she said, pulling the headphones from her ears, then, with a twinkle in her eye. 'Fancy seeing you here, what are you doing in a place like this?'

Helen began to feel better almost at once. 'Heaven knows. Oh, you know, they probably-'

'-Do.' Grace finished Helen's sentence and they both laughed. 'Come on, you look like you need a drink. Let's see where John hides his communion wine.' She abandoned the bath towel duster and linked arms with Helen as they set off towards the vestry.

'Or tea would do,' suggested Helen.

'Okay, tea. We'll have the kettle boiling in no time. So tell me, why the long face?'

Jim Barnett slipped back into the vestry and retraced his steps across the room and out into the little corridor behind. He knew the kettle was in the office so slipped beyond it to the toilet and closed the door just as the two women entered the corridor. He glanced at the sink and hoped the kettle had water in it.

A half-full kettle provided all the water they needed. Helen and Grace settled down over a cup of tea and talked through Helen's news. Grace was deeply disappointed that Helen had to go. She had been getting used to having a female ally around the place. On the other hand, Helen could always come back and visit for holidays and she could visit Helen in America, go to Disney World and stuff.

Eventually their talk wandered onto Helen's trip to Fife, how they found the dead Templar and all about his ring and dagger.

Suddenly a body appeared in the doorway. Elaine McPhee stood holding the bath towel duster. 'Grace, will the church clean itself?' She looked at Helen and gave her a polite nod. 'It's yourself, I see.'

Grace stood up. 'We've just taken a break and Helen had news to share. Did you know she's not able to stay on when her year's up?'

Elaine could be grumpy and uncompromising, sometimes to the point of harshness, but she was not given to lying, and certainly not to her daughter. She tried to avoid answering the question and turned to Helen. 'I've just been speaking with John. He confirmed you won't be staying on, I hope wherever you go you'll find a place you can call home.'

Helen noticed Elaine had not answered the question. 'I'm sure I will, but I'll be sad to go. And you know this place was starting to feel like it could have been home.'

'Aye, well, I'm sure it's for the best in the end. I know you'll not find John stinting in your praise if you need a reference.'

Helen smiled acknowledgement at her, but references were the last thing on her mind. She could never understand why the elder was always slightly frosty with her. She knew it was nothing to do with her being a woman. She had seen Elaine mixing with enough women clerics to know that it was not a theological problem for her.

'Did you hear about the skeleton Helen found in the dunes, Mum?' asked Grace. 'He had a gold signet ring and a silver dagger.'

'Yes, John told me, though it doesn't sound like anything that should be of concern to us. Just let's pray somebody gives the man a Christian burial at long last.' It was clear from her tone that she wanted the issue closed.

Helen did not let it rest. 'I did say a few words over the bones before they were moved.'

'Well, God bless you for that,' said Elaine, with a sincerity that warmed Helen a little and confused her too.

Helen smiled and nodded her head slightly in acknowledgement. 'Perhaps we'll have a proper little service for him when the archaeologists are finished. Maybe we could even bury his remains here. They really deserve to rest in consecrated ground somewhere,' she said.

'You know I think you might be right. I'm sure John would favour that idea too - you should put it to him,' said Elaine.

There was a sudden knock on the doorframe directly behind Elaine. Startled, she turned as they all looked through the doorway to see Jim Barnett.

'Oh, where did you come from?' asked Elaine. Her voice expressed a degree of surprise that did not register in her craggy features as she gave Jim Barnett a slight welcoming nod.

Barnett responded with a rueful grin. 'Hi everyone. Sorry if I made you jump, Elaine. I think I left a notepad after the meeting the other night and came back to look for it. I heard voices so came straight through. Don't suppose anyone saw it or handed it in?'

Barnett had taken his chance to slip from the toilet and glide to the open office door. Once there, those inside would never be able to tell from what direction he had come. And having overheard the whole conversation he was satisfied that Helen and Grace knew nothing of any interest to Cassiter. As for McPhee, she was still just that grumpy old git who could only be improved by a good kicking. Barnett would be prepared to help out with that if the opportunity presented itself.

Helen responded promptly. 'Nothing was handed in that I know of. Did you find anything in the church, Grace?'

Grace shook her head as they all instinctively looked around the office. There was no sign of the notepad.

'Oh well, it was worth a try. I must have dropped it on the bus. I'll go and check with the bus company's lost property office. Thanks for your time though, and I'm sorry for causing any bother.' Barnett turned and headed off, keen to be away and content he could report that other than a little safe that he had yet to open, the church was clean and certainly these three seemed to know nothing.

Elaine half stepped into the corridor and called after him. 'Aye, good luck with your search. If it does turn up here we'll let you know.' She stood for a moment in silence, watching the now closed door, her stoic face not betraying the slight sense of puzzlement she felt.

Chapter 11

WEDNESDAY 5th JUNE

DCI Robert Wallace stood in the back garden of the manse looking up towards the kitchen window. In front of him and directly beneath the window, Detective Sergeant Brogan was crouching down and scanning for footprints or any other clue. Nothing. Days of early summer sun had baked the ground hard. He tilted his head up and considered the kitchen window too.

'What do you reckon? About eight feet?' asked DCI Wallace.

The sergeant continued his own appraisal and then stood to reach a hand up towards the windowsill, which he could not quite reach. 'Nine I'd guess,' he replied, stretching up on tiptoes.

Wallace growled an acknowledgement. The robbery team had branded it an opportunist crime, junkies or kids out for a quick profit. There would not be much effort put into catching them, particularly as it seemed they had not actually got away with anything. But experience and a dislike of coincidences was making Wallace cautious. This was a quiet road in a safe area. If the police were involved in the lives of its residents once in ten years it was remarkable. Now, in short order, a former resident with live connections to the place had been murdered and then his old house broken into. He had to consider the possibility of a link, no matter how unlikely.

The kitchen window opened and John Dearly leaned out. 'This is definitely the window he got out of; got in too, I'd imagine.' He pointed over the policemen's heads towards the bottom of the garden. 'He headed that way before disappearing into the shrubbery. I think he managed to get over the wall there or through the back gate into the cemetery, but that's not been opened in years so I'm not so sure about that.'

DCI Wallace nodded an acknowledgement. 'We'll go and have a look around down there now. Then we'll just see ourselves away, minister. You've been really helpful again and I expect results will start to show soon enough now.' With a single wave of his hand, he bade goodbye to John Dearly and signalled his sergeant to follow him to the back of the garden.

'Anytime chief inspector, I'm always very happy to help,' said John Dearly. With Helen beside him, they watched the policemen disappear in the direction John had indicated.

Wallace growled at his sergeant - the normal introduction to any pertinent observation Wallace wanted to share with his subordinates. 'Whoever did this break-in was fit and trained. Jumping down nine feet onto hard earth is a recipe for broken ankles.'

'Yeah, and to start off with, they got the window open without any damage,' agreed DS Brogan. 'It doesn't fit our local crime profile. No reports of similar break-ins.'

At the bottom of the garden, they pushed through the shrubbery to reach a stone built boundary wall. Set within it was a little wooden gate. A private access from manse to cemetery. Sergeant Brogan rattled its handle; it was shut tight. 'Just went over the wall probably,' he said.

DCI Wallace nodded agreement. He didn't believe in coincidences but still couldn't see any direct link between the two crimes. While he had spoken with John Dearly several times, this was the first occasion he had considered the property itself to be of interest but he looked like drawing a blank here too. The old minister was trying to help but clearly knew nothing, and the young American girl was pleasant enough but she had nothing of use to add either. There was a link; he could feel it in his bones, but what it was he couldn't begin to think.

Wallace turned and pointed back towards the house. 'Come on, let's get away. I need some time to think.' He led DS Brogan off towards the front of the house where their car was parked. Crossing the back lawn, he could see John Dearly and the Johnson girl through the kitchen window. A pair of innocents he thought, but if the connection was here, he'd find it; he just needed a little more thinking time before speaking to them again. It was just possible that someone knew something, even if they didn't know they knew.

• • •

Set on the northern side of the church, the vestry and little church office behind it were always sheltered from the sun so it stayed cool even on the warmest of days. Anticipating the chill, Helen had brought a jumper along and now she pulled it on. She had filled the kettle and set it to boil while John was busy at the desk, sorting and re-sorting papers. She knew that the new presbytery clerk was ruffling both John and Elaine's feathers and could see that John was not looking forward to James Curry's visit. Though knowing John's dedication and Elaine's unmatched efficiency, she did not really understand what could be causing so much concern.

Helen drew a couple of chairs towards John's desk, placing them each at forty-five degree angles to the desk front, trying to create an environment where they could all sit and talk together as a team rather than being seated in an oppositional stance from the outset. John nodded acknowledgement of her efforts and then lapsed back to paper shuffling.

Just as the boiling kettle switched itself off, they heard a voice calling in the church. Helen stepped out of the office, along the little corridor, through the vestry and into the nave. A middle-aged man stood near the top of the aisle. She remembered him from the Moderator's reception; James Curry had arrived.

Only the thinnest of painted smiles crossed James Curry's face as he stretched out a hand, greeting Helen with formality and little warmth. 'Ah, Miss Johnson, again, the *temporary* assistant,' he said.

She chose to disregard the put down. 'That's me,' Helen replied with the warmest of broad smiles, hoping her pleasant response would smooth things a little. She could understand at once why Elaine had taken against the man. 'It's nice to meet you again.'

Curry nodded, he did not bother offering Helen any polite response; clearly she did not merit it.

'Is that the way to the office?' asked Curry while pointing towards the vestry from where Helen had just emerged. Almost before she had acknowledged his question he was setting off, leading the way.

Helen felt so sorry for John. His look of dejection told how unwelcome the visit was.

Curry did not hesitate. Lifting one of the chairs Helen had positioned earlier, he returned it to the side of the room before sitting in the remaining chair. No place for Helen.

John did not even bother offering his hand, giving only a shake of his head to decline Helen's offer of coffee. The visitor accepted. While Helen prepared his drink at the back of the room, Curry started the meeting without her.

'Now John, you and I are going to need to have a chat about some of the practices in this parish, things I think we want to be putting behind us now. But let's save that for another day. I'm sure you and I can sort out those little anomalies, yes?' He looked at John and gave the same thin painted smile that Helen had received.

John gave a little non-committal shrug that James Curry took as acquiescence.

'Good,' said Curry, 'but today we need to explore something very delicate. Curry paused for just a moment, forcing John into a nodded acknowledgement.

'Now, I've only been in this role a short while and you know what? Everywhere, in all the parishes in our presbytery, I see nice straight lines. Happy compliance, people fitting in. Then I turn to St Bernard's and it sticks out like a sore thumb. I have no intention of exercising the complaints against you today, one thing at a time, yes? First, I really want to understand this source of funds the parish has. It makes no sense to me at all.'

Viewed from Helen's position at the back of the office, John looked beleaguered behind his desk. As a matter of principle she disapproved of any financial misbehaviour; she held John in the highest regard, couldn't believe he would be involved in anything underhand, yet James Curry was here, he must have a reason to question John. She hoped it was a misunderstanding. She could not help feeling a pang of sympathy for the older man, held at bay by this luminary. Whatever he wanted, she hoped it could all be resolved amicably.

Helen placed a mug of coffee in front of the visitor. He scarcely acknowledged her and stretched out his legs ensuring there was no space to return the second chair to, even if she wanted. She retired to the back of the room and sat on a little chair beside the door.

James Curry took a tentative sip of the coffee - it was too hot and he tutted disapprovingly. He could not feel Helen's indignant scowl on his back, though it registered with John and he smiled fleetingly to himself.

'Now, John, today's little visit is quite informal and I certainly have no intention of trying to press you into doing anything you don't want. And after all, I don't have any powers here, I'm just an advisor, a guide, little else, but…' Curry paused and for a moment stared down at the fingers of his hands which were now pressing together to form a little steeple as he rested his wrists on the edge of the desk in front of him. The silence was not an invitation for others to speak.

At last, he continued. 'But John, I'm very worried about you, worried about St Bernard's, and I'm worried about the presbytery too. Reputations can be so easily damaged; misunderstandings, mistakes, mysteries even, and who knows what? Above all, John, my job is to protect, to shepherd the parishes in my presbytery. I consider myself responsible for their good order and making sure we all follow the rules.'

John was not quite sure where James Curry was going but indicated his agreement by inclining his head while half raising a hand from where it rested on his thigh and then he let it drop down again. He replied softly, partly cautious, partly just weary. 'Of course, who could disagree with such a sentiment? But what's it got to do with St Bernard's?'

James Curry's thin painted smile flitted around his lips. 'John, we're all friends at this table; in the end we're all on the same side. We all want to help and serve our people, want the best for every parish. However, John, I have a real concern, and you know? I don't understand what the big secret is. Why can't I see the source of St Bernard's funds? In my experience, secrets tend to be covering up things.' James Curry's smile had vanished, just a cold expression remained.

'John, I won't have my presbytery enveloped in a scandal. I think we need a good deal more openness here. You really need to share the facts with the presbytery.' Knowledge was power and James Curry wanted it.

John was drained but exasperated. 'What scandal for Heaven's sake? We do nothing wrong, our accounts are inspected every year and they're spotless. The presbytery is always happy with them. You know your predecessor never raised any issues. This is nonsense, it really is.'

'Let me be blunt, John, there are things about your parish that make me unhappy. I don't know how your predecessors managed to wangle these little informal concessions, these little unofficial twists in the rules, but be under no illusion; I intend to see those kinks ironed out. I want this parish to be conforming like all the rest. Oh, I know, you seem to have friends here and friends there. Everybody likes John, don't they? Everyone apologises for him - *Oh, don't worry about John and his lot, they go their own way, but it's all right, they always end up at the same place as everyone else.* Well, let me tell you, it's not all right, not in the modern Church and not on my watch. Trust me, it will change. It will. But that's for another day. First of all, there's this money question to address.'

From the back of the room, Helen was unable to get a handle on what Curry was really pushing for. But she could see that John was being pressed and was very uncomfortable.

'John, all I want is for you to show willing. I want my presbytery to be leading from the front, keeping everything in order. A model of propriety.'

Pressed as he was, John was not going to give ground easily. 'Look, there's no scandal, nothing underhand in our accounts. You've seen them, the government's seen them. What more do you want?'

'Yes, John, I have seen them and I have to say they are in good order. That's why I'm more than happy to encourage you to co-operate with me. To satisfy me that there's no need for an investigation, before one even starts. Let's just nip it all in the bud, hmm?' Curry leant back a little, tilting his head a fraction and arching an eyebrow, inviting John to respond.

'Of course I want to help. There's never been any question over St Bernard's. There's nothing to hide, there's nothing to show. I don't know what I can do to help.' John gave a shrug. 'I'm at a loss to know what to say.'

'Well, John, it's very simple. You make cash gifts to several local organisations each year, and I know you have every right to do that. I understand you have the funds, so that's fine.' Curry leant forward a fraction, quietly placing a hand flat on the desk. 'The problem is I need to know the source, need to know there is nothing that compromises my, our, presbytery. Nothing questionable going on.'

'I don't have the slightest idea what you're talking about. There's nothing questionable to rule out,' said John.

Curry had been weighing up the options. If there was a scandal, he wanted nothing to do with it, but this was his patch now and he needed to minimise any possible risk. And if there were to be a threat of scandal on his patch, it would be here, where they couldn't follow the simplest of guidelines. Every irritation in his working life seemed to lead back to St Bernard's and he was going to sort it, once and for all. 'John, I don't doubt things are as they should be, I have every confidence. But I think you should make a little time to provide whatever is needed, for clarity's sake. Our hands are clean so let's show that they are, it makes sense. I must urge you to help me.'

John pulled himself up in the chair a little. 'Well, what exactly would helping mean?'

Sensing progress and keen to close in on a conclusion Curry tried to wrap up the discussion. 'I think we should set some dates to start building a proper understanding of things, don't you?' he said.

John nodded, resigned, he was thinking about Archie. Compared to that, what did all this really matter anyway?

James Curry smiled contentedly. 'Good, we can sort things between us. John, I'll need to see your list of giving. I'm quite keen to understand the rationale behind your choices and see when these regular annual gifts started and why, that sort of thing, nothing you shouldn't be able to sort out easily enough. And I really do want to understand where the money comes from. Shouldn't take too long, we'll put the whole thing to bed in no time. Probably put your mind at rest too, what with this new government initiative on old trusts and the like, I'd like to know we have a clean bill of health there while I'm at it.'

James Curry half stood and then a thought struck him, from the parish's annual accounts he knew St Bernard's received a big payment each year, a very generous six-figure sum. He couldn't help but ask. 'John, how much is this mystery fund of yours worth?' Curry tried to make the question sound light, inconsequential, but he was suddenly intrigued to know.

John appeared withered and shrunken behind a desk that only a month previously he had so confidently filled to overflowing. He was grieving, tired and drained. He seemed a beaten man. He threw his hands up a little way and let them fall onto the desk, didn't look at the man in front of him, focusing instead on his thumbs. 'I'm not really sure; most of it's not in cash. But, there's a good bit more than you might think.' His voice trailed off in despair.

'Oh,' said Curry, 'seven figures? Eight perhaps?'

John just shrugged, lapsed into silence and made no attempt to get up. Watching the meeting unfold from the back of the room Helen found herself conflicted. She believed surplus wealth should be used where it would do the most good, yet she had found herself wanting to intervene to protect John from the onslaught. She was not happy with the pressure being applied; it seemed very threatening.

Then came the shock of hearing that St Bernard's had an old trust fund that might be worth millions, but it seemed John could not afford to extend her stay at the parish. She was being moved on and had obviously not been given the whole story. What were John Dearly and Elaine McPhee hiding? She had come to realise they were thick as thieves. Perhaps that was it? Even though it was hard to believe.

Helen realised John was not going to stand, so she stood and took control from the back of the office. 'Perhaps I can show you out now? I think John needs a minute or two on his own.' Helen could sense James Curry's feeling of triumph and did not really like it. She pulled open the office door and the man walked out, bristling with satisfaction. Concerned with his own thoughts, the girl's existence scarcely registered with him. Helen saw his expression as they moved out through the door and into the corridor. Curry's look of triumph showed he had achieved whatever goal had triggered his setting up of the meeting. But it was the intensity of his expression that shocked her. She had seen dominant and controlling men in Africa, witnessed their obsessive drive for power, and Curry's look was unpleasantly familiar.

Having guided the man out of the church she watched from the little window beside the door. Saw the triumphant expression still set on his face as he got into his car. Whatever John Dearly's reasons for hiding the fund, Curry's motivation seemed to stretch way beyond the public good. She could not work out what his angle was but felt instinctively that she did not like what she was looking at.

If only she could get John to talk to her, perhaps she could help him. He had always been kind to her, treated her so well throughout her stay, and yet all along he had been keeping secrets, holding back information. Did her father know about this trust fund? Surely not. Clearly, the parish could afford to keep her on for longer if it wanted, but it seemed not. Yet nothing was justification for today's bullying tactics against the older man, her father's old friend. First, she would put aside her own hurt and see what she could do to help him and then see about this money and its proper use.

• • •

Cassiter was at his favourite spot by the window. He watched the cityscape, the passing traffic and the people while he carefully weighed up the situation. He had received Barnett's report and reviewed his team's analysis of the contents of the church office computer. While things were not quite as clear cut as he would like, for the time being he would run with Barnett's view; in the light of Dearly effectively sacking the girl, clearly, she could not be involved.

But Dearly. Dearly, Dearly, Dearly. He must be involved. His response to learning of the skeleton in the dunes - that was not polite or passing interest; that was almost obsessive fascination, almost Parsolesque. Why did he need to see the dunes dagger so urgently, was he going to try to deprive Eugene Parsol of it? What had he rushed off to check in such a hurry? Dearly demanded further investigation, he needed to be pressed. Dearly was the key, and that little safe Barnett had found in the vestry might prove very interesting.

Cassiter would have liked to wait a while, dig a little more, see how events were related. That was not possible; Parsol was now equally agitated about the dunes dagger. He wanted it, wanted it now, and whatever Archie Buchan and John Dearly had hidden at the church was also to be gathered in without delay.

Cassiter was to redouble his efforts. Everywhere. The move on the university had not produced the desired results and in spite of his earlier concerns about avoiding unnecessary attention, Parsol had now changed his position. Cassiter was to strike where necessary, as quickly as possible and collateral damage was no longer a concern. The prize was in sight and no cost was too high. Get the daggers and destroy any supporting evidence trails, wipe it all away, completely. Cassiter knew that such a brazen push might endanger some of his operatives, but that was just how things were to be.

Before taking any further action, he needed to double check that no trail could lead back to him. Then he would get working on two fronts, would gather in both the daggers. Still, at least the Johnson girl's loose-tongued chatter in the manse kitchen had told him exactly where the dunes dagger was. MacPherson had it in his home, its acquisition would be about as easy as it gets. He returned to his desk and started running his private security checks, getting the team moving, digging. Preparing for his big push.

Chapter 12

THURSDAY 6th JUNE

DCI Robert Wallace glowered at his phone; he had just finished the most difficult of conversations with the chief constable of Scotland. The man seemed to have less interest in the actuality of events than in ensuring the media was given a positive news story before the weekend. The chief constable certainly projected a great public image, but he hadn't reached the top by being a nice guy and simply treading the beat for twenty odd years.

It was clear to Wallace that for all the chief constable's management skills he was a slippery devil and more a politician at heart than a policeman. The media was whipping up a public panic over the killing in Dunbar, the chief constable wanted - no, demanded - progress. Wallace could tell he'd need to be careful. In spite of the meddling and attempted micro-management from above, if anything hit the fan, Wallace knew he'd be standing alone.

Wallace was tired. It was over five weeks since the old minister had been murdered. Each night he was sleeping less than the one before, his wife was unhappy and his teenage kids were moaning constantly since he'd announced that next month's family holiday might need to be cancelled if he didn't get on top of the case soon. He reckoned that his time in the force was probably up. It wasn't the same police force he'd signed up to. Don't think, follow orders, fill in forms, carry the can: a rubbish job. Once he'd solved this one, he was thinking of calling it a day.

He stopped dwelling on his own circumstances and turned his thoughts back to the case. It was so unusual, there should have been clues and it should have been wrapped by now, but nothing. Nothing at all. No forensic clues, nothing on CCTV, no patterns, no previous form to trace, and other than the worried and the cranks, no public tip offs. It was as though a ghost had appeared, brutalised the old man and then just vanished.

Wallace allowed his methodical mind to pace steadily through everything they knew and it didn't take long to cover the lot. The one chink of light was the break-in at the minister's former manse. Wallace could not accept it as a coincidence. Both crimes were remarkable because they were not in patterns; they were unexpected and unattributed. Yet they were linked: by the victim. It was all he'd got to work on so that's where he'd focus.

Tactfully, his team had made themselves scarce when the phone call had come through from Scottish Headquarters. Now he needed his sergeant back.

'DS Brogan. Where are you? Let's get everyone together. Come on, I want to go over everything again.' Wallace shouted and people started to appear as if by magic, in less than two minutes his team had reassembled.

'Could the motive have been gain or profit of some kind? We didn't think so, he seemed quite well off but nothing was stolen from his home anyway. He had nothing worth killing for. No enemies. Just a quiet old man in a quiet little town. What was the trigger? Sort that and we are on the way to finding the killer. Most victims know their killer. Did he?' Wallace arched an eyebrow to emphasise the question.

DS Brogan fired back a response. 'We've checked the family. His nephews and nieces weren't anywhere near Scotland when he was killed,' Brogan was listing with his fingers as he spoke, 'none of the other residents were physically up to it, the care workers were all accounted for, that only left the local church congregation and most of them were involved in some midweek meeting or other with the minister. Everyone Archie Buchan knew or had regular contact with has some sort of alibi.' The sergeant stopped listing; he had nothing more.

Wallace would not accept defeat so easily. 'Look, Buchan's circle of acquaintance had narrowed hadn't it? Eventually that's what age does to you, to all of us. Now we've got his old manse being broken into, in a street where they've forgotten how to spell crime. Come on, Christ, there must be a link. It's always the Church, isn't it? The Church.' He paused for a moment and frowned.

'I want to go over his old church connections again, every bit. Re-do profiles of all the key people, trawl through that congregation, who doesn't fit? Are there grudges? Mysteries? Things done when he was minister, things left undone. I want to know the lot, got it?'

DCI Wallace looked around his team and could see they were all tired. He knew they had all been burning the candle at both ends. It was a skeleton squad, including himself only a dozen were working on the crime now, though the force's PR team somehow managed to give a very different impression.

Truth was there were just not enough resources, they were stretched everywhere as the force quietly shifted more and more staff away from operations to the backroom. A growing band of paper police, tasked to check and record the achievements of a dwindling frontline; methodically processing detail of activities to feed plenty of positive statistics and management information up the line and out into the media. Wallace gave a wry smile as the team dispersed to review existing information and trawl again for fresh leads; this just wasn't his world anymore. He glanced appreciatively at DS Brogan who had not moved away, anxious to support his boss.

'If there's some live connection between Buchan and his old parish I want to know what we've missed. We need to know, now let's get back on the trail.'

DS Brogan nodded. 'The current minister, he's been helpful every time we've spoken to him. You don't think he's involved do you?'

DCI Wallace had a thoughtful look on his face as he absently watched the rest of his team filing out of the office. 'John Dearly? No, I wouldn't think so, he strikes me as straight up and down,' he turned back to fix the sergeant with a confident stare, 'but there is something there, something we don't know. I can feel it in my bones. If he or somebody else there is hiding something, holding anything back, I want to know. Maybe there's something of value in the old church or manse, whatever it might be we need to find out. There have been two connected crimes with no obvious gain for anyone. That makes me think the gain is still to be made - the crimes aren't done yet. We need to wrap this fast before there's another. Right now things can only get worse.'

Brogan feared his boss was right though he couldn't imagine any crime being worse than what had happened to Archie Buchan.

• • •

A couple of care assistants pushed wheelchairs out of the dining room while a little cluster of residents sat tight in their chairs waiting for walking frames or supportive arms to get them back into the lounge. Two or three of the more agile ladies were up, shuffling towards Helen, determined to talk to a fresh face.

John regularly took his communion services out into the community, to reach those who couldn't make the regular church services. The outreach rotated through a list of destinations and today the service was in the Sunnyside Rest Home. Helen knew it was something that John loved to do and she had been happy to join in the visits and support the services.

Today she felt it was John who had needed support, he had waivered once or twice and that was just not like him. She watched him reverentially lifting and wiping the old communion set: the little cup and plate, the neat cross. It was a compact set and each part fitted perfectly into the ageing wooden carry case, perfectly made for the job.

As John bent forward to pack the set away, she was suddenly aware of a tear in his eye. Puzzled, she looked again, but John was lost from her view as the elderly ladies finally reached her and clustered around. Smiles and greetings and chatter demanded her attention and by the time she could refocus on John he was composed and the carry case closed. She would need to speak properly to John about how he was feeling. Could she help him? She resolved to set some time aside at the start of next week to sit down with him and clear the air, understand her own future and maybe help him get a grip on his too.

CHAPTER 13

FRIDAY 7th JUNE

The day opened bright and sunny. A cloudless light blue sky promised a long hot day, but at just after nine in the morning it was still cool and comfortable for brisk walking. Cassiter had left his New Town office and taken a southbound bus out of the city centre. He was heading for the affluent residential district of Morningside.

He travelled unnoticed, anonymous. Leaving the New Town, the bus headed up Lothian Road; passing the green-coppered dome of the Usher Hall to his left, and to his right, Festival Square and the financial quarter. Here the inner city streets were lined on both sides with sandstone tenements, mostly occupied at ground level by pubs, clubs, shops and restaurants, the upper floors a mix of offices and residential.

Driving on, the bus passed through the Tollcross district. Then there was a subtle change in the architecture as it skirted the green of Bruntsfield Links. The tenement flats seemed to be less pressed, less compressed, even the windows of the sandstone buildings seemed just a little larger; the bus had moved into traditional middleclass territory. The route ran on across Holy Corner with its four church buildings, one on each corner, and thence into Morningside; home to the young professionals who had yet to flit to suburban family nests, home to the middle aged returning from the outer suburbs and home to the determinedly affluent singles. A bustling mix of people: minding their own business and paying their own way.

Cassiter got off the bus just after Morningside Station, the CCTV coverage petered out around here and he was safe to take a leisurely and unrecorded stroll. He headed east along Cluny Gardens to Blackford Pond with its ducks and swans and mothers and toddlers. Now the tenements had surrendered to a mix of stone built houses and bungalows, greened with gardens and boundary hedges. Then he turned north, weaving through the mix of suburban residential roads leading back towards the city centre and John Dearly's manse.

In his shoulder bag he had a white disposable forensic suit, some small tools and a further change of clothing for use on his exit journey. A retreat that would go as unnoticed as the approach.

Cassiter was not far from the manse now. He had a single earphone in place, it was providing a live audio feed from his hidden spying devices in the manse and he had been monitoring the situation since setting off from his office. It was clear that Dearly was following his normal Friday routine. Having re-turned with his newspaper, the minister was now settling down for a quiet, undisturbed morning.

The walk had been pleasant, giving Cassiter an opportunity to consider events without any disturbances, clearing his thoughts before the action.

All of Dearly's behaviours made him the key suspect, and his unhealthy interest and frantic questioning about this other dagger that had been found in the Fife dunes just confirmed his guilt.

Having reviewed transcripts of the police visits to the manse, it was clear that the police were at a loss, grasping at straws, and that was heartening, it meant he had more time to complete the mission for Parsol. Dearly had not told the police anything of relevance. To Cassiter, there were only two possible explanations for that. The first, that Dearly knew nothing -

Cassiter had deduced that was not the case. The second, that Dearly was hiding something, even from the police. That must be the case and left Dearly an open target.

Continuing his northerly stroll along the main road, he passed a little side road off to the right, a neat residential road populated by impressive sandstone houses. He glanced right and counted several houses along until he spotted the manse; he marked it in his mind and continued his unbroken journey on up the main road. The stone built garden walls to the rear of the houses combined together to form the southern boundary of a great rectangular cemetery, exactly as Fiona Sharp had described.

From either end of this southern boundary, the walls extended northwards to define the eastern and western cemetery boundaries, and these were eventually linked together by the north wall, and so enclosed the whole cemetery. Cassiter was walking north up the main road, following the course of the western wall, some way ahead he could see Dearly's church sat near the northern end of the cemetery. Just ahead of him was a small wrought iron gate set into the wall, a little used pedestrian access to the cemetery.

Cassiter ducked through the gate into the stillness beyond. It was an old cemetery, for the most part populated by the long forgotten dead. Very few empty lairs remained, and most of them in older family plots. As a result, there were few visitors now, but the council still maintained it all in good order, helped by regular anonymous donations. He turned hard right, working his way through a confusing series of internal section walls and then found himself heading south along a little path that tracked right round the inner side of the cemetery wall. Unseen, he was now headed back towards the houses he had just passed.

Confident in his seclusion, Cassiter walked quietly along the path, heading for the section of garden wall that backed onto the manse. He had reports of the back garden's layout from both Fiona Sharp and Jim Barnett. These had been cross-referred with a web accessed satellite picture. He knew exactly how to proceed.

Cassiter stopped at a little wooden gate that was set in the southern cemetery wall. It gave private access between the back garden of the manse and the cemetery. He took a short steel pry bar from his rucksack and wedged it between gate and frame, low down near the ground and close to the locking bolt Barnett had described. One firm heave and the old wooden frame splintered. He moved up to the top of the frame and repeated the action, then carefully put his pry bar back in the rucksack and pulled out a forensic suit. He put it on.

For the next minute or so he needed to know Dearly was away from the kitchen and its rear facing windows while he forced entry. He produced a new pay-as-you-go phone and selected its sole pre-entered number. The phone dialled out. A moment later, his earphone filled with the sound of the study phone ringing in the manse. The overlapping sound feed from the kitchen told him Dearly had now left the kitchen and was heading towards the study.

Without waiting for Dearly to answer, Cassiter gripped the gate handle and twisted it open, then leant his shoulder firmly on the gate. With only the slightest resistance, the bolts parted from the splintered frame and the gate swung open. He entered the garden, pushed the gate shut behind him and sprinted to the back of the house where he grabbed a garden bench and dragged it beneath the kitchen window. From Sharp's report, he knew this was an easy point for entry and exit, and knew from Barnett that they had done nothing to reinforce it since the break-in. He was through the kitchen window before John Dearly had hung up his study phone on the missed call.

John walked back into the kitchen wondering who the caller was, telling himself they would call back if it was urgent. In the meantime, he had plenty to be getting on with. As he stirred his mug of coffee, he heard a sound behind him. Turning, he was confronted by an average sized man dressed from head to toe in a white forensic suit. John's mouth dropped in shock. 'What the? What are you doing in here? Who are you?' he demanded. His voice started to raise slightly as possible answers filled his mind almost as he voiced the questions.

'Get out. Get out of my house!' John fumbled in his pocket for his phone, pulling it out he frantically tried to speed dial Elaine.

Cassiter had crossed the room before John could key in any logical sequence. He struck the minister a single blow hard to the side of his head, sending him sprawling to the ground. The phone dropped unused and Cassiter kicked it away to the far end of the kitchen. Stooping, he gripped one of John's wrists and twisted it behind his back, the minister groaned in pain. Using the twisted arm, Cassiter started to pull him up to his feet; John complied in an attempt to reduce the excruciating pain in his shoulder.

As John rose, he protested, started to show signs of resistance. Cassiter hit him again with a tightly clenched fist to the temple, the blow so violent that it caused John's knees to wobble beneath him. The wafer thin forensic glove did nothing to cushion the attack. The only thing that kept John on his feet was the lurching counter pain in his twisted shoulder joint that became more intense if his body dropped, increasing the torque and ripping his arm further out of the joint.

Cassiter dragged John to the end of the kitchen table and forced him to sit on it. Confused, John looked at his assailant. 'Who are you? What do you want? What's going -' Another fist, this time straight in the face. It stopped the talking as John rolled back onto the table groaning and clutching his face with his hands. Blood streamed from a broken nose, spreading quickly to cover his hands and the cuffs of his shirt.

In those few moments of chaos, Cassiter's expert hands had cable tied John's ankles to the table legs. John was so preoccupied with his broken nose and torn shoulder ligaments that for a moment he was not even conscious of the constraints. By the time he started to process events it was too late; he was sliding into shocked confusion and fear. What was happening to him? Lying flat on the table, his legs were bent over its end, beneath which his ankles were now firmly secured to the table legs. Who was this silent attacker?

John struggled to rise, one hand covering his broken nose, the other a lever to help him up. In his dazed and shocked condition he had no defence when Cassiter smashed his fist into the hand John was using to protect his nose. John wailed as his own hand compressed the broken nose in an agonising press. He slumped back on to the table, tried to roll to one side, to escape. His bound ankles held him in place, in pain and confusion he wriggled his hips trying in vain to find the forlorn comfort of the foetal position.

Obsessed with the immediacy of his own pain he was quite unaware of what Cassiter was doing. That a tie had been slipped over a wrist did not register until he felt the pull as Cassiter dragged on the line, steadily, inexorably inching his arm away from his bleeding face, stretching it out beyond his head. The damaged shoulder ligaments meant no resistance could be offered. His head rolled from side to side in a frantic attempt to see what was happening as his arm was tied off to one of the legs at the far end of the table. Stuck on the table with three limbs tied, John was now very frightened, eyes wild with growing panic, his one free hand flew back and forth; now cradling his broken nose then clutching the torn shoulder ligaments of his bound arm.

John wriggled his free hand in futile resistance as Cassiter fixed a tie to it. Firmly, irresistibly, Cassiter drew it tight, steadily stretching John's arm out above his head and then securing the line to the remaining free table leg. John was spread-eagled on the table, could not move save a little hip movement and his fingers wriggling forlornly on the end of tightly secured wrists. 'Help! Help! For God's sake, somebody help me,' he shouted as Cassiter stood watching in silence.

Cassiter gave a little smile and disappeared from Dearly's line of sight. The noise was of no concern, double-glazing and detached stone built houses made for excellent soundproofing.

John rolled his head from one side to the other but could see nothing and every roll accentuated the pain in his nose and face. He stopped struggling and let his eyes fix on the ceiling. 'What in heaven's name do you want?' he said, frightened, but he was not a man who would surrender without a struggle. 'Whoever you are, you've made a mistake. Just let me go, you can escape if you do. There's money you can have, but please stop this. I don't know what you want...' The silence continued and fear seeped deeper into his bones. 'Hello? Hello, are you still there?'

At the far end of the kitchen, Cassiter was enjoying the scene. He savoured the moment while he prepared himself for the task ahead. He watched the minister, listened to his cries, the begging for a response, for some acknowledgment that this was reality. Cassiter noted the very slight upward lift in Dearly's tone as his own silence fed the victim's anxiety. Then it was time for work. He returned to his victim.

John sensed Cassiter lean over him and rolled his bloodied face to focus on his assailant, hoping to find some sign, to find out who he was, why he was there, why this was happening. 'Why?' John asked, 'What's this about?'

Cassiter did not answer. He looked closely at John's broken nose and then stretched out and gripped it, rocked it to and fro, felt the broken bone click against itself and could almost feel the screams of pain that rolled out to fill the kitchen. After a few moments, he stopped and waited, allowing his victim's surge of pain to subside slowly. 'Hello John, I'm here for the dagger,' he spoke in a calm and quiet voice.

'What? What are you talking about? Are you mad? I don't know what you're talking about. Just let me go, please. Please.'

'Now, John, I want you to know that I don't have to be bad to you. I don't want to see you suffer, but I've been watching you, listening to you. I know you know. So give me what I want and your suffering can end, eh?' He leant across and squeezed the broken nose again.

Cassiter marvelled to himself at how tough some of these old ministers seemed to be. He thought about old Archie Buchan and now here he was with John Dearly, both supposedly men of peace, but they could certainly take a good beating, even if they didn't like to give it out. He rather admired them, felt the challenge offered was worthy of his skills. He set to with enthusiasm.

Time seems to pass more quickly when you're having fun, thought Cassiter. All of Dearly's fingers and thumbs were broken and twisted but still this old man was putting up resistance. Where did he find the strength? He wouldn't mind some of it himself. Not even trained combatants normally resisted so long. Cassiter was quietly impressed, if not a little frustrated.

'Last chance to tell me, John, before I start to get rough,' Cassiter leaned back across the table and gripped John's face, turning his head so he could look into John's eyes. He spoke quietly to the moaning man. 'John, nothing can be worth suffering for like this, surely? Just tell me what I want to know and you can relax, we'll make it all end.' Cassiter tilted his face down and arched an eyebrow in question. 'Hmm, going to tell me?'

John Dearly was not a fighter; on the contrary, he was the archetypal pacifist. But he was also a man of honour, and he would not betray his task or his friends. Lying on the table, amidst the glimmers of conscious thought that still visited him, he understood that what had come to him today was what had previously visited Archie, and given the chance would visit his friends next. In his weakened state, he gasped out resistance. 'I can't tell what I don't know. Now please, just end it.'

Cassiter was not happy with the answer. 'Wrong answer, my friend. I'm afraid it's going to get a little rough for you now.' Once again, he disappeared from John's view. Staring up at the ceiling, John offered a prayer to God, forgave his assailant and begged for release from his torment. He could hear Cassiter rummaging through drawers and wondered what would come next. He did not have long to wait.

Cassiter reappeared. He pushed a heavy meat tenderising mallet and a handful of steak knives in front of John's face. 'Last chance, John. I don't know why you are holding out on me. After all, it won't benefit you, will it? And don't think I won't visit your friends, as many as I have to. Your pretty little assistant, Helen isn't it? She's next. She's going to suffer like you. Worse in fact, oh yes, much worse, I have some special little tricks for young ladies. John, believe me, she's going to hate it.' He waved his tools in front of John's face again. 'Last chance, John, it's going to start getting a bit nasty now. So why not do us all a favour? Tell me where the dagger is.'

'I don't know what you mean,' gasped John, 'don't hurt her please, she's an innocent.'

Chuckling quietly, Cassiter disappeared from his view. 'I know that but you're not innocent, are you? You're making me do it. When I visit her, which I promise I will, it's all down to you, and I'll make sure she knows who to blame. Anytime you want to tell me, John, just sing out. Meantime, I've got work to do.'

John heard a thud, then another. For a moment he couldn't place the sound. Then a fresh tidal wave of pain came rolling up his right arm, overriding that of his brutalised hands, and smashing into his consciousness, hammering him into a hellish present. He did not know what was happening, just knew it was too much to bear.

Cassiter swung away with the tenderising mallet, driving a steak knife through John's wrist. The sharp point had plunged between the two bones of his forearm while the serrated edge simply sliced through muscle, tendon and blood vessels without resistance. The real pain, the pain that was overwhelming even that from the already shattered fingers, was coming from the blade's serrated edge as it sawed into and through bone on its journey to the tabletop. Cassiter carried on hammering, pinning John's wrist to the table.

Satisfied that the knife was fixed firmly in place, Cassiter stopped. Making his way around the table, he paused and leaned over John's face. Smiling, he waited patiently for his screams to subside into a desperate whimper. 'That wasn't so good was it? I think that hurt you quite a bit. More to come though,' his matter of fact voice took on an almost cheery note and he disappeared from John's view, making his way round the table towards the unblemished wrist, 'unless you've got something you want to tell me?'

John knew what to expect now and could feel Cassiter pressing the point against his wrist, selecting the place of entry. 'No. Please, I beg you, no more. In God's name, man, please stop,' he muttered the words in desperation, did not really expect any remission.

'Not good enough, John, you have to tell me what I want to know.' Cassiter watched the old man's head rock from side to side and could hardly believe the defiance in him. Accepting his refusal to speak as an invitation to continue, Cassiter drove the second knife into John's left wrist, crucifying him on the table. He relished the man's screams, a sound that never failed to invigorate, but Dearly was not breaking. Cassiter could see the blood now flowing over the edge of the table down onto the floor. Dearly had fainted, he probably would not last another quarter hour. Cassiter's mind flicked back to Dunbar, he did not want to lose another customer before he had what was required.

Cassiter got a jug of water and threw it into John's face. John moaned and spluttered, opening his eyes to face his tormentor.

'Wake up man, I've got something else for you now,' Cassiter was about to step up a gear and time was becoming a key issue.

The doorbell rang. Cassiter froze, and instinctively he clapped a hand over John's mouth, though John's tortured mind had not registered the sound.

Then a key turned in the lock and Helen's voice called out. 'Hi John, it's only us.' She was leaving the porch and entering the hallway. 'Elaine and I just need the parish contacts list for the new...' she stopped in mid-sentence, puzzled by a strange moaning sound that came from the kitchen.

They hurried into the kitchen as a white clad figure streaked in bloody red disappeared into the cemetery, slipping unnoticed through the quietly closing gate in the garden wall. They both gasped in horror at the kitchen table, at John and the butchery. They rushed to him.

Elaine pulled out her phone and immediately dialled for police and ambulance emergency. Helen was struggling with the awfulness of it all while drawing on her professional training and experience. She could see John was dying, was only moments from death. There was neither way nor time to treat his wounds. She leant over him and gently stroked his forehead then kissed his cheek.

Elaine's normally impenetrable face was dark, a raging thunder. Her eyes carried tears of angry grief that dripped down onto the tea towel she was now holding against John's belly, a futile challenge to nature, which was steadily forcing his innards out through the mighty eviscerating slash Cassiter had inflicted with a third steak knife before leaving.

John watched them through blurred eyes, but the presence of his friends registered. 'Be careful, be careful. Elaine, they want...' his husking voice trailed off.

Elaine could not bring herself to speak. She could only look John in the eye and nod as his voice trailed away.

John managed the faintest of smiles in acknowledgement, finding strength from an unknown reserve he spoke again. 'Elaine, take care of them, I'm done now.' He strained against the pain and rolled his head to look at Helen. 'Around my neck..., take it.'

Helen still held her face close to John's, her hands cradling his head. She just nodded at him, gently kissed his cheek again. 'Don't worry, an ambulance is coming, we'll get you sorted out. Just relax, don't try to speak. You're with people who love you now. It's going to be all right,' she lied.

A fleeting and desperate glint flashed in his dulling eyes. 'Helen, take it! On the chain. Please, please listen. It should be held by the minister, always. I want you to take it. Take it now,' he gasped desperate words. His eyes closed, though her hand, which was supporting his head, could still feel a tension in his neck while he fought for the last scraps of life, holding on against all odds.

Helen looked at Elaine. 'What does he mean?'

Through guarded sobs, Elaine simply pointed unsteadily towards John's neck. 'He means you to have it... Do it now so he knows. At least let him die with some little peace of mind.'

Helen could sense just the slightest of nods in John's neck and head, could feel him urging her on. With her free hand, she pulled open his bloodied shirt and reached in. She stopped, frozen. Around John's neck was a heavy gold chain. She had seen one just like it before, in the dunes of Fife. On the chain was a ring she had also seen before. The golden Templar signet ring.

'Take it,' Elaine barked at her, 'take it!'

Helen could feel John's head trying to nod encouragement, feel his desperation. In a blur of confusion and grief she took the bloodied chain and ring from around his neck, felt his neck relax.

John opened his eyes and smiled at her, a sense of relief anesthetising the pain for just a fleeting moment. 'Thank you. Thank you,' the urgency in his voice as he tried to speak was quite distinct from the pain that was now reasserting itself fast. 'Tell no one, promise, tell no one you have it... I'm sorry, but...' his voice trailed off and his eyes closed for a moment, then his voice came back in an urgent and desperate burst. 'Elaine, Elaine, where are you?'

'I'm here, John. I'm here. Hush your voice now, just take it easy, old friend,' she said.

With a huge effort, John turned his head towards the sound of Elaine's voice. 'You take care of her, Elaine. Make sure she understands. Support her. You were right, Elaine, I should have listened to you.' His voice was wafer thin and fading. 'Promise me you'll help her. Give her a chance...' his voice trailed off into silence and Helen felt the last vestiges of tension slip from his neck muscles. He had gone.

Helen pressed her lips against his cheek and kissed him goodbye. Then she glanced up at Elaine with a look laden with anger, sadness and a hundred questions. She turned back to John, her face still close to his and blessed him silently. Straightening up, she stepped back from his body as police and paramedics rushed in and came to a shocked halt at the sight of the butchery before them. Without thinking, she slipped the ring and chain into her pocket and moved close to Elaine for mutual support.

Chapter 14

SATURDAY 8th JUNE

Helen and Elaine were taken from the manse to St Leonard's Police Station on the city's south side. There they had given statements, been gently questioned, politely pressed and tested while the police tried in vain to understand the inexplicable. Wallace had led the interviews and he could tell the women were in shock.

A good guide to murder investigation was that the last person to see a victim alive was probably the killer, but even the wildest fantasy could not put them in the frame for this; they were both completely devastated, traumatised. He believed them - they really did have the misfortune to stumble into a scene from hell. Perhaps if they had arrived a little earlier, things might have been different; on the other hand, this killer was clearly violent and unswerving. If they had arrived earlier, perhaps he'd now be dealing with three corpses instead of one.

Finally, frustrated, the police allowed them to leave in the early hours of the morning. Sam had been waiting to drive them both home. He had Elaine's daughter Grace with him. The young woman was completely distraught, worried for her mother and crushed at the loss of the nearest she had ever known to a father figure.

As they walked towards the parked car, Helen had tried to question Elaine, desperately tried to get some grounding, some foundation on which to build an understanding of the madness that had just happened. Elaine had just waved all her questions aside. Instead she had offered a meeting at the church office at lunchtime, noon.

Though Helen needed answers, Elaine was simply not ready or able to give them. Her voice was as gruff as ever, but her eyes showed grief for John and something else, real fear. Quite unexpectedly, surprising herself and the others, Elaine gave Helen a hug. Helen hugged her back, no words or sounds, just the comfort of a lingering physical contact, sharing a point of space together. Helen felt a wetness on her cheek where their tears met and mixed. Tear sisters, bonded forever through shared grief and horror. As they separated, Elaine had stooped, apparently to rub an aching calf muscle and by the time she straightened up the stern exterior had returned. Helen would never refer to the moment, but now knew Elaine for a kinder woman.

DCI Wallace and Sergeant Brogan silently watched the scene play out from a first floor window in the police station. They saw how Sam carefully shepherded the ladies to his car and guided them in one by one. Wallace wondered about the driver. Another line that needed to be followed up.

• • •

Outside, in the pre-dawn darkness the air was cool, but in Helen's flat it felt cold. She was shivering, sitting at the dining table, a half-empty bottle of wine in front of her and a glass in hand. Sam sat next to her with his arm round her shoulder. He was keeping silent, allowing her time to think. John's gold signet ring sat on the table in front of them, the gold chain still threaded through it.

Helen had given Sam a full account of what she had seen at the manse, John's death and the subsequent police investigations. She told him about John's insistence that she take his ring and how Elaine had hurriedly warned her to say nothing of the ring to the police. She had kept quiet and was now beginning to question the wisdom of her decision.

The ring glistened in the electric light, a thing of beauty that contrasted starkly with the previous morning's scene. She had scrubbed the chain, removing the blood that had settled between the links. She had felt guilty at washing away part of John but had been unable to look at the chain while it was so brutally stained.

While working in West Africa she had coped with some horrible scenes and man's inexplicable lust for blood; she was no stranger to cruelty and brutality. However, somehow this was different. This was a western capital city, supposedly liberal and law abiding. She shivered. The closeness to her, the intimacy of this killing, it was something sharp and the victim a dear friend: just hard to absorb, hard to comprehend what had happened. And what maniac would do such a thing to John? And why?

Sam stretched his free arm across and refilled her glass. She gave it a little wave in thanks and rocked her head closer to him. His arm around her shoulder pulled her in still closer, lending moral support. There was nothing he could say to make this better for her, for either of them.

'What I don't understand,' she said for what seemed a hundredth time, 'is what John was doing with this ring and chain? I mean, look at it! It's identical to the one you found in the dunes.' She took another drink, emptying the glass. Sam half-filled it again and before he could pull the bottle back, she bumped the glass firmly against the neck of the bottle, ensuring he topped it up properly.

'It's a real mystery,' agreed Sam. Then there's the other dagger at the museum - I wonder if they have a ring there too.'

Helen turned to Sam. 'What if John had a dagger too? Maybe it's a big kind of a set. You know, three of everything, not two like we were starting to think before. What do you say?'

'It's possible,' Sam conceded. 'Based on each artefact we've seen so far it's quite probably a set. But remember, the museum dagger had a numeral IV, so if we are thinking sets, it could well be more than just three parts. We will only know if we can compare all the parts. I'll have to press MacPherson about getting proper access to the dune dagger and hopefully we'll get some joy from Suzie at the museum. I'll ask her about the ring. It may be there's one in their collection that they have not quite linked together,' he said, thinking carefully about what they knew as the fingers of his free hand gently drummed on the table.

He was trying to make links where he felt there should be some, but the gaps were too big for any of it to make sense. All he knew was that it was becoming quite dangerous to be linked with Helen's parish. Thankfully, it was the summer holidays now, the students were finished and he could devote more time to keeping an eye on her.

• • •

Cassiter had finished reporting to Eugene Parsol. It had not been a happy interview. Parsol had been almost frantic with fury; both at the failure to find a dagger in the manse and at the ghoulish reports that were now breaking into the news bulletins. It was such a bizarre killing that reports were spreading like wildfire around the world. Parsol did not care about the minister's death, but he was concerned that the publicity would obstruct retrieval of the daggers. Cassiter assured him otherwise and that plans to secure the daggers were in hand.

It had been very unfortunate that the Johnson girl and that elder had arrived unexpectedly, but in Cassiter's experience, any man with information would break and spill what he knew under much less pressure than he had applied. Normally such extreme treatments were reserved as punishments, when the answers didn't really matter, and with ample time to allow bodies to be disposed of afterwards.

Parsol's last comment before hanging up the phone was to insist that he would not accept any delays over the other dagger. It must be collected immediately, before it could disappear. He would still be arriving in Edinburgh next week and expected results on his arrival.

Cassiter was not happy with this close supervision. Principals, with their need for instant results, could often get in the way of his work. Further, there seemed to be an implied threat and Cassiter did not like threats.

Almost all of Cassiter's clients failed to recognise that his activities had made him wealthy, very wealthy, and while he lived an invisible life in a world of shadows, he liked his life, didn't aspire to anything else. These days he worked for the pleasure of the job and a desire to maintain his reputation as *the man who does*. His exorbitant fees were simply a measure of his success, not the motivation for delivery. He was certainly more powerful and wealthy than many of his clients, though few would ever realise it. He knew Parsol did not fall into that category, but nonetheless he did not appreciate any attempt at threat or intimidation, even when the man making them really could back it up.

In the meantime, he would secure the dagger that Mac-Pherson was holding.

Then, as the furore subsided around St Bernard's he would turn his focus on the woman elder. She was the only person left who could, who must, hold the answer. He had reviewed his recording of the women's reactions and conversation at Dearly's side as he died. The elder had clearly implicated herself by pressing the Johnson girl to conceal evidence from the police, though once again, the girl had seemed uninformed, an innocent abroad. But what exactly was it that she had taken from the dying man?

It was something small, certainly not what Parsol was after; he'd have noticed something as big as a dagger himself while he was in the kitchen. Her body had been in his camera's line of sight, blocking his view. It was interesting but not crucial today. He'd look into it later.

Cassiter turned his attention to the dagger that was currently within his reach. The BBC's recordings had already been purged without incident. If BBC staff did ever look for the pictures, their absence from the archive would seem like a simple human error. Now he had prepared plans for the Fife dunes dagger's recovery and his team briefing was ready. But before issuing instructions, he wanted to review the Dunbar memorial service pictures again.

Barnett, his man inside the parish, had been submitting reports rather late for which he would be dealt with later. What concerned him now was that one of the submissions reported chatter that suggested two priests, perhaps Greek or Italian, certainly of some Mediterranean origin, were at the wake. Yet he had no photographs of them, and this was causing him a problem. They had somehow attended the wake and left without making even a ripple.

He could not find them anywhere. No hotels, no guesthouses. No CCTV at airport passenger arrivals or anywhere else for that matter. Lack of information was always the biggest danger. Fiona Sharp was good, but she had missed them. Where were they and were they involved? Another loose end to be tied off.

• • •

At twelve noon, Sam accompanied Helen through the vestry and into the little corridor beyond. They could hear murmuring voices as they took the few steps to the open office door. The sound stopped as they reached the doorway. Inside were half a dozen church elders.

Elaine sat in the minister's place behind the desk. A scattering of drained tea and coffee cups indicated the meeting had been running for some time. From the expressions on the elders' faces, it had not been an altogether easy session. Elaine hesitated and then decided not to challenge Sam's presence. His being there was against convention, but these were not conventional times.

Bethany and Cathy, the two older ladies who generally made it a point of principle to oppose Elaine's plans, leapt up as Helen appeared. They had been quick to befriend Helen when she first arrived in Edinburgh and they rushed to her now. Anxiously they enquired after her welfare. Bethany shuffled the chairs to fix Helen a seat between theirs.

With greetings and lengthy commiserations exchanged, the meeting settled down again. Business resumed, Helen sandwiched between the elderly ladies.

From her place behind the desk, Elaine brought the meeting to order and briefly recapped the previous day's events, her words frequently echoed by tuts and sighs of distress from the others. Then she paused. She had not told the others everything that had happened when she and Helen had found John and it could not be put off any longer.

What Elaine said first was as much for Helen as it was the others, they were all familiar with the parish's traditionally unorthodox succession arrangements. 'You all know the choice of a minister is not imposed from outside. It is made inside the parish by the nominating committee who make a recommendation for the congregation to vote on. It's our job as elders, with advice and support from presbytery, to make sure the committee is convened and goes on to select the right minister for our parish.

'In other parishes that would normally mean a gap between one minister finishing and a new one being selected and appointed. By tradition, and with the good fortune and luxury of our resources, St Bernard's has always,' Elaine paused for a moment, looked around the room and then continued, 'always carefully made selection of a successor minister well before any changeover was called for.

'The person chosen would have worked for some time as an assistant to the incumbent minister before being called, so one minister can prepare and hand over to the next.' She paused again and noted the elders were all nodding agreement. While it had never been spelt out to Helen, she had come to realise this in the preceding months. She nodded too.

Elaine resumed. 'Keeping to our parish's tradition was always going to be difficult. We all know administration and control of church affairs has become tighter with every passing year. Clearly, I wasn't involved when John took over from Archie, God rest them both, so I don't know how the Kirk Session handled the business then. It was a different world, no computer records and people did things face to face. I've been struggling for a while to work out how to comply with Church rules and still organise things our way.

Things have got even harder since James Curry has been appointed as presbytery clerk. He's made clear he's not going to allow us to deviate from the rulebook. Although now John's gone, there can't be a period of overlap for handing over the parish reins anyway.

'We have no choice but to follow the rulebook now and that should please James. He and the presbytery will provide the approved support and oversight, helping us to form a nominations committee to select a new minister.' Elaine stopped and looked around the group.

'Elaine, what about our traditions though? Don't they count for anything?' asked Bethany. Cathy nodded support for the question and the others around the room joined in.

'Not as far as James Curry and the rulebook are concerned. His view is simple. Whatever happened here in the past should stay in the past. Whatever old boys' network allowed our tradition to continue is gone, it's finished. We'll comply with the rules or I don't know what will happen.' She looked around, gauging the responses.

The older ladies had been appointed elders around the time that Archie had handed on to John so many years before. As well as any, they understood the importance of continuity in the parish and had seen it function smoothly in the past. Elaine could sense their resentment and confusion as they glared at her; it was clear that the two older ladies considered that Elaine was failing in her role.

Elaine wanted to put their minds at rest and resumed her explanation. 'We will follow the rules, that's for sure. I don't want anyone from the outside pointing a finger at us.'

'But the continuity is already broken,' objected Bethany. 'What are we to do about that? The knowledge is gone.'

'They are two different issues,' replied Elaine. 'Listen, I think we can follow the rules and still maintain our traditions.'

'How?' demanded Cathy.

'Yes, how?' echoed Bethany. 'I think it's all over now. It all died with John.'

A muttered chorus of resigned agreement ran round the group. Helen began to feel edgy. The raw emotion of yesterday's events demanded answers and this conversation was revealing nothing. She wanted to know what was going on, this was all a mystery to her. She was just waiting to get some sense from the meeting. Nothing she had heard yet cast any light on events.

Elaine cut in over the fading dissenters. 'Like I said, separate issues. We will comply with the church rules and the presbytery clerk will have no grounds to complain about our attitude, alright?' Elaine could be very fierce when she started laying down the law and the rest of the group shifted and nodded an unhappy acquiescence.

'We will follow the rules, we will be seen to follow the rules, but you know what? I am pretty confident that a shortage of potential ministers, and letting it be known on the grapevine how pleased the congregation is with one person in particular, should ensure we get who we want without any lengthy contest being necessary.'

'Alright, so we can follow the rules and get who we want, but that doesn't alter the fact we have broken the tradition, the new minister will not have been introduced as has always been,' said Bethany.

'And who would we choose now? Who do we want?' asked Cathy.

Elaine nodded an acknowledgement while holding up a hand, the open palm pushing gently towards Cathy, signing she should hold on a little longer. Then she threw Helen an apologetic look. 'Of course, because John did not plan to leave us, we had no succession plan in place. It's no secret around this room that I was not happy with John giving you a year's placement as an assistant when we should have been focusing on selecting his long-term replacement. John would have been retired in two or three years and we were running out of time.' Again, a round of nods seemed to support Elaine.

Then a flash of resistance came from one of the elderly ladies sitting beside Helen. 'I never understood what was wrong with Helen anyway. I can't think what you have against her,' said Cathy, her hand rested on Helen's arm and squeezed it as she spoke.

Elaine nodded in the old lady's direction. 'Thank you, Cathy. I acknowledge your support for Helen, yours too, Bethany,' she nodded her head towards the second elderly lady who was maintaining a firm grip on Helen's other arm. Cathy smiled back at Elaine while leaning her shoulder very gently in against Helen's upper arm in a signal of support.

Elaine continued, finally letting her gaze return to Helen. 'I admit I spoke against Helen being appointed as assistant, and for what it's worth I think John eventually came to agree with me. He had finally accepted the ideal candidate would come from here, would be able to appreciate the history, and would have the strength and motivation to keep our traditions.' In spite of her gruff ways, it was clearly not easy for Elaine to expose her personal views and she had to pause again for a moment to collect her thoughts.

Helen had never considered herself a candidate and was slightly surprised to realise that some at St Bernard's had even been thinking about her as a possible successor minister one day. She really just wanted to know what was going on and took the opportunity to interrupt. 'Where is this meeting going? It's all very well liking me, or not, but I want to understand what's happening. You know what? I don't care who you give the job to, but I do want to know what got John Dearly killed yesterday.'

The elders looked down, away, anywhere to avoid her eye. They all turned expectantly back to Elaine who was weighing up how far she could go in explaining the situation in a single sitting.

'First, understand, I know everyone thinks I'm old fashioned, I cling to traditions that are probably past their time. I was never really against you, Helen. I was against putting a young woman, a modern young woman, who did not understand the situation, our history, into what could one day become a challenging, even dangerous position.'

Helen frowned. 'Well, I don't know what could be more dangerous than yesterday, do you?' The two elderly ladies nodded in agreement.

Elaine held Helen's gaze for a second then she nodded too. 'Exactly my point. The danger is real. John wasn't convinced, you know. Over recent years he had started to think it was all lost in the past, argued that we kept it all going for tradition's sake and nothing else.'

'What danger? Kept what going?' Sam had been listening carefully, but he was now getting frustrated. For all the talk, there were still no answers to explain the horror of the previous day.

Elaine sent him a black look as she barked across the room. 'You have no voice here. Please allow those who should speak the space to do so.'

Undaunted, Helen cut in. 'Sam's with me, and when he speaks, he speaks for me. If you can't accept that, then this meeting is going nowhere, it's over right now and we're out of here.'

Sam threw her a look of thanks as the elderly ladies muttered supportive sounds.

Suddenly, less certain of her place, Elaine seemed reluctant to challenge Helen and a little hesitantly nodded an acknow-ledgement to no one in particular. 'If I might continue?' said Elaine. 'This is a parish with a special history and tradition. Unique, I believe. Most of us wanted a strong minister to carry on our tradition. From our own roots, our own history, mentally and physically strong,' she gave a shrug and thought of big John Dearly, crucified on the kitchen table.

'Perhaps when evil comes physical strength is irrelevant. Yesterday I saw real strength of character in you, Helen, how you responded to that nightmare.' She stopped speaking, trying to force the vision of suffering back down into the subconscious place from where it had just emerged again.

Helen shared in the same recurring vision, but without the causal knowledge and like Sam now just wanted answers, nothing else. 'Elaine, physical strength, mental strength, whatever. You and I have just seen hell. Tell me what I need to know so I can try to understand what happened, please. I can't be expected to go home to the States and live any sort of life without knowing why that happened. For the love of God, just tell me! Just cut to the chase now. All right?'

Sam nodded agreement, the two elderly ladies were suddenly still, suddenly noncommittal, concerned over what Elaine could or would say.

Elaine did not speak to Helen as she continued. Instead, she was focusing on the elders again. 'You know my views. You also know that John Dearly, in spite of his reservations, which had grown in recent years, cared for his flock above everything else. He cared for us, and he did care for our traditions too. I don't know who his killer was, but irrespective of what the papers are saying I believe it was not some religious madman, and I believe John must have realised it too.' A ripple of disquiet ran round the room at this unexpected revelation. If not a madman, then what?

Elaine pressed on. 'In John's last moments, through all his pain, the only thing that mattered was that the ring was passed on, the task continued. That he still had the ring on him shows he had not given up on our parish's tradition altogether. He had not abandoned it and in spite of the torture and his suffering, he kept faith with us and our history. In the end, he must have realised that the threat was real. He gave Helen the ring, made her promise to keep it. He made me promise to support her.' She had to stop as excited whispers erupted and flowed around the little group.

Suddenly, Bethany and Cathy were both speaking to Helen, firing a series of questions at her in excited voices. 'You got the ring?'

'The man didn't steal it?'

'You have it now?'

'Where is it? Let's see.' They shook her arms gently, trying to extract a response to all the questions at once.

Helen nodded. 'Yes, I've got it, look,' she flipped undone the top two buttons on her blouse and pulled out the chain and ring. All the elders were delighted and the two old ladies both reached out to touch it. Elaine seemed happy with the responses and for a moment she showed just the hint of a sad, sad smile, but almost immediately was arching an eyebrow and waving her hand, describing a small circle in the direction of Helen's chest - perhaps there was a little too much undergarment and associated flesh on public display. Helen threw back a slightly quizzical look as she allowed the ring to slide back against her skin and fastened the offending buttons.

It seemed to Helen that revealing the ring had produced a disproportionate response from those around her and she did not understand what Elaine had meant by, *supporting her*. She began to suspect that no definitive answers were going to emerge from the meeting, Helen got ready to stand. 'Well this is all very well, but it explains nothing to me. I really don't want to carry on with this mystery. And what did you mean by supporting me? Wasn't that just talk in a crisis, a dying man's confusion?'

Sensing that time and the meeting were running against her, Elaine abandoned her plan to explain everything in a carefully balanced sequence of revelations over several days. 'It means that John nominated you as the successor minister and he made me promise to support you,' she said.

'What? Wow. You've got to be kidding, right?' Helen was shocked.

'No, I'm not joking,' replied Elaine. 'However, technically it wasn't in John's gift. As I said - it's the task of the nominations committee. It's for the elders to inform succession decisions, according to the rules, which we are now following to the letter. John is not allowed to influence the selection of his successor.'

Elaine felt the looks of defiance from the suddenly invigorated elders and hurriedly continued. 'But I know he was trying to maintain continuity at the end. To help us, guide us, as Archie did for him, and countless others before them; Helen, I'm a woman of my word. I want you to apply, we'll follow the rules to the letter, but I will be supporting you and I fully expect the others will support your selection and then recommend you to the full congregation.' A murmur of consensus ran quickly through the group.

Helen was still trying to come to terms with John's death. Now, she had been nominated to succeed him instead of getting ready to fly home to her family in New England. She needed some time to think. To think about her future, about Sam, and about all this danger stuff. It was like something from a gothic horror. Maybe New England was a safer bet.

Once the murmuring had subsided, Helen thanked them for the invitation but insisted she needed a few days to think things through, still needed to understand what had happened and why, before any decision could be reached. She could see the disappointment on the faces around the room, but really needed time to come to terms with everything. Needed facts, facts she was clearly not going to get today.

She and Sam left the room and a rising babble of confused and excited voices followed them down the hall and through the vestry, finally dissipating within the silent cavern of the nave. They walked out through the silence, still with more questions than answers.

Chapter 15

SUNDAY 9th JUNE

So soon after the butchery, Helen had not felt able to lead a service in John's church, or anywhere else for that matter. A guest minister had stepped in and Helen had been happy to take a place in the congregation close to Elaine and Grace, finding some strength amidst the congregation, a great family of friends. There she had spent an hour going through the motions while her mind had churned, demanding answers of God. She had not heard a reply.

The guest minister had the sensitivity to realise this was not a day to prolong the post service formalities. After delivering his commiserations and sympathy, he had slipped quickly away. The congregation had done the same. Many of them had really wanted to stay and talk, but had been scared away by the media pack that was gathered outside.

As the last of the churchgoers left, Elaine was able to close the great doors at the front of the church. She locked them from the inside and walked quickly back through the church to join Helen in the vestry. The room was always cool, this morning it felt cold. Even in her uniform tweed, Elaine shivered.

Helen greeted her arrival in the vestry with a drawn smile. 'I can't remember when I found a service so hard,' she said.

Elaine nodded. 'Aye, it was hard this morning. Those journalists didn't help though. Vultures.'

'You know, I think one was actually recording the service - so disrespectful.'

'Aye,' said Elaine. She had suspected the same thing, but right now, she just wanted out of the church. 'Come on, we'll go out the back way.'

Helen felt the same need to be out in the open and followed her into the little corridor behind the vestry. They walked to the end and the heavy wooden door that led out to the back of the church. Elaine unlocked the old door and pulled it open letting daylight flood in. There were no journalists at the back of the church and the two women slipped out, pushing the door shut behind them. Elaine hesitated for a moment, and then carefully locked the door. Then they were away and heading down the path for a little gate that led them directly from the rear of the church into the cemetery.

The pair walked in silence while weaving a path amongst the graves; steadily working their way deeper into the forest of stone until eventually they were invisible from the church. Now completely alone they let their pace ease, and by some unspoken agreement, they settled on one of the gravel covered pathways that criss-crossed the cemetery. Helen linked arms with Elaine and instantly she felt the older woman tense, almost bridling at the sudden physical contact. Then Elaine relaxed, perhaps suddenly realising how alone she really was and for once welcoming proximity. She allowed the link to remain and both women found comfort in it.

They walked for a few minutes, moving deeper and deeper into the cemetery. The serried ranks of headstone slabs were interrupted by an occasional stone angel and a scattering of imposing Celtic crosses, some towering so high they seemed to be reaching for heaven. The pair talked, dancing around the issue like sparring boxers until Helen finally took the bull by the horns.

'Elaine, I need to understand what's happening. I'm flattered you have said you want me to be minister and will support me. I understand there are procedures to follow and it's not in your gift so let's just see how things play out. I'm with you, okay? Just, there's so much stuff I don't understand. You need to give me some answers.' Using her own linked arm, Helen squeezed and joggled Elaine's arm hard against her side, encouraging her, coaxing her. 'Okay?' She turned her head to look into Elaine's eyes and the two women came to an involuntary halt. Their eyes were only inches apart. 'I need to know what I'd be signing up to, right?'

Each saw sadness and worry in the other's eyes. Elaine was motionless, thinking, holding Helen's gaze. The closeness of their bodies, the intensity of their gaze and their unswerving focus might have easily been misread by an observer. This was not romance though; this was a desperate search for truth and trust. After a long moment Elaine nodded, sighed, and started walking on. Helen matched her step for step, keeping arms tightly linked.

'Well?' asked Helen, expectant.

'I'm not sure where to start,' replied the older woman.

'Anywhere you like, just fill me in, please.'

'You know, I've been here so long I can't remember when I wasn't a member of this parish. My husband died when I was young, Grace was just a baby then and it was John's support that got me through.' Elaine could feel Helen's arm squeezing tighter still against her own, offering sympathy and support.

'John was a good man,' said Helen. 'You must have become so close.'

'We are, were… Grace and I would have been lost without him and I'll never forget that. I trusted John without question, he was good through and through. Stood by Grace and me, and never sought anything in return.' Silent tears were running down Elaine's face, unbroken streams finally unleashed.

'He did so much for us it was only natural I took on more and more tasks to help him. It wasn't long before I became an elder. I was quite young for the role, but he encouraged me there too.' Through the tears, she gave a fierce, defiant laugh. 'Oh, we had our moments though, believe me. He could drive me to distraction. He was too good, needed to be toughened up. I tried. Oh, I tried all right. You know, no matter how hard I pushed him he still stayed calm, relaxed, ready to see the good side in people.' A bitter tone entered her voice. 'See where all his goodness and forgiveness got him?'

She stopped and turned to Helen again. 'God forgive me, but if I ever get my hands on who did that to my John I'll, I'll…' Her voice trailed away lost in a huge sob. Helen was crying too and the pair cradled and hugged each other.

Set close beside the path was a little bench, and almost without realising, they found themselves sat. As Elaine's composure slowly returned she produced tissues from her jacket pocket, the pair dabbed and wiped. Suddenly, Elaine let out a chuckle, smiling through the tears as she recalled fondly how impossibly liberal John could sometimes be, and especially when he would not take her concerns seriously.

Elaine took a deep breath and then let it out in a long slow sigh. 'So you want to know. Well I'll tell you what I can. I guess I was John's trusted lieutenant. You know this parish has one or two independent ways, things that James Curry wants to put a stop to.'

'I guess so,' said Helen, 'but I'm not sure exactly what his problem is. What's wrong with local customs?'

'Church rules, I suppose. But this is a very old parish. St Bernard's church building is only a couple of hundred years old but the parish roots go way back. And we've got one or two things we do our own way that don't quite fit the modern rulebook. It was all right in the past, and even quite recently, back when John was taking over from Archie. The world then was more about who you were, who you knew and maybe just getting the right bits of paper signed off for the record. These days there are rules and records and you can't move for computer controls and oversight. One of our little quirks is the selection process - you know about this, but the presbytery clerk really is determined to put a stop to it. Then there's the money.'

Helen tensed at the mention of money. The trust fund that had been causing such a stir last week. 'That's what James Curry is really nosing around into. Isn't it?'

Elaine nodded agreement. 'Yes, though believe me, Helen, the money and its use is as clean as a whistle, everything above board. Everything. John would never do anything deceitful.'

Helen smiled acknowledgement. 'So why the big secret then? What was he hiding?'

'Nothing. Well, it's not so much to do with the money. It's more the traditions. And I guess that's where you come in.'

'Me?' asked Helen. 'What do I have to do with it?'

'John trusted me but there were some things I didn't know. It's all about hand me downs, stories from the earliest days of the parish. There's stuff from then that I don't know about. Things that one minister handed on to the next, which is why the parish had its own little recruitment tradition. The current minister needed to know who the next minister was to be able to brief him - or her, now - old church rituals or something.' Elaine was suddenly sounding a little vague.

'So that's what this ring's about?'

'I think so,' agreed Elaine.

'I can't keep John's traditions going if I don't know what they are. Will you tell me what to do?' Helen was sounding sceptical. 'I might not even want to be involved. It all sounds a bit iffy to me. Why can't we just hand it over to the police?'

Elaine gripped her wrist and squeezed it. 'Nothing John Dearly did was iffy. He chose you, gave you the ring and made you promise to keep quiet. I don't know what's going on, but how many church ministers do you think are killed in Scotland in a year? None! Then Archie is killed, then John. I don't think that's a coincidence, do you? He begged you to keep it secret, please, it was his last request, let's respect that, don't tell the police about his ring. He begged you on his deathbed not to reveal it and you gave your word.'

'I know and I have kept quiet. Obviously, I've told Sam and you told the elders yesterday, but I don't understand why I've to keep quiet. Why did he want me to keep it from the police? I don't understand.'

'Whatever it signifies, he carried the ring all his working life. It mattered to him and we should respect that. I can't see his life's work discarded, wasted. He was the best person I've ever known. His beliefs are my beliefs. I can't bear to see his trust broken.' The tone in Elaine's voice was almost pleading, revealing another layer of vulnerability whose existence Helen had never suspected.

Helen was not entirely persuaded but she could see Elaine's sincerity and allowed herself to concede, for now. 'Okay, I'll go along with this for now, but I still need to know the full story. I'm not committing to anything without the facts, right? In the end, if the ring's material, I'm handing it over to the police right away. Understand?' Helen was not concerned with keeping traditions or secrets if it put her on the wrong side of the law, but she could tell it had meant a lot to John and just as much to Elaine. She would keep quiet for now.

Elaine nodded acknowledgement. 'I know some things, procedures and processes but I don't know the whys and wherefores. It was always John's secret, not mine. To be honest, I supported it because it was part of the parish, the minister's thing. I've never known anything different. I think we should see Francis Kegan. He and John go a long way back and were as thick as thieves. If anyone can give you the full background, it's him. He'll speak to you, I know he will.'

• • •

DCI Wallace had sat through the church service. Apart from the media prowling the edges he had not seen anything that struck him as out of the ordinary, nothing to attract his attention. Afterwards, he decided to take a walk before heading home for Sunday lunch. He had promised his wife he would not be late and after all the recent domestic turmoil triggered by this case he knew he had to keep his word. Nonetheless, he needed to clear his mind and so opted for a stroll through the quiet of the cemetery where he could put his thoughts in order.

As he wandered amongst the gravestones, a movement caught his eye and his observer's instinct brought him to a sudden stop. He was pleased it had. Sat on a bench perhaps twenty paces ahead of him were the two women who found John Dearly's body. What were they doing here? Consoling one another? Perhaps, but this was a lonely place to give support. He couldn't make out what they were saying but he'd stop and watch a little. Who knew what this was all about?

Chapter 16

MONDAY 10th JUNE

The media storm had grown over the weekend and police officers were posted outside both the church and the manse. Helen was relieved, thankful for the protective blue barrier that kept the paparazzi at bay. Now safely ensconced in the church office, she sipped at a strong coffee and tried hard to ignore the ghoulish headlines staring up from the morning newspaper that lay on the desk.

She was functioning physically but was quite detached from life around her. The daily routine seemed of no consequence and she really did not want to confront the events of recent days. Staring hard at the desk's worn and mellowed wood, she absently traced patterns in the grain; keeping her mind busy on nothing.

Elaine sat at the other end of the desk; neither woman had chosen to sit in the seat behind it. In the absence of a minister, it was probably Elaine's place as Kirk Session clerk, but as assistant minister, Helen might have staked a claim. Today, both had subconsciously decided to leave John's seat vacant as a mark of respect. The phone on the desk was silent now - its constant ringing had prompted Elaine to unplug it at the wall and Helen had not objected.

Traumatised by events, neither was feeling ready to face the world, but it kept turning and it seemed with scant regard for their pain or loss. Both were ill at ease with what was about to arrive.

James Curry had been in touch. He would be with them at any moment. Under the circumstances, this was not unusual; a parish would expect its presbytery to rally round at a time of crisis, to lend whatever support it could. Curry's note did make reference to their loss and offered support, but it seemed to suggest that he also had other business he needed to address today.

'You don't have to be here you know, I can deal with it,' said Elaine.

Helen pulled herself into the day and shook her head. 'No, it's alright, I'm fine, perhaps we had better see him together, moral support, safety in numbers and all that stuff. Though technically I think you're in charge at the moment. What do you think? Curry might be just delivering his condolences.'

Elaine grimaced. 'Well his is not a face I want to see here just now, and I wouldn't bank on him calling round just to be nice,' she said. 'He's a heartless one. John wasn't keen on him, for all his clean cut public image. He's one who shouldn't bank on his maker being that pleased to see him when his time comes.'

A rapping knuckle on the vestry door brought them both up short and an inappropriately cheery voice called out. 'Hello, anyone home? The police let me through, I've shown myself in.' James Curry walked through the vestry and on into the little corridor leading to the office. 'Don't get up on my account. Quite understand. I'll see myself in.' Then he was there, framed in the doorway. They both turned to look at him and their hearts sank yet further.

Curry syruped into the room, he parroted a worried concern that was belied by the enthusiastic tone in his speech, which he could not quite suppress. 'Elaine, my dear lady. Helen too,' said Curry, turning to them each in turn. 'How are you both bearing up? Awful business. Tragic. Inexplicable.'

Elaine was careful to be holding the coffee pot in her right hand as she stood to greet the presbytery clerk. She waved the pot in his direction, offering him both the hospitality of a coffee and a hollow excuse for not shaking hands. Instead, they exchanged brief head nods in greeting. Elaine tilted the pot towards a tray of clean cups and James Curry nodded acceptance of the offered hospitality.

Helen remained seated at the end of the desk, avoiding the hug of condolence that she feared would come if she stood. Instead, as Elaine poured everyone coffee, Helen stretched out an arm across the corner of the desk to shake the presbytery clerk's hand. Greetings over, Curry picked up a chair from the side of the room and purposefully placed it in front of the desk.

It had been a surprise for Curry to find Helen there at all. He put it down to a combination of some misplaced deference on the part of that dullard McPhee, while the pushy American girl clearly did not understand the proper parish protocols. He had expected to find the senior elder behind the desk, filling the leader's role until the parish selected a new minister, which with his guidance and support was going to take many months. Then he'd ensure a nice, conventional, compliant minister was selected. Job done.

Now was the time to break up McPhee's little coven, time to dismantle their traditions once and for all: James Curry had it planned.

After the short exchange of pleasantries, James Curry plunged straight to the point by addressing himself to Elaine. 'Now, Elaine, my dear, I know you and the other elders will be anxious to ensure parish affairs are kept appropriately during this difficult time. Don't you agree?' he did not allow Elaine the time to reply. 'You really must have things in order for the next minister, whoever he may be,' Curry paused, turned and gave Helen the slightest of smiles. 'Someone quite special will be needed here, don't you think? After all the urr... All the unpleasantness.'

Curry turned his head towards Elaine again, addressing her alone. 'Of course, presbytery knows the responsibility for appointing a new parish minister ultimately rests with your nominating committee. A grave responsibility for you and the other elders involved,' he stretched out his hands to embrace the whole parish, 'and that is your responsibility. We will guide you and you know you can rely on my support throughout, but ultimately it will be the congregation here that makes its choice,' James Curry fixed Elaine with a steely gaze. 'And perhaps we might hope for a more conventional procedure too. I want to regularise things here. Get a level playing field for the next minister, that's important don't you think?'

His smile gave no warmth. 'However, we do still have these concerns about certain financial arrangements that might not be as they ought. I met with John Dearly to discuss that very issue,' he turned pointedly to Helen, 'and you will recall, young lady, John agreed to co-operate with an informal investigation. He agreed in a gesture of goodwill and public spirit that St Bernard's would provide what information might be needed - so heading off any risk of our needing to implement a formal investigation and perhaps, helping to avoid a financial scandal.

'Now, in the light of circumstances surrounding the pre-vious two ministers' mmmh..., ending, we think it's all the more important to do that investigation quietly and at once, don't you agree?' He fell silent, sent Elaine a smug smile and waited for her to agree.

Elaine stared back without returning his smile. 'I don't think you understand the situation here, this is turmoil; we've no time to help informal investigations. No time to help any investigations. We've got to appoint a new minister, there's a murder investigation going on and there's a parish to run.'

Curry smiled back at her. 'Now don't you worry about a thing, we thought a helpful gesture might be appreciated. The presbytery thought I should personally make myself available to support the running of the parish in the interim. I'll just beaver away in the background, nobody will even notice me. It will give you all the peace of mind that things will be as they should be for the next minister, allowing you to concentrate on pastoral business and the appointment of a suitable new minister. Oh, and the time to give access to any and all financial information that might be needed. What do you think?' Curry paused, contented.

Confidently, he lifted his coffee cup and sipped. It was nice coffee, but not quite the quality he liked. As he intended to spend some time here, the first thing he would do is upgrade the coffee quality. St Bernard's could afford it.

Elaine sat silently. The prolonged presence of such a senior administrator was not normal, nor was it necessary. But she was cautious, St Bernard's had always sought to keep a low profile, avoiding attention or comment for any reason. Recent events had forced it into the limelight and the close interest of the presbytery's senior administrator was undesirable, but so was the attention that would be attracted by resisting such interest.

Curry relished Elaine's discomfort as he allowed the silence to stretch. Finally, accepting the prolonged silence as acquiescence, complete surrender, he carefully drained his cup, put it on the desk and pulled out a slim pocket diary. 'Now, Elaine, firstly is there any more of that coffee available? Perhaps you could top up my cup, hmm? Then we need to fix some dates for me to attend and get things underway.

'I don't think we should wait until after the funeral - with the police involvement that could take a little while. Best if I set aside a couple of days a week to support you, perhaps Tuesdays and Thursdays? Shall we say starting this Thursday? Of course, I'll need access to the accounts and records and so forth, and I'd expect the parish's support in every way. What do you think?' Curry started to enter diary dates but stopped short as his proposal was challenged.

'I think you've skipped a line somewhere, James,' said Helen. Quiet spoken, confident and masking the growing irritation she was experiencing over this smug man. She could tell he was little more than an apparatchik, making the wheels turn to best suit the system, to protect the system and his place within it, and with no concern for the thoughts or feelings of those affected. John Dearly had not liked the man, had been right about him all along, and she was not about to let him push in over John's dead body.

Curry paused and peered over his glasses. 'I beg your pardon, my dear. Did you say something?' Turning his head towards Elaine, he asked theatrically. 'Have I missed something, Elaine? I can't imagine what.' Turning back to Helen, he gave her a disdainful look. 'And I'm not exactly sure what purpose you serve in this meeting anyway, Helen. A transient parish assistant has no role or voice in this essential work.' He tutted, chiding her like a naughty girl, then looked back at his diary to complete his arrangements. 'Now, as I was-'

'Listen, yes, I am the assistant here but I am an ordained minister too. This is not an empty place where you can just roll up and wipe John Dearly away. I'm here as part of the existing parish team and I'll be supporting Elaine and everyone else too, believe it,' said Helen. She met and held Curry's glare as his head snapped up.

'What?' Curry's voice betrayed sudden and intense irritation.

She nodded, giving him a sweet smile of confirmation. 'That's right, I'm still here. John trusted me, wanted me. And you know what? When the time comes, I'll be putting my hat in the ring too. I hope you think I'll be a really suitable new minister.'

Curry almost sneered at her. 'There's a selection process, advertising the post, whittling down, then the congregation have to make the appointment. I don't know what silly dream you're having but why don't you go and pack your bags, and let Mrs McPhee and I sort it out? Hmm? There's a good girl.' Curry swept her aside, blustering himself back into control, but it was short lived. Even as he half turned in his chair, directing Helen towards the office door with his pointing hand, he was brought to a halt.

'She is part of our parish team. I know the parish wants her to stay. I hope, no, I believe she will be selected as the new minister,' growled Elaine. Her voice made clear that there was no scope for give and take. She had hoped to keep things as low profile as possible, to put up with Curry's arrogant and superior behaviour, and hopefully avoid the issue of succession altogether today. However, once Helen and Curry had clashed that hope had vanished and Elaine stood beside Helen at once.

'Rubbish! You can't make that decision. It's not in your gift. Church rules are quite clear, and make no mistake; you'll be following the rules to the letter. It's for the parish to form a nomination committee with the guidance and oversight of the presbytery, to follow a selection process, to deliberate and recommend a minister to the congregation,' said Curry, confident of his ground. 'And then the congregation will need to vote acceptance.'

'Yes,' Elaine replied, 'and we'll follow the rulebook to the letter, with your guidance and support, I'm sure. But the other elders and I have conferred, taken soundings around the congregation. Oh, it'll have to be seen to go through process, but rest assured we know who we want right now.'

Helen stood up, fixed Curry with her gaze and gave the sweetest of smiles while pointing at herself. 'Me, a minister,' she said, as her head tilted slightly to one side and she nodded and arched an eyebrow, seeking his acknowledgement. She spun her finger pointing round the room in a little circle, 'My place, my people. Yes?'

Curry leapt up, his chair falling over behind him, the carefully cultivated veneer cracking to let his irritation show through. He directed a blast at Elaine. 'Impossible, you can't do this! It's completely irregular, against every procedure. I demand you stop this charade.'

Elaine looked at him, her craggy features betraying none of the turmoil she felt inside. 'We'll follow the rulebook, every letter just as you direct. But in the end, everyone wants her. She will be the new minister once the processes are followed and complete.'

Curry felt a rage bubbling up; he could suddenly feel his access to parish records and the source of the parish's secret bequest slipping away.

Curry was in no mood to surrender meekly. He would force this parish into line. 'Never! I'm not standing for it. This is absolutely wrong, and I'm going to make a full report on it. Don't think you'll stand in my way. I don't know what you are up to, but I'll have you all out. Out for good!'

Helen repeated her sweetest of girly smiles, pushing Curry's blood pressure up yet another notch. 'We're not up to anything here,' she said, 'I know I will have to follow process to take up the post, but I'm qualified and I'm wanted, and there's nothing you or anyone can do to block that. And you know it, friend.' Helen had spoken gently, now she mimicked his own earlier gesture, directing Curry towards the office door with her pointed hand. 'Of course we will welcome any advice you might want to give us. After John's funeral, not before.'

With an unintelligible splutter, Curry glared round the room and then turned abruptly away. He stalked out and slammed the office door behind him. That bang was closely followed by two more as he stormed through the vestry taking out his anger on those doors as he passed.

Helen and Elaine stood in silence for a moment looking at one another. Helen stepped round the desk and hugged the older woman. Still unaccustomed to such expressions, Elaine responded awkwardly, half hugging Helen, half patting her back. Helen sighed, long and loud, and then stepped back. Taking one of Elaine's hands between hers, she rubbed it gently. 'You know, Elaine, I don't think we made a friend there.'

'I don't think he has a friend anywhere,' Elaine's deadpan response broke the tension. For the first time in days there was something to laugh at, even for a few moments.

'And did you see his face? I wish I'd a camera.'

'Aye, he was sick, for sure.' Elaine paused; she fixed Helen with an eye that seemed to twinkle for just a moment. 'I take it that's an official yes then. You're staying?'

Helen gave a wistful smile. 'There are so many questions that still need to be answered. I'm sure things will work out, but I need to talk it over properly with Sam and my family back home first. Okay?'

• • •

Neither radio nor TV news was on in Helen's flat. She and Sam both knew the only story in town; they knew it better than the media. Sam was turning fish suppers out of their paper wrappers on to plates - this had not been a day for home cooking. Helen joined him at the table, setting down mugs of hot tea. The day had gone in a flash and while there was no doubt James Curry would not let things rest, there were so many other issues to think about, so many puzzles to solve, and right now the man was way down the list of worries.

Helen's day had been topped off on a brighter note by a call from home. Her father was worried about her. John Dearly had been his good friend, he needed to pay his respects and he wanted to be near his daughter too, but his own poor health prevented travel, so a phone call was the best he could do for now. Just hearing his voice had been a release mechanism and she'd poured steam and tension down the line until his ear burned. She was his daughter so he didn't mind, though he worried about some of the things she confided.

The rushing release of words had helped her, and by the time Sam arrived, she had regained some equilibrium.

'You know, I think Elaine is a really good person after all. I'd always felt she had something against me, but it's just she's looking out for the parish. She's taking me to visit Father Francis on Tuesday evening. They're going to explain, I hope. Though how a catholic priest fits into the picture, I don't know.'

'Wasn't he a good friend of John's?' asked Sam.

'Yeah, very good friends, with my father too, from way back, when my family used to visit years ago. Before my time.' Helen placed salt, vinegar and sauce on the table as they both sat down to eat. 'It's going to be interesting to hear what they've got to say. It's really strange. All these events must be connected somehow. It seems too much of a coincidence that John had a ring just like your Templar's skeleton from the Fife dunes.'

'True. But I guess if Francis is the gatekeeper, we'll find out soon enough. Now let's eat,' said Sam, getting started before the food cooled.

Chapter 17

TUESDAY 11th JUNE

MacPherson was sitting in the lounge reading his copy of *The Scotsman* while waiting for his wife's summons to eat. Politics, international disasters, even his beloved dagger from the dunes, all had dropped well down the editor's list of newsworthy stories. Instead, the paper's front page and several of the succeeding ones were dedicated to a brutal and apparently ritualistic murder in an Edinburgh manse. Police were remaining tight lipped about the event, releasing only what they really had to. In the absence of all the facts, speculation and fear were growing to fill the gaps.

Once links had been made with the recent murder of a retired minister in Dunbar, the media had shifted its mood into a ghoulish ecstasy and two distinct theories had now formed. One argued that some kind of random satanic serial killer was on the loose, the other that the killer was somebody who held an extreme grudge against the parish where both men had served.

He was horrified by the story and felt a little concerned that one of his lecturers had a connection to the parish. Though Sam Cameron's girlfriend had come across as a nice young woman. The whole business was so, so unfortunate, it seemed you couldn't turn around for suspicious deaths right now. Consoling himself with another sip of Scotch, he wondered what had happened to his evening meal. His wife was always organised and he had expected a call to table before now. He listened carefully - the aroma of her excellent cooking had worked its way to him from the kitchen, but no sounds accompanied it.

He rose and followed the smell down the hall and into the kitchen. A couple of pots bubbled away on the hob. On the worktop beside the cooker was a steaming casserole, fresh from the oven, but the room seemed empty. He went to turn down the heat under the boiling pans before they could bubble over.

A sound made him turn, but instead of his wife, he faced Fiona Sharp. A younger woman, petite, encased in a forensic suit, strands of blond hair, it all registered fleetingly in his eye. Before he could say anything, she delivered a sharp blow across his knees using a telescopic police baton - he went down. Instinctively, he gripped his knees. The pain was agonising, worst in his left knee, he knew immediately the cap was split. Between his groans of pain, he started to shout at Fiona Sharp. 'What the hell do you think you're -'

He was forced into silence by a size three shoe, neatly packaged inside a forensic bootee, it fitted snugly across the side of his neck, pressing it flat to the ground. His skull tilted back slightly and his right cheek and lips pouted like a gasping fish.

'Lie still. Shut up,' Sharp's higher pitched voice and piercing commands cut through and dominated his own protests. 'If I press just one bit harder your neck will snap. If you press back against my shoe, your neck will snap. Don't move.'

MacPherson was silent and still. His eyes scanned the room, worried for his wife, searching for some hope. There was none. Behind the now closing kitchen door stood a big bear of a man. Like the woman, he was dressed in a forensic suit. Robertson held Sarah tightly; she was silent. MacPherson could see why, her mouth had been stuffed with a cloth, strands of which protruded out from around the edge of a layer of tape that fixed the gag in place. The tape had been wrapped round her head several times ensuring it would not slip and she could not make a sound. Her nose and eyes were not covered, and those frightened eyes stared back at him, hoping for salvation.

Robertson threw Sarah onto the ground and she broke her fall by landing on her hands and knees. He raised his boot and brought it down on her back, applying more and more pressure, forcing her steadily down and into a prone position. 'Lie flat. Face down. Legs together. Arms wide apart,' his shouted orders filled the room and demanded instant response. Frightened and cowed she obeyed at once, while MacPherson watched, immobilised, desperate, and impotent.

In total control, Robertson knelt and bound Sarah's legs together with more of the tape. Satisfied with his work he stood. He looked down at her and prodded her rib cage with his boot. Sarah looked up at him from the corner of her eye. 'You, listen,' he shouted at her, 'don't move your hands or arms or I'll break them. Do you understand?' She nodded and lay very still.

He turned his attention to MacPherson. 'Legs together,' he ordered.

'I can't, my knee's broken,' said MacPherson. His hand was clasped over his left knee. He could feel the huge swelling, and the slightest movement sent pain surging through his body like a shock wave, which crashed abruptly against the immovable size three pressed into his neck.

The big bear did it for him. MacPherson screamed at the pain, as his kneecap finally separated into two and the various parts of that most complex of joints ground and grated. He passed out. By the time he regained consciousness his legs were bound with tape and his hands taped behind his back. The pain in his leg was almost overwhelming, but strangely, he found some tiny comfort now the shoe was off his neck. Looking along the floor he could see his wife, still lying flat. He could see little tears of fear glistening and reflecting the kitchen's electric lights as they ran down her nose and one after another dripped onto the floor tiles.

Robertson and Fiona Sharp were seated at the kitchen table. They had helped themselves to food from the casserole and were enjoying it. He took a second helping, grunted in appreciation and offered the serving spoon to her.

Sharp held up her hands in protest. 'No, no, I've had my fill, thanks. But you take some more. It's good, isn't it? Pity to see it go to waste.'

As the big man continued to eat she looked down at MacPherson, looked into his pained and angry eyes. 'You okay down there? Good. You'll just have to wait 'til we're ready. All right? Won't be long now. Your wife's a great cook by the way, saved me having to bother with anything else tonight, thanks.' Fiona Sharp wondered if there was a container anywhere handy, she wouldn't mind taking a doggy bag away with her.

'What do you want?' said MacPherson. In spite of his pain and confusion, he tried to sound reasonable, conciliatory. 'We have money, and valuables, just take them. You don't need to hurt us any more. Why are you doing this to us? Please, just take our things and go.'

Sharp looked across the table to Robertson, they laughed. She looked back at MacPherson. 'We don't want your money, professor. We're just professionals doing our job, that's all.' She tilted her head to one side, then over to the other side as though she were playfully communicating with a little child. 'That's all,' she smiled sweetly, tilting her head again. 'That's all.'

MacPherson did not understand and the look of confusion on his face made her smile again. She leant forward slightly and in a mock conspiratorial voice whispered at him. 'It's nothing personal. We've got a job to do and you're the job, that's all there is to it. Nothing else.' Sitting up straight again she nodded and smiled at him. 'Now are you going to be a good boy and do as I say?'

Anger swelled up in MacPherson and he swore at her, the madwoman would not get any help from him. He quickly regretted his response. She stood up and walked across to Sarah, placing her feet firmly on his wife's left arm, pinning it to the floor. Meanwhile, the big man had picked up one of the pans that had continued to boil on the stove. He walked across the room and put his boot on Sarah's right elbow fixing it tight to the floor. Then, slowly, slowly, he emptied the pan of boiling water over her right hand.

Sarah's mouth was full of cloth, she could not vocalise, yet MacPherson could hear a long despairing squeal that seemed to first whistle through her nose and then to pulse directly through her taught neck as her vocal cords stretched and contorted in an attempt to express the agony and distress her body was experiencing. She buckled and convulsed as the water continued to pour. MacPherson's mad, angry cries of protest were simply ignored until the pot was empty. Sharp and Robertson stepped away, leaving Sarah to curl into a whimpering protective foetal ball, carefully encircling her right hand, an untouchable bloated balloon. The pan was tossed aside.

MacPherson glared up at them. 'What in God's name are you doing this for?' he bellowed.

The big man stooped and shouted directly into Mac-Pherson's face. 'Shut up. Shut up or she gets the other pan. Do you want that? Hey? Hey? Do you want that? On her face next? Do you want that?'

Across the floor MacPherson could just make out Sarah quivering in renewed terror at the threat of more boiling water, quickly he averted his eyes and shook his head in submission, seeking to placate the madman.

Sharp pulled a chair away from the kitchen table and placed it facing MacPherson. She sat down and then leant forward placing her elbows on her knees and resting her chin on her cupped hands. She looked at him and thought for a moment before speaking. 'You see, prof', it's like I said, we're professionals, and we do what needs to be done to achieve our goal. That's our job and we're good at it. You can help us do our job or you can be awkward and make my friend here very angry, but I don't think you want to be awkward, do you?'

MacPherson shook his head. 'Whatever you want, just say. Anything, anything at all, but don't hurt my wife again. Please.' He was in agony with his broken knee but he had forced the pain from his conscious concern as he worried over his wife. 'I'll do whatever you want. Just leave her now. I beg you, don't hurt her anymore.'

Sitting up straight, Sharp stretched out a foot to tickle his ribs gently. 'There's a good boy. You see it's easy isn't it? You do as you're told and no more suffering, okay?'

MacPherson nodded.

Sharp cast a triumphant look towards Robertson who was out of MacPherson's sight. Then she looked back at her prisoner. 'Where's the blade?' she asked.

MacPherson looked at her blankly. 'What? What blade? What do you mean?' He was silenced by a trim little shoe cracking into his mouth. He gasped, jerking his head back and blood ran from his mouth onto the floor.

Sharp shouted at him. 'When I want you to ask me a question, I'll tell you. Until then, just answer mine. Now where is that old dagger you found?'

Realisation suddenly dawned on MacPherson. 'Oh God! This, all this is for that old trinket. Why? What can it be worth to do all this?' Sharp jerked her head and Robertson picked up the second pan of boiling water, he started towards Sarah.

MacPherson caught the movement in the corner of his eye and called out. 'No. No, wait. I can help you, please no more for her, please. Please, just leave her now, I beg you.' Robertson stopped halfway across the room and looked towards Sharp.

'That's better. You're learning, professor, we're back on track again,' she said, giving an approving nod and Robertson returned the pan to the hob.

In less than ten minutes, they had what they wanted. Tucked away at the back of a cupboard in the master bedroom was a combination safe. They took the dagger, ring and chain from it. From the desk in MacPherson's study, they gathered all the official university photographs and the memory stick with the original picture files. Sharp loaded her gibberish virus to MacPherson's personal computer, set it running and left it to do its wipeout task. Mission accomplished. Almost.

The pair returned to the kitchen where MacPherson lay, sullen, angry, confused. Sarah was exactly where she had been left, the only signs of life a constant and quiet shivering accompanied by a low whimpering. Sharp looked down at MacPherson. 'Well, I think we're about done here, unless there's anything else you want to tell us?' MacPherson was silent and Sharp laughed. 'No? Oh well, time to go then.'

While she spoke, Robertson had been playing around with the cooker. He had switched off the burning hobs and set the oven to auto ignite in five minutes. Meanwhile, the main gas pipe was severed, allowing gas to flood into the kitchen. He nodded to her and they walked calmly out of the kitchen. As he passed Sarah, the big man emptied the second pan of boiling water across her back. She arched and writhed in distress. MacPherson roared in rage and Robertson looked back, smirked and closed the kitchen door behind them.

In the hall, he dragged an occasional chair across to the kitchen door and wedged it under the handle. Even if Sarah could crawl to the door through the renewed pain, she would never be able to open it.

Just inside the front door, the pair paused and removed their forensic suits. Sharp opened her rucksack and stuffed the suits on top of the stolen artefacts and a container of stew she had bagged. They stepped outside, their shoes scrunching the pebbles as they strolled down the drive. Then they were out on to the quiet residential road and blended into nowhere before the neighbourhood was shattered by the sound of a gas explosion ripping the MacPherson's kitchen to pieces.

• • •

Francis Kegan's living room was a cluttered patchwork of furniture that had accumulated over many years, nothing quite matching and everything just slightly threadbare. The priest seemed to have jammed furniture in everywhere. Helen sat in a worn though comfortable armchair. A glass of wine in her hand and a little bowl of mixed nuts within arm's reach. She was ready to hear whatever Francis and Elaine had to say.

Francis was sitting opposite her, settled in his favourite chair. Forming a link between the two chairs was a broad sofa where Elaine sat. After the initial pleasantries, Francis re-emphasised what should have been obvious to everyone in the district. While he was a Roman Catholic and John a Presbyterian protestant, they were, had been, the closest of friends. They had worked together for thirty years or more and had finished off more bottles of Scotch than he liked to think about. He stressed that Helen needed to understand everything that happened here was rooted in the past. A past from before the Church split. A time when one God had only one Church.

Helen interrupted him; she had not come for a history lesson. She wanted the facts. Francis promised to get to the point, but he and Elaine needed to paint the background first. It was what John Dearly would have done himself had he lived. Helen allowed him to continue.

Francis fixed Helen with a slightly cautious stare. 'You already know the parish is old, very old,' he watched for her acknowledgement. Helen nodded. She had read the church histories as soon as her father had told her of the offer of an assistant's post. Francis continued. 'That's not so remarkable in itself; there will be scores of other churches that can make a similar claim of ancient roots.

'In some respects, the fourteenth century, when your Fife Templar was alive, was just like today. Greedy people and power brokers mixing religion and politics to find advantage, trying to exploit good to build strength for themselves. It seems as though it's always been like that,' Francis paused and took a mouthful of Scotch. 'It probably always will be.

'I think Elaine has already explained about the parish's quirky recruitment process?' he looked from one woman to the other and both nodded agreement.

'So, in John's parish the Church rules are followed just like everywhere else, but with a local variation. Here, the elders chose John as their minister, as you would expect, but under the guidance of Archie, the then incumbent. Just as Archie had been chosen a generation before with help from the then incumbent, and so on, back as far as you like. And now they will choose you, with an input from John,' Francis paused and turned to Elaine for verification.

'That's right, it's how we've always done it,' Elaine confirmed.

Francis resumed his account. 'So, you see, John and Archie both belonged to an old tradition and now you are drawn into that tradition too. They were specially selected and entrusted with something in the parish, something more, some extra responsibility beyond the pastoral. Once they had taken on the commitment they were obliged to sustain it. And I… We,' Francis swept his hand round to include Elaine, who nodded in agreement as he continued, 'we supported them, first Archie and then John. We supported them because they were our friends and we cared for them. It's your responsibility now and we'll help you too.'

'But what is it, Francis? You've told me zilch. I need to know what it's all about if I'm going to take it on board,' Helen was anxious to have the facts, the information she needed to reach any decision. In spite of telling Elaine she would like to stay, there were questions that needed to be answered first.

Francis threw a worried glance at Elaine and drained his glass. 'Right,' he said. 'Here we go', and pouring himself yet another drink from the bottle at his side he started to explain. 'What I tell you now I learnt from John during more than thirty years of trust and friendship. I'm telling you because he can't. Sadly, I can't tell you everything because I don't know the whole story.

'First, you have John's ring, it's a fourteenth century signet ring.'

'Yes, I know, Sam looked at it for me. And it seems identical to the one we found in the dunes up in Fife.'

Francis nodded. 'I think they are identical in almost every way. I think they are part of a set.'

The evening slipped by as Francis told his story. He explained how during one of their whisky nights of many years before, John had told him in confidence how the parish was even older than many realised. There were some documents tracing its origins all the way back to the independence wars with England, to the time of the Templars. Though it was just a regular church, of course, nothing to do with the Templars; or so Francis had thought at first. But John, and Archie before him, had kept something secret, some sort of parish history, some task to do, and it was all a bit vague.

Francis knew that Archie had always viewed it as deadly serious, but John himself had come to think of it as really just a fable; nothing ever seemed to happen, no purpose to it at all. Just old trinkets, except of course there was the trust fund that pumped in a shed load of money every year. That was very real. John liked the money, did a lot of good with it, discreetly of course, but that was John for you.

Francis explained about the Templars. An order of holy knights who were once headquartered at the Holy Temple in Jerusalem and whose purpose had included the escort and protection of pilgrims. They became highly trusted and respected throughout Europe, were given lands and established a form of banking that supported commerce across the continent. While always serving God with their swords, they rejected personal wealth. And so, collectively, they became a rich organisation. Above all things, they became a very, very, rich organisation. So rich the Templars could bankroll kings and countries. That made them important, made them enemies and ultimately made them vulnerable.

Anxious to get a handle on current events and suddenly suspecting where the story was leading, Helen tried to ensure Francis did not stray into speculation and rumour. 'Oh for heaven's sake! Not another silly fable. I'm not playing along with any silly boys' games of treasure hunts or Grail quests and such nonsense. I'm sorry, tangible facts only or I'm off directly to the police.' She stood.

Elaine reached up a hand to restrain her as Francis leapt up. 'No, no,' he said. 'You've got me wrong. This isn't some fantasy. I tell you, I've checked things myself. I couldn't just take it at face value either, really, it's history. Well, as far as I could tell some of it checks out anyway. Wait a few more minutes; hear me out. Helen, remember, Archie and John didn't kill themselves.' More than anything, his final sentence made her think; she paused for a moment and then sat down again.

Francis quickly resumed his account. He explained how, in 1307, perhaps in an attempt to solve his own problems including a financial crisis, King Philip of France suddenly turned on the Templars. With his puppet Pope, he promoted charges of heresy against all the Templars everywhere. He seized their lands and had many killed, but the problem for Philip was that a small fleet of Templar ships had warning of his purge and just managed to escape from France, carrying away much of the Templars' treasure and secrets. The problem for the fleet was they had nowhere to go. Having been accused of heresy, they were unwelcome in every Christian country: except one.

The pope had previously excommunicated the Scottish king, Robert the Bruce, in response to his murdering John Comyn on a church altar. This placed all Scotland beyond the reach of the Pope and the rest of the Christian world. The Templars already had lands in Scotland and so it was a natural destination for those fleeing the French king. And one important base in Scotland was nearby, just outside Edinburgh.

Helen interrupted, attempting to short circuit Francis' story. 'Yeah, you're slipping right back to the old myths, that's Rosslyn, right? Sam and I took a run out to see it a couple of months ago. The chapel's just beautiful and really amazing inside but -'

Holding up his hand to stop her, Francis shook his head. 'No, no, not Rosslyn, that came a little later. Though it is a beautiful place, I agree. Back in 1307 the Templars had a base in Scotland in a little village we now call Temple, just a short way from Rosslyn. I'm sure you can work out where the village name comes from.'

Helen interrupted again. 'Are you trying to tell me this butchery we're seeing is just about some weird cult, built around old wives' tales and half-forgotten myths, about a lost treasure that's probably a complete fiction?'

Elaine glared at her. 'John Dearly and Archie Buchan didn't belong to a weird cult. They were good men, honest men, Christians. They served the people and the Church. Men you could trust, who committed their lives to the service of God. And by God, didn't they show us that in the end?'

Helen fell silent. She could see she had hurt Elaine. She nodded agreement.

'The problem for the Templars', Francis continued, 'was they couldn't be sure it was safe to store their secrets at Temple. This part of Scotland was a war zone back then, with Scots and English forces ranging back and forth. The skirmishing bands from both sides would have been careful to avoid the Templars on their own patch at Temple, but the knights must have expected that eventually one king or the other would muster enough strength locally to overpower them and seize what was theirs.

'Though Bruce eventually proved to be a great Scottish king, he had a reputation for changing horses and having a darker side too, which was why he was excommunicated in the first place. Having seen what King Philip of France had done, the Templars probably feared the temptation of their wealth would eventually be too great. I don't think the Templars wanted to hold their secrets within reach of any king.'

Francis fell silent for a moment, glanced ruefully into the whisky glass in his hand, sighed, and then continued. 'Now I'm putting this story together from snippets gathered over a lot of years and a lot of whisky. I don't have the details, the full story, that was John's secret. I do know Temple was amongst the Templars' last secure refuges and it had become vulnerable too.

'According to John, it was decided to split up the order's secrets, or rather to create and divide up some sort of message about the location of their secrets and wealth, which had actually been hidden by the fleet that fled France in 1307. John never said what the message was or how the parts of the message were dispersed and hidden across the Christian world, other than they were carried and guarded by the most trusted of knights.

'Their task was to keep the parts of the message hidden and secure until they were to be recombined to serve the cause, ensuring in the meantime that no one could snatch what remained of the Templars' power and wealth.'

'So you guys are holding some super-secret treasure message?' said Helen, still unconvinced and on the edge of leaving.

'Well, no, not us. We are just supporters of an old and trusted friend. You on the other hand may well hold a part of the message, along with several other unknown holders.'

'People are dying over this fantasy,' Helen glanced at Elaine, 'sorry, but that's how I feel. And you know, it's got to stop. We've got to put a stop to this nonsense. Right now, before anything else happens.'

Francis and Elaine exchanged worried looks. It was clear that they had not got the message across as they had hoped. 'We don't understand what's happening any more than you do,' said Francis, trying to placate her. 'Helen, we don't know what the killer wants. We just know it is happening and we certainly don't know how to stop it.'

'John and Archie were the men with the full story; they might have understood what is going on and how to respond, but they are dead. We're all in the dark,' said Elaine.

Helen was unimpressed. 'You must have some idea of who would do this, or at least what's triggered it? Listen, John was kind to me, I liked him. He was a good friend to my father. They clearly trusted each other. I love this place. But what you're telling me is, if I stay, I'm bound into some secret group, every member of which is getting killed over an old wives' tale? Let me tell you guys, it's not a big selling point.

'Why aren't you telling the police? They should be all over this like a rash. For Heaven's sake, old Archie's gone, John's in the mortuary beside him, who's next? Come on; let's level with this policeman, Wallace. He seems a straight guy. Let's tell him what we know and forget all about this history nonsense. Okay?'

Both Francis and Elaine looked crestfallen, the meeting was not going as hoped and neither could actually offer any good reason that might persuade Helen to stay. Elaine tried again. 'John was desperate, and he gave you his ring, passed on the trust to your keeping -'

Helen stuck a hand up cutting her short. 'But he didn't tell me what it was, did he? I didn't know I was going to be involved in murder and God knows what else.

'You know what guys? I'm finished here. I'm out. One of you can have the ring and be Mr Mysterious. I'm going to speak to Wallace.'

'But we can't,' said Francis. 'The trust runs in the parish, it's the tradition.'

Helen stood up. 'Well not any more.' Her phone rang and she stopped talking to glance at the display screen then looked up. 'It's Sam,' she said and answered the call, relieved at any opportunity to break if even for just a moment.

'Hi Sam, things are pretty heavy here right now. What's up?'

She listened carefully, suddenly looking pale, and sat down again as Sam continued to speak. Her audience could just make out the sound of Sam's voice across the silent room. They had no idea what he was saying but they could tell it was not good news. Helen promised to join him at once and hung up the call.

She paused for a moment before breaking the news. 'Sam's boss and his wife, the MacPhersons, they're both dead. There was an explosion in their kitchen earlier this evening. Sam doesn't know any more than that. I said I'd go right round to him now.'

Francis and Elaine both leapt up. 'For God's sake, be careful,' said Francis.

'Aye, they were involved with the things found up in Fife,' said Elaine.

Helen paused for half a moment to consider the suggested link then shook her head. 'No, don't start building any more conspiracy theories. It was a domestic gas explosion. Just an awful accident.

'You know, we were there for a meal just last week, she was such a nice person, him too.' Helen picked up her light summer jacket.

Francis hurried to help her put it on while still trying to persuade her to take care. 'It would do no harm to take precautions -'

Helen cut in. 'That's enough, both of you,' silencing them while shrugging off Francis' attempts to help her jacket on. She treated them to a schoolteacher's waving finger and a parting volley. 'And I haven't finished with this whole mystery business yet, don't think I have. It's just going to have to wait. We'll speak tomorrow and I want us all to go to that detective together, right?' and she was gone.

Chapter 18

WEDNESDAY 12th JUNE

Helen sat alone in the manse study. The warm morning sun was blazing through the window, but it could not take the chill she felt out of the air. Through the study's open door she could see across the hallway to the kitchen door, closed now and sealed with police tape; the room beyond held frozen in time pending completion of the forensic investigation. She was unsure whether or not she felt grateful to DCI Wallace for having authorised her access this morning. She had needed into the manse so she could gather what was required to deal with urgent parish tasks, but the atmosphere was horrible, still, cold. She did know she was grateful for the policeman guarding the front door; she did not particularly want to be alone in the manse right now.

A commotion at the front door pulled her thoughts into the present. She could hear a familiar voice arguing with the policeman. It took a moment for recognition to filter through to her consciousness and then she hurried towards the noise.

Julie, the student from the dig in Fife, was trying to get past the policeman; he was big, she was small, no contest. But she was ably holding her own in the verbal exchanges as Helen joined the policeman on the step. After some pressing and assurances from Helen, he relented and allowed Julie in, on a promise that his superiors would never know.

They stood together in the study, and without a word, Julie stretched out her arms and embraced Helen. The bleak atmosphere that had filled the study lifted slightly as they shared care for one another.

Julie leant back and looked at Helen. 'Davy and I are so sorry about what happened to the minister. It's sick, it really is.'

They separated and Helen gave a despairing shrug and waved her towards a chair. 'I know, it's so horrible, but I don't really want to talk about it, I can't talk about it,' said Helen. She sat back in the chair behind the desk, looking a little lost and waved a hand in the direction of the policeman at the front door. 'I don't think I'm even meant to talk about it.' She shrugged again, half raised her hands, open palmed, and let them fall back in a gesture of helplessness.

'I'm sorry. I didn't mean to pry. We just wanted you to know we are all thinking about you. The whole class sends their love. Most of them have gone home for the summer now, but everyone's been sending messages, so I've come for them all. We're so sorry and everyone's thinking of you. It must be awful with your family so far away. Though at least you have Sam here.'

Helen nodded. 'Yes, I've got Sam here and he's a big help.'

Julie tried to manoeuvre away from talking about John Dearly, but her subconscious would not let her leave the subject of death altogether. 'The city seems to be going mad now, killings everywhere. Did you hear about the MacPhersons? You know, our department head, him from the dig?'

Helen gave a slightly weary nod. She knew all about the MacPhersons. Last evening Sam had been visited by the police who were trying to piece together what had happened and thought he might be able to provide an academic angle. It seemed the police were becoming regular visitors now. Last she'd heard they were working on the theory it was probably a robbery gone wrong, very wrong, and that the thieves were after something of great value, something from the university perhaps. Could Sam help them identify what it might be?

Surfacing from her thoughts, Helen realised that Julie was babbling now. Trying to avoid further mention of the Dearly murder at all costs she had latched on to the MacPherson case as an escape route. 'It's so weird. The latest on the news is that they were after some valuables, but what is worth enough to kill two people for?' - Then she hesitated, annoyed with herself. She should have given some thought to what she was going to say before arriving. Perhaps she should make her excuses and leave?

Helen was pleased with Julie's company, happy with the presence of another friendly human in what right now felt a dark place, but she wanted the girl to be quiet. Julie was clearly a kind-hearted soul, but probably just too young to appreciate the weight of the situation, the depth of the emotional trough she had stepped into. Suddenly, however, Helen latched onto a key phrase from Julie's continuing babble:

'... and the news was saying they think the killers may have been a gang stealing to order - after some ancient artefacts like the ones we all found in Fife, you know, the gold signet ring, the dagger -'

'What? What are you talking about? Where did you hear that? Tell me again. How do you know that's what they were after?' Helen's voice was suddenly very focused, she was right back in the day.

Startled at Helen's dramatic change of tone, Julie quickly expanded the story. 'The radio was just speculating, reporting a rumour. That was all. Though Davy had reckoned it might be right, the ring and dagger were probably worth a fortune to a specialist collector. And you know what? Davy had been speaking with a post-grad student who is working on campus over the summer. Apparently there is no trace of the photo-graphs and records of the dagger at the university any more, somebody has wiped the lot away, so it doesn't exist,' Julie paused for dramatic effect.

She gave Helen an earnest look and continued to explain. 'Davy says the thieves think stealing all the photographs of the dagger makes it unidentifiable now, hides its provenance. Probably stole it to order, and now there is no photographic record it ever existed at all. Got clean away.'

Helen felt a growing knot forming in the pit of her stomach. Perhaps Francis and Elaine were right. It was already clear the MacPherson fire had not been an accident. Was it just coincidence or were they really murdered for the dunes dagger? And was that because some fanatical private collector wanted it or was it because it was part of a Templar set? If so, what did it signify? And now the dunes dagger was lost completely. She had not given Francis and Elaine a chance to explain properly the previous night, but clearly, if even a fraction of their story stood up, then losing the dagger could not be good.

Julie continued. 'They think they've wiped the record, but Davy has pictures of it too. He took them with his phone while helping the photographer at the dig site,' Julie was proud of Davy's ingenuity and gave Helen a smile while pausing to allow space for Helen to recognise Davy's accomplishment.

Helen was electrified. 'He has pictures? Where? Where are they?'

A little surprised by the urgency in Helen's tone, Julie explained that they were still on his phone and that he'd just left for Oban. He'd gone home for a few days. Helen could get copies of the pictures when he got back to Edinburgh.

Francis' words of caution from the evening before finally resurfaced and for the first time frightening links tried to join in her mind. Was she being stupid? Perhaps, but in the morbid cold of the manse study the possible risks of involvement suddenly seemed very real. Urgently, almost frantically, Helen told Julie to warn Davy to tell nobody else about the pictures until he got back to Edinburgh. Then she and Sam would meet him. Holding them might be dangerous, he shouldn't open the pictures, transmit them, shouldn't even think about them. Shouldn't let anyone know he's got them.

Helen gripped Julie's forearm, compelling her to make eye contact. 'Tell him to keep quiet, just in case.' Helen let go of Julie's arm as she nodded a slightly puzzled agreement. 'And Julie, you too, hey? Let's just sit on this ourselves until Davy gets back, say nothing to anyone, okay?'

As Julie nodded further agreement, Helen bundled her out of the manse as quickly as she could. On the way out, they passed the police forensics team going in to do a final inspection of the kitchen. Helen pointed Julie in the direction of her student flat and then set off alone to link up with Elaine at the church. There was no point in trying to call Sam yet; he was away with some of the university's sub-aqua club, wreck diving in the Firth of Forth. He had taken a day out to clear his mind after the fire at the MacPhersons' home, an event that had now become altogether more sinister.

The phone rang in the empty study and after several rings, the answer phone machine kicked in. One of the passing forensic team paused in the hallway to listen.

'Hello there, message for Helen Johnson. This is Suzie Dignan from the Museum. Sam said I could pass on a message via you if he's unavailable. I can't get him on his mobile phone, so perhaps you could pass this on, please? It's about our old Templar artefact, the dagger that he was so interested in last week; I've found more information about it for him. I'm going away for a week on holiday, so if he wants the info quickly he'll need to get in touch before the weekend. Give me a call here at the museum and we'll make a plan. Bye for now.'

The answer phone clicked off and silence returned to the room. The forensics man shrugged and headed back to the kitchen, just a message for the parish assistant, obviously it had nothing to do with John Dearly. If they pushed on, the team could get finished with the manse today.

• • •

Leaning forward at her desk, the rather sour faced receptionist gave a little smile that did nothing to improve her countenance.

A headphone played back the audio in her left ear as experienced fingers edited it down to a single audio file; she saved it. Later she'd prepare a full transcription of the day's recording from the manse; right now, she knew the highlights would be most welcome. Stretching across her desk, she jabbed the intercom button and waited for a reply.

'Yes, what is it?'

'I've an audio recording from St Bernard's manse that you might want to hear, sir.'

'Right, let me have it now.' Cassiter cut off the conversation and turned to his computer, waiting for the audio file to arrive.

• • •

Davy McBain drove his mother's 4x4 slowly along Oban's George Street. Through gaps in the oncoming traffic, he could make out one or two boats in the harbour. He had seen the same scene almost every day for the first eighteen years of his life and every time he came home, its beauty stirred a quiet thrill of pride inside him. Wherever he went in life this would always be home.

Leaning back into the driver's seat he stretched, relaxed, turned up the music and let the drivers round about him stress. Having stocked up on booze at the supermarket he had chosen to drive the longer way home, he was in no hurry. His parents were away for a short break, so he had taken the opportunity to return home, helping them out with a bit of dog sitting, and catching up with old school friends too.

Barty, the family's ageing and overweight black Labrador, watched him trustingly from inside the safety cage at the rear of the car, his tail beating out a constant welcome home against the cage sides. Between Davy and Barty was the beer, securely stacked on the rear passenger seat. His mother kept a well-stocked kitchen so there was always plenty to eat, that together with all the drink he had just picked up would ensure the old gang could have a proper catch up session. A boys' night in. Drink, food, friends and films: great.

There was no particular reason why Davy should have noticed the white transit van behind him, nor the slim man behind its steering wheel; he didn't notice. Passing the railway station on his right hand side he entered the one-way system and lost sight of the boats as he cruised towards home. The white van allowed a discreet distance to open up between them and then matched his speed, tracking him, unnoticed.

Davy took a left exit from the one-way system. Driving on, he wove a route up hill and moved into the popular Pulpit Hill residential district, its views across the water ensured it was always in demand. He slowed and pulled into his parents' driveway. The van passed on by.

A little way along the road, the van slowed and then stopped. Jim Barnett watched in his wing mirrors as Davy opened the rear hatch. An old black dog struggled down; it clearly had some hip problems. Satisfied, Barnett drove off, turned and cruised back past the house again. He followed the road away from the house, establishing an exit route as Davy lifted his beer stack from the back seat and headed for the house. Barty waddled behind, tail still wagging contentedly.

Having loaded the beers into the fridge, Davy opened a bottle for himself and got busy grilling sausages for the gang's tea. They would want to get something in their stomachs before the serious drinking started. Barty hovered, hopeful that a sausage might reach him. The front door was unlocked: while there is crime everywhere, local people in small towns are generally about as safe as you can get.

Music covered the sound of the front door opening and the quiet steps of a slim man coming down the hall. Barty heard nothing since he was pretty well deaf anyway and right now he was intent on demolishing the large meaty sausage that Mrs McBain would never have allowed to reach him. Davy was busy turning sausages and listening to music, but he heard the kitchen door opening.

'You guys are early, come on in. Beer's in the fridge. Help yourselves,' said Davy, his back to the door as he kept his concentration on the grilling sausages. He looked round to see which of his friends had arrived and was puzzled to see a strange man dressed in a white forensic suit. The man was moving very quickly across the room towards him. Davy raised the turning tongs in the man's direction and challenged him. 'Who the hell are you? Get out of here before I call the police.'

The man did not stop, closing the gap between them in an instant. He brushed aside Davy's tong wielding hand, gripping the wrist and twisted it violently. Davy's body turned in an automatic response that sought to relieve the impossibly painful stress on elbow and shoulder joints. Jim Barnett kept the twisting pressure on and Davy's whole body continued its involuntary turn until he was again facing the cooker. Then Barnett applied simple forward pressure to the wrist and with a cry, Davy found himself propelled against and then bent double over the worktop beside the cooker.

In a single, seamless movement, a hand slid round Davy's waist and patted his crotch, feeling for a phone. Found, the hand slipped into Davy's trouser pocket, removed the phone and Barnett pocketed it just as Barty caught up with proceedings.

It had taken the old dog a few moments to realise that the man in the kitchen was unwelcome and a few moments more to waddle across the room. He growled fiercely and ignored the pain in his ageing hips to lurch up onto his hind legs. Placing his forepaws on the intruder's back, Barty leant in to worry at the intruder's neck. Had Barty been two or three years younger, the outcome might have been very different, but he just didn't have the speed or body strength needed anymore. Barnett pulled his hand out of the pocket into which he had just deposited Davy's phone. The hand now clutched a knife, and a metallic click rang out as the blade sprang open and locked.

The knife swung up over his shoulder then down, plunging the blade into Barty's neck, then slicing down and embedding into the dog's shoulder. Barty howled and tried valiantly to bite at the attacking hand, but the agony in his hips and his bloodied neck and shoulder forced him down. As Barty slipped off the assailant's back towards the floor, Barnett kicked back hard, catching the dog's muzzle. Canine teeth bounced down on the floor tiles, unheard in the commotion of music, shouts and howls. A second kick that the dog was too old and too shocked to avoid sent Barty sprawling into oblivion.

Barnett turned his attention back to Davy, who remained pinned against the worktop by his twisted arm. The target needed to be disposed of now while he was trapped. But the knife was out of reach, embedded in the stupid dog. It was necessary to improvise; he glanced around to see what could be used.

One of Mrs McBain's heavy copper pans was sitting on the top of the cooker. Clean, shiny, brutal, lethal. Not his favoured technique, but a solid bludgeoning did generally deliver the goods. Barnett stretched his free hand across the cooker, clawing with his fingers he coaxed the pan handle into range and then gripped it firmly; he swung it up in a great arc over his own head and back down on to Davy's.

Davy gasped then groaned, stunned, and dazed. With the second blow he slipped into unconsciousness, the resistance eased from his muscles and he dropped to the floor. Barnett stood over him and gave a wry smile; sweets from a child, he thought, just like taking sweets from a child. He raised the pan to deliver the third blow, the killing stroke. The doorbell rang, the front door opened and the voices of several young men called out as they spilled into the hall.

Barnett was already out of the back door, had sprinted away round the house, down the drive and into the road before the boys discovered the kitchen chaos. By the time anyone had set off down the drive in pursuit, Barnett was in the van and driving calmly away, heading for the car park at the cemetery on the A85 road just outside town.

Defeated, the chasing boys turned back towards the house and then the quiet street burst into life. Ambulance and police sirens wailed as emergency vehicles raced up towards the house in response to an emergency call from one of the boys. Two more boys emerged from the house carrying Barty between them. They held Barty wrapped tight in his own bed blanket; their progress was marked by a trail of red blood drops along the pavement as they hurried for the local vet's.

Turning gently into the empty car park opposite the cemetery, Barnett came to a controlled halt; he pulled the handbrake on but left the engine running. He got out of the van, calmly walked to the back and swung the doors open. Without hesitation, he slid out a long plank, allowing one end to rest on the van floor while he lowered the other to the ground, forming a simple ramp. Then he jumped into the back of the van, peeled off his bloodied forensic suit and shoes and threw them down. He pulled on leathers, boots and a helmet, then rolled a motorbike down the makeshift ramp and stood it a little away from the van.

Having kicked the motorbike engine into life he left it ticking over and returned to the rear of the van where he pushed the plank back inside. He jumped back in to retrieve a petrol container and started pouring petrol all around the cargo bay, being careful to soak the four other plastic containers of petrol that were stowed inside. Then he moved round to the cab and soaked the front seats. Stepping back, he splashed it across the exterior too, particularly the driver's side door. From a safe distance, he fixed a cloth wick into the nozzle of the nearly empty petrol can and lit it, then threw it into the van. The petrol soaked interior ignited with a whoosh and flames spread rapidly throughout the van.

A little over three minutes after driving the white transit van into the car park, Barnett was riding out on a motorbike. Careful to stick to the speed limits, just another unremarkable tourist biker on the road south. Helmet on, engine running, he heard nothing of the explosion, but his wing mirror did show the flash behind him as the forty gallons of petrol stored in the back of the burning van exploded.

• • •

Helen stood in the middle of her living room. Her phone call over, she stared pensively at the handset, tapping her fingers on its display screen. Finally, she threw a worried look across the room towards Sam, pushed the phone into her pocket and sank down on to the sofa beside him.

He had been listening to the one-sided phone conversation with growing alarm, and now put a comforting arm around her. 'Go on then, tell me.'

Helen twisted on the sofa to look him directly in the eye. 'That was Julie, your student, you know? Davy's friend.'

Sam nodded. 'Yeah, of course. What's up? What's her problem?'

Helen shook her head. 'It's not her with the problem, it's Davy - he's been mugged. No, he's been beaten to within an inch of his life. They think the attacker did try to kill him, but he was interrupted. Julie's frantic, has no one to turn to, most of the class are away for the summer now and she has no close family. She's getting a train up to Oban in the morning to be with Davy, but doesn't want to be alone tonight. I've told her just to come round, she's welcome here.'

'Of course she should come and stay, but tell me the details before she arrives,' said Sam.

Helen recounted the whole story that ended with the police and everyone else being puzzled why the thief seemed only interested in his phone, not his wallet or anything else of value. After she had finished, both sat in silence for a moment. They knew exactly why the phone had value; it held the only surviving photos of the dunes dagger, for which it seemed the MacPhersons had already been killed. It must have been why *they* targeted Davy. The question was who were *they*? And what really made the information so valuable?

'What I can't get to grips with is how did they know Davy had the pictures? Davy and Julie knew, and we did too. Nobody else,' said Sam. He looked at Helen for inspiration.

She shrugged. 'And he only went up to Oban first thing this morning, how would anyone even know he was there?' She paused and gave a slightly despairing grin. 'Somebody is a hell of a lot better tuned in than we are, that's for sure.'

They lapsed into silence again, puzzling, trying to understand what had happened and why. Suddenly Sam leapt up from the sofa. 'Of course, you're right. You're absolutely right!'

'What do you mean I'm right? I haven't said anything,' said Helen.

Sam shushed her and disappeared, returning with their coats. 'Grab your toothbrush, we're going out,' he said, chivvying Helen along, neither allowing questions nor giving answers. Something in Sam's military intelligence training was waving a red flag to his concerns, triggering latent thought patterns, bringing old cautions back to light. In moments, he had her out of the tenement flat and heading down stairs. 'Text Julie, tell her to go to my place, we'll meet her there. Come on, let's go.'

Once in the street, they walked quickly away from Helen's home in Causewayside. Round two street corners and they were skirting the south side of the Meadows, the wide green expanse of public park that separates the city's cramped Old Town from its more spacious neighbours in Marchmont, an ever-popular area for academics.

They hurried on. Overtaking courting couples who strolled arm in arm in the warm evening light; being overtaken by joggers running the tree lined length of Melville Drive, the arterial road that cuts right through the heart of the Meadows. A chorus of voices rolled across the road as footballers called encouragement to one another in half a dozen impromptu games scattered the length of the park.

As they walked, Sam outlined his idea that perhaps somebody really was, just as she had said, 'better tuned in'. In fact, was really listening in. As ludicrous as it sounded, her flat and the manse might be bugged. It also explained how whoever was involved would have known that MacPherson was keeping the dunes dagger in his home. Helen had been incredulous at the thought of being bugged. She had nothing of value or interest to anybody, but as they walked on and she thought it through her feelings turned to outrage that anyone might bug her home or the manse.

Then she surrendered to a growing sense of guilt. If her conversation with John had told *them* where to find the dunes dagger then she had unintentionally signed the MacPhersons' death warrant. They would also have known that John Dearly was alone in the manse. And of course, they would have heard that Davy had pictures and was going to his family home in Oban.

Helen reached for her phone and called the only person she could think of. Elaine. On hearing the suggestion, Elaine had been far less circumspect than Helen had expected. In fact, Elaine agreed with Sam's analysis, told her to stay away from her home, the manse and the church until she had sorted something out. She would get back in touch as soon as possible, when they could make a plan for the morning. Her parting was rueful; if only she had thought of it herself earlier, people might still be alive, including John Dearly.

Julie arrived at Sam's flat just after they did, so there was no opportunity to speculate further about the wider issues. To support the girl, all the conversation revolved around Davy's awful experience. Later in the evening, Elaine phoned Helen back; a member of the parish had worked for the police as a civilian IT and surveillance technician before becoming a private security consultant. He was going to scan all the properties in the morning, off the record.

They arranged that Helen would take Julie to Waverley Station and see her on to the morning train to Oban and Sam was to meet Elaine outside Helen's home at ten o'clock sharp.

Chapter 19

THURSDAY 13th JUNE

Morning found Sam's flat with a slightly less fraught atmosphere than the night before. Julie was now calmer, having had the opportunity to process the incident overnight, and perhaps more importantly, she had received an early morning call from Davy's mother, who gave a health update and shared a long and reassuring conversation. Overnight, Davy had been transferred to hospital in Glasgow and having cut short their trip away, his mother and father were there at his bedside. They were looking forward to meeting Julie there.

With Julie in the passenger seat, Helen drove Sam's car off in the direction of Waverley. They planned to stop off at Julie's student flat on the way. She needed to collect some things to take with her. The previous evening she had been too upset to think about anything as mundane as a change of clothes.

• • •

Sam retraced his route of the evening before. Now the Meadows were quieter. Just a scattering of dog walkers and a few late starting office workers cutting across the grass towards the city centre. A great green space left largely vacant for the birds that strutted to and fro, searching for whatever treats and treasures they could find.

Turning back into Causewayside, he saw Elaine McPhee and an earnest looking man about his own age standing at the entrance to Helen's stairway. As Sam joined them, he couldn't help but notice the difference in their attitudes.

Elaine seemed tense while Scottie Brown, the security consultant, was enthused. Scottie shook Sam's hand as Elaine made the introductions and explained to Sam that they had started earlier in the morning and had already swept the church. Sam felt a sickening lurch in his stomach as his fears were confirmed; they had found a listening device in the office.

According to Scottie, it was top quality kit. The best, a real Rolls Royce. It seemed he viewed the quality of the device as far more noteworthy than its presence. They entered Helen's flat in silence. It took less than twenty minutes for Scottie to declare the flat clear and it was still well before eleven when they set off for the manse.

There was no policeman on duty at the manse now. The forensic team had finished their work the previous afternoon and media interest had moved on quickly, as it always did. Once again, the trio took the precaution of maintaining silent mode as Elaine produced her set of keys and opened the front door. Working from the front door inwards, the hall was declared clean first. Then the living room too.

They all instinctively shivered when they entered the silent kitchen, felt it bleak for such a lovely summer morning. The clear space in the middle where the kitchen table had once stood told a bitter story. Almost at once, a screech drew their attention to where Scottie was scanning the smoke detector. He gave them the enthusiastic thumbs up of a professional succeeding at his work. Pulling a chair to beneath the smoke detector, he climbed up and quickly extracted a tiny camera and listening device. There he paused for a moment to inspect it with an appreciative professional eye before continuing the sweep.

• • •

Sitting in her office, buried far away from the museum's public galleries, Suzie Dignan allowed her fingers to stroke the museum dagger. Then they trailed across a gold ring and chain that had been delivered to her from the museum's secure storage facility. In a plastic sleeve beside them was a sheet of paper, appearance giving away its age: foolscap paper, a small font, closely typed with narrow margins and little white space. More modern was the set of sharply focused photographs that she had pulled from the museum's photographic records.

Suzie had scanned and printed a full set of copies for Sam. Now she was quietly relishing the moment when artefact and history merge to tell a story. Putting historical artefacts into their proper contexts and telling their stories was her life's work. She always felt a special thrill when a story or snippet of information could bring some long forgotten or neglected object back to life. This was one such moment. She allowed her hand to continue its glide slowly over the artefacts, exploring their textures, imagining their owners, their lives and dreams.

She had unearthed the museum's paper record from deep in the archives; files that were themselves close to becoming historical objects in their own right. They were scheduled to be digitised but the archives were vast and steadily expanding as more material came in. The digitization process could never be fully complete.

Notwithstanding the thrill of discovery, today was becoming a little frustrating. She wanted to share her news with Sam, but he had not returned her call of yesterday, and she was going away for a week's holiday with her sister and baby nephew. Unless he got in touch soon it was all going to have to wait until she got back.

Suzie came to attention as her phone rang. It was a call from the main reception desk. A packet had been delivered for her and one of the porter staff was on the way up to her office with it. Hanging up the phone, Suzie stuffed the document copies into an envelope, sealed it and scribbled a message on the front.

For collection by Sam Cameron, Uni. Archaeology Dept.
You'll find these interesting; let's meet when I get back
from hols.
Call me.
Suzie.

She was distracted by her phone ringing again and dropped the envelope into her desk's mail tray. Sitting on the side of her desk, she answered the phone. 'Hello, Suzie Dignan speaking.'

The museum's switchboard operator replied. 'Hi Suzie, you've got an outside call, from the university, he works with Sam Cameron, his assistant I think. Sorry, I missed his name.'

'No problem. Just put him through, thanks,' the line clicked through but there was only silence, though the line was clearly still live. 'Hello, Suzie speaking…' while she waited for the caller to speak a porter entered with a small packet, she waved him in, stretching out her hand for the packet. As he handed it over, the porter pointed at her mail tray and she smiled, nodding agreement. He picked up the contents and left: carrying the mail and her cheerful smile down the corridor with him.

The office fell silent for a moment as she waited for her caller. 'Hello, it's Suzie here, can I help you?' She could almost sense somebody at the other end of the line, somebody listening in the silence. 'Hello, hello, it's Suzie here. Is anyone there?'

A deep and muffled voice suddenly broke the silence. And, it wasted no time on pleasantries. 'Suzie, is that you?'

Suzie was relieved to have a response at last. 'Yes, it's me. Look, I need to link up with Sam Camer -'

'You've just had a packet delivered. Yes?' the voice swept aside her words; a voice used to giving orders, one that did not anticipate argument.

Without thinking, Suzie responded. 'Yes, it's here with me now but -'

'Open it now. It has something you need to see.'

Suzie was feeling a little put out by Sam's assistant's attitude. 'Look, I think you had better put me on to Sam please. I'd rather speak to -'

Once again, Suzie was cut short. 'We've got your baby nephew and your sister too. If you hang up or shout out, they're dead. Now, shut up. Don't speak to anyone. Open the packet.'

A chill of fear ran through her body, and she glanced around her empty office. Alone. She trapped the handset between her chin and collarbone and used both hands to scrabble open the packet and pull out the contents; her heart sank as she recognised her sister's phone, unmistakable with its shocking pink cover encrusted with diamante. 'What's going on? What do you want? I don't -'

'You were told to shut up. Speak only when you're spoken to and do exactly as you're told or they're dead. Do you understand?' The voice fell silent, waiting for an answer.

'Yes, I understand,' said Suzie, as silent tears of worry and fear welled up in her eyes. She stood, suddenly a little girl, vulnerable, unsupported.

The man's voice resumed. 'Good. Do as I instruct and they will be released unharmed,' her sister's phone began to sound its familiar ring tone as he spoke. She gasped in shock and stared down at the phone. 'I am going to hang up now, and you are going to answer your sister's phone. Answer it now.' The landline went dead as the caller hung up.

Suzie stood stunned for a moment, dead handset in one hand, ringing phone in the other. The familiar ringtone suddenly seeming harsh, it blared at her like an emergency siren. The ringing persisted until Suzie's mind focused. Throwing down the dead handset she quickly answered her sister's phone, raising it to her ear and calling out. 'Jenny? Jenny, are you all right? How's little Joe, is he all right? What's happening?'

A chillingly familiar voice cut her short. 'Shut up and listen.' She fell silent at once as the voice continued. 'I expect absolute obedience, anything less and they die. Do not make any phone calls. If you do, they die. You will not speak to anybody, even in the passing. We are monitoring your every move. Do you understand? Speak now.'

Behind an involuntary sob, Suzie answered. 'I understand.'

'Good, do as I instruct and they will be fine. It won't take long, behave and you can all be together by teatime. Now you have the dagger, the Templar dagger?'

Suzie was taken aback at the question. 'The what? What would you want with that?'

'Do you have the dagger?' the voice offered no explanation.

Suzie allowed her eyes to settle on the dagger. Only moments before, she had been happily considering its story. Now it had assumed an air of true menace. The voice gave her instructions that were not to be deviated from. With no time to think or weigh up the dangers involved, she executed the orders.

She dropped her white lab coat, pulled on her light summer jacket, grabbed her shoulder bag and stuffed the dagger, signet ring, chain and all the original documents and photos into it. Then scribbled a note announcing an early lunch date and posted it on her desk. She left her office, walked along the corridor, took the stairway leading from the staff work area to the public galleries and hurried on. In only three minutes she was outside and turned left to head along Chambers Street.

She followed the instructions precisely. Instructions planned to confuse any attempt by others to trace her steps: moving her quickly away from the security camera coverage of the main thoroughfares. Walking to the end of the street, she dodged the traffic to cross George IV Bridge and weaved behind Greyfriar's Bobby, the famous statue of Edinburgh's faithful little Skye terrier. From there she ran down Candlemaker Row towards the Grassmarket. At the bottom of the slope, she turned right and hurried on. A little while later she turned right again, suddenly finding herself in one of the ancient, narrow and twisting lanes of the Old Town.

Beyond the first twist, and clear of any CCTV coverage, sat a black Land Rover Discovery, engine running, facing away from her and up the slope. The smoked glass prevented her seeing the occupants as she approached, but she had been seen. The nearside rear door swung open as she reached it. As instructed, she got in, silently and without fuss. The Land Rover immediately drew away from the curb and disappeared round the next twist in the lane. Moments later, it emerged into the flow of mainstream traffic heading south out of the city.

• • •

Standing still in the chill of the manse's kitchen, Sam and Elaine watched Scottie Brown continue his methodical sweep of the room. A momentary and perverse sense of satisfaction at being right had visited Sam. It faded very quickly, was replaced by a grinding worry. This find was further confirmation that they really did face danger. They faced a truly organised threat, one that could and would go to extreme lengths to achieve its aims. Finally, Scottie stopped and gave them a disappointed shrug, nothing else found; the room was now all clear. He led them across the hall into the study and started the same silent and methodical sweeping process.

Scottie found nothing in the study and ended his sweep of the room by sitting in front of the computer. He plugged in a portable hard drive from where he ran a security scan. The search had hardly started before the computer screen started flashing up a warning, something had been found. The expert allowed the scan to complete before executing a rapid and baffling series of keystrokes that moved and quarantined the infection on to his portable hard drive. He unplugged it and declared the computer clean. He wanted to take a closer look at the bug later, but it too was definitely state of the art. He threw an appreciative glance towards Sam, adding that whoever installed it had full control of the computer, including its camera and microphone.

It took less than half an hour more to sweep up the stairs and through the bedrooms and storage. Eventually the manse was declared clean and Scottie really started to enthuse over the quality of the bugging devices. The equipment quality told him this was an operation mounted by a high worth, high skill organisation, but it did not indicate which one. He speculated that either it would be a top end corporate or perhaps even a national security agency and they sometimes overlapped. He had no way of telling which.

From the landing at the top of the stairs, they could hear the phone ringing downstairs in the study. It quickly cut to answer phone. Whatever the message was, they could not make it out from so far away. Sam looked at Elaine. 'I suppose we had better go and listen to the messages, just in case there are any urgent ones that you or Helen might need to deal with,' he said.

Scottie needed to get away, he had paid work to be doing, but once he had a chance to study the bugs he would pass on anything he learnt. He warned them not to hold their breath, such high quality devices were designed not to be traceable. They were meant to be anonymous. He laughed at the answer phone with a parting shot. It was an old model, with a simple form of call screening. As it recorded an incoming message, it played through the loudspeaker at the same time. Any incoming messages recorded would also have been picked up by the bugged computer's live microphone. He hoped there was nothing sensitive in the recorded messages.

Sam and Elaine saw Scottie off and then they settled down at the desk with a notepad and started to work through the messages. It was a lengthy task. Helen had noted and cleared some of messages the morning before, but had not had time to listen to them all and yet more had poured in since then. Messages seemed to come from all quarters. From distressed parishioners, well-wishers and friends of the church, some from journalists, a tele-salesman, and scattered through the other calls were a few ghoulish and malicious messages revealing the sicker side of modern society.

Suddenly, Sam tuned in a little more intently and Elaine caught his eye as the bouncy voice of an enthusiastic young woman played out:

'Hello there, message for Helen Johnson. This is Suzie Dignan from the Museum. Sam said I could pass on a message via you if he's unavailable. I can't get him on his mobile phone, so perhaps you could pass this on, please? It's about our old Templar artefact, the dagger that he was so interested in last week; I've found more information about it for him…'

Sam barely listened to the rest. 'My God, when did that come in?' he looked at Elaine, aghast.

'You'll need to call her right away. If they heard that message she's a sitting duck, God help her. Do you have her number handy?' said Elaine. Her face showed little emotion but her tone told Sam that his own fears over the girl's safety were shared.

Sam fished out his phone and called Suzie's work number. It was answered at once and a reassuring telephonist confirmed that Suzie had only minutes before gone. She had seen her leaving, probably for an early lunch. Sam asked her to ensure Suzie phoned him as soon as she got back. The telephonist was silent for a moment. Then, puzzled, explained Suzie had already been in touch with his office. In fact, the telephonist had herself put the call through to Suzie from Sam's assistant only a little while before, there was no doubt.

Sam didn't have an assistant. He hoped the chatty receptionist had made a mistake, hoped Suzie would call him back through the afternoon.

Chapter 20

FRIDAY 14th JUNE

The green pedestrian light shone and a little crowd of pedestrians joined Cassiter in crossing Princes Street to reach the Foot of the Mound. There he paused and looked up the Mound. The short stretch of road snaked like an umbilical cord away from the elegant New Town and up the ridge into the Old Town, joining the two halves of the city. Here at the foot was the National Gallery of Scotland. It was staging an exhibition that he had been meaning to visit and he hoped to take it in before lunch.

He remained stationary for a moment longer, briefly savouring the thought that he had just entered his own landscape. This was the scene he watched every day from his office window, a constant frame with ever changing details.

Then he turned into the Princes Street Gardens, down the steps, past the floral clock and on into the gardens. He passed mature trees, the varied greens of countless shrubs, and ahead of him were great stretches of carefully tended lawn. The gardens were once the site of a stretch of water known as the Nor Loch, in past times it had provided a watery defence at the foot of the castle rock. Now drained and landscaped, the location provided vital space in the heart of the city.

Cassiter moved at the steady pace of mister average. His destination was the Royal Scots War Memorial, an impressive arc of dressed stone blocks. As perhaps the world's oldest standing infantry force there was a lot to commemorate. It was a quiet spot in an otherwise busy park. A neutral open-air venue, perfect for a meeting with a very private, very security conscious man.

Ever cautious, Parsol had chosen not to visit Cassiter's office, avoiding establishing any concrete evidence of a relationship. A chance encounter in a public space was just that, a chance encounter.

Approaching the stones Cassiter could clearly see the whole pathway as it curved round to the other end of the memorial. Two middle-aged women were standing at the main stone, they moved off as he approached. A bunch of flowers left behind hinted at a little of their story.

From the far end, three men approached, walking in a ragged file perhaps three or four metres apart. The uninformed might easily have assumed they were unconnected. The first and last in line were well built and in top physical shape. Cassiter admired the guards' physical condition with a professional eye. He watched as they discreetly allowed the spacing between them to shrink as the departing women passed by. Nothing was taken for granted. Then, as if by magic, the gaps opened again, allowing the middle man space. He was the leader, tall and upright, though an expertly cut suit masked where his shoulders were just starting to slope with the encroaching years: years attested to by an impressively controlled quiff of silver grey hair. Eugene Parsol.

Parsol carried himself with the confidence that screamed aristocrat. Cassiter had dealt with Parsol frequently enough over the years to understand this was no façade. Parsol came from an old family, old money, he expected to lead, expected to be followed. He was never disappointed. Cassiter did not know what Parsol's interest and motivation in this business was, but knowing the man as he did, knew it would be significant and unswerving.

Though not a recluse, Parsol rarely met his business associates face to face, preferring the anonymity of distance. However, very occasionally, the prize was big enough to lure him away from his chateau. This was most certainly one such occasion.

Cassiter stopped to admire the main stone and the leading guard passed behind him, pausing a little beyond to look intently at the next stone in the memorial arc. The second guard held his position at the rear of the group, seemingly studying the preceding stone. Parsol joined Cassiter at the main stone. Both men looked and spoke towards the memorial, limiting the opportunity for any distant microphone to focus on their voices.

In spite of some very public blips, Parsol was pleased with progress. He had known all along that a dagger, the key dagger, was concealed in this part of Scotland. Now its location was narrowed down to a single place. While it hadn't yet been found the evidence all pointed in one direction. St Bernard's. That Cassiter had discovered and recovered two further daggers was a startling bonus. They would be needed in due course, but they were of little value without the key dagger.

Parsol continued his study of the stone as he spoke to Cassiter. 'We are delighted with the progress. I checked the two daggers you secured and they are entirely authentic.'

'Well, you don't think I would waste time faking something, do you?' Cassiter spoke respectfully to the older man, his client, but without deference. Cassiter was nobody's man.

'No, you are always reliable, for me and for others. I do not doubt you, but who knows what criminals and forgers have got up to through the ages?' Parsol hesitated for a moment before continuing. 'But... I, we, are proposing a change in your contract.'

Cassiter tensed. He liked a deal to be fixed in advance, it was always crucial to have a clear understanding between himself and the client. Any ambiguity or change could lead to disputes, which were very bad for business. He gave a grim and knowing smile to himself: ultimately, changes were more usually bad for the client's business. 'I don't normally expect changes, you know that,' he said.

Parsol waved a hand in a small calming gesture. 'You misunderstand. Our need is made more urgent by the public nature of recent events. We are delighted with your results, but now we need more. More quickly. It was always going to happen, once the genie was out of the bottle. Then others could start taking an interest and we can't kill everyone who gets involved.' He gave a short chuckle. 'Or can we?'

Cassiter thought carefully for a moment before answering, his voice flat. 'Death is an excellent silencer, in the short term. We can contain the spread for now, but eventually the police have to tie together all the deaths, it's unavoidable. I have taken care to ensure there is no trace back to me and my people, but this is all taking place very close to home. Eventually there will be a slip, it's human nature. I prefer my people to be active further afield. What exactly is the change you propose?' he turned his head and for the first time looked at Parsol.

'Our deal was…' Parsol turned towards Cassiter, each holding the other's eye for a long moment before turning back to the monument. 'Our deal *is*, at present: your regular retainer fees, all your team's expenses met without question and a million Euros for delivery of the dagger, the key dagger, and any associated documentation. And, of course, your usual per capita fee for removing any, uhhhh, loose ends that might compromise the plans. I think that's what we had agreed?' Parsol gave a little cold smile and tilted his head very slightly.

Cassiter nodded. 'Yes, so why seek to change it now?'

'You misunderstand. We have no intention of cutting fees. On the contrary, it has been decided that possession of the artefacts is now of extreme urgency. Matters must be brought to a conclusion immediately. We want to incentivise progress, that's all. You will be paid a million each for the two daggers already delivered, and now we will pay five million for delivery of the outstanding dagger, plus all the usual allowances, of course. But it must be concluded quickly, before the authorities make the inevitable links and engage properly with your, our, activity,' he paused for a moment. Then gave the cold smile again as he turned both his open palms towards Cassiter, 'Well? A good offer, yes? But can you deliver quickly? Time is everything now. Everything!'

Cassiter's brow furrowed very slightly. 'We know the church, we know the people. But still, there is no sign of the dagger. If it is there you will have it, but if not -'

'It is there, for sure. You will get it. I know you, Cassiter. I will be staying in Edinburgh for one week and I want to leave with that dagger in my possession. Are we agreed?' asked Parsol.

The very slightest dip of Cassiter's head showed an understanding had been reached. Without further exchange, the pair parted and continued their separate ways around the monument.

Chapter 21

MONDAY 17th JUNE

Helen, Sam, Francis and Elaine had gathered at the manse. All were sickened at the loss of so many innocent lives. Knowing they might have done more, not knowing what *more* might have been. Now they sat ranged around the study desk, a worried group. Francis looking a little defensive, Elaine as impenetrable as ever, Helen desperate for answers and Sam increasingly worried over the disappearance of Suzie Dignan.

Suzie had not returned his calls before the weekend and he had already checked to establish that she was not at work in the museum this morning. According to a very cautious telephonist, she was unavailable, away on a week's holiday. However, Sam had also spoken with a colleague who split his working time between the university and museum. It seems the corridors were awash with rumours about a staff member having gone missing along with some artefacts that were in her charge.

They could just make out a vacuum cleaner buzzing on the upper landing. Grace had started to give the manse a thorough clean, a final goodbye to John. The mechanical sound ended as she switched to using a hand duster.

Helen was sat behind the desk, arms resting in front of her, hands wrapped around her coffee mug. She pulled them all to order. 'Right guys, I don't understand the back story that you were trying to explain the other evening, but I… We,' she spun a hand out to include Sam, 'we are kind of floundering. We've had attacks, murders, robberies, the manse bugged, the police all over us, a girl's gone missing from her work, and hey, who knows what else?' Her arms rose up from the desk, pointed to Francis and Elaine. 'You guys have to put it on the level now or Sam and I take this whole shifty mess to the law.'

'You can't do that,' Francis spoke with a resigned tone.

'And what's to stop us?' There was an edge to Helen's voice that none of them had heard before.

'Because they won't believe you. At best they'll think you're mad, at worst, guilty,' said Francis.

'Come on, you can do better than that. There's evidence, I don't buy we'd be in the frame,' said Helen.

'Well, the police have made no arrests. It's clear they have no real idea who they are looking for. They will be under real pressure to show some progress. There's no evidence because the people involved are clearly professionals,' Francis turned to Elaine, appealing for support.

'Aye, in fact the only thing that links all the crimes together is us, our little group,' Elaine spoke in a slow deliberate tone.

'What? That's rubbish,' Sam was outraged at the suggestion.

Francis cut back in. 'Rubbish it might be, but Elaine's right. Oh, I know the link to Archie Buchan's death in Dunbar is a bit tenuous, but even there I'm sure the police could easily build something out of the parish connection, and if not the police the media could for sure. For just about everything else we have direct links, contacts, proximity, relationships, the works.' For a long moment, Francis stared hard into Helen's eyes, then turned to Sam and continued. 'Once they run out of bogymen, we're bound to be considered.'

'But there's nothing of substance. No case against us could ever stand up to any sort of scrutiny,' said Sam.

'Yes, but perhaps more importantly, once you put your head over the parapet you become a media target. How many times have we seen innocents pilloried by the tabloids because the papers need someone, anyone, to rage at in the headlines? They'll worry about the truth later. You'd do nicely as a story just now. You just have to open your eyes and you can see them all around. The press are on the prowl, desperate for an angle: something, anything to feed the story. Don't make yourselves, don't make us all, the story, please. Once the media starts and momentum builds the police will get dragged along too,' said Francis.

Helen and Sam were shocked; this was not how they had envisaged the discussion panning out.

Sam glared across the desk. 'No, I can't accept this. We've done nothing wrong, what could the police charge us with?'

Francis looked at him, arched his eyebrows and shrugged his shoulders. 'Think about it, you tell me. In fact, the more you think about it, the more involved you seem. As I say, the media are not going to worry about proof. Right now, they have readers desperate for information. The press will have you guilty and hung long before the police can confirm your innocence.'

'You should listen to Francis, listen carefully,' said Elaine.

Francis continued. 'Who was the last person to see John Dearly alive? Helen and Elaine were there when he died. The police didn't see anyone jumping out of the kitchen window, did they? No. Who's filling in John's job? Helen. Who was at the MacPhersons' home for a meal the week they died? Helen and Sam. Who worked for MacPherson? He was Sam's boss.'

Francis gave a theatrical shrug and then continued. 'None of it's evidence worth a penny in court, but the tabloids aren't in court, they just need villains today, it's their oxygen. And what would make a more sensational headline than a female minister involved in bumping off her predecessors?'

While the others argued, Helen had been thinking. It was dawning on her that preposterous as Francis' suggestion was, it just might make sense to a policeman looking in from the outside while being pressed to show some progress, any progress. 'All right guys, let's not get bogged down in a who looks most guilty contest. Given time, we know the police will sort out right from wrong; in the meantime, Sam and I need to know what's happening now. Let's just say we agree not to walk right out of here and over to St Leonard's Police Station. Let's say we don't hand over John's ring and chain; then you have to tell us what's happening. Is anyone else in danger? What's triggered all this? What happens next?'

Sam added his burning question too. 'And what about Suzie? Is she in danger?'

Francis shifted uncomfortably in his seat. 'Where to begin?' he mused, looking from Sam to Helen and back again. 'I don't know the poor girl or her role, but if she does have any involvement in this… Maybe she is, well… I'm sorry, but maybe she is in need of our prayers. May God protect her.'

Sam growled across the table. 'No. No,' his head bowed, shaking in angry despair. He banged his fist onto the desk. 'I should never have given her the number here.'

Helen stretched out a hand and squeezed his arm. 'We don't know anything for sure. She might just be away for the week as she said. Right now, you must have hope.'

Sam looked up at her, grateful for her moral support but completely unconvinced. 'You think?'

Having made a start, Francis did not want to surrender the initiative again. 'Don't blame yourself for this, Sam', he said. 'Phone message or none, I think if she could give them access to something they wanted then they would have found her sooner or later, with the same end result.'

Helen needed to get an explanation. 'For Heaven's sake,' taking a breath she continued, speaking slowly, forming each word carefully, and emphasising each with a pointing finger jabbing in Francis' direction. 'Francis, tell us what's going on. Now.' She sat up straight, picking up her coffee mug in both hands, taking a sip, all the while holding Francis with her gaze. 'We're waiting.'

They sat in silence as Francis tried to explain, attempting to finish off his history lesson of that earlier evening, the night the

MacPhersons had died, which now seemed such a long time ago. Helen felt tired, drained, battered by the deaths, but she forced herself to stay completely focused.

He told again of the Templar ships, fleeing just ahead of the king's attack. The ships were thought to have been laden with the Templars' treasure and banking assets and perhaps with more spiritual treasures too. Eventually they arrived, one by one, slipping into the Firth of Forth, making for the only really secure sanctuary left to them in Europe: Scotland. And ultimately, to the village of Temple.

His understanding was that when the ships arrived they had no treasure on board, but they did carry many knights, perhaps the final mustering of a significant Templar fighting force.

Francis continued, explaining that it was unclear exactly what happened to the fighting force or the treasure. It seems likely that a group of Templar Knights served with Robert the Bruce in his war against Edward of England. Perhaps it was some sort of payment in kind. Bruce needed fighting men and the Templars needed sanctuary: a marriage made in Scotland. It seems the only loser was Edward when his army was destroyed by the Scots at Bannockburn.

Of the remaining Templar Knights, some stayed at Temple and eventually moved on or just faded into history. Most of the story is in the public domain and anyone could piece it together given time and desire. But there was more: other knights had been sent away, dispersed on a mission. All Francis knew was they carried parts of a message. What that was, he did not know. The story lay in John Dearly's keeping and he had guarded it closely.

But once, long ago, John had let something slip in the midst of a particularly heavy whisky evening; then immediately regretted it and made Francis swear half a dozen oaths to keep his secret. Whatever it was had been hidden in a set of daggers. In some way, the blades were meant to be a message to the whereabouts of something very important, maybe the lost Templar treasures. John had never said what, nor did he ever talk about who had the daggers. Perhaps he did not know and had certainly never shown Francis one.

John had said the daggers were dispersed across Europe, protected, hidden, waiting for a time when they would be reunited to somehow reveal the Templars' secret message and restore their position.

Helen had sensed the direction of the story and was almost unsurprised when Francis went on to reveal that John, and Archie before him, had occupied a place of trust, passed on from one carefully selected and recruited minister to the next: quiet, discreet, a line unnoticed and unbroken over time. And now, finally, there was Helen, unbriefed, facing a threat that none of them could quantify or identify, protecting something unknown, whose whereabouts and purpose were equally unknown.

Helen and Sam had to take Francis' account at face value. It was incomplete, riddled with holes, an incredible story that even a fortnight ago they might have dismissed as delusional ramblings. But the artefacts, the trail of death and pain that was weaving through their lives and coming inexorably closer by the day, it all needed an explanation and this was the only one on the table. And incredible or not, there was no doubt the daggers existed.

Sam again raised the idea Helen had in the long ruminating hours after John's killing; perhaps John had a dagger too? It would be consistent, whatever the true purpose. In any event, it seemed clear that people were dying because of them.

Then there was Xavier, continued Francis, the Sardinian priest who was even now preparing to travel back to Edinburgh. The origins of his connection remained unclear to Francis, but the man had maintained a close relationship with Archie and John. He might have at least some of the answers that died with John Dearly. Francis also trusted Xavier implicitly, and it seemed trusted friends were in short supply right now. He urged Helen to speak with Xavier before making any decisions; perhaps he could shed more light for her.

When Francis had finished there was a long silence, finally broken by Helen. She sighed. 'Wow. Wow. Wow,' she said slowly, then looked at Sam. 'What do you think?'

'Well,' said Sam, 'the history bits might just about fit together. I could follow that, no problem. And I can, I *will*, check it out in more detail. But do we believe the story? Is there a more credible explanation? Is there any other explanation?'

Helen fixed him with a telling stare. 'I think we need to walk and we need to talk. What do you say?'

Sam took the hint. 'You're right. I need some fresh air after that lot. Something to eat, too, suddenly I'm hungry.'

Helen promptly stood up. 'Great. Let's go now,' she said. Turning to Francis, she continued. 'We will need to talk more, a lot more. Can you spare some time later? Or maybe tomorrow? I'll call you, but I really want to talk with Sam alone now.'

Francis and Elaine were both uneasy, unsure if enough had been said, unsure what else could be said. Francis shook Sam's hand rather solemnly and then turned to Helen. 'You know, Helen, John was my dearest friend. We have been sharing and helping each other for over thirty years. At the end, he chose you to carry on his tradition. If you stay, I will do my best to support you. No matter what.'

Helen stepped towards the old priest and hugged him. 'I know you will, and thank you Francis, this is hard for everyone. I'm just struggling to understand. I don't want to let you all down, let John down either. But I need facts, need to understand what this is all about.' Sensing Elaine had experienced enough hugging in recent days; Helen just gently rested her hand on Elaine's upper arm and pressed a little. Then, with a shrug and an apologetic, almost plaintive look, she left. Sam at her side.

Francis and Elaine stood feeling the world continue to spin around them. Who next? Who next?

• • •

The rest of the morning had come and gone in a flash. Helen and Sam had shared a long walk, stopping off at the church to pick up the communion set; before lunch, Helen had another residential home to visit, a service to conduct in John Dearly's stead. They walked towards the retirement home through what she could not help but feel was now *her* parish.

• • •

The service over, Helen headed for home and welcomed a quiet hour or so alone to mull things over before she finally made a phone call to her father. From their regular long distance conversations she knew he was worried, and feeling a bit guilty too. After all, it was he who had sent her here, to what suddenly seemed nothing like the safe and cosmopolitan city he thought he knew.

In the end, she half wished she hadn't called him. She was worried sick by all the seemingly senseless violence and killing. Now she had set him worrying again, and he was 3,000 miles away and unable to help.

A text alert sounded on her phone. Helen grabbed the communion set in its carry case and headed for the door. Sam had collected his car on the way back from campus; he was now parked outside her flat's main door, waiting, engine running. He saw Helen emerge from the common stair and reached over to turn down the volume on the car radio.

She jumped into the passenger seat, slipped the old case to the floor and leant towards Sam as he turned his face to hers. They kissed, a light brushing of lips, just enough to convey a message.

'Thanks for picking me up,' said Helen.

'No problem, I'm done in the office and I'd rather be with you right now. It's all so mad,' said Sam.

'Well let's go then, Mr Cameron, and don't spare the horses,' she buckled her seatbelt and settled back for the ride.

It was only a five-minute journey to St Bernard's, one that Helen had done countless times, but today she didn't want to go into the church alone. It wasn't her way to be afraid, but she just wanted a friendly soul beside her.

They discussed what she had said on the phone to her father. Helen believed in telling the truth, but on this occasion was now wishing she had said less than she did and perhaps telling him might even have put him in some danger: Archie, John, the MacPhersons, Suzie, Davy and Barty the dog, she'd covered the lot in an unstoppable torrent. Mention of the MacPhersons triggered a memory for Sam.

'Oh, here, in my jacket pocket, there's a letter for you. It came through the university's internal mail. MacPherson must have dropped it off.'

'Let me see,' Helen stretched across and rummaged in Sam's jacket pockets, finding the envelope and pulling it out. She sat back and with a little shiver opened the envelope. To her surprise, it wasn't from MacPherson but from his wife.

Helen,

Mission accomplished. MacP will be grumpy if he finds out, so don't spill the beans. Come and see me, we'll crack this one together!
Sarah.

'What on Earth is this all about?' Helen puzzled for a moment. Then she read it aloud for Sam. 'Got any idea?' she asked.

He shrugged. 'Not a clue, do you think she sent you the wrong message?'

Helen looked again and dismissed his suggestion. 'No, she's addressing me directly, but it doesn't make any sense.'

'Maybe she was planning to share another bottle of rosé with you? Or maybe she'd been drinking it herself?' suggested Sam and he got a smart dig in the ribs.

'Sam! Don't talk about her like that. The poor woman's dead.' Helen's reprimand was meant but her tone was light. 'No, this message certainly meant something, but I guess we'll never know. It's so sad, she was asking me to visit, and now she's gone.'

Sam swung the car off the road and into the car parking space beside the church just as the radio news caught his attention. He pushed up the volume. They both listened in horror as Sam's fear of the past few days became real.

'... until next of kin have been informed, the police have refused to identify the body of a young woman that was found earlier today floating in the Firth of Forth, off Cramond Island. Some have speculated she may have been walking back from the tidal island and been caught out by the inrushing tide. A spokesman for the Queensferry lifeboat said many people are cut off each year at Cramond Island and rescues are commonplace.

The police would not comment on any link with the missing museum worker Suzie Dignan, but did confirm they were no longer actively searching for her. The police also confirmed that no missing artefacts were with the body found at Cramond. For the time being, police are referring all questions about missing artefacts to the National Museum of Scotland.'

Sam flipped the radio off and leant forward, pressing his head hard against the steering wheel. 'Oh God, I knew it,' he said, leaning back, staring up at the roof. 'What the hell's going on, Helen?' He turned to her and she stretched out a hand to touch his arm. 'I brought her into this mess, and she didn't deserve it. She was a really bubbly girl, kind, good hearted. Now she's dead,' he banged his fist on the wheel. 'Dead for helping me.'

Helen gently rubbed his upper arm, then slid her arm round his neck and pulled him towards her. He responded and for a few moments, their heads rested against one another.

Pulling apart, Sam's voice was altogether harder, once again focused, determined. 'What's happening here? What in God's name is this all about? Surely nothing can be worth all this slaughter?' He sighed and closed his eyes for a moment, composing his thoughts. 'Come on. Let's get your communion set locked away. We can try to fathom it all out later.'

'They've got the museum dagger, haven't they?' Helen was still not sure why the daggers were so important, but once again, somebody thought them worth killing for.

'Seems that way.' Sam slammed the car door shut and they linked arms as they stepped towards the church entrance. Suddenly, more than anything else, Helen just wanted to see the old reassuring face of her father. She knew he could not just make things right as he used to back in her childhood. But she still longed for the reassurance and stability that only a good father could bring. She wished he was here but knew his health wouldn't let him come.

The church doors were closed. DCI Wallace had insisted the church be kept locked when unattended. Helen unlocked the doors, slipped inside and keyed in the alarm deactivation code. Together they proceeded down the centre aisle. Other than their movement, the church was quite still. Helen had grown up in and around churches; busy or quiet, for her they were comfortable places where she never felt alone. Yet today she was glad of Sam's presence. They hurried to the vestry where Helen locked the communion set in the safe.

As they retraced their steps she locked the vestry then paused for a moment in front of the cross and bowed her head slightly, wanting to say some words for John, for Archie, for the MacPhersons, for Suzie. Who else? Who next? She prayed the killing would end.

After a minute she stopped. 'Come on,' she said, linking arms with Sam again. 'Let's go.'

• • •

Now, late into the evening, the wine bottle beside the sofa on Helen's living room floor was three quarters empty. They had talked everything through, over and over again.

Eventually, Helen tried to sum up their position. 'So, *they*, and we don't know who *they* are, seem determined to kill anyone who has contact with these daggers, and they want to collect the daggers. All for reasons we don't know, but it might have something to do with an old treasure. They got the dunes dagger we found in Fife and they got the museum dagger that your students spotted. We don't know how many more daggers there are or where they are, or for certain what they are for, but

Francis thinks there might be several. And it seems they are all somehow linked together with St Bernard's, and they want whatever that link is too.' She looked at Sam for confirmation. He smiled encouragingly and Helen continued.

'You believe there's a chance there might well be a dagger here in St Bernard's, we don't know for sure, but I'm going along with you on that just now. Whatever they want from here is clearly important, because it seems this place is where everything revolves around. Unfortunately, the only people who could have cast light on this were Archie and John, and they killed them both. God! Who are *they*?' Helen's casual invocation of God's name passed without note.

'Every death seems to have some link to us. It's getting so it's not safe to know us. Looking at it from outside, each incident seems isolated, motiveless, though clearly the more we see the more there must be a plan or reason behind it. We just can't work out what it is or why people we know are being killed.'

'Yes, but there must be information somewhere. Something that will help us understand,' said Sam.

'Francis and Elaine have told us what they can, but really that's little more than a mix of history lesson and folklore. We can't really see what all that's got to do with today's events. What's more remarkable is how little the pair actually know.' Helen paused, looked at Sam, he nodded agreement but remained silent.

'I don't know what John got himself mixed up in. Was he really a good guy? Was he a villain? Where do Francis and Elaine stand? And, now…' she threw her hands in the air, tilting her head to one side and adopting an incredulous tone. 'Now the pair of them say this guy Xavier is flying in from Sardinia, in a private jet no less, and apparently he might have some answers. I know he was here for Archie Buchan's memorial service, but I never met him. Do we trust him? Do we run for the hills?'

Sam's arm was draped around her shoulder and his hand squeezed it gently, expressing something between support and consolation. He gave a little wry laugh. 'At least we don't have any money worries.'

Helen turned her head to look at Sam and gave him a rueful theatrical grin. 'What do you think buddy? It's a mess, that's for sure.' She raised her wine glass. 'Next time I want a work placement, remind me not to take my pop's advice. Let me make my own arrangements, okay? Anyway, as you say here in Scotland, slàinte.'

She drained the glass and stretched forward to put it down very carefully on the floor. Then on a second thought, lifted it again, a flick of the wrist tilted the glass fractionally towards Sam, a clear request for a top up. He responded at once, picking up the bottle and filling her glass.

'Seriously, it is a mess. I don't know what to do. There isn't enough information to make any decisions,' she said.

'I know. Everywhere seems dark. I can't see a way ahead either. Maybe we just need to sit tight a little and think it all through again,' said Sam.

Helen nodded glumly as her phone chimed to signal the arrival of a message. Checking it, she exclaimed. 'It's from my pop - *some pictures in the cloud for you. Come home quick.*'

They scanned the pictures her father had sent. They were old. A young Peter and Joan Johnson holidaying in Edinburgh; Archie Buchan, even then he seemed old; a young man, straight, tall, unwrinkled, and unmistakably John Dearly; and Francis, slight, youthful but instantly recognisable by the broad smile and head tilt. They laughed and for a minute were carried away from the pressures of the moment.

The last picture had them puzzled; it was a christening. Her mother was sitting, holding a baby, surrounded by the usual family suspects. And clustered around the picture's edge were others who Helen had come to know more recently.

'Is that you?' asked Sam.

'I don't know, I've never seen this picture before, it must be one of us kids, but I didn't think any of these guys came to the christenings.'

'Well, you wouldn't know would you?' Sam pointed a finger at the screen. 'Who's that Latin guy? Did you have the inquisition at your family christenings too?'

'I don't have a clue, but I tell you what, I'm phoning someone who does.' She called her father as she spoke.

'Hi Pops,' she said as the phone line opened.

'Helen? Helen, how you doing, honey? Your mom and I are worried sick. What's happened now?'

His voice faded slightly as he turned away from his phone. 'Joan, it's Helen calling again, she's on the line now.'

'Pops, I'm doing fine, you don't need to worry, honest. Sam's with me and we'll get through this for sure. And you know what? Nothing bad has happened since my last call.'

'That was only nine hours ago, honey.'

'Yeah, believe me, here that's an improvement.' Helen felt her spirits rising; he always did that for her.

'Your mom thinks you should be coming home now, can you do that?'

'I don't know. I'm a material witness, so I don't think the police will want me to go far right now. And anyway, I've got unfinished business here.'

Her mother's voice came through clear and worried. 'Don't you get involved there, you hear, Helen. You need to get home, now.'

'Right Mom, I don't think I can though. But listen, I'm not alone. I'll be fine. I've got Sam with me. Tell you what; I'm going to put the phone on speaker so he can hear too.'

She looked at Sam and he nodded.

'Pops, speaker's on now.'

'Hi Sam, good to speak with you at last. Though not good times.'

'Hello Mr Johnson, good to speak with you and you too Mrs Johnson. And I agree it could have been under better circumstances.'

The small talk of introductions never really got started as Helen cut back in. 'Pop, tell us about the christening photo.'

A laugh rolled down the phone as Peter Johnson considered his daughter's question. 'It's your christening, honey.'

'But I see John and Francis there. I didn't know they came to my christening,' there was a thrill in Helen's voice, a relief to be diverted from her current hell even for a few moments.

'Oh, they all came for yours. Archie too, even Xavier.'

'You know Xavier?' Helen cut in, at once excited and surprised. 'You know Xavier? Who is he? What is he? Who don't you know? Tell us about him. He's coming here to Edinburgh now. Who is he?' she demanded.

Down the line, she could hear her mother's excited chatter in the background. Clearly, she approved of Xavier. Peter Johnson's sigh of resignation was perfectly audible down the line, cajoled by his wife on one side and his daughter on the other; it was as though there was no distance between them.

'What can I tell you about Xavier? He's a priest from Sardinia. I first met him years ago when John and I were still assistants. He was a bit older, had already taken on his own church, as I say, it's in Sardinia. Clearly, John and Xavier were from different denominations, spoke different languages, normally they would never have met. I think they became friends because their respective parishes were linked somehow. Don't ask me how; I haven't a clue. Anyway, our paths used to cross most summers, quite a gang in our day, John, me, Francis, and of course, Xavier...'

Sam prompted him to go further. 'What's the man like? He seems a bit of a mystery.'

'I haven't seen Xavier in years, but we've always kept in touch: letters, more emails now. I have been expecting him to retire for years. Then again, when do priests ever really retire?'

Helen could picture him rolling his eyes, half mocking his vocation.

'When they go to meet their maker,' said Helen, 'which won't be for a long time yet where you're concerned. Now, tell me more about Xavier.'

'There's not much more to say. Yes, self-confident, and always seemed in control. Not just of himself, but always the things and events around him too. Warm, friendly enough. But doesn't do much small talk even when he gets to know you.' The line fell silent for several moments as Peter Johnson marshalled his thoughts.

Quite suddenly, he resumed, 'What I do know is that one year, way back, your mother and I had gone over to Edinburgh for our summer holiday during the Festival. We'd been on a night out, a meal, some show or other and once we'd got back to the manse your mother had gone to bed while John and I sat up half the night sharing a drink and putting the world to rights. That summer John was a bit perturbed, excited even. Archie Buchan and he had just got back from a trip to Sardinia; they had been over for a funeral, for Xavier's predecessor, I think.'

'That's right, I remember the time, it was a funeral in Sardinia,' confirmed Joan Johnson.

'Anyway, John went a bit mysterious on me; I put it down to the drink. He rambled on about some responsibility or a task or something and Xavier's name cropped up more than once. I don't remember the details now. We'd both had a fair bit to drink. All I do remember is it's the only time I ever saw John get moody. I think I'd laughed at his idealism or dreaming or something and he didn't like it. The evening ended and we never spoke of it again.'

Once again Peter Johnson fell silent, and for just a moment listened to his grown-up youngest daughter's breath down the line, wondering where all the years had gone. 'Over the years your mother and I would visit John, mostly during the Festival - she's told you about the trips often enough and you know how much she loves a show.'

Helen prompted him. 'I know she loved it here, why did you stop coming?'

Peter Johnson laughed again. 'That's easy - family happened! As you and the rest of the brood were growing up, it started to get just too expensive. And when the little trust fund your mom's parents left her went down the plughole in some investment shenanigans back in the 1980s, well, that mostly put an end to our regular trips. It was a poor minister's life for us after that. We couldn't go over there for holidays and leave you lot home alone. Could you imagine the gossip?' They both laughed at the thought of his congregation's response had they ever found the Johnson children abandoned.

Peter continued. 'Anyway, in those earlier years, before the holiday trips went out of our price range, ours and Xavier's paths crossed quite regularly and we got to know each other well. Your mother approved of Xavier you know, and she's a good judge of character.'

'Oh, but she married you,' said Helen. A conditioned response to a long running family joke.

'My point exactly,' said Peter, taking the jibe in good spirit, 'and she always sticks up for you too. No matter what you've done to my blood pressure over the years.'

'Whey, let's hear it for mom,' said Helen, raising her wine glass and clinking glasses with Sam. Helen leant towards him, whispering theatrically. 'You are going to love my mom,' then spoke back to the phone. 'You tell him, Pop.'

For just a moment, there was a tricky pause. Helen realised she had told neither Sam nor her parents that she had ever considered such a meeting.

Sam digested the possible implications of such planning. 'Well… I'm sure I'd love to meet her,' he said.

Peter Johnson rolled in to his daughter's rescue. 'Ha,' he cried, 'ha, women, they're always at least a step ahead of us men and of themselves sometimes! Eh, Sam?' They all laughed the implication away, though it had planted a thought in Sam's mind that he would need to revisit in the future.

'Look at the time, I'm going to have to close the church up,' said Peter Johnson. 'It's been a long day and you don't solve many problems with a tired mind. I'm a morning person anyway.' Then he gave Helen a real surprise. 'You've met Xavier too, you know? When you were just a toddler we went to Sardinia for a summer holiday, stayed with him. Remember?'

'Never! I don't remember.' Helen was startled by the revelation.

'Perhaps you wouldn't recall. You were just two or three. Xavier was really taken with you. Not too talkative with adults, but he loved little children, a natural with them. Odd, really, when you consider he became a priest.' He could sense Helen's disbelief and Sam's amusement. 'Oh yeah, you followed him around, inseparable for days. You wouldn't believe the tears when you weren't allowed to go into the confessional with him.'

Helen was only half-convinced. 'Get out of here,' but a smile showed she was thinking of the mysterious Xavier in a different light. He couldn't be all bad.

'It's true, all true,' chimed in Joan Johnson's more distant voice.

'How come nobody's ever told me this? John never said,' Helen was learning things about her life she'd never dreamt of.

'Sure, they all came. It probably never crossed John's mind to mention it. Now, let's speak again tomorrow. You take care of yourself, and you too Sam.'

'Love you, Pop.'

'Love you too.'

And the line went dead as Peter Johnson hung up.

Chapter 22

TUESDAY 18th JUNE, DAYTIME

Helen had church work to deal with and once again found she needed to spend part of the morning in the manse. She was still very uneasy with what had happened there but had to come to terms with events. Anyway, Grace was to be there too, supervising a team of security fitters who were booked in for today, so she wouldn't be completely alone. Leaving Sam on the doorstep, she stepped into the manse.

Meanwhile, Sam found himself with time on his hands. He made his way towards the city centre, once again heading for the museum, a bunch of carnations in his hand. An entirely inadequate gesture to show his feelings, but he wanted to do something. He turned into Chambers Street and forced himself to enter the building without a pause; if he stopped, he would probably not go in at all.

Once inside, he did hesitate for just a moment, then steeled himself and headed straight for the reception and enquiry counter. As he approached, he realised it was the same receptionist on duty as the day he had first met Suzie. She greeted him with a professional smile, but without recognition. He nodded back and there was a moment's silence as he considered what to say.

'How can I help you?' asked the woman.

Sam responded, still slightly hesitant. 'Morning. I wonder, I've got these flowers, I thought I'd hand in. They're just a token, well, to mark… For Suzie, you know she's died.' It was lame and he knew it sounded pathetic, but what do you say? He gave his bunch of carnations a little wave.

The receptionist's face changed from efficiency to a mix of warmth and sadness. 'Oh, that's so nice. Thank you,' she said, leaning across the reception counter to take the flowers. 'I'll have them taken up to her section right now. What a kind thought,' she gave him a smile of genuine warmth. 'It's so sad. And strange too. She was such a good swimmer - raised money for charity, swimming and all sorts. We don't understand how it happened,' she paused to admire the flowers. Then leant still further towards him and added in a conspiratorial whisper. 'And it's so weird; nobody here believes Suzie would take stuff. She lived for the job; everyone loved her.' Sam nodded and was turning to leave as she stopped him.

'Sorry - you haven't written a card,' she said.

Sam hesitated, feeling the need to leave, and shrugged. 'It doesn't matter; I'm thinking of her, that's what counts.'

'No. Wait. At least let me write your name down. Her friends and colleagues will appreciate it,' she smiled at him, beckoning him back to her, a pen in her hand. 'Just your name, please?'

Reluctantly, and now a little self-consciously, Sam returned to the counter and gave the receptionist his name. She wrote it on a note and slipped it amongst the flowers. Sam nodded a goodbye to her; he could finally leave, albeit his nagging guilt remained completely unassuaged.

'Hold on,' she called, stopping him for a second time, 'I remember you now. You were here visiting Suzie the other day, weren't you?'

Sam half turned back towards her and nodded acknowledgement. Then he watched as the receptionist suddenly disappeared from view, bending down to pick out something from a storage shelf fixed beneath the counter. She resurfaced with a broad brown envelope.

'Suzie must have sent this down for your collection before, before, well…' her voice trailed off as she slid the slim packet across the counter towards him.

'You'll need to sign for it,' she said, reaching for a receipt pad.

Sam signed, thanked the receptionist and left. He resisted the urge to open the envelope in the street. Instead, he headed straight for his office at the university. With the teaching year over he would be able to sit quietly and evaluate whatever Suzie had left him and consider the wider problem that was threatening to overwhelm Helen's and his own safety too.

• • •

Helen sat at the desk in the manse study, revising her work schedule for the week. Grace came in carrying mugs of coffee and chocolate biscuits. She took the chair next to Helen's desk. Helen smiled a thank you to her while finishing off the work schedule.

A minute or so later, Helen stopped, put her notes aside and grabbed her coffee. She looked across at Grace. 'Grace, sorry, I really had to get that finished while it was fresh in my mind. It seems an age since we last spoke properly. How are you bearing up with everything?'

Grace looked vulnerable. 'Oh, not very well really, but I guess we're all having it bad. But what about you? Poor John, he died in your arms. I know - my mum told me, though she wouldn't give me any details.' Grace almost didn't want an answer, a little afraid of what Helen might say.

She had never known her father. After he died, John Dearly had gradually evolved into almost a father figure for her, a surrogate uncle at the very least. Under John's watchful eye she had spent countless school holidays bouncing around the manse, the church and the graveyard while her mother was at work. Grace and John had become friends, more: trusted confidants, a shared and faithful affection.

The conversation moved on, touching this and that, but for once, both found it a little stilted. They worked around topics that Grace clearly felt too big to explore, and Helen was determined to avoid. Having become mindful that anyone coming into contact with the whole Templar dagger thing ended up in danger, she was not prepared to discuss anything that would put Grace in harm's way.

The pair, who had always found conversation so easy, suddenly had nothing to say. Grace stood, muttering uncomfortably about checking up on the security technicians. Helen stood too and came round the desk towards her. Then, as if by some instinctive synchrony, arms wrapped round and the pair embraced; two gently rocking bodies pressed against one another, leaning, supporting. Two friends joined in grief and worry; the stilted tension vanished while they shared a moment of mutual comfort and support.

Eventually their whispered babble subsided, the pair separated in a more comfortable frame of mind, but Grace left with a parting comment that stoked up all Helen's previous concerns. 'I'd have those security boys get up to the church next. Somebody's been at the doors. I know it, the locks opened far too easily when I was up there cleaning first thing. It's as if someone has done something to them, oiled them or something. Should I tell these guys to see my mum about it?'

'You don't say? That's really important. Can you tell your mother right away? I'll check it too. I'm to meet the police at the church at eleven thirty. They want to look around again. Probably ask more questions too. Though I guess we should be pleased that DCI Wallace is being thorough.'

Grace grimaced. 'Rather you than me. I always feel on edge with the police. I don't know, it's as though you're worrying you've broken a law without knowing and they'll pull you up.'

'I know, but don't worry. No one will be looking at you for answers to this stuff.'

'Hmmm,' said a slightly pensive Grace.

'In fact I'd better get over there right now. Don't want to keep the police waiting. I'll be back for lunch though. See you then.'

Helen headed straight away to the church and Grace stood at the study window to wave as Helen passed. Once Helen had gone, Grace remained, still, thoughtful, her fingers press hard against the windowsill.

• • •

DCI Wallace was standing on the step leading up to the church doors. To one side and just off the step were DS Brogan and three of the team. They were going to have a good hunt about. If there were any evidence in the church that linked these crimes, his team would find it.

He watched Helen carefully as she approached. Like everyone else, she had to be assessed, evaluated, but his gut instinct screamed innocent. Yes, everyone's a suspect, but if she was a serial killer, then he was a Russian ballet dancer. Yet there was something about her, he couldn't quite put his finger on it, just a feeling.

With a nod of his head, he acknowledged her wave and smile, and waited for her to join him on the step.

'Good morning detective,' greeted Helen. 'I'm not late, am I?'

'Morning there. No, you're spot on, we just arrived a couple of minutes ahead of time.'

Wallace stepped to one side, allowing Helen access to the door handles and locks. She produced a set of keys and opened up. The easy turning lock registered at once, though not sure a properly working lock was the sort of thing DCI Wallace was looking for, she determined to follow it up with Elaine as soon as possible. Stepping inside, she keyed in the alarm code before it could trigger. Then she invited the police in.

'I don't know quite how long this will take. Not sure what we're looking for until we see it,' said Wallace.

'Take as long as you like, but I don't have long detective. I've plans for lunch at the manse. Do you want the keys? How should we handle the lock up?'

Wallace took the keys. 'Are these for all the internal doors too?'

'Yes, but not the rear exit door behind the vestry,' said Helen.

Wallace gave a little growl, holding out the keys for DS Brogan to take. He looked back at Helen. 'Under the circumstances, you should set the alarm when we're finished. It's not good policy to share alarm codes, even if it's with the police.'

'What do you suggest then?' Helen was quite relaxed about leaving the police alone in the church but security was the order of the day. Perhaps more to deter ghouls and voyeurs than to keep the killer at bay. It seemed pretty clear a locked door was not the sort of barrier to stop him if he wanted to strike again.

'My sergeant's got your mobile number. I'll have him phone you once we're done and you can come back across to set the alarm. How's that?'

Helen smiled agreement. 'Great, I'll go for that. Now is there anything I can explain about the building before I leave?' She pointed up the aisle. 'I'd appreciate it if your men treat it with respect,' she looked expectantly at Wallace.

'Don't worry about that Miss, we're not heathens,' Wallace paused, eyeing one of his more dishevelled detectives. 'Well, most of us anyway.'

'The vestry is over there, on the left hand side, you go right through it to get to the church office. Feel free to look at anything you want. Just make yourselves at home. I'll collect the keys when I come back to reset the alarm.' Helen made to leave. 'If there's nothing else, I really need to get back to the manse.'

Wallace nodded agreement, but just as Helen turned to leave, he stopped her with a question. 'Oh, by the way Miss, I wonder...'

Helen turned back to hear what DCI Wallace wanted.

'The MacPhersons. Well, Sarah MacPherson, actually. I know you were there for a meal the week before they were killed, but I'm not quite clear how well you knew her. Were you good friends?'

'I'm sure I've already explained this to your sergeant.' She knew she had. 'I met Sarah once and only once. She was a lovely woman, a generous hostess and she didn't deserve to die.'

'And you're sure that's the only contact you ever had with her?' DCI Wallace's voice was relaxed, almost gentle.

'Absolutely. Oh, no. She sent me a note, a letter actually. I didn't get it until after... Well, after she was dead.'

'A letter. That's very unusual today, isn't it? Don't people mostly text or message or something these days? Why write, I wonder? What did she want?'

For the first time in her dealings with the police, Helen suddenly felt under the spotlight. 'I'm not sure, it was a bit vague. I think she just wanted me to visit, that's all. And writing? I guess that's just the sort of person she was. Stylish, but a mix of creative and traditional.'

'I'd quite like to see that letter if I may?' said Wallace.

'I don't have it with me. It's at home. I can look it out for you tonight.' Helen was relieved the questioning was limited to the MacPhersons. At least she did not have to sit on any information about them.

'That's fine, if you look it out and let me know, I'll have somebody drop by and pick it up for me...' Wallace left his sentence unfinished as his mobile phone rang. He reached for it while waving a silent goodbye. She did not need a second chance to leave.

• • •

Helen returned to the manse just as the workers' drilling and banging silenced for lunch. Back in the quiet of the study, she sat and considered what had happened and what they could do to protect themselves from whoever their enemy was. She smiled wryly; in all her time in West Africa, she had never thought of the militias there as enemies. Yes, they were misguided. Cruel, certainly. And sometimes simply evil. But they had not really been her enemies, just part of a wave of madness that swept up and brutalised whatever it touched. The wave did not worry who you were, was not in the least selective. If you met the wave, you met cruelty or torture or death. Sometimes all three. If you could run from the wave, you did. The wave didn't care; if it missed you, it just took the next person in line.

What she faced here was different. This was focused, aimed at her friends, her loved ones and aimed at her too. She would not run from it. What she had also learnt in Africa was that in the end a wave of madness did not kill or rape or brutalise; when the wave broke, you were always faced by an individual. To survive, the individual had to be stopped. She had survived then and she would do so now.

Her thoughts were brought to an abrupt end by shouts at the front door.

'Pizza. Pizza delivery for Johnson. Come and get it.' Francis' voice carried through the house as only a preacher's can.

She jumped up, pleased to hear his familiar voice. Then she headed for the hallway where Grace was already holding the front door open. Framed in the doorway was Francis with an arm full of pizza boxes. Elaine was in the doorway too, and wedged between the pair was an older man with tanned Latin looks and dressed in the formal black of a Catholic priest. It could only be Xavier. Angelo followed a pace behind.

Introductions were made, the dining room was quickly filled, and with a practiced hand, Grace spread out plates and organised drinks for everyone.

Francis started opening boxes and sliding them around the table. 'Take a slice. Take two, plenty to go round.'

Helen found herself sitting at the head of the table while Xavier had quite naturally slotted into the chair at the opposite end, Angelo to his right hand. The others filled the seats as they could. Elaine was looking gingerly at the pizza. She didn't think there had been a pizza delivery to the manse before, ever.

From behind her, Grace stretched an arm over Elaine's shoulder, pointing to one of the boxes. 'You like mushrooms, Mum, that'll be a nice one,' she said. Elaine did not respond, so Grace leant right round her, picked up a slice of pizza and dropped it on her mother's plate. 'Excuse fingers.' Then she was off round the table, pouring out glasses of water for everyone.

Elaine took a reluctant bite and secretly enjoyed it, though her unswervingly stern countenance made clear to anyone watching that she was eating under sufferance. A little while later, Grace noted a second slice shift smoothly onto her mother's plate.

Midway through the meal Sam arrived, triggering another round of introductions and enthusiastic greetings.

By the time lunch was over, Helen had definitely taken to Xavier. He had an air of leadership, you could just sense he was a man who could and would make the hard decisions, yet he was courteous and considerate to those around him. She could understand why her mother and father had befriended him, even though he was clearly not predisposed to idle social chatter. In his younger days, he must have been the epitome of the tall dark stranger.

Eating done, they migrated to the study and took seats around Helen's desk. As everyone settled, Elaine sent her daughter out of the room. Grace started to object but then let it go and set off upstairs to resume the cleaning she was doing so diligently in John's memory. Helen was delighted that Grace was not being exposed to anything that might put her at risk and she could tell that Elaine shared the same feelings.

The meeting started gently, a continuation of lunch's conversation, with invitations repeated and promises given to visit Sardinia, the States, to come back to Edinburgh for the Festival later in the summer. For a moment the meeting hung in the air with nobody quite willing to take the next step.

Xavier took the initiative. His aging voice gentle yet confident; his accented Italian English delivered in a calm matter of fact way, as though proposing a parish outing. 'We need to plan what to do. We need to face this threat that seems all around us. We need to come up with a plan to protect our friends here in Edinburgh,' his arms swept open to include all those present, 'and of course to protect those of us who have travelled from afar.'

A murmur of agreement rippled around the room, but Xavier held his hand up for silence. 'Of course, such a thing is always difficult, here doubly so, as the central party,' he nodded towards Helen who looked slightly startled at the label, 'is not so aware of her position or responsibility.'

He pouted, shrugged and turned his hands in towards his chest, pointing at himself. A single flowing gesture that disclaimed any responsibility for drawing Helen into the problem. 'John Dearly took her as his assistant, not me. Maybe he did not plan for that to last forever, but he died when he died. John gave her the ring. He asked her to stand for him.' His hands raised and fell back into his lap, a resigned acceptance of what was.

Elaine nodded. 'It's true,' she let her gaze roam round the room. 'John's last gasp committed to Helen, before my eyes. But without him here to support us it's going to be difficult to achieve his last wish, difficult but not impossible. We'll need to be strong now the presbytery clerk is trying to exert his influence over the parish selection process. But in the end, he can only advise, he can't make the congregation choose someone they don't want. I'll stand for John's last wishes no matter what, I'm with Helen for sure,' she looked towards Helen, face fixed, but eyes defiant, almost angry.

Helen couldn't help smiling to herself. Elaine seemed to be getting back on form. Helen wouldn't fancy James Curry's chances in a standoff between the pair now. But the threat they faced from outside was another thing altogether.

The room fell into silence for a moment and then Helen spoke for the first time. 'Innocent people are dead and it seems more are at risk. I don't want any special focus on protecting me. I can stand on my own two feet. There are plenty of others to be concerned about. Everyone needs the same care and protection.'

As a child she had always kept pace with her big brothers and their friends, running, swimming, playing ball, joining in whatever they did, while still managing to remain her daddy's little girl. Much later, in preparation for joining the church, she had shared long private talks with him, much of it about her time working in West Africa. Yes, she knew she could stand when the call came, and she wasn't a little girl any more.

Xavier nodded acceptance. 'Good, because this is a time of risk,' he looked around the room, his dark eyes betraying no concern for self. 'Risk for everyone. We must all be ready, be careful,' he gave a dry laugh. 'For me, it is not so bad. I am old anyway, but most of all I have Angelo.' Xavier waved towards his assistant and continued as Angelo gave a stiff nod. 'They will find Angelo a hard shell to break.'

Francis laughed quietly. 'Xavier, I know you know it. I think you mix up our sayings on purpose. You mean Angelo is a tough nut to crack,' he said. The mood lightened slightly and everybody jumped at the chance to smile for a moment.

Xavier waved a dismissive hand, mocking himself. 'Hard shells, tough nuts, who cares? Neither falls apart easily, eh?' Then he bluntly drew the group back to the problem. 'Now what do we do?'

Helen had a stack of questions that she and Sam had talked through endlessly over the preceding days and she took the opportunity to direct the discussion. 'Well, I need to know what these blades or daggers are for. Why are they so important that people are being slaughtered for them, and why now all of a sudden? If they've been around for so long what's triggered all this now? And you know what? How come I've never heard of all this stuff before?' She looked accusingly at Francis. 'You seem to be in the thick of all this. And my father tells me he knows all of you. Seems like Sam and I are the only ones out of the loop. Let's start by levelling with everyone, what do you say?'

Xavier responded first. 'Francis knows more than he should and certainly more than is good for him, I think. But that comes from a long friendship and too much of John's fine Scotch.'

'Helen, I've already told you what I can. I know just enough to understand there is a problem but not enough to provide a solution,' said Francis.

Xavier looked around the room. 'So, it must be for me to tell the story now. Yes?' The silence around the table answered him clearly.

'You will wonder how I know this and I will tell, but first some story. The Templar treasure... I know Francis has already explained how the Templars ended up here; what is not clear is what happened to the treasure. It was enormous, and bankrolled a good part of the Christian world. The French king seized a lot, but the main treasure escaped France with the Templar fleet and was then hidden away; nobody knows where.

'In those final days, the Templar leadership worried about their hidden wealth, knowing it was coveted by every king and villain in Europe. They worried that their treasures, God's wealth, might somehow fall into the wrong hands or perhaps even be lost forever. Ultimately, to protect their wealth for the future, they devised a plan to keep their secrets safely hidden and secure until they could emerge again, reclaim their wealth and resume their place in the world. They put that plan into operation.

'Then, as formal dissolution of the order became fact, many of the knights simply vanished into history. Others allowed to transfer, becoming knights with the order of Hospitallers of St John. As they were absorbed into their new order, Templar power and influence faded. But the most senior Templars were not so lucky; the leaders were taken and tortured, long and slow, hurt in unspeakable ways. Not to extract confession and repentance, that could be drawn from any man in a day: less than a day. This torture went on and on.

Why? To extract from the leadership the hiding place of the Templars' wealth.' Xavier paused for a moment. His dark eyes roamed around the room, he coughed, drank from a glass of water and sighed.

'But the Templars' plan worked perfectly. It had been so carefully designed that no man alive knew the full story and that included the leaders of the order. Even under the harshest torture, they could not tell their tormentors where the treasure was; they did not know. The secret was spread around, dispersed among a group of loyal knights, each of whom had only part of the answer, and none knew to where the others had travelled. All anyone knew was they had dispersed away from the hub, the heart; away from Scotland. It was the perfect protection for the Templar's treasure, but tragically it guaranteed those poor leaders the most awful of deaths,' Xavier was shaking his head.

The room remained in silence for several moments, and then Helen spoke. 'So, once again, this all just comes back to money? People are dying, being butchered and brutalised today because of a medieval treasure hunt? Tell me that people do not still believe in this stuff today.'

Francis looked at her carefully and spoke in an almost hushed voice, his tone carrying a hint of reprimand. 'They do believe, and you see the results. Pray God now holds John Dearly's soul safe; for those people's beliefs sent him on his way, and Archie Buchan and all the others too. Don't discount the savagery that greed and a lust for power breeds, Helen. It's always been here and it always will be.'

Xavier nodded and continued. 'You should believe it because I say it. And you have the evidence in your ring. Look, me too.' A ripple of surprise ran through the group as from beneath his collar he pulled out an ancient gold signet ring, strung on a heavy gold chain. 'This is the token to identify the task bearers. Each tasked to protect a part of the secret of the common wealth until called back together.' He dangled the ring, swinging it gently on its chain. 'And you?' he asked, fixing Helen with his gaze and tilting his head forward slightly.

Reluctantly Helen reciprocated, slipping a hand inside the collar of her polo shirt and pulling out her signet ring; she did not need to look closely to compare them, even the gold chains were clearly identical. She looked at him grimly and felt a slight sense of foreboding as she allowed her ring to swing in time with Xavier's, back and forth, back and forth. He gave a knowing nod, and slipped his ring away. The rest of the room had fallen silent watching the exchange with fascination and anticipation.

Xavier maintained his eye contact with Helen. An intimate link in a full room. 'So now you know how I know. Just like you, I hold a ring. Well, maybe more like John; he and I were told, inducted, we knew what was involved. You? You knew nothing.'

Sliding her ring out of sight, Helen tried to pick up her questioning again, all the while trying to suppress the surge of excitement that had come with the revelation that she was not alone. Xavier held a ring too. 'Okay, so there's lots of money and greed driving this…' her voice trailed off in response to Xavier's arching eyebrow as he leant back one shoulder and took a short sharp intake of breath, making clear he had not finished speaking. 'Sorry - Xavier, you have something more to say?'

The old Sardinian leant forward again. Resting his elbows on the table, he pushed his forearms a little forward while turning his open palms towards her. 'Greed and money? Yes, you are right, but look around you,' his hands swivelled a little to embrace everyone. 'What have we got in common? Faith. What did the Templars do when they weren't fighting or supporting trade? They praised God and prayed and gathered things, holy artefacts of the faith, from anywhere and everywhere. Especially from Jerusalem,' his hands rose in the air in a display of apparent exasperation.

'This is not so easy. It might be wealth that motivates our oppressor; it might be a thirst to find the ancient collection, the religious artefacts that defined our faith. Who knows? So we must make no assumptions about who we face and why they are coming. Yes?'

'Well that's progress. We find a clear motive; then it gets muddied,' said Helen. 'Is there anything we actually know for certain?'

Xavier allowed a space for others to contribute. No one spoke. He resumed. 'It might be human greed for treasure. It might be a zealot's desire to obtain holy artefacts. We don't know. How can we know? But unfortunately, it would seem those things we do know are known to our oppressors too.' Xavier paused again and looked down at the corner of the desk in front of him. Palms flat down, he applied a steady downward pressure and watched the tips of his fingernails whiten as the blood beneath was forced away. He was about to break his second secret of the day; a secret he and others before him had kept for a very long time, and it was not to be done lightly.

Helen watched Xavier's almost theatrical delay. She repeated her question. 'Well, Xavier, what do we actually know?' She waited as Francis leant forward in expectation. At last, and quite unexpectedly, he was going to learn the secrets that John Dearly had hinted at in moments of indiscretion but ultimately had kept all those years. Secrets that had eventually condemned him to an early and awful death.

Elaine sat stoically listening. She was as interested as the others, but years of restraining her emotions had left her face a near involuntary mask. She would have been a great poker player if she had approved of gambling.

Without looking up from the desktop, finding some comfort in his unmoving hands, Xavier explained what he could. 'So, it was arranged that no man knew all the details of where the Templars hid what was hidden, how to access it and what it contained. In those times they did not have computers and things to hide information in, but they were just as clever as we are today, and they could devise their own schemes to hide things. The knowledge was to be split up, dispersed and held apart until the time was right.

'Henri de Bello was a senior Templar Knight. Old, a thinker, his fighting days long behind him, based not far from here at the preceptory in the village of Temple. I think, a headquarters in Scotland? He was clever, one of their best thinkers and, crucially, he was dying - steadily and inexorably moving towards his God. He was the last man to be trusted to hold all the knowledge of the Templars' secret wealth and his impending death meant he would not live long enough to fall into the hands of their enemies. In those days, death was the best keeper of secrets. Perhaps it still is.

'The story passed down to me tells us that de Bello chose daggers from their Jerusalem treasure. There are nine, each exactly the same, perfect.' A murmur ran through the group at this revelation - it fitted with Francis' story. Xavier continued, 'Pure silver, and ceremonial, the blades are too soft for real fighting, but ideal to carry a message that would never change over the years. Pure silver lasts a very long time, it does not waste away quickly like iron.

'Henri de Bello made a message. It was engraved in sections across the blades of the daggers.' Xavier paused at Sam's excited eureka cry.

'Of course,' said Sam. 'All the patterning and lines on one side of the blade, they seemed random -'

'But not if they line up with other blades, like sections of text,' Helen cut in, finishing his sentence.

'And all together they provide the full message. Brilliant!' Francis finished off the deduction.

Xavier was nodding. 'Yes, yes you have it. And the legitimacy of each task bearer is signed by the ring they carry.' Then he gave one of his characteristic shrug and pouts. 'But is it so easy? No. Not at all.' The excitement subsided as they waited for Xavier to continue.

'What is the message? I don't know. Do we know where to find the other daggers? No. Have we got the dagger that Sam found in your Fife sand dunes? No. Have we got the museum dagger that Sam tracked down? No! But somebody has and they want more.'

'We're back to square one then. In fact, we're worse off than when we started,' said Helen. 'We don't know who wants the daggers and they have two already. They have part of the message already. And you know what? I don't have a dagger to go with my ring.'

Sam frowned. 'Yes, it seems whoever it is has a head start. But what are we in for? To stop the killing or to find this treasure?' he shifted his gaze from Helen to Xavier. 'What's it to be?'

'Xavier, what do you think?' asked Helen.

The old man stretched his hand out, rested it on Angelo's forearm and squeezed affectionately. 'I have protected my part of our secret for all my working life. I'm old now, what I think matters less each day. I have had my time. For me, the days are already starting to feel too long, I don't much care when I meet my maker now. Angelo here will soon take over from me, as you have from John Dearly. It is for you younger people to decide the course soon. But I would say this, for me - and I know for John Dearly too - life is always more precious than money. Lives should come first, always, and then you can worry about money.'

'Hear, hear,' Francis cut in to support Xavier and slapped his hand on the desk. 'You can always dig more gold, but a life lost is lost forever.'

'So how do we stop these killings? How do we put an end to it all? Do we just give these mercenaries or zealots or whoever they are, what they want? I guess that's the dagger from here,' said Sam. He stared around the group. 'But we haven't got it to give.'

'Here's a radical thought,' said Helen. 'There's a detective over in the church right now, why don't we go and tell him? Put it all in his lap. They'll work out it's nothing to do with us soon enough.'

Xavier nodded acknowledgement. 'I understand your view, Helen, but you have seen what these people are capable of. They are driven; do you think the police can stop what is happening? They haven't managed so far. Yet Sam is right as well when he says we don't have it to give, to buy them off. But I wonder, even if we could give them what they want, would that stop the killing? I don't think so. Everyone who has had even the slightest contact with our secret, knowingly or otherwise, has been killed.

'None of them could have caused any harm, and they would never have known the significance of what they were dealing with. They were just loose ends to be tied up. I don't think the killing will stop just because we tell the police or they get what they want. It might even speed up the killing as they try to seal their plans. We will all have to be silenced too. Who knows, if you tell your detective, perhaps you are signing his death warrant too.'

Helen looked away, thinking about the others who had died just because they knew, even when they didn't know they knew. Could she live with herself if she knowingly triggered DCI Wallace's death too?

'So, we need to protect ourselves. But how?' said Helen, she couldn't see a way forward.

Xavier had slumped a little. Suddenly drained, his age showing, it seemed to be something of an effort for him even to raise his arm. He managed. He pointed a single finger up. 'One,' he said. 'I have friends who could help but they are far away. For now, we must see to ourselves.' A second finger pointed skywards. 'Two, they don't yet have all the daggers, so they are still in the dark.' A third finger went up. 'Three, I think the daggers they have already seized were just good fortune, thrown up by chance and Sam's unrelated efforts. They took them because they could.' Xavier paused for a moment, collecting his thoughts or his breath, or both.

Another finger popped up. 'Four. There must be a way to find the other daggers, to call them back together. Perhaps, that might be the purpose of John's dagger, Helen's dagger now, as it sits here at the heart, I don't know. But there must be a way, a device, something, and it must be here.'

His thumb rose joining the fingers to make an open palm. 'Five. The killers are here only because they knew a dagger, the key dagger, was here in Scotland. The one from which all the other daggers travelled away so long ago. Only those who were originally entrusted to protect the daggers, the sections of the message, whatever it is, could possibly know of the message's existence and the place from which they all originated. Only one of those could know there was a message to find. So the killer must be a task bearer, must have their own dagger,' Xavier stopped talking and let his hand drop. Those around him stirred and shifted, shocked by Xavier's deduction.

'Wow, that is crazy,' said Helen. Though, like the others, she was struck by the simple logic. 'It's sick. I thought you guys, us guys... We are meant to be the good ones. This lunatic is one of you, one of us, I guess. And he was after John all the time. Now he's coming after me? For what? My ring? A dagger or some other device that I don't have, that nobody has ever seen? Unbelievable. Mad. God help us all!' She threw her hands up in despair.

Xavier briefly raised his own hands, mirroring Helen in sympathetic agreement. 'Yes, it is mad, but logical. Each of the daggers is engraved, but not with words; just a series of interwoven lines that will somehow combine. A code, I don't know how, that is the essence of it; none of the task bearers could ever read or know the message they guarded. On their own, each of the daggers is useless. To track down and get all the other daggers they would need the one from here, St Bernard's. The one John had and hid. Your dagger.

'You are at the centre Helen, your blade is what they want, that's why they're here. Oh, they will want mine too, but yours is special. Also, I think if it's not your blade, then in your church's possession is hidden something that will say where the other daggers were sent. There must be a way to gather them all back together again; a way to reassemble the parts of the message when the old Templars needed it again.'

Elaine, who had been sitting quietly throughout the meeting, finally broke her silence. 'What I don't understand, Xavier, is if none of those guarding the daggers knew where the others were, how come you and John Dearly were friends? It doesn't make sense to me.' She was not accusing Xavier of anything underhand, but it was an anomaly that did not fit with the old priest's story.

Everybody bristled cautiously as soon as the question was asked. Angelo sensed the change in mood at once and tensed. Xavier waved him to ease.

'It's a good question, my old friend,' Xavier smiled at Elaine and spoke with careful measured words, 'and the answer is also built on friendship. Not mine and John's, no. A friendship much older. When Henri de Bello sent out his knights from this place, they went with their tasks, probably knowing they would never return or see their friends and comrades again; knowing that the return of the daggers might take more than their own lifetimes.

'Like the others, my predecessor, who was sent to Sardinia so long ago, was probably resigned to never seeing or hearing from those old comrades and friends again. Each had set out from Scotland to their own secret destination, carrying away their tasks, scattering across the known world.

'Supported by a little group that had travelled with him, my predecessor quietly set up a small holy community and chapel. Doing good, helping, serving, becoming accepted, growing into and becoming part of the community and always waiting, always ready for the call were it to come. It never did.

'But one day, many years later, ships from Scotland did come, though not with a message for our hidden knight. Driven wildly off course by a fierce storm, they were pausing, recovering before continuing on their journey that would take them to Avignon, in the south of France. They had messages for the Pope, seeking forgiveness for King Robert's crime of murdering a man at the church altar - to have Scotland readmitted to the Christian world, to see the excommunication lifted.

'On board the Scottish ships was one particular man, once a Templar Knight too, but now a highly respected Edinburgh priest. He travelled at the request of the Scots king, to provide spiritual support to the travellers, and to support the petition to the Pope.

'By chance, that priest was from here; Archie's, John's... Helen's predecessor. The forced stop in Sardinia and the Edinburgh priest's chance visit to a local chapel brought two old friends and comrades back together. Reuniting two men whose bond of trust had been forged in battles in Europe and Palestine, who had served in peace together, had fled King Philip of France together and had finally been separated to serve alone, in secret; surrendering old friendships to protect the Templars' wealth and power.

'Once reunited it was a bond that remained unbroken. A friendship and a shared secret burden that passed quietly and unremarked down the years until here we are today. Though I should tell you I know of no others anywhere.' Xavier ended with an emphatic shrug.

'But this is still only part history, part hand-me-down story. There are no facts to build a plan on,' Helen looked round the group for inspiration.

'It may be story, but there is stuff to go on,' replied Francis. 'Two daggers have been stolen, people killed to get them. So somebody puts a serious value on these artefacts and this story. You and Xavier share a common strand of the story, with identical signet rings. In the absence of a better explanation, I fear we must accept the story. We know the threat is real, know the danger exists, and we must challenge it somehow. In the meantime and in the absence of anything else, I for one am happy to accept Xavier's account.'

'If we could find the other daggers before them, perhaps we could finish this somehow,' said Sam. 'They thrive on secrecy. If we could get the whole story together and somehow make it public, then we would cut the ground from under their feet. There's no point in killing to keep a secret everyone already knows.'

Sam's suggestion was sketchy, but it was an idea. Nodding heads marked the progress of excited agreement as it rippled round the room. A chink of light? A way out? A straw to clutch at, certainly.

Helen looked at Francis and Sam. 'Yes, but we can't do anything if we don't know where the other daggers are. Nothing will work if we don't have this key dagger, the parish dagger, which might point us to the others. So we need to find it first.' She turned to Elaine. 'Have you any idea at all where it might be? Any clue, any secret place that John might have used?'

All eyes turned to Elaine as she shook her head. 'I've no idea. I knew about the ring, obviously. I knew that our parish had a different selection process for its ministers and that John held something in trust that was for the minister only and secrecy was paramount. I knew we had a long history and he had a trust fund for public good; but I've never heard anything about a dagger and never seen one either. Though, if it were a special secret known only to the minister, I would never have known, would I? It'll be hard to find. Let's face it, John and all those before him have had a long time to find a hiding place.' Faces dropped around the room at this cold shower.

Helen looked at her. 'You're right, but have you ever looked for it, I mean actually gone hunting for it?'

Elaine shook her head again. 'No, of course not, never, but then none of us knew there was a dagger to find, did we?'

The meeting was interrupted by Helen's mobile phone ringing. She looked to see who was calling, excused herself and answered the call. After listening briefly, she spoke into the handset. 'That's fine. I'll be along as soon as I can. Just give me a few minutes.' She hung up the call and looked round. 'The police have finished; they didn't find anything of interest. I'll need to go over to the church and lock up.'

A round of nods acknowledged she needed to go and she decided it was time to set some plans in motion. 'Right, this is what I propose. We need to move fast before anyone else gets hurt, and let's not forget that soon enough the police are going to start asking Sam and I difficult questions. You've all warned me there are no suspects and when that happens the media will simply find someone for a story.

'I don't fancy being locked up while the police try to solve the apparently insoluble. If we can track down the guilty, we can somehow deflect the police onto them and minimise risks to innocent lives: ours, the police or the public. From what I'm hearing here, we have a better chance than anyone else.

'Sure, they have a start on us, snatched our two daggers, but doing nothing is not an option. Our first step must be to get up, get out and find this parish's dagger. Let's find what we can and see where that takes us, let's get ourselves some advantage. We've been taking a mauling. Now let's turn it around, right?'

A cautious nodding of heads told her that the others were with her and she pushed on. 'Let's search the church, check it over, every floorboard, every stone, the works. Find the dagger. I know the police have just searched the church. But as we've already heard from Elaine, if you don't know it's there, you don't know to look for it. Right now, we have an edge. Let's use it, let's get ahead of whoever's coming at us.'

Chapter 23

TUESDAY 18th JUNE, EVENING

Sitting comfortably in the swivel chair at his desk, Cassiter gazed out of the office window, observing the first signs of rush hour as the early birds tried to steal a march on the homeward journey. Having reviewed progress and planned his next steps, he was feeling reasonably contented with the world. This job for Parsol was now moving steadily towards completion.

He did not really like working on his home patch, but if his people could function successfully pretty well anywhere in the world, they could do it here too, as they had been demonstrating so admirably. True, one or two overzealous moments had caused Parsol some passing concern, but by and large, things were proceeding as they should be.

There was just one dagger left to find in the city and he knew where to look. He also knew who to ask; that old church elder McPhee would be helping him with his enquires soon enough. Cassiter smiled to himself in anticipation and spun his chair away from the window. He pulled a memory stick from his jacket pocket and inserted it into a port in the desktop computer. Navigating his way to the location, he saw the two expected folders, each one containing the downloaded contents of a mobile phone.

He opened the first folder and reviewed its contents. Davy's pictures of the dagger were there. He looked at them closely, admired the boy's camera work and then continued scrolling through the pictures. He lingered for a moment, admiring some revealing pictures of a pretty girl that she really ought not to have let the boy take. Cassiter decided to keep those pictures too. He liked the look of this girl, and anyway, you just never know when material like that might prove useful. It was certainly not the sort of thing she would ever want leaking into the public domain. He searched on and finally decided there was nothing else of interest and closed the folder.

The boy had had a lucky escape in Oban and would need to be removed as he just might be able to identify Barnett, but it could be left in abeyance for now. There were more pressing issues to address. He would have a nasty accident when Cassiter was ready.

Cassiter turned his attention to the other folder. The contents of Suzie's phone were quite uninspiring. Pictures of friends and babies. Benign, much as the girl herself had proven to be. She'd been no threat beyond her immediate engagement with the issue, but that had been enough. A remarkably radiant character inside, but such a plain exterior, and for one moment her naive sincerity had almost been disarming. Even when frightened for her life, she had still seemed to care so much for her family. Worried about their welfare ahead of her own.

He did not put any store in family loyalty himself, but it had offered him such a wonderful lever to work with, to ensure her compliance. It had been quite touching to see how she obeyed his every instruction, believing he would keep his word, faithful to her loved ones right to the very end. Stupid girl.

Of course, he'd lied; her family had never been taken. As soon as she had gone to work on the Thursday morning, his man had done an emergency gas safety call to her home, and in the process stolen her sister's mobile phone and clipped the house's phone cable: simple but effective. The young mother had sat at home, incommunicado, innocently nursing her baby, completely oblivious to her sister's pointless sacrifice.

Cassiter didn't bother looking at any more of the domestic messages from her life. The girl had presented no risk. He closed her folder and dragged it to the waste paper basket. He turned his thoughts to Elaine McPhee.

• • •

A fruitless afternoon spent searching in the church had left Helen drained. She had wondered what they would find that the police had missed, but they had to start somewhere. Eventually, she left the others in the church and returned home to link up with Sam who had been asked to pop back to campus. Since MacPherson's death, additional work had started to filter down the management pyramid on to his desk.

Helen leapt up as the security entry phone buzzed; she went to the front door and answered. Sam's voice announced his presence at the street below and she pressed the entry-phone button to release the street-level door. She opened the flat door for him and headed off to put on the kettle, stopped and altered course for the fridge. He would probably prefer a beer.

Sam didn't get a chance to speak as Helen shoved the beer into his hand, pulled him onto the sofa and bemoaned their fruitless afternoon's search. She threw out questions on Xavier's story, the threat they faced and their decision to fight back. He listened quietly as Helen's words and rhetorical questions fired off like a stream of machine gun bullets. Finally she stopped. 'Well, what do you think?' she asked.

As Sam weighed up his answer, she jumped up, took his now empty beer bottle and headed for the kitchen. 'You'll want another one of these, and you know what? I need some wine,' she raised her voice a little so it carried from the kitchen and the tone was laden with indignation. 'Whoever these bad guys are, they've got the daggers. We lost out on them before we even knew there was a race on. It's sickening, you know, we had both of them within our grasp and now they're just gone.'

She returned from the kitchen with the drinks. 'It makes me so frustrated that these evil…' she paused and struggled for a word from her regular vocabulary to describe them and then gave up. 'These evil Bs have bullied, spied, tortured, robbed, killed, and now they're walking away with whatever it is they wanted, Scot-free. And there's nothing we can do to stop them.'

Reaching the sofa, she thrust the fresh bottle of beer into Sam's outstretched hand and sat back down beside him. She paused just long enough to take a big mouthful of wine and savour the slight burn and kick it gave as it ran down her throat. 'It's just so frustrating.' She drained the wine glass and refilled it from the bottle that had accompanied her from the kitchen.

Sam squeezed her knee and let his hand slide lightly up to the soft of her thigh and squeezed again, rubbing gently. 'We'll get through this. But we need a plan and we need to stay strong too,' he said.

Helen put the bottle down and took a drink from the refilled glass; she savoured the taste and swallowed, then took a second mouthful. 'I can stay strong. Don't worry about that, but a plan? Plan for what? The problem is we don't know who we're dealing with or what we're up against.'

Sam nodded understanding, his hand still gently rubbing her thigh trying to give a little comfort. 'Well, let's top that glass up first, I've got things to tell you too and a drop more wine won't go amiss; in fact you might just need it.'

Helen turned her head towards him with a slightly puzzled look. 'Why? What do you mean?'

'When I left you this morning, I took flowers across to the museum as a mark of respect for Suzie.'

'I know. So what's new?'

'Well, where to start? Let's say it ties in with your latest information pretty closely.' The contents of Suzie's envelope had been surprising but he had not mentioned it at their earlier meeting, allowing Xavier space to tell his story. It was starting to heat up now he had taken the time to think it all through. Inside the envelope he had found a copy of the museum's own record of what they knew about the artefact's story. Suzie had also tracked through the photographic archive to find good quality images of the dagger, ring and chain.

Sam explained how the museum dagger had a long history, a clear provenance; the old widow who had donated the artefacts had included her family's history and records as part of the gift, and Suzie had managed to dig them out of the archives. The family record traced all the way back to the beginning of the fourteenth century and a knight, Bernard de Bras, who Robert the Bruce had made a lord for his part in the wars against England. Whoever this knight was, there had been no record of him or his family in Scotland and then suddenly there he was leading a small group of fighting men in support of Bruce.

Who knows, perhaps he was one of Xavier's task bearers who simply got caught up in Bruce's northern civil war, then was dragged to the south into the main war. That could also explain how de Bras suddenly led a larger force. Once he was obliged to come south with Bruce, perhaps the remaining Templar Knights from the preceptory at Temple had joined with him. He did well, was made a lord and rewarded with lands. In fact, he did very well, becoming one of Bruce's closest confidants, a member of his inner circle.

At the end of Bruce's reign, Bernard de Bras was part of the old guard that carried his heart south on a crusade to fight the Moors in Spain. By that time, de Bras and many of his band were older, truth to tell, far too old for campaigning abroad.

The fighting was fierce and there were many casualties, but de Bras and his men seemed to fight with a wild and almost inexplicable fever that many remarked on. They seemed to seek victory without any thoughts of death. Eventually, they got both. He died with his men, standing in the face of a frantic Moorish attack against the Christian army, providing a determined suicidal block that held the Moors back until the Christians could rally and take the day.

Bernard de Bras had never married. Of course, if he were a Templar Knight it was not allowed. So when he was killed in Spain, his brother inherited the title and thereafter the family remained as small but steady players in Scottish life right up to the First World War when the family's two sons were killed. They were junior officers, leading platoons in the same battalion, both died at the battle of the Somme in 1916.

Their father could not cope with the loss of his sons and was dead within a year and the family line came to an end. No distant cousins or whoever to step in, the Great War had taken them all.

Eventually, a forerunner of the National Museum ended up receiving a bequest from the dead man's widow: family papers and a stack of money for the preservation of various artefacts. Included amongst those things were the dagger and gold signet ring, but the old lady had not told them much about these artefacts. Only that her late husband had always identified them as the family's most precious possessions. He kept them locked in the family safe and allowed only his sons to see them and then only very occasionally. The family story had it that they had passed from the first lord to his brother and then down the line over successive generations.

Pausing for a moment, Sam looked at Helen. 'The old widow had no idea why the things were so valuable, but we certainly do,' he said.

Helen nodded agreement. 'You bet we do, but knowing the story's not any good to us is it? They've got away with the dagger already. Both the daggers.'

Sam grinned back at her. 'Yes, they have, but we don't need the museum dagger. We've got copies of the museum's photographs and we know the scale. If it really is part of a message, as Francis and your new friend Xavier say, then the picture should do just as well as the original dagger, shouldn't it?'

Helen looked carefully at the picture Sam had produced, saw the logic in his argument and suddenly felt a surge of excitement displacing the mood of gloom that had settled over her.

'Too right it should.' She leapt up and strode to the window. In silence she looked out at the city, watched the buses and cars passing beneath. People just following their ordinary lives, all quite oblivious to the events besieging her and her little band. She looked up to the clear blue summer sky above the tenement roofs, searching for some inspiration.

Sam was just beginning to get anxious about her when she spun round. 'Sam Cameron, you are smart, you know that? Just when I was lost, in you come with an answer.' Pacing quickly back to the sofa, she bent down and kissed him enthusiastically. She pulled back, looked him in the eye, then kissed him again.

Straightening up, she took his beer bottle. 'You won't be needing that just now, there's some driving to do. We need clear minds if we are going to put together some sort of defence. I don't know how it will work out yet, but I know they've just lost their edge.' She took his hand and pulled, though he didn't need much encouragement to stand. 'Maybe we really can mount a bit of offence too. What do you say?'

'Well, if they are coming after us as Xavier thinks and we can't look for police protection since we might put the police themselves at risk or even be seen as suspects ourselves, then I'm with you,' he replied. His voice sounded confident, though Sam was not sure what could be done. He just knew he did not fancy sitting and waiting for a knock on the door, whether it was a visit from the police or someone altogether more sinister.

'The question remains, what should we do?' said Sam.

'Let's start by getting the others up to speed. Your news is important. It's a break and it's independent confirmation of Xavier's back story. So you and I, all of us, now know there really is a history to this. And a threat too, not just some coincidence of evil.' She paused for a second before continuing. 'And you know what? Your envelope from Suzie tells us no matter how ruthless they are, how clever and determined to gather in all the evidence and information, they are not infallible. If they missed those,' she pointed at Suzie's envelope, 'then just maybe they missed something with your dunes dagger too.'

The pair headed out of the flat as Helen tapped in the speed dial for Elaine; hopefully they would still be searching the church, and the sooner they all got the news the better.

• • •

At the church, the others had been locking up when Sam and Helen arrived. They had been excited by Sam's news and heartened by the revelation their opponent was not infallible. But taking their lead from Xavier, they determined to break for the evening - it had been a long day.

They all agreed to meet again in the morning to resume their search. Xavier looked particularly drained, the whole business and his long journey had caught up with him, simply exhausted the older man.

• • •

Back at Helen's flat once again, Helen and Sam had eaten a quick snack, neither feeling inclined to tackle a full evening meal. They were back sitting together on the living room sofa, taking a few minutes' break, quietly thinking.

Helen looked across towards the pile of old parish papers she had brought home with her in the hope she might unearth some clue, anything that might lead them towards this parish dagger. She had found nothing.

Jingling a set of house keys, Sam tried to introduce a change of tack. 'Do you fancy coming with me?' The police had asked that his department check MacPherson's house to establish if any university valuables were there. Particularly those things an archaeologist might have about the house, things that the police might not recognise as valuable.

The idea did not appeal to Helen, and she declined, but it did trigger a thought in her mind. She went over to the bureau and looked out Sarah MacPherson's letter. The police wanted it. What had it said again? It deserved to be treated with respect, as it may have been the last thing the poor woman wrote. She read it again, thinking of her, hoping for her.

Helen,

Mission accomplished. MacP will be grumpy if he finds out, so don't spill the beans. Come and see me, we'll crack this one together!
Sarah.

Helen weighed up the letter, yet it still made no sense to her at all. She passed it to Sam and asked him what he thought.

He read it and handed it back. 'Haven't got a clue,' he said. But a moment later he was on his feet, suddenly very excited. 'Let me see it again.'

Taking the letter back from her he re-read it. Then with a triumphant smile, he waved it at her. 'I think I know what it means. Look, here,' he handed the letter back to Helen. 'Think, what did Sarah do?'

Helen was puzzled. 'She was an artist,' she said.

Sam nodded. 'Yes, but what sort of artist?'

'A sculptor?'

'Not just any sculptor, she worked in metals,' he took the letter back from Helen and tapped on it. 'Look what she wrote: *Come and see me, we'll crack this one together.*' He looked at Helen meaningfully, expectantly.

Helen was tired and fed up with games. 'Sam, just tell me, what does it mean?' She was finding it hard to get excited while thinking about the threat they all faced.

Sam took her gently by the shoulders and looked into her eyes. 'What do sculptors do with metal?' He paused for a moment, giving her shoulders the lightest of squeezes. 'They cast things. And what would Sarah have cast that could be of the slightest interest to you? That would make MacPherson grumpy?'

The penny dropped. 'The dagger! She cast the dagger.' Helen was suddenly buzzing too. 'She told me not to worry when we left their house, remember? She said she'd make sure we got access to the dagger, even though MacPherson was being awkward about it. She's cast the dagger!' Helen took a deep breath, letting the thrill subside. 'Sam, we could still have access to your dunes dagger. This is big news. But, where would she have put it? Wouldn't whoever killed them have taken it?'

'I don't know,' said Sam, as he waved MacPherson's house keys again, 'but I know how to find out.'

· · ·

Sam parked the car in the driveway of the MacPhersons' house. From the front, there was remarkably little damage. Some flowerbeds had been churned up by emergency vehicles and the side gate that gave access to the rear gardens was off its hinges, knocked aside in the initial rush of the rescue crews.

They sat for a moment looking up at the grand old house. Its faded golden sandstone and comfortable rectangular symmetry exuded a reassuring sense of strength that belied recent events.

Helen suddenly shivered, remembering the laughs and fun she had found here, the wonderful food and sparkling hospitality Sarah had offered her visitors. She wondered at the hell that had visited and steeled herself to go inside. It suddenly seemed a less attractive idea than it had even a few minutes before. A sinister though unspoken threat now seemed to hang over everything.

Both hands still on the steering wheel, Sam pulled himself a few inches forward and theatrically squinted through the windscreen, peering intently up at the house. He blew a noisy breath out through his teeth, leant back again and turned to look at Helen. 'Well, let's get it over with, shall we?' Sam shared Helen's sudden change of mood and she found a little strength from that. She was not alone in her disquiet.

Just like the front façade, the inside of the main house was remarkably undamaged, though the taint of smoke hung in the atmosphere. The sturdy wooden fire door that led from the back of the hall into the kitchen had withstood the original blast. It now had a strong hasp and padlock on it, preventing access to the wrecked kitchen. Apart from the smell of smoke, it was hard to tell there had ever been a fire.

Sam inspected the padlock and shrugged. He had not expected it to be there, but on the other hand, he had arrived with no real preconceptions. Quietly and methodically, they searched the house, room by room. Sam examined items that might have some particular value or academic interest or simply belong to the university.

He was making notes as they moved through the house. Once he had typed it up, the list would go to the police and to the MacPhersons' solicitor, to inform their arrangements for short-term security and eventual distribution of the estate. Helen searched for signs of Sarah's cast without success.

Finally, with a growing sense of anti-climax, the pair moved into the smallest of the rear facing bedrooms, the last room to search. It took only minutes to establish that the room contained nothing of interest.

'Looks like we've drawn a blank,' said Helen. 'Do you think they got away with her cast as well as the original?' her voice was sad, and it wavered as she glanced through the window. The outside of the bedroom window was streaked with soot from the fire. It allowed only a blurry view out over what had been the original single story kitchen and beyond into the secluded back garden. 'Oh my God, Sam, look at this.' She pointed out of the window, down towards the kitchen.

Sam joined her. He looked out and down across the kitchen, and instinctively put his arm around her, providing comfort, finding some too. From this angle, it was clear why the kitchen door had been fitted with a padlock. It was now, in effect, the back door. The kitchen fire door had deflected the blast energy back into the kitchen, which was all but destroyed. Just a charred shell remained. Windows blown out, ceiling down, the roof and slates lost: a bombsite. Everything completely written off with charred roof beams and rafters left open to the sky.

'Well, we're not going to find anything down there,' said Sam.

Helen nodded. 'You're right. God bless them. What an awful way to go. What a cruel thing to do,' she shook her head despairingly. 'Who are we up against here, Sam? I just can't get my head round it. It's so, so alien.' She pressed her head against the window frustrated. 'And they must have got the cast too.'

Sam looked beyond the charred kitchen. 'You know, Helen, I'm not sure about that.' He pointed across the garden towards an old single story outbuilding that was partially concealed behind mature shrubs at the bottom of the garden. 'We've seen no sign of where Sarah worked in the house. If you had all sorts of sculpting tools and furnaces and the like, you'd need a lot of space and want to keep it all together, like in a -'

'Workshop!' Helen finished his sentence.

It took only a minute to lock the front door, pass through the broken side gate and follow the path down the side of the house into the back garden. The acrid smell of recent burning was much stronger here, hanging in the air. It caught in their noses as they hurried past the kitchen annex and across the lawn. Without stopping, Helen threw a silent blessing over her shoulder and promised herself she would return to the ruined kitchen at a less frantic moment.

As they got closer to the outbuilding, it became clear it was well maintained and still in use. At one time it would have been the workshop for gardeners and the handyman, but not anymore. Nicely symmetrical, a broad door was set at the midpoint of the building while to either side full sized windows let light flood inside. The faded golden stone had a rougher finish than that which faced the main house, understandably so since the original builder would never have envisaged that first owner spending any time here.

Sam was trying to open the locked door using the bunch of keys.

Helen went to the window on his right and peered in. 'It's the workshop, Sam. I can see stuff.' She returned to Sam at the door. 'Come on, are the keys working? Let's get in.'

A distinct click answered her as the third key Sam tried turned smoothly, unlocking the door. He pushed it open and they both stepped in. The space was bigger than they expected since the building was deeper than it was wide. Off to the right were rows of tools and raw materials, welding kits, a portable hoist and various art works that may have been finished or abandoned, or were works in progress, just waiting for Sarah to provide a finishing touch of inspiration. It didn't matter now.

Helen and Sam began to search; if there was something to be found, this is where it had to be. The middle of the room was a clear open space, scrapes and marks on the concrete floor showed this had been Sarah's working area for larger scale jobs. It was empty now. To the left, under the window, was a workbench where she must have done smaller tasks, it too was empty. In a corner at the back of the room were a desk and filing cabinet, beside them two doors that led away into a kitchenette and toilet.

The pair were running out of places to look, beginning to doubt there was anything to find in the workshop. Finally, they traced their way along the rear wall towards the furnaces. One was small, the other bigger.

Helen pointed at the rack beside the small furnace; she glanced at Sam who nodded agreement to her. Quickly, she stepped forward to look more closely at the chunky shaped mould. Around twenty inches long, six inches wide and perhaps two inches deep. If anything was going to be the mould of a dagger it was this, and it was heavy. There was definitely something inside. Helen felt her hand trembling slightly. 'How do we get it out?' she asked.

'Crack it,' said Sam, matter-of-factly. 'Crack it carefully.' He pointed towards a little mallet that sat in a rack next to the furnaces. 'That should do the trick.'

Helen did not need to be prompted twice. In no time, the mould was broken and a beautiful replica fourteenth century dagger rested in her hands. They both checked anxiously for markings on the blade; they were there. With some cleaning up these would stand out as clearly as the day they had been engraved on the original dagger. She felt a surge of pleasure rush through her. At last they had something, something tangible, and taken together with the pictures of the museum dagger they were on a level playing field again. Perhaps they could now start to make some headway. For the first time, there was a real flicker of light at the end of a very dark tunnel. She did not fully appreciate the significance of these ornamental weapons yet, but at least they had something.

Chapter 24

WEDNESDAY 19ᵗʰ JUNE, AM

Elaine and Grace McPhee walked up the drive to the manse and made for the open front door. As they passed the study window, they saw Helen sitting behind the desk. Francis sat at one end, leaning forward, elbows on the desk's edge. Helen gave an enthusiastic wave from behind the glass, beckoning the two women to come straight in.

As they entered the hall, Sam emerged from the kitchen carrying a tray. 'Just in time, morning coffee for everyone. You come through too, Grace. Join us for a drink before things get started,' said Sam.

Grace smiled and nodded grateful acceptance, pleased that Sam included her as an equal. The others did not want their meeting disturbed, so today Grace had the job of housekeeping, waiting for the delivery van that was bringing a new kitchen table and chairs.

A squeal of taxi brakes heralded the arrival of Xavier and Angelo. They were all coming together to make a plan. A plan for their own survival.

Coffees finished, Grace left the study and headed upstairs to start sorting John Dearly's clothes in the master bedroom, its windows faced out across the driveway, well placed so she would see the furniture delivery van when it arrived.

Helen called the group to order, and they responded without question. That she was the youngest in the room and still knew only part of the challenge they faced did not seem to matter.

Everyone felt more positive now the information engraved on the two stolen daggers had been recovered - whatever it meant. They were back level again.

Helen reiterated Sam's suggestion that finding the solution and placing it in the public domain might be their best hope, perhaps their only hope to thwart their attackers, to bring the business to a close. Xavier had applauded the idea but cautioned over the danger. Those arrayed against them were not small-time locals. They faced a serious threat, an international threat that was focused, rich in resources and clearly very well informed.

In spite of a shared resolve to turn the tide, they did not even know their enemy, though they agreed with Xavier's earlier suggestion that whoever it was would themselves need to be a holder of one of the daggers; it did seem the only way the killer could have come across information about the daggers and known that Scotland and Edinburgh was at the heart of the puzzle.

Sam insisted the best way to discover who they were up against was for them to track down the other dagger holders, to rule them out, one by one. And that would leave their enemy exposed. Though they would have to be careful such a hunt did not carry them straight to the killer's door. Unfortunately, they did not know where John Dearly had hidden his dagger, which somehow seemed to be the key to finding all the other daggers and their holders.

While the previous day's search of the church had proven fruitless, it was agreed that Elaine would return to the church and resume the search. Francis could not help at once; he had to attend a long-standing engagement with his bishop, but promised to join Elaine at the church as soon as possible.

Sam also had to leave for the moment. He had been invited to visit DCI Wallace at St Leonard's Police Station to deliver his report on what if anything he had found in the MacPhersons' house, and, to answer a couple of questions, which was slightly disconcerting. Sam had no intention of telling the police what they had found in the garden workshop, but nonetheless was happy his report on the contents of the house itself would be comprehensive and truthful. He promised to return as soon as possible.

Xavier had paused to read some messages on his phone before announcing that he would make both himself and Angelo available later that morning and would help wherever they were needed most. First, he wanted to spend a little time on his own church's business that was being neglected in his absence.

The meeting ended on an optimistic note as the furniture delivery van arrived and Grace came downstairs to oversee installation of the new kitchen table. In just a few minutes it was in place, the house was quiet and the people all gone about their business, leaving Helen and Grace alone in the hall.

Helen was not quite sure what to do with Grace. They were friends but she did not want to drag the girl into the firing line. She needed to get Grace away from the manse, so she could get on and search it discreetly. She thought she could scribble down an urgent shopping list and wondered if Grace might go to the shops - but before Helen could suggest it, Grace broke her train of thought.

'Helen, we need to speak.' It was a tone that stressed urgency and as Helen tried to delay, Grace continued. 'We really need to speak now. Whatever else you have planned today, give me ten minutes first, please.' Grace did not wait for a response but turned and headed into the kitchen.

Helen followed her, figuring ten minutes either way would not matter and if nothing else, it would enable her to write a longer shopping list. Sight of the new kitchen table triggered a shiver right through her body. She forced herself to sit, being careful not to take the place John had normally used.

She looked at Grace who seemed a little on edge, seemed to be almost avoiding her eye. 'Grace, what do you want to tell me? Are you in some kind of trouble?'

Grace hesitated, and then shook her head. She sat down in the place at the kitchen table she had considered hers all her life. 'No. No, I'm fine, you don't need to worry about me, but you're in trouble, I know that for sure,' said Grace.

'What do you mean, Grace?' said Helen. Her guilt at keeping Grace in the dark was assuaged by the knowledge that it would keep her safe, but she could not allow Grace to start ruminating on half-truths and guesses. She could now see that Grace would need some explanation of events. The truth, but perhaps not complete; enough information to keep her content, but not enough to put her at risk.

They looked at one another, neither quite ready to start.

'Well? What's bothering you?' Supportively, Helen reached across and squeezed Grace's forearm as it rested on the new table.

'You're looking for something,' said Grace, a statement not a question.

'Yes,' said Helen, trying to think where the conversation was heading. 'I am looking for something. Something of John's. How do you know? You shouldn't be worrying about it though,' she hesitated for a moment. 'It's just something I need to find so I can do the job properly. If, when, I take over his post.'

Grace fixed her gaze down on her hands and nodded an acknowledgement. 'It seems you've got everyone looking for it, everyone except me. Francis, my mum, Sam, even Angelo and old Xavier are getting stuck in, but you're keeping me out.' She looked up, fixing Helen with an almost defiant stare. 'I grew up here. The church, this manse, they were my playground. John looked after me here. Let me help out over school holidays when my mum was at work. This place and John mean just as much to me as to anyone else, maybe more.'

Helen tried to placate her. 'I know that Grace, I know this is your home patch. I know you loved John too.'

'So don't leave me out then. I want to help too. I'm on your side, Helen. And I know stuff,' Grace was desperate to help. 'I may not be so clever, or some tough guy or heavyweight like the others, but you know what? I care too.'

Helen tried again to deflect her. 'It's not that easy, Grace. I know it sounds weird, but sometimes there is stuff it's better not to know. Safer not to know, even.'

Grace gave Helen an almost scornful look. 'You think I don't know? I'm not stupid. I told you I know this place, better than anyone alive, better than my mum even.' She stood up. 'Come on, follow me.' Leading Helen into the study, she switched the radio on and without speaking turned and headed up the stairs. Helen hurried after her, catching up just as Grace entered the master bedroom and slid open an air vent set in the wall. Instantly, the room filled with the sound of the radio flowing with perfect clarity through the air vent from the study below. Helen realised immediately what it meant.

'Grace, you heard all this morning's conversation?' said Helen.

Any sense of guilt at having eavesdropped had been swept aside by the growing sense of indignation over her exclusion and in the knowledge that she was the only one who could help solve the problem. 'I heard everything this morning, and the previous meetings too. And you know what? You're all wasting your time,' said Grace, with supreme confidence.

Helen was mortified. Grace had plunged herself right into the middle of the danger zone, made herself a target to be silenced too. She would have to warn Elaine and the others at once. 'Oh Grace, you shouldn't have done this, you don't understand the danger.'

'Of course I do. I've listened, I've watched, I've seen,' Grace was not making an apology for her actions. 'I've shared things with John too. Remember, for years I was his Grace, his little helper. I know exactly what you're all looking for, in fact, I know better than any of you. I know where it is.' Grace ran out of words. Her defiance spent, she turned away to stand at the bedroom window, looking out over the drive, her eyes full of tears; sadness for John, frustration at the way the others had excluded her, exhilaration at getting her message out at last, and, lurking in the corners, a growing fear at what might now be coming her way.

Helen was stunned by the revelation, but she moved instinctively to Grace's side, sliding an arm around her shoulder to support her. Grace was comforted by her friend's presence and bent her head towards Helen as they stood for a long moment resting against one another. Eventually, Helen pulled gently on Grace's shoulder and turned her back into the room, pressing a tissue into her hand.

'Friends?' said Helen.

Grace nodded again and they both smiled. Helen kissed her cheek and led her towards the stair. 'Come on girl, I think you and I need to put the world to rights,' said Helen.

Helen could tell that Grace was not going to be fobbed off and maybe she really did have the information they needed. If so, Grace more than anyone else had to be within the circle of friends, to receive what little protection, if any, they might be able to offer. As soon as the pair had settled back at the kitchen table Helen tried to phone Elaine. She needed to know that her daughter was becoming involved.

When Grace realised who Helen was calling she had given a resigned shrug of agreement, accepting that Helen would need to make the call. Elaine did not answer her phone. It would be safe in the pocket of her jacket and that was invariably left hanging in the vestry while she worked in church. She probably could not hear it ringing. Putting the phone down, Helen turned her focus back to Grace.

'Well, Grace, what is it that you want to share with me?' asked Helen, feeling guilt at allowing her in still deeper, but real excitement too. Perhaps Grace really did have the answers they needed.

Grace grinned nervously at her. 'I know you are looking for a dagger, and I know you'll never find it. John had a great hiding place; no one would ever think of looking there. It was just sheer luck that I discovered it, and it was the only time I ever saw him even close to being angry with me. He made me promise never to tell. I never have,' said Grace. She looked at Helen and waited for a response.

Helen nodded, considering carefully the implications of Grace's words. A sudden thought crossed Helen's mind and she pulled Sarah MacPherson's reproduction of the dunes dagger from her bag. She placed it slowly on the table. 'Does this look familiar?' she said.

Grace gave a gasp. 'Where did you get that from? How did you get it?' she said, puzzled. Then, on turning the blade, she visibly relaxed. 'Oh, it's not the same. It's not John's dagger, similar, but not the same.'

'How do you know it's not the same?' said Helen, surprised at Grace's confident assertion.

Grace allowed her fingers to trace the pattern engraved on the blade's side. 'That's easy, they look the same in almost every way, but this one has a pattern on it, and this single Roman number, see? John's blade has no pattern, just a random column of Roman numbers engraved down the blade. Like this number here, but lots of them, different numbers.'

Helen's mind was buzzing, she almost had to pinch herself; the parish dagger really existed, it was within their grasp. To be able to describe the difference, Grace must really have seen the parish dagger, must really know where it is. At last, they were going to get ahead of the game. She fixed a calm face and pressed Grace for details. 'So, where is it then? What hiding place has been so good that nobody, including your mum, has ever discovered it?'

Grace gave a knowing smile and felt a burden sliding off her shoulders. 'I only found it by accident, years ago. I'll show you. It's in the church. We can go over there now.'

Helen wondered why Elaine could not find it. She knew the church so well and yet her daughter had managed just to stumble across it. Well, they would know soon enough. 'Come on then,' she said, standing, 'your mother's over there now. Let's go and surprise her.'

Grace stood up to follow Helen out of the manse. 'I'm only going to show you, Helen. John made me promise to keep it a secret. He said it was a great secret that had lasted for years, and only the minister should know it. Then, of course me too, because I found it. But he knew he could trust me.'

Sensing Grace's concern, Helen gave assurance that she need show only her. Then, as a minister, it would be up to her to decide who needed to know, who to share the secret with. She could feel that Grace was not entirely happy with this response, but they left the manse and turned out of the driveway onto the road, walked the short distance to the corner, turned right to head north along the main road to church. They reached the church's great doors and found them closed and locked.

Helen knew immediately that things were not right. Elaine should be inside searching for the dagger. She could see the newly installed alarm system's active light was out, so the system was disabled. This didn't make any sense. If Elaine was here, the doors should be open; if she had gone away, she would surely have switched the alarm system back on. Helen tried her key in the lock; for some reason the door was jammed. With growing unease, they walked quickly down the side of the church to the rear access, the old wooden door set at the end of the short corridor behind the vestry. It was securely locked too and only Elaine carried that key. Helen tried Elaine's phone again, but it rang out without answer.

Grace tensed and pressed her ear to the outside of the old wooden door. A very faint ringing could be heard from the inside, the sound becoming clearer with recognition. 'It's my mum's phone, it must be in her jacket hanging in the vestry,' said Grace. 'She can't have left the building. She always keeps her keys in the jacket too, with the phone.' Her voice was breaking as worry for her mother started to take a grip. 'She must still be inside, so where is she? Why isn't she answering her phone?'

Grace banged on the door with her hand, but it was tight fitting and solid hardwood. It scarcely made a sound in response to her blows. 'Mum. Mum. Come on, open up. Mum! Mum! We need in. It's me and Helen, open up,' her voice rose in volume and pitch as anxiety bit deeper. A couple of kicks at the solid wooden door generated no significant extra sound and Grace stepped back, scanning up the soaring wall of the church in a futile attempt to spot a way in; there was none.

As Grace continued to beat on the door, Helen phoned Sam. His phone went straight to answer phone; he must already be in the meeting with DCI Wallace. Perhaps she should just phone the police directly. Suddenly, Grace turned away from the door and raced back the way they had come while muttering what seemed like garbled nonsense. Helen ended her call and gave chase, hoping to calm Grace down.

• • •

From behind the vestry's net curtains, unseen eyes watched them go. Satisfied, they turned to focus on activity within the church. 'They've gone. Carry on, while we can.' The voice delivered perfect English but with the slightest of French accents. The women would certainly raise the alarm, but he had been assured by Cassiter that the police response time would be about twenty-five minutes, perhaps even thirty: much longer than might normally be expected for the city.

Cassiter, ever resourceful, had organised his people to create a scattering of diversions across the city if required. They were now required: a car crash, a tenement fire, some yobs brawling, a nasty assault on two elderly ladies as they made their way to their local pensioners' club, and a firearms incident in

Leith, the city's port. Cassiter sent a single letter text message that launched his mini crime wave. Time was tight but still on their side. Every officer on duty in the city would right now become very busy dealing with a flurry of serious emergency calls. Very soon the force would be putting out requests for reinforcements from neighbouring areas. A securely locked church door and the alarm not sounding would hardly be a top priority for the emergency call handlers right now.

With an encouraging wave of his hand, Parsol started his two guards back to work. Elaine's arms and legs were immobilised, tied tight to an office chair that had been placed in the middle of the vestry. The two men resumed their steady assault. After each blow to her face or head, a gasp of pain slipped through her teeth and out of the vestry into the nave where it seemed to fill the whole church. Then as silence returned, the next blow was delivered, triggering a further wave of anguished sound and a fresh spattering of blood onto the old and threadbare rug that covered the middle of the vestry floor.

Cassiter and Parsol stood in silence, watching the men work. The guards were enthusiastic in their task, but Cassiter was a little disappointed in their traditional approach, confident that for all their blunt force his creative brand of interrogation would have brought answers more quickly. A sustained beating like this was certain to break the woman's jaw quite soon and one thing he knew was that people with broken jaws did not say very much. But Parsol paid the bill so he could choose the tune.

Like the other men, Parsol was dressed in a disposable forensic suit. He felt slightly uncomfortable in it; but was nonetheless enjoying the spectacle. However, not to the exclusion of his main goal. And as the blows steadily turned Elaine's face to a swollen bloody mess without producing answers, he was becoming frustrated. He looked beyond the guards and their violence, focusing once again on the church's safe, now empty, its door hanging open. The fool McPhee had actually carried the key to the church safe on her personal key ring.

He crossed the room to the table where the safe's contents had been placed for inspection. His first scan had been fruitless, now he decided to go over things again. To the sounds of Elaine's breaking body and her cries of pain, he gathered the contents back into a pile and methodically reviewed each item. Papers, cheque books, various statements, some small trinket boxes and the carry case for the church's old set of communion silver: nothing. He looked at the communion silver disdainfully; these Scottish churches were so austere, so plain.

Then, on an impulse, he grabbed the carry case and emptied out the silver. Plate, cup and cross tumbled onto the table and clinked together as they landed. Parsol shook the empty carry case, heard nothing. He produced a knife and slashed at the velvet lining, ripping it out so he could look into the carcass of the box. Nothing, it was empty. Parsol cursed and threw it down onto the table.

'Make her speak. Make her speak, now!' said Parsol, urging his men on. They picked up the speed of delivery, a synchronised attack, one from the left, one from the right, blow after blow. Elaine's head now had no time to recoil or settle from one blow before it was being propelled in the other direction. She was not going to last much longer.

Cassiter gripped Parsol's arm. 'She's not going to speak like this. Time's running out, perhaps you should let me take over?' he said, his voice steady and unflappable. All the while, he discreetly eyed the woman's tightly bound hands. The skin showing one or two blemishes, marking her progress into middle age - some wrinkling too, but nonetheless, slim feminine fingers, exposed, defenceless, flexing and clenching in response to each head blow she received. He felt a stirring in his belly as he imagined how she would squeal under his touch.

Parsol acknowledged the suggestion, but thought he would persist with the guards a little more; she could not hold out much longer.

• • •

'Grace, slow down. Running about is not going to help anyone,' said Helen, as she finally caught up with the girl halfway back to the manse. She gripped Grace's arm and applied just enough weight to make her slow up.

Grace resisted for a moment; then allowed Helen to pull her to a stop. She turned to look Helen in the eye and waved back towards the church. 'Helen, we've got to get in there. I know my Mum's inside and if she's not opening the door then what's stopping her? We've got to get her out now.'

Helen did not bother answering the question directly. She had a dark fear that she knew exactly what was stopping Elaine and if they didn't act at once, it would be too late. It was clear that Grace shared that same fear. How do you break into a church with reinforced wooden doors? Helen did not have an answer.

Grace did. She headed off again, making for the manse. 'Come on, I know what to do. There's a way, I'll show you.'

This time Helen did not try to stop her, but kept pace as they ran together along the road. Arriving first, Grace rattled the door handle in frustration. 'Open it, quick,' she shrieked.

Helen eased her to one side, unlocked the door and they both stepped inside.

'Lock it,' said Grace.

Helen looked surprised, hesitated and then decided to humour the girl and locked the door from the inside.

In the hallway, Helen finally got the chance to challenge Grace. 'Grace, what on Earth are you doing? We've got to get your mother out, not lock ourselves away in here. Wait a moment, just stop!'

'Down here,' said Grace, ignoring Helen's instruction, heading off along the hallway and through the access door to the basement stairs. 'There's another way into the church,' she shouted over her shoulder as they hurried down the stair into the basement. The stairway down and the basement passage at the bottom were well lit by a series of powerful electric lights. The walls of rough-hewn sandstone had never been bleached by acid rain or burning sun and they appeared as clean cut today as the day they had first been set in position.

Leading off the passage were doorways into a series of four big storerooms, two to the right and two to the left. Several times she had been into the first of the storerooms, the biggest room where old parish records and mementos of previous eras were stored. These rooms were to have been part of her search target for today, before this latest problem had arisen.

Grace quickly led Helen past the last of the doorways and four metres further along the passage came to an abrupt end, just about where it should, at the edge of the building's foundations. Helen pressed her hand on the solid wall and turned to Grace. 'Grace, there's nothing here. We need to get back to the church now, raise the alarm and try to force our way in somehow,' she said.

Grace shook her head and pulled Helen back from the dead end, then stepped into the place Helen had vacated. 'Trust me, just watch,' she said, pressing her body and face up against the dead end wall. Slowly she slid her feet apart, steadily sliding them out across the passageway's flagstone floor. Her feet came to a halt against the bottom of the sandstone walls. She twisted her ankles to force her toes out against the lowest sandstone blocks. Raising her arms she stretched her hands out as far as she could, her body seemed to describe a saltire cross against the dead end wall. Her hands carefully felt the stones above her head. Selecting particular stones, she pressed these too. The four invisible pressure points activated in unison, triggering an almost inaudible click and the whole end wall against which Grace was pressed simply disappeared.

Helen looked on in disbelief. The wall had slid away to reveal a dark chasm, but then a series of lights started flickering into life, lighting a stairway down.

'What on earth is this?' said Helen.

Grace looked at her and gave a fierce grin. 'Told you so,' she said. 'Come on. This leads right into the church.'

They both stepped into the secret stair and paused. Helen noted that the false wall was in fact a finely crafted door dressed with a thin veneer of stone. Grace selected spots near the top of the secret stairway and repeated her previous foot slide motion against stones at the base of the wall, this time triggering a closing mechanism. The wall closed behind them and they were sealed in.

'Always close the door,' said Grace. 'I'll show you the trick later.'

Helen nodded, a hundred questions buzzing in her mind but she knew they would have to wait. If Elaine was in trouble, there was not a moment to lose. By the time they reached the foot of the stair Helen guessed they must be six, maybe seven metres below ground. Another dead end; Grace repeated her stretch and flex exercise and with another almost inaudible click the blank wall in front of her opened. It led directly into a black space, then more electric lights started to flicker on and Helen saw it was a tunnel that stretched off into the distance. Once they were in the tunnel, Grace paused briefly to close the door; it slotted back into the wall, smooth, featureless, invisible. The pair set off at a run along the well-lit and perfectly crafted tunnel.

Helen focused on keeping pace with Grace, yet she could not help but marvel at the tunnel. It was dry, the air was fresh and the evenly spaced lights ran away into the distance until finally vanishing around a gentle bend. The uniform const-ruction meant it was hard to judge distances with any accuracy. Grace stopped abruptly and Helen bumped into her, they held onto each other for a moment to avoid falling. Then, steadied, Grace started to cast about, searching out a particular sequence of stones where the walls met the tunnel floor.

'Where are we Grace? What is this place? Whose is it?' said Helen, firing out questions between gasps as she caught her breath again.

Grace had found the stones she wanted and was pos-itioning her feet to either side of the tunnel floor. 'It's our tunnel and we can get into the church here. It links the manse, the church, and somewhere else too. I don't know where it ends up. It just seems to go on forever. John made me promise not to go and see, so I didn't.' Grace started to press her feet out against the stones. 'Step back a little, you're in the door's way.' Helen took two paces back.

The now familiar sound, that almost inaudible click, signalled the opening door. It slid back to rest at the point where Helen had been standing. Beyond the newly open doorway, more lights flickered on automatically to illuminate a stairway that rose steeply away from them. They entered.

Once Grace had closed the tunnel entrance behind them Helen went to lead but Grace held her back. 'I know this bit, you'll have to let me lead,' she said.

Helen nodded. 'Be careful though, we don't know what's up there.'

The pair moved silently up the stone steps and then came to an abrupt halt at a dead end. Helen felt no surprise this time as Grace spread her limbs, wedging her feet against the lowest row of stones to either side of the top step, her hands stretched up above her head and pressed into secret places. The click sounded first and then the dead end wall at the top of the stair slipped away. The stairway lights behind them shone out to illuminate a wood panelled space, for all the world like some giant broom cupboard beneath a stair. She could not place where they were in the church. Then in a flash it dawned on her, the inverted staircase she could see running up the side and spiralling over their heads was certainly the underside of a staircase. There was one in the church, built into the great pulpit. They were beneath the pulpit.

With another almost inaudible click, the space suddenly went dark as Grace closed the stairway door behind them. 'Keep close to the side, next to me,' whispered Grace, as she tugged Helen back against the now closed stone door. Helen could sense Grace's hands moving firmly and confidently in the darkness above her head and then suddenly a crack of daylight appeared above them, quickly broadening out until the space above them was all daylight. The pulpit floor had dropped smoothly down, light flooding in behind it to illuminate a short stepladder that would carry them up into the pulpit and allow them to walk down the steps into the nave. It was the perfect concealment of an access point: no trap door; the whole floor was the door.

This time Helen did not allow Grace to take the lead. She gripped the little handrails and pulled herself up the stepladder. Slowly she emerged into the pulpit and allowing her head to rise above it, she looked around. There was nobody in sight so she climbed out cautiously onto the pulpit's top step and then hurried down into the body of the church. Grace was right behind her. They stood in silence. Helen had a restraining hand on Grace's arm, listening to nothing, not a sound.

Just as Helen decided it was safe to search the building, the silence was shattered by a howl. A woman's long and agonising cry rolled out from the vestry and circulated round the church, bouncing across the nave. Both feared what the sound meant and raced for the vestry, Helen leading and Grace behind but making up ground fast. As they reached the vestry door Grace hit the front.

In the vestry, Elaine McPhee remained tied to the chair; crouched beside her was Cassiter. Elaine's body arched against her restraints as Cassiter worked the little finger of her right hand. It was snapped at both the first joint and the knuckle. Cassiter was busy grinding the parts of the broken digit back together, like a mortar and pestle, his actions triggering repeated and unbearable jolts of pain. Cassiter did not expect her to hold out much longer, but to accelerate the process he would snap the next finger. The guards had been stood down and now watched Cassiter at work; fascinated at the level of pain that was being generated for such little effort. They made mental notes so they could use the same technique in the future.

Cassiter did not have a chance to defend himself as Grace burst in. Throwing herself across the vestry, screaming and swearing in rage she rushed at Cassiter's crouching form. Her foot caught him square in the back sending him sprawling across the floor. Grace reached her mother and knelt to kiss her face, to touch her, but she stopped herself, aghast, confronted by the swollen mess that had once been her mother's face and frightened that any contact would cause further suffering.

Helen caught up with Grace and at the same moment they both saw Elaine's right hand, swollen, the little finger obscenely distorted, still attached but somehow no longer part of the limb. Neither of the young women had a chance as the two bodyguards, lacking in imagination but strong on reflex, moved into action.

The larger bodyguard circled Helen's waist with his left arm and lifted her bodily off the ground. He tilted her over and held her locked tight like a parcel tucked under his arm, then moved her away from the chair, restrained her flailing right hand with his and let her legs kick out vainly into empty space behind him. A little woman like this? It was too easy. He looked to Parsol for instructions.

The second bodyguard punched Grace hard in the back of the head jolting her forward. As she staggered, he moved in close. He quickly secured her in a headlock with his left arm; trapping her head tightly and keeping her bent double to the waist. He swung his right arm round to bring the flat of his hand hard into her face. He forced his hand tight over her mouth, muffling her outraged cursing, threats and objections. The bodyguard grinned triumphantly at his partner, and then he smirked at Elaine McPhee whose eyes no longer registered pain, just despair for her daughter.

Cassiter pulled himself up off the threadbare rug, handkerchief dabbing at the little trickle of blood that seeped from the graze on his chin where it had rubbed into the stick hard carpet fibres. He was about to place a carefully aimed kick between Grace's legs when Parsol intervened. 'Stop. Hold them tight, but don't hurt them, yet,' he said.

During the commotion Parsol had manoeuvred himself to the vestry door that opened into the little corridor. He was carefully positioned, half in and half out of the doorway, just in case a retreat had been called for. Now it was clear his men had things under control he could exploit this interruption.

With a quick and rueful glance at his bloodied handkerchief, Cassiter stuffed it beside his phone in the pocket of his forensic suit. Then he joined Parsol at the doorway. 'We've got ten minutes at most before the police arrive and we become trapped. We must get what we need now,' said Cassiter.

Parsol nodded. 'Let's carry on with the old woman; you were doing such a good job before we were interrupted. If she won't tell us herself I think the ladies will want to give us what we need to know very quickly,' he said, allowing a little smile to spread around his mouth. Then he spoke to his bodyguards. 'You two, turn them around so they can see the old woman's suffering. Get them in close. I want them to feel her pain.'

The bodyguards responded at once. Grace, still in the vice-like headlock, found herself turned to face her mother. The other bodyguard, carrying a now unresisting Helen still locked under his arm, moved to stand beside his colleague. Confidently he released her right arm, which she allowed to drop down towards the floor. She did not cry out when the guard used his now free hand to take a strong grip of her hair, jerking her head up so she looked directly at Elaine.

Cassiter stepped away from the door and once again crouched beside Elaine. He smiled up at the two younger women. 'Well ladies, ready for a show? We're in a bit of a hurry now so I'll have to push on. Just tell us where the dagger is and it will all be over. Simple. The ball's in your court, ladies,' and as he spoke Cassiter reached out and took Elaine's broken finger and twisted it a little as he smiled serenely at Grace. Elaine's scream filled the room but Grace could respond only with a futile, anger driven struggle.

Helen's captor was enjoying the spectacle and pleased he had the easier girl to control; he relaxed a little to take in the show. He could see that after the little refresher tweak, Cassiter had now abandoned the broken finger and taken the woman's second finger in his hand. A firm and unrelenting pressure was now bending it out of line, it would break at any moment and the guard was watching carefully; this time he wanted to see the woman's face just at the moment it snapped.

Helen was ready. She thought for a moment of her darkest days in Africa. When you strike, strike to win. The tips of the fingers on her left hand were curled in tight to make a blunt faced wedge. She twisted her whole body half a turn from the waist so she was looking up into her captor's face, not even registering the pain as her hair came out in his hand. For a fraction of a second he was surprised at how agile she was and how his grip on her hair had suddenly gone. The initial surprise was replaced by shock as Helen continued the momentum of her body twist, swinging her left arm up from below and thrusting her wedge shaped hand up hard into his throat, pushing his Adam's apple back deep into his neck, crushing into his windpipe.

The guard dropped with a gasp and a whimper, clutching his throat and thrashing his legs in an unsuccessful search for relief. The second guard was only just registering that his partner was down as Helen scrabbled up to her knees and punched him hard in the groin: once, twice, he had no defence while still holding Grace, three and out. In just a moment, Grace was free and her captor lay on the ground writhing. She gave him a kick as she moved to join Helen who was closing on Cassiter.

They all froze in response to two shots Parsol fired into the ceiling. 'Stay still. Move and you're dead,' said Parsol, from his position at the door. He pointed the pistol towards Helen and Grace.

Cassiter rose, grinning. 'Nice try ladies, but not up to the mark I'm afraid,' he said, then paused to listen. The sound of a distant siren wormed its way through the vestry window; he turned to Parsol, 'Police. We have to go.'

Parsol nodded agreement. 'Yes, but we have too many loose ends here. We must tidy things first.' He waved the muzzle of his pistol towards his men who lay completely disabled on the ground, 'Can they move?'

Cassiter stooped to check them, then shaking his head he glanced back at Parsol, 'Not in the time we've got.'

Parsol nodded an acknowledgement. 'Well they'll have to stay too,' he said, turning his pistol on the guard with the damaged windpipe. In an excellent demonstration of marksmanship, he stretched out the pistol, gripping it carefully with both hands and shot the man in the head twice, dead. He trained the gun on the second guard. Both hands, a steady stare down the barrel, he could see the guard, one hand grasping his groin in nature's response to the blows received, the other outstretched towards Parsol. A futile barrier raised by a defenceless man, able to comprehend what was about to happen but powerless to respond. He looked up at the pistol in fear, then suddenly averted his gaze, dropped his hand, resigned. Two shots and he was dead. This did impress Cassiter and he made a mental note of Parsol's shooting ability.

'Now, let's get rid of the rest of them, shall we?' said Parsol. He turned the gun towards Helen, who glared back at him. She stood defiant yet resigned, with one comforting hand resting on Grace's shoulder while the girl knelt trying to protect and share a last moment of love with her mother.

Cassiter nodded, but was mindful of the distant sirens. 'Yes, but do it now, we need to be gone,' he said.

Helen stared at Parsol and his pistol as it lined up on her face. This was the end. She was angry at these monsters and at herself. She did not fully understand what had happened but knew she had let her friends down. For one moment she even registered sadness that she had failed in her task, whatever it was. Evil was triumphing and John's trust in her had been misplaced. She had led the people she loved and trusted into terrible suffering and there was nothing she could now do, except pray. She pulled her head fully upright. Glaring defiantly back along the barrel into Parsol's eye, Helen started the Lord's Prayer. 'Our Father, who art in heaven, Hallowed be thy name…'

Parsol gave a little laugh as she prayed, and then spoke over her prayer. 'Little lady, you should have given me what I wanted. It's too late for you now, and certainly too late for your prayers. I don't think your God hears you, hmmm?' As he spoke he steadied the pistol with both hands, fixed his final aim but didn't fire, he seemed frozen. Helen had seen the accuracy of his previous shots, and she could not understand why she was still alive. She continued her prayer, determinedly holding his eye.

She noticed Parsol's head seemed to twitch very slightly, jerking a little away from the doorframe. As it moved, it was followed by the silver barrel of a neat little pistol pressed hard against the side of his skull.

'I think, perhaps, God does hear her prayer,' Xavier's voice spoke from the gloom of the corridor.

Cassiter spun in alarm as Angelo pushed Parsol clear of the doorframe by applying more pressure against his skull with the pistol's muzzle. Xavier stepped round to take Parsol's pistol from his hand. 'Mine now, I think, yes?' Xavier pointed the pistol at Cassiter. 'Don't move. I would hate to have to shoot a man in the house of God, but if needs must, well…'

Xavier looked over to Helen. 'Say nothing, we must get rid of these dogs first,' he said. 'Then we fix things.'

More out of disbelief than agreement, Helen nodded. At that moment she didn't much care what Xavier meant by *get rid of*, was just pleased her people were still alive. She did wonder for just a second about priests with guns, but then it did not seem the biggest issue of the moment and she pushed the thought aside. Xavier and Angelo guided Parsol and Cassiter away down the little corridor towards the old wooden door. Helen registered that it was now open but didn't question how Xavier had managed that.

Helen went to help Grace untie her mother; with her nurse's training, Helen could help Elaine, but not much here.

It may have been better to sit tight, but nature kicked in. Fight or flight. With the first rush of adrenalin subsiding, primeval instinct overrode everything: flight. Helen and Grace struggled to get Elaine away from the danger zone. They got her to her feet and hurried her through to the nave, up into the pulpit and down into the dark space beneath. Elaine was too dazed and hurt to register any surprise as Grace opened the doorway into the stair beneath.

With them safe inside the tunnel, Helen headed back towards Xavier. She could not understand why the police had not arrived, but perhaps she could stop any more killings.

Moving through the vestry, she opened the door that fed into the little corridor beyond, and her senses were assaulted by the roaring engines of a police helicopter as it arrived above the church. It seemed to be hovering directly beyond the open door; she knew it was close, she could feel its downdraught blowing right along the little corridor. Xavier and Angelo were between her and the door; beyond them, and controlled by the pressure of pistol muzzles in their backs, were Cassiter and Parsol. They were all stood just inside the doorway, invisible to the helicopter and its camera that was recording every visible detail of the scene while transmitting a live radio account back to the police incident commander and his control team.

• • •

In his control unit, the incident commander listened impassively to the audio feeds from his teams. He waited, building a full picture in his mind's eye before committing his force. Following a passer-by's report of a woman's tortured screams and then gunfire from the church, his men had closed the road immediately in front of the church. Now it was clear of civilians, allowing his squads unfettered access once he gave the word, and he was almost ready. Just waiting for the armed response units that were due to arrive at any moment. They had been delayed following their attendance at a bogus firearms incident on the other side of the city, in Leith.

In the meantime, the incident commander wanted a complete visual scan of the area from above - he still didn't know if this was a robbery gone wrong, some sort of religious terrorism or perhaps a domestic flare up that had gone way over the top.

Whatever the cause, he was taking no chances. He had reports of people running about in the grounds, cries of pain, sounds of gunfire and the church's great wooden doors were jammed shut, barring access. Now the scene seemed suddenly quieter and as he had a helicopter available, a few moments spent appraising the situation could save lives. His squads were champing at the bit to go in, once the helicopter sweep was completed and the armed response teams had arrived he would unleash them all.

• • •

In the vestry corridor the engine roar subsided as the helicopter veered away, circling to look at the other side of the church and then to sweep on out across the cemetery; to give the incident commander the full picture he wanted.

Xavier pressed the pistol harder into Parsol's back. 'I think it is your lucky day today,' he said. Then, aware that Helen was behind him he spoke to her over his shoulder so Parsol and Cassiter could hear. 'We can leave these two for the police, yes? Justice for them and it keeps our hands clean,' he flashed her a dry smile as he finished speaking.

'Perfect,' said Helen. 'We've moved Elaine, but we need to get back to her now.'

Xavier nodded and turned his head back towards Parsol, he leaned forward close to his ear. 'You are finished here, there is nothing for you. You have lost,' Xavier spoke quietly, almost hissing the words. Then he leant even closer so Parsol could feel his breath against his neck. 'Who are you? Why did you come? Where did you come from?'

Parsol turned his head just enough so their eyes could meet. Xavier almost recoiled as he saw a cold and dispassionate blackness in Parsol's eyes, but forced himself to stand and hold the man's gaze.

'You don't need answers to your questions, priest. All you need to know is I never lose. Remember, I never lose,' said Parsol. His calm voice carried a heavy threat that seemed completely incongruous as he had a pistol stuck in his back and was about to step out into the arms of the law.

'Well, I will just have to live without your answers. Time for you to go now, time to meet justice. Time to meet the police, I think,' said Xavier. Pressing pistol muzzles forced Parsol and Cassiter out through the doorway, then Angelo slammed the door shut, locking it with the key Xavier had received from the team he had recently sent to test the church's security. They had not been impressed with the locks but had given them a good clean and oil.

Xavier turned to Helen. 'Now, you know this place. Is there a way out for us? That would be good for Angelo and me. May be good for all of us, yes? I don't think we would be able to explain that little thing away,' he said, nodding towards Angelo's neat little silver pistol as it disappeared into the young priest's jacket.

Helen nodded. 'Grace has a way. Let's go,' she said.

• • •

The helicopter was now out of sight as it continued its sweep of the area. Cassiter gripped Parsol's arm, pulling him along the side of the church away from the main entrance and back to the rear, towards the cemetery. 'Come on,' said Cassiter, 'we have a minute, maybe less before the police move in and are swarming all over this place.'

Parsol followed his lead. Under the circumstances content to trust the local man, particularly as that man was Cassiter. 'Can we get away?' said Parsol as they hurried round the corner of the church, heading for the little rear gate that led directly into the cemetery. Ahead they could see the helicopter moving away from them as it continued its sweep.

'You don't think I would have put all my faith in your two numbskull bodyguards do you?' said Cassiter, still holding Parsol's arm and hurrying him along. 'I'm free because I always have a contingency plan.'

As Cassiter fished in his pocket for a phone, Parsol stumbled against the cemetery gate, dragging them both down, the contents of Cassiter's pocket emptied out. 'Be careful man, damn it, you'll get us both caught,' snapped Cassiter as he scrambled to retrieve the phone, it was unbroken. Straightening up they pushed on into the cemetery, Cassiter pressed speed dial as they ran.

Cassiter's phone rang out once. It was answered immediately. He spoke calmly into the handset. 'Action. Action now,' then he hung up and continued the retreat.

Unnoticed in all the turmoil, Fiona Sharp sat in her car. It was parked just over the wall at the northern end of the cemetery, well beyond the police cordon. She held a little signal control box in her hand. To the left side of the box was a master power switch; strung out in line to the right were five little press button firing switches. Above each switch were sets of LEDs: red, amber, green. She flicked on the master power switch and the LEDs above it started to shine. Amber for a moment then flashed red before settling to a steady green, confirming the device was ready for transmission. The five sets of LEDs to the right were flashing red, amber and green simultaneously. As the transmission sequences readied, the lights one by one switched to amber and finally all glowed a steady green. The device was armed.

With her thumb, she pressed the first firing switch. The LED above it started to flash red as a short-range signal beamed out and activated the first of the packages that a scruffy looking hoodied skateboarder had concealed inside the cemetery's northern wall earlier in the morning. The packages sat roughly spread out along the wall, waiting. For a moment nothing happened, then with a flash and roar several military issue Thunderflashes exploded. She pressed the second firing switch and a flash of light and billowing cloud of smoke supplemented the first blast.

Mirror, indicate, manoeuvre. She pulled smoothly away from the curb and pressed the third switch. Behind her, the road disappeared in a fog of smoke billowing over the cemetery wall. As the roar of the blast subsided, she drove calmly away into the city traffic, pressing the final two switches. More and more smoke billowed out filling the northern part of the cemetery. The police helicopter spun to focus on it, occasional flashes could be seen from inside the swirling opaque mass, possible gunfire?

Parsol and Cassiter continued their hurried move south, to some extent sheltered from above by the partial canopy of tree cover as they wove a route between the gravestones. Behind them, the police teams were pouring into the cemetery from the main gate. Most headed for the smoke and explosions, some headed towards the church. Others started to fan out and search methodically between the graves while keeping a wary eye on the swirling inferno of smoke and explosions. A police team spotted Parsol and Cassiter just as they slipped through the pedestrian access gate near the south-western corner of the cemetery; the little-used wrought iron gate that Cassiter had used on the day he killed John Dearly.

The pair emerged into the road. A scruffy young hoodie who had been sitting quietly on the pavement adjusting the wheels of his skateboard stood up. Without acknowledging them, he threaded a chain through the gates, and then padlocked it shut. Long before the pursuing police arrived, the hooded skateboarder had vanished, a freewheeling citizen skating into anonymity.

Police radios crackled in frustration. Trapped behind the locked gate, the officers could see nobody in the road beyond. Was it a false sighting? Meanwhile, Barnett drove off, his anonymous white works van pulling calmly away from the cemetery, on through the streets, blending into the traffic and away from the scene.

• • •

The sound of explosions outside the church hurried Helen back along the corridor into the vestry, close behind her came Xavier then Angelo. She was surprised to find Grace had returned from the tunnel and was busy scooping the communion set back into its carry case.

'An excellent idea, Grace,' said Xavier. 'Let's leave it looking like a robbery gone wrong, a falling out amongst thieves. Quick now, grab the papers and other things from the safe too.' He pointed at the rug spattered with Elaine's blood and the now broken chair she'd been tied to. 'Angelo, roll all that up and bring the bindings too.' Xavier beamed a slightly incongruous smile towards Helen. 'The two we let go are not the talking type. Professionals. They will say nothing to the police. So, if possible, we don't want to leave anything concrete to place Elaine or any of you in this mess.'

As Xavier stepped closer to Helen, he carefully wiped his prints off the pistol Parsol had used to kill the guards, and then tossed it down onto the ground. 'Now, you said we have a way out. Perhaps this is the moment to leave?' His suggestion was underscored by the sound of running boots passing outside the vestry window, a door handle rattling in vain against its lock, then vigorous kicking on the old wooden door.

Helen nodded. 'Come on, we'll make it if we're quick.' She grabbed Elaine's coat from behind the door as they rushed out into the nave and filed up the steps into the pulpit. One by one, they slipped down into the space below.

An echoing crack came from the front of the church. It was followed by the sound of cautious boot steps spreading out slowly through the nave. They were out of time; the police were in. Grace crouched low on the pulpit steps, keeping her head beneath the rim of the pulpit banister as she urged the others down into the tunnel. Only she knew how to close the pulpit entrance, she needed to be last.

Another crash, this one from the direction of the vestry. The police had now broken open the old wooden door; they were coming from two directions. As the first policeman emerged from the vestry Grace disappeared from view, slithering headfirst down into the space beneath the pulpit, where Helen caught and helped steady her. Grace finally clicked the floor of the pulpit shut as an armed policeman cautiously led his squad around the base of the pulpit. A moment later, the slightest of clicks signalled the sliding shut of the stone doorway into the tunnel stair. For just a second the policeman paused, thinking he heard a sound, but then dismissed it as he and the team continued their search of the church.

At the foot of the stairway, Grace triggered the closing mechanism and the tunnel door slid shut. They were all sealed in. Once Grace had checked on her mother, she pointed in the direction that she and Helen had come from just a little while before. 'This will take us to the manse,' she said. They set off, Grace leading.

For a little while nobody spoke. Xavier was inspecting the construction work as they passed along. He was visibly impressed, from time to time allowing his hand to stroke the clean, dry stone of the walls and then scuff his feet against the still sharp edges of the slabs beneath their feet. These were stones perfectly assembled by real masters of the construction trades, built to last a lifetime. Many lifetimes.

'Helen, this is a great surprise. In all my years of visiting here I had no idea such a thing existed,' said Xavier.

'Me neither. Join the club,' said Helen.

'It is magnificent. The stonework, so good, so powerful, so...' he allowed his eyes to stretch out ahead to where the tunnel vanished in a gentle bend. 'So consistent.' He turned to look over his shoulder at her. 'I know John did not like spending money but clearly his predecessors were happy to.'

'I guess so,' said Helen. They lapsed into silence, their footsteps punctuated only by the sound of Elaine's quiet, rhythmic groans as she leant on Angelo step by step.

In the quiet, Helen considered the tunnel properly for the first time, its origins and purpose. A tingle of surprise, or perhaps it was excitement, was bubbling inside her. It was competing with the remorse, guilt even, which she felt over what had taken place behind them at the church and for her own part in the violent struggle.

Helen wondered what exactly John Dearly had passed to her: the mysterious trust fund, the tunnel, Xavier and Angelo, and to say nothing of the missing parish dagger that everyone seemed to want so desperately and whose location nobody knew. But no - her thoughts froze - Grace knew where it was. It took a mighty effort not to shout out to Grace and demand an immediate answer, but she made herself wait a little longer.

The distance from church to manse was only a few hundred yards, but they were pacing themselves for the slowest, and it was all Elaine could do to shuffle along. Eventually, Grace called a halt. Then she did her now familiar foot spread and ankle wriggle to reopen the stairway up to the manse and to safety.

Chapter 25

WEDNESDAY 19ᵗʰ JUNE, PM

With only a domestic first aid kit available in the manse, there was nothing Helen could do for Elaine's broken hand except carefully guide the arm into a supporting sling. She cleaned up Elaine's face as best she could and tried to sound positive for the groggy patient. However, in addition to the hand she could see both cheeks were broken, along with a broken nose. The jaw had to be fractured too and there was a lot of dental work to be done, to say nothing of the deep shock that was setting in.

Elaine urgently needed hospital treatment, but they were loath to phone for help. A call from the manse for an ambulance would attract immediate attention. It would be like firing a distress rocket, calling in all the emergency services that were massed just up the road at the church.

Helen was finishing Elaine's first aid treatment as Francis arrived back from the meeting with his bishop. She could hear the terse account Xavier was providing without really focusing on the detail; instead, she concentrated on getting Elaine ready to move. Francis looked shocked, listened, nodded, understanding some bits, incredulous at others, and he asked only a few questions. It was clear he understood there would be a time for explanations, but that was not now.

Francis agreed to take Elaine direct to hospital in his car. A nasty fall at home while decorating the stairs, falling headfirst and a hand caught in the banister on the way down. The explanation was flimsy, would not really account for the injuries properly but when delivered by the local priest, with the patient and her daughter in full agreement, it should ensure there was no immediate link to the major on-going firearms incident. Hopefully keeping the police out of things for a while. Grace promised to phone with any news once the hospital had taken a look at Elaine.

Wounded away, Helen finally sat down and was swithering between a large glass of wine and a strong coffee just as Sam arrived; dropped at the door by an anxious DCI Wallace, who waited only long enough to check that Helen and the others had not been embroiled in the incident. Satisfied they were safe in the manse, the policeman raced away to the church. Sam guided her towards the coffee option. He sat and listened to the account delivered jointly by Xavier and Helen.

In the process of unpicking events, it finally became clear why the police had taken so long to arrive. Once gunshots had been reported the unarmed police had sealed the area and waited for the armed officers to arrive, and that could sometimes take a little while, particularly if having to travel from another firearms incident.

Helen relaxed, just a little; she lent her head on Sam's shoulder and sighed. Sam placed his hand over hers and pressed it gently. She twisted her hand so their palms touched; pressed back, felt his warmth. Then the doorbell sounded, a klaxon tearing at their moment's peace, quickly followed by vigorous banging on the door.

They all tensed and Angelo rose to answer the door. 'No wait,' said Helen. She stood up and headed for the front door. 'This is my patch now. Whoever it is will want to speak with me.'

A police constable was at the door. 'I'm looking for Miss Johnson, the assistant minister,' he said.

'You've found her, what can I do for you officer?' said Helen, straining to keep her voice at what might sound a stress free tone. She did not recognise the policeman so he must have been drafted in from one of the other areas to help today.

The police constable looked a little surprised at her accent; he had not been expecting an American. 'You're Helen Johnson? From the church?' he asked, waving a hand in the church's direction.

'That's me, how can I help?' said Helen.

'We've been trying to phone you but it kept going to your answer phone, didn't you hear it ringing?' said the policeman, his voice slightly aggrieved.

Helen gave him the warmest smile she could muster. 'Oh sorry, we've spent much of the morning below ground. You know, down in the basement, gathering old parish papers, parish business, that sort of thing. I must have missed your calls officer,' said Helen, a slight hint of contrition in her voice. 'But please, won't you come in? Tell us what's happening at the church. My friend arrived a little while ago and he says the street's cordoned off and full of police. What's all the commotion, do you think I should be going up there now?'

The constable did not want to enter, annoyed that he had been sent away from the action on a simple errand - he wanted back to the locus as soon as possible.

'Well, we like to think explosions, theft, a gunfight and dead bodies in a church is a bit more than just a commotion,' he said, then paused for effect. He was quietly pleased at Helen's shocked reaction. Mellowing, he proceeded to deliver his message. 'DCI Wallace has asked that you stay where you are. We think the immediate danger is past, but he wants you to keep inside and ensure the property is secured.'

'Do you think we are in danger officer?' she asked.

'With mad stuff like this going on everyone's at some risk. We can't quantify it yet. Please do as he asks. And he wants to know if any of your congregation would have been in the church this morning?'

'I can't say exactly, off hand. Why? Is it important?' Her tone was becoming more anxious, which the policeman attributed to her lack of information and worry about the incident.

'There are dead bodies in the church. We need to know if they are from your congregation or outsiders.'

'My God!' Sam pressed forward to the front door, putting a protective arm around Helen. 'We'll stay here officer, but what's happened? What can we do to help?'

The policeman switched his focus to Sam. 'Who are you sir?'

'Oh, yes. Sam Cameron, I'm Helen's…urgh, Helen's partner. What do you want us to do?'

'Stay indoors, secure the premises. And can you start to phone around the congregation? Ensure everyone's safe, see if anyone is unaccounted for. DCI Wallace said he or his sergeant would be along in a while. If you can get that information, it would be a big help. Is that clear?'

Sam nodded and Helen started to ask a further question but the policeman lifted a hand to cut her off. 'Now don't worry, just do as the DCI asks and you'll be all right. We have it covered, and everything is under control. I have to get back. Can I tell DCI Wallace you are doing as he asks?'

Helen hardly had time to nod before the officer was running back towards his car.

'Secure the premises now please,' he shouted towards them as he jumped into the driver's seat and fired up the engine. The patrol car pulled out of the drive and raced back to the church and the action.

Helen felt an overwhelming surge of relief that she had been spared revisiting what she knew to be a very messy crime scene and had also avoided having to answer any questions for now. The only worry was that the authorities now had free access to the church. While her little team had already carried away the papers from the safe, who knows what else they might find. Her stomach twisted a little, they might even find the dagger.

• • •

Evening had settled slowly over the city and with it descended some semblance of calm. DS Brogan had called round briefly. He gave little away but was happy that Helen had been able to account for all the congregation. He specifically warned her not to approach the church; it was a major crime scene. Tomorrow DCI Wallace would probably want her to accompany them through the church, to identify anything that was missing. In the meantime, could she think of anything that might have triggered the incident? Any people with a reason to be in the church today? Then he had left, content in his mind that Helen was an innocent abroad, floundering about for an explanation and as mystified as everyone else was.

Now in the twilight calm, Helen sat on one side of the new manse kitchen table, her back to the window. Everyone was there: apart from Elaine who was safely installed in the Royal Infirmary. The doctors had not yet decided what should be done about her hand. The finger was so badly damaged they had deferred any decision until the next morning.

Helen had just finished a short prayer for Elaine's recovery, and a little wryly, added thanks that the hospital had accepted Francis' dubious explanation of what had happened to her. Whether or not they believed the story was another matter, perhaps it had just been convenient for everyone to accept it at face value. In any event, right now, the police were far more interested in gunshots and murders and so Elaine's unfortunate domestic decorating accident had slipped under the official radar.

On the table were piled all the papers and other items they had managed to bring away from the church that morning.

'I think we have taken a step forward today,' said Xavier. He raised his hands, pushing away any objections. 'Yes, yes, I know it has been a bad day. Men dead, poor Elaine... But think, those who would hurt us, our enemy, they have faces now. We know how they look, so we know them,' he looked around the table, stretched his arms out to include them all in a circular sweep. 'We don't sit frozen in the headlights now, we know what's coming. We know who is coming, yes?' He looked around, seeking agreement. 'Yes? Yes, you understand?'

After a moment, Sam responded. 'You know, Xavier, I think you're right. We are facing a threat, so it has to be better to know what it is and where it comes from.'

Helen nodded. 'Well we don't know much yet, but we do know their faces. I agree with Xavier too. It's better to know where a threat comes from rather than to just sit and wait. And in the end they are just men.'

'But, is this even a conflict we should be involving ourselves in?' said Francis. 'There must be a way of bringing this to a conclusion? Pray God there must be some way to end it all, surely?'

'They want the parish dagger,' said Helen. 'Give them the dagger and they might go away. But as Xavier said before, I don't think they will. I think that once they have the parish dagger we are all disposable. Until then maybe we have a chance, and they will be very careful around here now, that's for sure. The authorities are on alert and we have shown we are not the pushovers they obviously thought.'

'But we still don't have the parish dagger anyway,' said Sam, 'and I'm not happy with Helen being in the firing line, nor you either, Grace.' He paused.

Helen nodded acknowledgement of his concerns and turned to Grace. 'A first step is to understand what cards we hold. What do you say Grace? Can you, will you bring us the dagger?'

Grace looked uncomfortable. Earlier she had assured Helen that there was nothing to fear over the police or anyone else searching the church, they would never find the dagger. Now, however, the moment had come, Grace knew it, Helen knew it, everyone knew it. Grace needed to share access to the dagger, tell them where it was. If it was the key to the mystery, it was essential they should all be focusing on it.

'Well Grace, I guess it's now or never,' said Helen in an encouraging tone.

Grace looked at Helen while determinedly avoiding eye contact with the others. 'I know you have to know where it is, Helen, but John made me promise never to tell. It was something he would only pass on to his successor; that's you. I know he chose you, so telling you won't really be breaking my promise, and John needs me to do it for him, and to show you the things he can't,' Grace paused for a moment. 'Are you really sure you want me to tell everyone?'

'Grace, I think this is a problem that is going to need many minds to solve,' said Helen. 'The people here were John's friends, and each one of us is still in danger until we unravel the mystery. Please, now is the moment for trust, for keeping faith in one another.' She stretched her hands across the table and pressed her palms down on to Grace's hands, encouraging her, steadying her nerve, feeling the girl's hands tremble beneath her own. 'Please?'

After a long pause, Grace took a deep breath. 'Okay,' she said. 'If you think that's what John would have wanted I'll go along with you.' She slid her hands free from under Helen's and with an outstretched arm pulled the communion case towards her. She removed the cup, plate and cross, placing them in a row on the table. She lifted the box with its ripped lining and gently stroked the damaged cloth back into place. 'I've polished this wooden box a hundred times over the years, cherished it for John, and kept it looking beautiful.' The group began to suspect there must be a hidden compartment that Parsol had missed, but then she put it down on the floor beside her feet.

The room was in silence. They could feel Grace's discomfort, indecision; no one wanted to be the person that distracted her or dissuaded her from revealing the secret. Grace looked at the friends gathered round the table, she reached out and gently laid a finger of her left hand on the cross, she allowed the finger to trail down, lightly caressing the stock and finally resting it on the base. She remained stationary in what seemed a moment of contemplation, perhaps even desperately holding out for some message or a sign of John's wishes from beyond the grave. No sign came.

Helen smiled encouragement. Then in one swift movement, Grace reached her right hand out and gripped the top of the cross while her left hand pressed down on the stock and base, holding it tight to the table. With a firm twist of her right hand, Grace loosed the top of the cross from the stock and drew them apart. As her right hand rose, it drew a shining silver dagger out from the stock. There were gasps of surprise around the room. Grace handed Helen the dagger and sat back quietly while the others leapt up and crowded round to look more closely.

Now Helen understood why the other daggers had seemed so familiar. Their handles and quillons were identical to the top half of her own church's old communion cross, something she had looked at, unseeing, so many times.

Eventually, Grace got the chance to explain that as a youngster she had been busy cleaning the communion set when she had knocked the cross onto the ground and the jolt had twisted the dagger free from the base, its scabbard. She had been horrified, thinking she had broken the cross in two. On closer inspection she realised it was meant to twist and come apart, then John Dearly had come in to see what the noise was. Finding her with the dagger and scabbard instead of a single cross, he had been obliged to swear her to secrecy, which she had kept until today.

Sam was carefully studying the dagger. It was clearly of the same ilk as the others. Where this one did differ was in the apparently random column of numerals engraved down the face of the blade instead of any engraved lines or wavy patterns. One common thread was the Roman numerals on each of the two regular blades also appeared within the parish dagger's numeral column. But this took them no further and with the patterns on the engraved blades not matching up in any way they still faced a dead end. Whatever the symbolism was, it was quite unintelligible, meaningless: Henri de Bello had done a good job.

'Well, I suppose that's what makes a good code. This dagger might be the key, but you can't decipher it unless you're meant to,' said Helen in pragmatic response.

Francis nodded agreement. 'I think it is the key. We just need to recognise the lock.'

Sam was less sanguine. 'Yes, but it's Helen who is meant to be able to read it, isn't it?' he said.

'Well, I can't,' said Helen, gently.

Francis nodded towards Xavier. 'According to Xavier your parish dagger is somehow the key and the hub around which the others are employed. Wouldn't it help if we had Xavier's dagger too? The more information we have the easier it will be to fill in the gaps, to interpolate.'

Xavier gave a slightly mysterious grin. 'Perhaps something can be arranged. But not today,' he said, flashing Helen a real smile and chuckling to himself. 'Tonight all I can say for sure is, like many people, I have always been fascinated by the use of Roman numerals. If I were pressed to pick a favourite, maybe I would like a seven.' Xavier looked at Sam as he finished speaking.

Sam was already checking the list of numerals. 'Seven, VII, it appears on the parish dagger too,' he said, looking back at Xavier.

Xavier gave a little nod. 'Yes, well, it seems a popular number. Now perhaps you will like it too, yes?'

Sam was nodding while considering what extra insight a number seven could bring them. Other than it also appeared on the parish dagger he could see none. 'There must be a pattern to this. For God's sake, we can put men on the moon. Surely we can break this old riddle?'

Francis leant across the table and tapped Sam's arm. 'You know, I wonder if we're going about this the right way? Perhaps there's another approach we should try, something we are missing? Let's sleep on it, start afresh tomorrow, what do you think?'

Sam shrugged. 'I don't know, maybe I'll keep at it a while longer,' he said.

Helen stood up. 'Well, Sam, it's been a long day and I'm beat too. Let's get some sleep now. Try again in the morning. Then we can put together a proper plan; try to solve this once and for all. What do you say? Let's all go home, take a break.'

Reluctantly Sam agreed, but made no move to rise; arguing that knowing the number on Xavier's dagger was not enough. They needed to see the pattern on his blade to build their understanding properly.

Xavier was already standing, leaning on Angelo's arm for support. He conceded that an arrangement might be made, but not unless they all got some sleep and he half waved half beckoned everyone towards the manse's front door. Helen took advantage to shoo them on from behind. It was late and a long day had passed.

• • •

Jim Barnett drove his white van northwards, heading away from the city centre. This late in the evening there was little traffic and he had to force himself to stay below the speed limit, staying inconspicuous, unnoticed. He had left behind the bustling city centre, the confident inner suburbs and then passed the sprawling Western General Hospital. Beyond it, he had slowed at an arterial roundabout and carefully selected his exit route.

Five minutes and several turns later, he pulled into a council housing scheme. Poor, fierce, proud. Here people seemed to get by in spite of the system, not because of it. The law didn't seem to help them much, so people mostly looked the other way. People were careful to mind their own business while struggling to live decent lives against the odds. Not somewhere to drop a fat wallet and expect it to be handed in, mused Barnett. He gave a little smile to himself, not somewhere to take a fat wallet in the first place.

Weaving through the housing scheme, he reached a children's play park. A small island of green, overlooked on every side by housing; flats, mostly three storeys high. The park was empty at this late hour as he pulled to a stop. Some way behind him a saloon car came to a halt, its lights went out as he switched off his own.

He carefully checked around, confirming his first impression that there was nobody on the street and then he went into action. Stepping out of the van, he opened the back door and pulled out a can of petrol. He emptied it over the roof, doors and driver's seat. He threw the petrol can back into the rear of the van and stepped back a little. Then pulled a cigarette packet from his pocket, took the last one, crumpled the pack and discarded it. Quietly, calmly, he pulled out a lighter and lit the cigarette. Drawing deeply, he savoured the sensation of smoke scraping at the back of his throat, rushing down to fill his lungs and the little kick as the nicotine flooded into his bloodstream. He blew the smoke out, took a quick breath, and then drew again on the cigarette.

He didn't flinch as someone came up behind him.

'Come on Barnett, let's go,' said Fiona Sharp. She threw a little signal control box into the back of the van and turned to go back to her car. 'Burn it.'

He shrugged and took another draw on the cigarette, held the smoke in for just a moment. As a car engine fired up behind him, he flicked the glowing cigarette end into the back of the van, turned away and walked over to the car.

From his place in the car's passenger seat Barnett could make out the flames taking hold in the rear of the van as Fiona Sharp drove past it. He gave a snort of satisfaction and they were gone.

Chapter 26

THURSDAY 20th JUNE

Sam woke at five in the morning. The street outside his Marchmont flat had not yet started to fill with the familiar rumble of urban noise and he lay quietly for a moment thinking through his idea. Then, leaping up, he ran into the living room and grabbed the photograph of the museum dagger. He looked at it carefully for a little while, considering the possibilities. Then he hurried to Helen's pillow and gently slid his hand under it, feeling carefully for the parish dagger and Sarah MacPherson's replica of the dune dagger, both of which Helen had decided to sleep with. She stirred and woke with a start and demanded to know what he was up to.

'I've had an idea,' said Sam.

Helen was still tired from the previous day's exertions. 'What time is it?' she asked, sitting up.

Sam sat on the side of the bed and waved the photograph of the museum dagger at her. 'Five o'clock and time to wake up. Look, it's what you said last night that's got me thinking. Both you and Francis.'

'What did we say?' Helen asked, still struggling to wake up.

Sam picked up the parish dagger. 'You said this dagger, your dagger, is the key, yes?'

'I guess so,' said Helen, 'but, it must be a weird lock.'

'It's not a key for a lock, more like a cipher, well no, not even that actually, I think it's really simple. Do you remember saying, let's put together a proper plan?' he said.

'Vaguely,' said Helen, 'but I just meant start afresh in the morning, think again, that's all.'

'Well, that's not what you said, and I think the whole engraving thing is not a message or text. It's a plan, or rather a map. And your dagger is the key,' said Sam. 'Look, take a regular map, think about how you'd read it when you go hiking. It's all folded and you see only the bit you're using. As you turn it, unfold it, there are lots more similar sized sections, all different but part of the same map.' He looked at her triumphantly. 'Each dagger's engraving is part of a big plan or map. Individually the lines are a pretty but meaningless pattern. Put them together and you have it. Your plan to the treasure or whatever it might be.'

Helen was interested but cautious. 'Okay, but if none of the lines join up how can it be a plan or map?' she said.

'Easy' said Sam, as he let his hand run down the list of engraved numerals on the blade of the parish dagger. 'See the list of seemingly random numbers? Well I don't think they are random at all. As far as we know, each of the other blades has only one numeral, and so far, each of those numbers is also found on the list of numerals that appear on your parish dagger. I think the parish dagger is the key or list that tells what order the other daggers must be laid in to make the map.'

Sam twisted the blade so Helen could see. 'Like this,' he said. Letting his finger trail down the parish dagger's blade again as he called out numbers in the order they appeared. 'Two, seven, three, eight, four, and so on.

'Because none of the patterns ever reach the edge of the blades there is always a little bit of map missing, so the daggers can't ever be lined up successfully by trial and error. I think once you have all the daggers placed in the right order you'll have a map with little strips missing at the blade edges; but if you are confident of the daggers' place order, it should be straight forward, easy even, to interpolate and fill in the little gaps.'

Helen was impressed by the idea, but could not quite see the end result. 'Hey that would be a really neat solution and if you're right, once you have all the pieces it really is simple. It takes us a good bit further on, but it doesn't solve the whole problem. There are no words, so how can we tell what or where the map is of?'

'Well, one thing at a time, let's build the map first,' said Sam. 'We know we have numerals three and four and their patterns don't remotely match up. That fits if we accept those two are not meant to be side by side because they aren't listed side by side on the parish blade. Now, Xavier has a seven, and the three and seven are next to each other on the parish blade. If we could line those two blades up, see if we could interpolate, fill in the gaps between them to link the sections of pattern logically. Maybe get on our way to building a map. See where it takes us.

'There must have been a template somewhere; an original map that they based their dagger engravings on in the first place. If we could somehow trace that template it would probably have words on it, who knows…' Sam shrugged.

'So where does that leave us?' she asked.

'With a lot of work still to do,' said Sam. He stood up from the bed and drew the curtains open. 'We've got to shed some light on this and do it without anyone noticing. Even if you wanted to tell the police that time has gone now.'

'So it seems. But there must be a way to reconnect with them, surely?'

'No. I don't think so. For days, weeks even, we've been withholding little bits of information, telling ourselves they're not so relevant, not really related. Now it's as clear as you like that every bit is linked, and God help us, you were all there at the killings yesterday. We've been obstructing the enquiry. We've withheld evidence. Even if they didn't think we were involved before, they would smell a rat now as soon as you mentioned any of it. There really is no way back.'

Helen swung her legs off the bed and onto the floor. Leaning forward she rested her elbows on her thighs and cupped her face in her hands. She blew a long slow breath out. 'We've cut ourselves off from the authorities completely, haven't we?'

Still at the window, Sam allowed the morning sun to bathe his face; Helen could see his head nodding as he replied. 'Yes, completely. I'm not happy, Helen. This could completely discredit me, you too, actually. Our professional reputations would never recover if it gets out.'

'Will it?' she asked.

'I hope not. But right now I do know we must be very careful, everywhere.'

'We should never have listened to Elaine and Francis with all their schemes to protect John's reputation and his life's work. It's probably going to wreck ours instead,' said Helen.

'Perhaps, but we have to do everything we can to prevent it, and let's be fair - they couldn't ever have anticipated any of this. They're innocent victims just like us and they're our friends. There are still killers out there and we are probably still the target. We need to solve this before those madmen regroup and come back.'

Helen checked her mobile messages and gave a groan. 'The police want to see me. DCI Wallace has asked if I can go to the church. He wants to do a walk through with me this afternoon, whatever that means.'

• • •

DCI Wallace had been watching Helen carefully as they worked their way round the church. She had pointed out little bits of damage, mostly caused by the police teams as they pressed into the church. She had answered his questions clearly, but without giving him any fresh insight into why the incident had occurred. He was prepared to accept she didn't have a clue.

The girl seemed a little vulnerable and seemed very slightly shaky when they entered the vestry, which wasn't surprising with his team bustling about, lifting fingerprints, taking photographs. And the dark congealed blood stains around those body outlines on the floor. It must all have been disconcerting. Particularly here in the vestry amidst the aftermath of chaos.

Helen had assured him that nothing was missing. Even the open safe did not offer any clue as to motive. The only things it normally contained of any value, and not much at that, was an old communion set in a carry case, plus some papers and a few bits and bobs. And they weren't missing. She had it all at the manse, for an inventory and some sort of evaluation that was underway.

With a sense of relief, Helen left the death scene behind as they stepped out of the vestry and into the little corridor. DCI Wallace led her beyond the old wooden exit door and out into the fresh air. From there he guided her along the path towards the cemetery gate where they had to dodge around a couple of officers who were intently scouring the ground. They were carefully gathering up and bagging everything that wasn't grass or gravel. Beyond them lay the cemetery; she had never seen it so busy. It seemed that dozens of police officers were engaged in a fingertip search. Radiating out from the gate, they were meticulously checking everything, lifting anything and everything that should not have been there.

'You're busy out here. Do you think you'll find anything of use?' asked Helen.

'If there's anything to find, we'll find it. Don't worry about that.'

'I hope so. Your men will be treating the graves with respect though, won't they?'

Wallace did not answer her directly. There were rules about graves and cemeteries but he had no intention of restricting his men unnecessarily. 'I'm very grateful for your help this afternoon but there is something else I'm going to need your help with, Miss Johnson.'

'Yes? Anything. I'll be happy to help however I can.' Helen surprised herself at just how innocent she could sound.

'We are going to need a set of your prints for elimination purposes. Yours and everyone else who had business to be in the vestry or office recently.'

'That's no problem, I'm sure everyone will want to cooperate. I can put together a list of names for you if that would help.'

'Thank you. I'll have someone visit you later to collect it, but they might not get round to you until this evening. Will that be time enough?'

'Plenty of time, I'll phone around for you, make sure everyone is expecting you. I'm sorry I couldn't shed any light on the identity of the men who were killed, or name who might have done it. I hope you find the killers soon. It's a real worry. Now, if you've finished with me detective, perhaps I could go? There are so many people that I need to speak to.'

Wallace nodded, gave her a smile and left her at the gate as he headed off into the cemetery. He liked the girl and was confident murder was not her game, but there was something about her. She had a secret she wasn't sharing, he'd bet on it. Still, he was too busy right now to worry about any side issues.

Chapter 27

FRIDAY 21st JUNE

DCI Wallace glared round the room. Forty-eight hours into this latest outrage and nothing. His team had not produced anything of note. Blank, zero, nadir. They needed to pick up the pace. The chief constable was demanding results; the man was being hounded by politicians and the media and he in turn was kicking Wallace.

His team had grown dramatically in size and they had explored every conceivable angle to establish why two unknown men should end up shot dead in an Edinburgh church. No ID on them, but their clothes were mostly French labelled, and they had forensic suits on too, which just made it all the more puzzling.

There was an obvious church link with the other murders, and he knew in his bones the MacPherson killings were linked too, somehow. This morning he'd also called in the file on the university's dead night security guard: no proof that it wasn't an accident but it happened at MacPherson's place of work - maybe there was a link there too. For now, he'd keep an open mind. One common theme that did stand out was the brutality, the heartless, careless dispatch of life. But other than a growing pile of dead bodies they had nothing, nothing at all. No suspects, no motives.

'Listen up you lot.' He raised his voice a little, though it was not necessary. The team knew they were up against it and were desperate for some leadership. The room fell silent.

'Today we're making a change. So far we've found nothing, no clues no leads. It's as though we're chasing shadows that just melt away, that leave no trail. Well let me tell you, I don't buy it. There must be something we're missing.

'There must be consequences, cause and effect, links. Nothing happens in isolation. We must find that link today. Today! Every day that passes lets the trail go colder. So we have a new approach. We're going to review every little thing that happened in this city in the 24 hours before and after the crime. I mean everything. Every parking ticket, every speeding car, every dog owner caught letting their dog mess the kerb. Speak to them all. Find out what they were doing and why they were where they were.

'If a wee girl lost her sweeties, I want someone interviewing her. I want to know what kind of sweets and where she last saw them. Speak to everyone. Assume everything matters now, no matter how unlikely.

'During that day things happened that we're missing, things we haven't linked together yet. Find the link, that's all, just find it. Any questions?' He looked around the room defiantly. Nobody spoke. 'Okay, team leaders, you have your task lists. Let's go then. Make today count, people. Make it count.'

Even as the teams filed out to start their information trawl, the team leaders were calling out instructions, starting to allocate work. DCI Wallace beckoned DS Brogan over. 'I want you to get on top of forensics. I'm not interested in a neat report next week, I want information filtered through as soon as it's available, no delays. And have every action double-checked. I don't want to give the chief constable the excuse to sack me before I get my retirement request in.

'Come on. Let's go over what we've got one more time.' As they began the rehearsal of events for the umpteenth time, they were interrupted by a uniformed constable.

'Excuse me, sir.'

'Yes? Reynolds, isn't it? What have you got?' Throughout his career, Wallace had taken a professional pride in knowing the people he worked with, and he had been around long enough to be able to put names to many of the city's longer serving officers. Though in the past year or so he had been feeling the call of retirement and was subconsciously less worried over fixing the younger officers' names. Reynolds was an old hand.

'Sir, I'm not sure if this is what you're interested in; it's a fairly regular occurrence over at my patch, insurance jobs mostly. But you said you want everything. Well, a white van was torched late Wednesday evening on the housing scheme I work. No one hurt, no damage to other property, so just run of the mill.'

Wallace looked at his sergeant. 'Nothing's run of the mill that day. A white van. Wasn't one seen leaving from beyond the far end of the cemetery? I think there was. Let's check it out now.' It took only moments to pull up the report. It was flimsy, there were umpteen white vans in Edinburgh, but a white works van had indeed been in the road at the time of the incident and one had been torched that night. It needed to be checked.

'Right now anything is a possibility, let's follow it up. Reynolds, where did the torched van end up, do you know what happened? Can we see it?'

'Yes sir. I only know about the incident myself because I was on duty that evening. It's not exactly a remarkable event over there. It's more unusual not to have a fire or something going on. I was actually just round the corner when it went up. The fire brigade had been called out to a rubbish bin fire and we always attend with them there, just in case the local kids take against the firemen for spoiling their fun.

'It was lucky; we actually got the van fire out before it burned out completely.'

'What? You saved the van, where is it now?'

'Well, it's in the vehicle 'pound sir. It's just junk now. I expect it'll go off for scrap eventually. But I don't know if it has anything to do with the killings.'

'Nor do I, but we're going to find out. I don't suppose forensics bothered going over it?'

'Sorry sir, they were all pretty preoccupied with the killings and to be honest, we don't normally bother for burnt vehicles unless somebody's hurt.'

'Okay. Brogan, get the van checked out as a matter of priority and Reynolds, that housing scheme is your patch, get over there and see what you can pick up. Have a nose around; if that's our van, I want to know anything else you can learn. Now let's get moving.'

'Oh, and Reynolds, thank you.'

'Sir.' Constable Reynolds acknowledged DCI Wallace and headed off for the scheme, hoping the lead was not a red herring.

• • •

Forty-eight hours without a death or an attack. In the crazy world they had been dragged into, it seemed almost like peace. There had been no further signs of trouble but Helen, all of them, worried it was just a façade of calm. Still, Helen hoped and prayed that the assailants really had withdrawn, scared off by the publicity and heavy police involvement. Xavier was less convinced and deep down she felt it too.

Right now things were quiet, maybe they should welcome that, count their blessings and pray the police would get the breakthrough that would lead to the killers. It was the one thing that would allow them all to relax again. And how they needed to relax.

Xavier and Angelo had flown home to Sardinia and flown back the next day with a photograph of a dagger, and it was engraved with the Roman numeral VII. On their return, they were accompanied by three of Xavier's parishioners, tough men whose rugged complexions suggested they might have spent a lot of time deep in Sardinia's wild and sun kissed hinterland.

Not the type of men you would choose to argue with. Now there was always at least one hovering around the manse, providing Helen with a second shadow.

Xavier's dagger photograph gave Sam a lot more to get his teeth into and he was devoting lots of time to prove his 'folded map hypothesis', interpolating between the engraved sections, but so far with uncertain success.

Also unresolved were the locations of the other daggers. They all accepted Xavier's view that the St Bernard's parish dagger was the key, either as Sam suggested or in some other way. In any event, the location of the other daggers must somehow be contained in the parish dagger or somewhere in St Bernard's or its archives. How else could the daggers ever be recalled and combined?

• • •

DCI Wallace eased his car to a halt beside the play park. Based on Constable Reynolds' description he reckoned he was just about where the white van had been parked. All around him, rising from behind low garden fences were blocks of flats, mostly three storeys high. They stood like sentinels watching over the children playing in the park. He had arrived a few minutes early for his rendezvous with Constable Reynolds so he leant back in his seat, relaxed and looked across at the children playing in the park. He smiled to himself.

The tranquillity of the moment was shattered by the sound of something landing with some force on his car roof. Jumping out of the car, he saw it was an open and excessively soiled disposable nappy. It left a yellowy smear behind as it slowly slipped off the roof and down the windscreen. He looked around, then up. Standing at a second floor window were two women of indeterminate age, anywhere between twenty-five and forty, both with blond streaked hair: one thin, one somewhat heavier. Even from this distance he could see that life had clearly not been kind to them. Based on their use of the nappy projectile he guessed nearer twenty-five than forty.

'Peado,' shouted the heavy woman.

'Pervert, get away from here,' shouted the thin one.

'Clear off or I'm coming down and believe me you don't want that,' the heavy woman's arm swung and a second nappy flew towards Wallace, he ducked and it landed on the road behind him.

'Cut that out, I'm a police officer,' shouted Wallace, as he straightened up.

'Aye, right,' shouted back the heavy woman.

The thin woman jabbed an arm out of the window. 'We don't button up the back, pal. We know what you lot are about.' She disappeared from the window and her friend was quick to follow her.

Wallace had hardly had time to compose himself before the two women emerged from the building's common stair. They came directly up to him. Wallace was aware in his peripheral vision that play in the park had stopped and the children were gathering behind the fence to get a better view of proceedings. He was fishing in his jacket pocket as the women arrived.

Heavy woman jabbed him in the chest and thin stood close beside her, fist clenched looking for an excuse to strike. A steady chant of, 'peado,' 'peado,' was rising from the children at the fence and Wallace noted one or two windows open in the flats as others took an interest in the show. The wonder of such areas was how residents never saw anything for the police but otherwise never missed a thing. He managed to get his warrant card out and thrust it towards the heavy woman who was just winding up for a further finger jab. It stopped her for a moment.

'I don't care if you are police, you shouldn't have been perving at our kids,' she said.

'What's to say you're not a peado anyway?' demanded the thin woman.

'I can assure you I am not. I'm waiting to meet a colleague, that's all.'

'Aye, right. You were leching at the kids, and I'll bet that card's a forgery,' said thin woman. In a harsh world, they looked out for themselves and their own, and necessarily assumed the worst of strangers. Strangers were guilty until proven innocent. That's how to survive.

Seeing the two women close up Wallace revised his age estimates. He doubted if either was much over twenty but they were not his main concern. More adults were arriving - two or three older women and a couple of men, each one of them looked ready and willing to dole out a bit of summary justice to a pervert encroaching on their patch.

'I was not looking at your children. I just glanced into the park.' Wallace was now backed up against his car, his body holding the door closed. He couldn't get in, couldn't get away.

With the crowd behind them, the two women were growing in confidence again. 'See you, I'm going to have you. I hate you peados, you hear?' The heavy woman raised her hand, pulling it back, readying a good swipe at Wallace's face.

'Hey, you! Chanelle McLean, what the hell do you think you're doing?' Constable Reynolds pushed through the little crowd to stand beside Wallace.

Unsure of how things were playing out, but recognising Reynolds' authority was probably going to spoil the show, the children's chant was replaced by a round of booing which gradually petered out.

The odds had shifted in Wallace's favour and Chanelle's hand dropped, but she didn't give any ground.

'Hey! Reynolds, he's a pervert, been spying on our kids,' Chanelle spoke with real anger and again she took a half step forward, thrusting her face towards Wallace's.

Reynolds forced himself between the two. 'Hold on Chanelle, you're going to get yourself into trouble here, he's my boss.'

'He might be your boss but he's still a perv'. We want him charged, he was staring at the kids and we can prove it,' she retorted, though giving a little ground.

Sensing his chance Reynolds raised his voice. 'All right folks, show's over. There's nothing here. Come on, move along.' The crowd rippled and stepped back a little, giving Wallace the space he needed to regain his dignity.

'Come on now, move on. Just a misunderstanding, let's be having you.' Years of experience in handling tricky situations on the street found Reynolds in his element. Almost before the crowd realised it they were dispersing, leaving Chanelle and her friend.

'I still say you're a perv',' said Chanelle, her friend nodded support.

Reynolds turned his attention from the dispersing crowd back to the two women. 'Come on now, you're talking nonsense, trust me,' he said.

Chanelle fixed him with a quizzical eye. 'Trust you? Why would we do that?'

Reynolds shrugged and gave a grin. 'Just because I'm telling you, alright?' The police weren't really welcome here. He was tolerated partly because of constant exposure and partly because there wasn't a person on the scheme that could honestly say he had misled or mistreated them. It was as close as they would ever get to trust and right now Wallace was thanking God for it and for decent coppers.

Chanelle glowered at Wallace. 'What are you doing here anyway? We don't want your sort here, right? Reynolds might have got you off the hook but we know what you were up to.'

DCI Wallace was confused. 'What do you mean, this is nonsense. I was just waiting here for the officer.'

'Aye, so you say, but we can prove different. You perverts, you're all the same, coming round here bothering our kids. Why not go and do it in some fancy middleclass area? Because the law would be on you there, that's why.' Chanelle had the bit between her teeth and was reluctant to give up.

'Look, I've told you who he is. He's not a pervert. Now cut it out or I'm going to take this further, right?' Reynolds' voice had lost its conciliatory tone. It was time to push Chanelle back a bit.

'We can prove it, we've got a trap. He was looking at the kids.'

'No, he'll have glanced into the play park just like anyone might. Now come on Chanelle, let it go.'

Something was not fitting quite right in Wallace's mind. 'What do you mean by, *prove it?*' he asked.

The thin woman butted in. 'Easy, we've got you on film.' She pointed back up to the second floor window. 'It's our peado cam. Anyone comes here now; we've got them taped. We don't need the law. We sort things ourselves.'

Chanelle nodded agreement. 'My uncle fitted it. You come down this street and we've got you, no bother.'

Wallace felt his chest lighten immeasurably: a street recording, perfect. He could almost kiss Chanelle; then he thought of his soiled windscreen and tempered his gratitude.

• • •

It had taken the best part of an hour of persuasion, cajoling, threats and promises to get access to the computer recordings. Wallace had noted Reynolds discreetly passing a twenty-pound note to Chanelle after which resistance had finally evaporated. He would have to reimburse the constable. Wallace had wondered for a moment how someone who appeared so poor could find the money for a state of the art computer and even a surveillance camera. Then he shrugged, so what, at least he had pictures.

He'd watched the scene play through four times. A van, a man, a woman, a car passing the burning van: unfortunately, the flames distorted the light as the car drove through the picture so the camera didn't catch the car's registration number. But if they were involved, he was closing in. Time for the tec' teams to get to work.

Wallace said his goodbyes and left Reynolds in the flat with the two young women. There was plenty to be chased up elsewhere. He hoped the other forensic reports would be filtering through by now and perhaps other leads were coming up. He headed down the common stair and out into the road, then stopped dead. For the first time in days he gave just the hint of a genuine smile. His car windscreen had been washed clean. In fact, the whole car was gleaming.

He glanced up to the second floor window where Chanelle's thin friend stood watching him go. He gave a warm wave and she gave a friendly grin in return and followed it with a very public two-fingered salute.

Still smiling, he opened the car door, and then froze. Something about the video recording niggled at him, what was it? He ran through the images in his mind and then quickly stepped back from the car. There in the gutter was a crumpled cigarette packet. Could this be the one discarded by the driver? He stared at it. Then saw another and another, there were four packets within twenty feet. At that moment some of the team arrived to harvest the IT and video files, he pointed them towards the discarded packets.

• • •

Cassiter was oblivious to the scene in front of him. The castle, the Old Town skyline, the lengthening shadows darkening the green of the municipal gardens, all things he normally lingered over. This evening they did not register, he was entirely focused on weighing up his options. Things had gone badly wrong, that was an occupational hazard, it happened from time to time. But there was a whole world for it to happen in, not here on his home patch.

The close proximity to home was a disaster. He thought about how events had played out. Could he have done things differently? For a moment he found himself regretting taking on Parsol's commission, but self-pity never delivered anything. He wondered exactly what prize could be so big it had lured Parsol out of his lair and into the front line; however, he was a contractor - ultimately, client motivations were not his concern. This job was of no consequence now. It needed to be removed from here, wiped away; some necessary sacrifices made to deflect attention.

He reached for his intercom and buzzed the sour faced woman. 'Have Barnett and Sharp arrived yet?' he asked.

'Yes sir, just a moment ago.'

'Good, come through, bring them both with you, and bring the rest of the team too. We need to start the house cleaning now.' He leant back and took a final quiet moment to consider again what needed to happen. He had no intention of doing time just for following his profession, yet with so much police activity they had to be prepared for every eventuality. The normal protocols would need to be enhanced, there was a lot to do, a lot to shift. This was going to be a long night. Finally, while he prided himself on his professionalism and very consciously did not get personally involved, those females at the church had to go: they had all seen his face. The old moaner, her daughter and the American, all three of them. As soon as things were tidied up here, he'd silence them. Forty-eight hours and things would be finally wrapped, but not before those women had identified the Latin priests for him. They had to be removed too.

CHAPTER 28

SATURDAY 22nd JUNE

Helen linked arms with Xavier as they moved slowly through the airport car park. Close behind came Angelo, watching, ready to rush forward should Xavier so much as threaten to stumble. Helen was determined it wouldn't happen on her watch, she wanted these moments together to be special. Sam was moving just ahead of the group pushing a trolley with the priests' bags on. Bringing up the rear was one of Xavier's parishioners. He strolled with an air of detached disinterest, but he constantly scanned, monitoring and assessing everyone; ready to strike down any threat in an instant.

It seemed events had finally caught up with Xavier. He looked his age; the sparkle had faded from his eyes. The rapid succession of journeys together with so much death and violence seemed to have worn down his normal quiet strength. Helen could feel how frail he was; she hoped he just needed a good rest. Whatever it was, now he needed to be home, quiet amongst familiar things.

Once over the pedestrian crossing in front of the main terminal entrance Xavier stopped. He pulled Helen to a halt too. Leaning in close, heads almost touching, he tried to force a cheery note into his voice. 'Now young lady,' he said, 'you promise to visit me soon, yes?'

'You can count on it, Xavier. But you recharge your batteries first, okay?'

'Pah, a day, two, I'll be fine. Bring him too,' he waved towards Sam who had already gone through the automatic doors ahead of them and was now waiting patiently for them to catch up. The two men nodded to each other through the glass doors. 'I think he can solve this riddle with you, for all of us. For sure, only that can make this hell go away forever.' His attempted bravado lapsed back into concern.

'I know, Xavier. But you've done your bit, you need a break.' She placed her free hand on his free arm and rubbed it gently. 'Come on, I want you well enough to visit. You rest, let's hope the police can capture the bad guys, hey? The detective seems pretty sure they will.'

'Hmmm, maybe, I hope so.' Clearly, Xavier was not entirely convinced. 'Stick together, yes? And be careful, for all of you.'

Angelo and the Sardinian parishioner were very close behind them now, creating a protective buffer to deflect the stream of tutting, glaring pedestrians whose passage through the automatic doors was being slowed. 'We go now,' said Angelo. His limited English left it unclear whether it was a request or an order.

Helen nodded and together with Xavier, she moved forward again, heading through the entrance doors and making directly to the private departures. At least Xavier would not be waiting for a scheduled flight.

• • •

For the first time since he had been called down to Dunbar to take charge of the Archie Buchan murder, DCI Wallace felt he might just be getting a break. It wasn't what he expected. At first sight it all seemed entirely random, unconnected; but once he started building a people chain, who connected to who, some dots were starting to join.

Forensics had lifted prints off all four cigarette packets. Two were children's hands, one a local ned who Reynolds knew and was going to speak to, though he did not think he could drive and was sure the whole business was well out of his league anyway. But the fourth set, prints unknown. Unknown but not unfamiliar.

Whoever this Mr Anonymous was, he had been busy. Had thrown down a cigarette packet beside a burning white van. Had left just a partial print on the blade of a knife used in a recent attack in Oban. Its handle was clean, and the blade smudged through the dog's flesh, but they had found a single fingerprint on the blade, just where it hinged into the handle - it must have been left at some point before, when being cleaned. And he had left prints in St Bernard's church office, the vestry, and crucially in several of the pews. He must at least have *something* to do with the church.

It all kept linking back to the church and the university too. Wallace trusted his judgement and was happy that Helen and Sam were not killers; that was for sure. But there was something going on in the background, he could feel that too. Perhaps he should bring them in again for a slightly heavier questioning session?

DS Brogan pushed his way through the scrum of officers who seemed to be congregating a little distance from the DCI. 'Mixed news, sir. Turns out the van was stolen. False plates and too badly burnt to get anything useful from it-'

'- and the good?' cut in Wallace.

'They found something in the back, burnt. It won't do much as evidence but they reckon it was some sort of remote control box.'

'Remote control for what?'

'They can't begin to say for sure. Though, we know of one remote control box that was used last Wednesday to fire off the decoy munitions. If that was it, then maybe that's what the woman in our video threw in the van.'

Wallace nodded, agreeing. He wished again that they could ID the faces. 'Where's my photographer? Where's Stephens got to? If he's moonlighting as a sports photographer at Tynecastle again I'm going to do my nut.'

'The football season's over boss, it's the close season,' replied Brogan.

Wallace grunted a response that hovered somewhere between acknowledgement and continuing discontent. He knew the season dates exactly, very rarely got to attend matches now but followed the results. He used to love taking his son and daughter to watch his team, the Hearts, but work had made a habit of getting in the way. 'Get Stephens over here. He promised to get me decent stills from that video recording, where are they?'

'Here, boss.' Stephens, the photographer, newly arrived in the office, was waving a large white envelope as he pressed through the rest of Wallace's team who had all fallen silent, tuning in, hoping for good news. 'You said get them to you by lunchtime, here they are.'

Wallace stretched out a hand for the envelope. 'What time do you have your lunch at, Stephens?' he grumbled, but his tone and the slightest of smiles made clear the arrival was welcome.

Wallace, Stephens and Brogan sat round the desk looking at the pictures, other copies had been channelled back to the waiting crowd.

'Good quality pictures, we could ID someone from these, easy,' said Wallace.

'Thanks, I do my best,' replied Stephens, taking the compliment.

'I don't know the man, never seen him before. But this woman, I know her face,' Wallace looked up, seeking confirmation, inspiration, tapping the photograph. 'But where? I've seen her recently, I'm sure.'

Stephens nodded. 'Now you mention it, she does seem familiar. I've seen her too. Just can't quite place her. Sorry, I'm stumped too.'

'Well I've never seen her,' said Brogan. 'So where have you two been hanging out together recently?'

'Well done, sergeant!' Wallace almost shouted as he leapt up and turned to the filing cabinet against the wall behind him, 'I've got it.'

DS Brogan looked a little puzzled, 'Got what?'

'Who she is. Look...' Wallace pulled out the file of photographs taken at Archie Buchan's memorial service. He started to flick them down on the desk.

'There! There she is, outside the Dunbar church,' he jabbed a finger down on a photograph featuring the media crowd. Wallace flicked down another picture. 'There again, yes? It's her?'

Brogan gave a little whistle. 'I think you're right boss, it is her! But who is she?'

Stephens looked a little bit sheepish. 'I don't know. I didn't recognise her. She's not one of the regular press photographers; I pretty well know them all. I thought if she's new maybe I could chance my arm for a date, but nobody knew who she was.'

Wallace tapped his finger on the picture. 'It all keeps coming back to the church, doesn't it? But still, who is she? Where is she?'

'Maybe I can help you there,' said Stephens, taking what remained of the photos from DCI Wallace. Flicking through them, he stopped and nodded to himself. 'Yep, this is the one. That's her car.' He handed back a photograph of a saloon car pulling away from the kerb. 'Snapped her driving off, thought I might have been able to trace her through the licence plate, try for that date. There just hasn't been time to follow her up.'

'Wallace took the picture and looked at it triumphantly then tapped it against the photographer's head. 'Lucky for you that you didn't, you old dog; that would have been breaching privacy rules. And you nearly tried to date the most wanted woman in the country. God knows what she would have done to a police photographer. Well, now we'll follow her up for you.'

'Sergeant, it's the same model of car as in the video. Trace this car number now. Let's get a team scanning every bit of

CCTV between that housing scheme and the city centre. Look for this model of car. We know she was there. Find her car and track it to its destination. Let's get moving now; I want everyone working on this.'

Chapter 29

SUNDAY 23rd JUNE

Helen and Grace supported Elaine between them as she shuffled along the ward. Elaine had had enough. Yes, she could cope with the rods holding her face together. Yes, she was unsure how the amputation of her finger was going to affect her, though she fully expected to cope. Yes, the nursing staff had been wonderful and yes, she was going home. She fully intended to be out of hospital by lunchtime.

The three women emerged from the Infirmary. Even in her discomfort, Elaine got an instant lift from the fresh air touching her face. Grace supported her mother with an arm while Helen carried Elaine's small overnight bag. They headed for the car park where Sam was waiting to drive them home.

'Everything's quiet now, Elaine, I really think they've been scared off. The detectives are confident of catching them too,' said Helen.

'Hmmm,' replied Elaine. She was not convinced that such violence would simply vanish, but things still hurt too much for her to argue, 'Hmmm.'

• • •

DCI Wallace was outside the police station. When he needed a break from phones and screens he'd step out of the building, move a little distance away from the front door and light a small cheroot. Now he was leaning against his favourite piece of wall. Basking in the sun, he alternated sips of coffee with gentle puffs as he allowed the latest information to percolate through his mind.

His team had traced the car registration and it had proven of no use. The car had been registered in the English Midlands to a business down there that seemed to exist only to host the lease agreement. It was insured with open insurance cover for any driver, the perfect arrangement to ensure legal compliance on the surface combined with comfortable anonymity. Still no name for the woman.

The team had found and tracked the car's travels on CCTV. Traced its journey into the city centre, saw it finally end with the car disappearing into an underground car park in one of the lanes behind Princes Street. Once they had fixed the location, the team had trawled back through old recordings and confirmed the car to be a regular visitor. So no woman's name but definitely a base. When he'd finished his smoke it would be time to strike. He could see several vehicles assembling in convoy across the road. He was trying hard to avoid the occupants' eyes right now. This would probably be his last quiet moment for some time.

• • •

Cassiter's team was waiting for him beside the reception desk. No emotion showed in the sour faced receptionist's eyes, and the rest of the team were all equally blank. They were experienced, knew the form and had all been briefed by the lawyer. If things did not go well then they knew how to respond; this was a nuisance and an occupational hazard, but they were not prone to panic. The slightest of clicks heralded Cassiter's arrival as his private office door opened.

He nodded to the team, if they were going to be busted it would be today. But everything here was clean, a legitimate international trading business with records to prove it. Certainly, the churchwomen could link him to events, but he had plans to remove the three women today. He gave a little smile. Before he let them die, they would tell him about the two priests: the final step in the purging.

He'd also taken the precaution of making one or two phone calls; there was no point in collecting people in high places if they were never used.

Time now to go and deal with the women. His team were to stay put, not trapped, not sacrificed; if Wallace was coming, it made sense to have everyone in one place, all singing from the same hymn sheet. And his was a well-practiced choir.

'Okay guys, you know the score. Sunday trading today, the world market doesn't stop for church services. Let's get to it.' Cassiter looked round at his little team and read the confident nods and grins. Two of his team were missing, Sharp and Barnett. They had made mistakes, it was clear they were compromised and now they were fulfilling a special task for him. He saw others exchange high fives. They would do. He nodded to sour face who responded with what passed as a smile and an unseen flutter in her heart as she released the lift door. It opened and Cassiter entered. Now for the churchwomen, a final sweep and everything would be clean, order could return to his world.

• • •

From just inside the entrance to the basement car park DCI Wallace looked over to the lift doors. This was an odd access arrangement and he was struggling to understand why the place was not on his radar. No one in the force had seemed aware of its existence. A small international trading company, no profile, no reputation, no form. The evidence pointed here, but it seemed clean as a whistle. What if he was wrong? He shrugged and knew it was time to move. Armed response teams were already in place, one in the fire escape, a second team gathered in front of him. They would go up in the lift first, just in case.

'Boss. Boss,' DS Brogan's urgent half whisper came to him from the lane outside the basement. Wallace turned and looked up the drive ramp to find out what could be so important to justify distracting him right on the kick off.

'What's up man?' he asked.

'They've found her car, boss. Over at Silverknowes, on Marine Drive.'

Wallace was annoyed at the interruption but intrigued too. 'What the hell's it doing there? Is she walking a dog or something? Have they got her? 'He fired out the questions, needing answers quickly in case they impacted on his next move here. Marine Drive was an isolated sweep of road to the north of the city. It ran along the foreshore, popular with lovers at night and dog walkers through the day.

Brogan joined him at the foot of the ramp. 'She's in the car, boss. A man too.' The absence of elation in Brogan's voice alerted Wallace to problems.

'And?' he asked.

'They're both dead.'

Wallace was stunned. 'What? How?'

'Shot. The patrol boys who found the car say they can see two handguns inside, looks like they shot each other.' Brogan gave a half shrug. 'They are clearly dead so the lads haven't opened up the car yet. Waiting for a forensics team, and you.'

Wallace tried to consider how this news should affect his approach here. One thing for certain, he wasn't buying any sort of murder-suicide pact. He nodded to Brogan and briefly patted the sergeant's arm, a mixed message: thanks and we'll work it out later. Then he turned back to look through the car parking bay towards the lift. Before he could order a move the armed response team outside the lift suddenly tensed, bringing their guns to bear on the lift entrance. The lift was descending.

The lift door opened and Cassiter stepped out directly into a storm of shouts. Cassiter knew the procedures well enough to present the safe response. Without a moment's hesitation he raised his arms and knelt, then lay down. Prone, he waited for the police to handcuff him. He cursed silently; he was not going to get to the churchwomen.

Wallace had watched the arrest from a distance - he did not recognise the man. Now he closed in, looked at the unfamiliar face for a moment then waved him away to the lockup. He pointed his team into the open lift doors, they moved in, the lift doors closed behind them and the assault began.

Chapter 30

MONDAY 24ᵗʰ JUNE

Cassiter sat in silence in a St Leonard's police cell. No emotion, no signs, motionless. But his mind was not still.

The police had come too early for a perfect wrap. Nevertheless, all the evidence at the office had already been removed or destroyed. He knew the police search would show only a clean little trading company.

Jim Barnett and Fiona Sharp had gone. Good operatives, but they had become expendable. They were too close to events; if any evidence was linking Cassiter to the crime it would be theirs. It did not matter whether or not they had really been compromised or allowed evidence to leak, their necessary and properly presented sacrifice would lead the police along another path; a lunatic couple, a modern day Bonnie and Clyde, choosing to exit together when they felt events and their rampage were running out of control. It had happened before and no doubt, it would happen again. So an easy option for the police - it would give everyone an out.

But he was puzzled. The police did not seem to be linking the three churchwomen as witnesses to the killings in St Bernard's. The women must have got out of the church somehow and kept quiet about their presence there. It was a bonus, certainly, but he didn't understand why they had kept quiet. They must have something to hide, something so big they were willing to withhold evidence from the police. It was excellent; they could link him to the crime scene and for whatever reason, they were staying silent. They could not change their story now without incriminating themselves for withholding evidence: they could not stand witness against him.

Had the police not arrested him, the three women would by now be dead - perhaps he could let them live after all, perhaps he should.

But there was another question - one that he had not foreseen and which he could not yet address. A question that had left Wallace and his sergeant looking so very pleased. Cassiter could not yet think through how to address it; this was an unexpected turn of events that would require some careful consideration. Or he might be inside for a very long time.

• • •

Unless it was part of an active investigation, DCI Wallace did not like making house calls, but this was one visit that had given him real pleasure. At the same time, he was wondering whether maybe it should be his last call too. Maybe he'd done his bit now; he should retire, time to get out while his wife was still speaking to him... While he still had a wife. He liked this American girl. He was sure she was holding something back, but for some reason it didn't seem to matter. She and her group were victims and he could report the all clear. It felt good, was what policing should be about. And he could read Brogan like a book. The sergeant was also enjoying delivering good news.

Bringing it all to a conclusion had been touch and go for a while. The little group in their eagle's nest of an office had put up no resistance; it had felt almost as though he was dealing with the military. Names, ranks... he'd half-expected numbers too. Then silence, they said nothing, as if they had a routine drilled into them. The offices had been clean, nothing shady, so suspiciously innocent it screamed guilty. For a little while he'd had nothing. It had all looked a bit flaky and of course, the chief constable had been wittering away in the background.

Predictable as ever, the man seemed more worried about the media image than the murders. He certainly seemed to like the desperate villains argument; Bonnie and Clyde, clean, simple, everything finished, neat and tidy. But Wallace didn't like it.

None of the suspects had behaved like normal folk; they had sat silent, unflinching, stoic. He'd had to admit he had nothing on any of those he'd lifted from their office, on the face of it, they did seem to be international traders, and initial feedback on the contents of their computers showed a real business. He knew they were involved but suspected he'd soon have to let them go, along with the sour faced receptionist, but their cards were marked. The slightest step out of line and he'd have them.

The man they had taken at the lift was the biggest mystery. Like the others, he had only spoken once, to identify himself as Clive Innes, then silence: cold, expressionless, detached. Wallace knew he wasn't a Clive Innes, regardless of legitimate documents that said he was. From his manner, he was a leader, *the* leader. But Wallace didn't have the slightest idea who the man really was. He was a ghost, a shadow and like the others had been in line for release; without evidence there was no sustainable charge. Then just when it looked as though his team had come up empty handed they got a break, they cracked it.

Wallace had been fending off some arrogant, high-priced lawyer when the call had come through from forensics. One moment the fat cat had been threatening action against the police for compensation - for wrecked careers, ruined reputations, the works. The next moment he was struggling to keep his feet, like a novice on an ice rink.

One little bit of steady police work had set 'Clive Innes' on a one-way trip to Saughton. No, Wallace corrected himself; he was not supposed to call it that anymore. They had to call it 'Edinburgh Prison' now. Perhaps that was another sign it was time for him to go. This was a new era when even the prisons were getting image makeovers. He grunted in disgust.

It was methodical police work that broke the case. A fingertip search and then DNA from a bloodstained handkerchief found near the little path behind the church; it put Innes right in the middle of the crime scene. Bingo.

Wallace had read the relief on the women's faces as he broke the news. He felt the atmosphere of fear lift. Had been happy to spend half an hour over a cup of tea, putting their minds at rest. There was a lot of work to do and more evidence to gather, a case to build, but they had their man and the evidence to hold him, nailed. Clive Innes was going nowhere, and Wallace knew it.

Chapter 31

THURSDAY 27th JUNE

On police advice, the elders had taken steps to ensure the manse was not left unoccupied. They had asked Helen to move in as a temporary occupant and she had readily agreed.

Helen and Elaine sat in the back garden of the manse. Both tucked under parasols, enjoying the still air and afternoon warmth while avoiding the direct sunlight. Helen shading her fair skin, Elaine keeping her wounds covered. It was a rare quiet moment for the pair to share together. They relaxed, having begun the process of steadily unwinding in the wake of DCI Wallace's earlier news. Helen did the speaking and Elaine gently nodded or shook her head in response, throwing in the occasional supporting mumble for reinforcement. It would be a while yet before Elaine was able to talk properly.

Scottie, Elaine's counter-surveillance expert, had been round the previous day. He had swept the manse again, just to give Helen some peace of mind. He gave the place a clean bill of health, but Helen was still just that bit happier chatting outside rather than indoors. She knew she'd get over it soon enough, but trust was still at a premium.

Scottie had not been able to shed any more light on the origins of the surveillance devices he'd found previously. They were certainly not currently available on the market, definitely leading edge. Must have been developed by a national security service somewhere, he didn't know which one. He didn't have any idea how Innes had been able to get hold of the technology, but clearly he had.

Alone together in the garden, Helen and Elaine had lapsed into quiet; contentedly thinking their own thoughts. Birds chirped and called in the warm air, tree leaves rustled faintly in the gentle breeze and Helen just enjoyed the tranquillity of the moment. It was rudely shattered by the ringing of the manse telephone. She had brought the portable handset out into the garden with them and now wished she had not.

Almost reluctantly, she answered the call. 'Hello, Helen Johnson speaking.' Then she fell silent, squinting slightly as she concentrated, trying to understand the message. 'I'm sorry. I don't understand you very well. I certainly don't know you. I think you've made some sort of mistake. Let's just leave -'

Helen fell silent as the caller interrupted her and good manners demanded that she listen a little longer. Having finally caught his name she took the opportunity to end the call politely. 'Herr Brenner? Franz? I'm sorry but I don't have the slightest idea who you are or what you're talking about. I think I'd like to end this call now...' Helen's voice trailed off as she noticed Elaine's movement.

Wincing at a series of pains, Elaine seemed to hurry in slow motion, sitting up as quickly as she could while nodding and giving a thumbs up sign. It was clear that Elaine knew who Franz Brenner was.

'Just a minute, Herr Brenner,' said Helen. She placed her hand over the phone's mouthpiece, while throwing Elaine a quizzical look. 'Who is he?'

Elaine mumbled urgently and rubbed her forefinger and thumb together, making a sign for money. Her speech was not clear at all, but Helen thought she could make out the word banker, and anyway, Elaine was clearly not threatened by the man's presence.

'How can I help you Herr Brenner? Where are you calling from?' Helen paused to listen to the brief reply, and then responded in turn. 'Oh, really?'

She looked at Elaine. 'He's parked in the driveway. Wants to see me. What do you think?'

Mumbling and nodding from Elaine made clear she thought it a good idea.

'Hello, Herr Brenner? I'm not sure what you want, but I have a few minutes. Why don't you follow the little path round the side of the house? Join us in the garden.' She ended the call and quickly stood, moving to wait beside Elaine's chair. The pair looked to the side of the house, waiting for the unexpected visitor to appear.

A slim man of middle height with short greying hair and solemn brown eyes stepped into the garden. Aged in his sixties, but a well-lived life had him looking little more than fifty. His dark blue business suit sported a fine pinstripe. Franz Brenner seemed every inch the conservative banker. Helen saw his smile and wave as he approached, it was clear he knew Elaine.

When he saw Elaine's injuries, a look of shock registered, fleetingly. It was quickly replaced with concern and finally returned to his composed business face. By the time he had reached the two ladies his hand was stretched out to greet them, Elaine first. They had met several times over the years, during Franz's previous visits to John. Good manners prevented him from commenting on Elaine's appearance, but the nature of her injuries demanded an account. Elaine would speak with him later, when she was better able.

Helen offered a hand of welcome too. Formalities completed, she quickly learnt that Herr Brenner, Franz, was indeed a banker. A private Swiss banker who had looked after certain affairs for John Dearly and he had travelled here to initiate a handover. Having followed recent events in the media his bank had some idea that things had gone tragically wrong. Then, when they were unable to contact Elaine any more either, he had travelled to Edinburgh. Business was business and no matter how insensitive the timing, he had to sort out affairs.

'I don't see what John Dearly's affairs have to do with me,' protested Helen. 'I am sure you could find a distant relative somewhere. I'm the last person who would have an interest in anything from him.'

'I would agree were I dealing with a family estate. But I am here for the trust fund,' said Franz.

'What trust fund is that?' asked Helen. 'I don't have the slightest idea what you're talking about.'

For just a moment, Franz looked confused. 'You don't know about the fund?' He looked at Elaine for some guidance. 'I… We had understood from Elaine that you were John Dearly's selected successor. Have I got this wrong?'

'Well, that's about the size of it, but it'll take a good while before the Church process is completed,' said Helen.

'I'm sorry? What has the Church got to do with it?' Franz sounded puzzled, again.

Helen was confused too. 'What doesn't the Church have to do with it?'

Franz looked to Elaine. She nodded and pointed at Helen. He took that as a sign to proceed. 'My bank administers a trust fund that pays out significant sums of money each year. Much of that does flow through St Bernard's. John's church…'

A little warning light was flickering in Helen's mind. 'Oh! That trust fund. Yes, I'm aware of it, but only in the passing. Why do you need to involve me? Surely the trustees of the fund have made the appropriate arrangements to benefit St Bernard's?'

Franz raised a hand slightly, excusing himself for a moment he paced steadily away down the lawn towards the shrubbery at the bottom of the garden. There he stayed for several minutes, staring intently into the greenery: thinking hard. He made a call to his office in Switzerland then another call. The two ladies saw but could not hear what was said.

In hissed half whispers, Helen tried to coax information out of Elaine. Her responses were pretty well limited to head nods and shakes. By the time Franz returned, Helen was none the wiser.

'Helen, this is difficult. Circumstances tell me you are the right person to speak to. Elaine seems to think so too. Yet... Yet, you know nothing. I do not understand how this can be.' Franz paused, hoping that some inspiration would come from Helen's side.

'Well, yes, I know nothing. I only learnt of your existence a few minutes ago. How could I know anything?' she asked. 'Why don't you tell me?'

Franz nodded slowly. He took a couple of paces back, ensuring he could see both ladies properly as he spoke. 'The trust fund. John was not the trustee. The senior members of the bank are trustees. John...' Franz paused again, before continuing. 'John was the beneficiary.'

'No!' Helen could not help but challenge the statement. 'I know the money was paid to St Bernard's, not to John.' She looked to Elaine for support. But the older woman was now perfectly still.

'He was the beneficiary. The trust fund has no direct link with St Bernard's. Money is paid to the church's account each year because John instructed it,' said Franz.

'I don't understand. How can that be? And anyway, what's it got to do with me?' Suddenly, Helen felt uneasy. The old concerns about John and the money came flooding back. Too many secrets.

'It is how it has been for a long time. Before John, Archie Buchan was the beneficiary. And many others before them.' Franz looked towards Elaine again. 'Have I got this right? Is she next?'

Elaine nodded in confirmation that Franz had understood properly.

'I'm not due any money,' said Helen. 'There must be a mistake.'

Franz tried a different tack. 'Do you have a ring, a special ring? Something you received from John.'

'Oh?' said Helen, now very much on her guard. Suddenly the ring seemed to weigh heavy round her neck. 'What's that got to do with it?'

'The ring identifies the beneficiary. If you have the ring, you must be the beneficiary.' Franz fixed Helen with a clear unswerving gaze. 'Do you have the ring?'

Elaine's mumbled encouragement filled the background as Helen held Franz's gaze, and thought very carefully. Finally, she nodded. 'I do have a ring. What of it?'

'May I see it please?' There was a slight tension in the man's tone. 'I must see it.'

Helen reached beneath the collar of her blouse and pulled on the gold chain, as it emerged into the sunlight the ring came too. Keeping the chain round her neck Helen allowed Franz sight of the ring. He smiled at her, and pulled a photograph from his jacket pocket as he stepped closer to compare properly. After a long moment, Franz stepped back, satisfied.

'It is the ring,' he said.

Helen nodded. 'We know. So what now? What does it mean?'

'I said the ring identifies the trust's beneficiary. But that's not enough to access and control the funds. You must have the account number too.'

The sense of excitement that had begun to build in Helen fizzled away. 'I don't have any number. I wouldn't know where to find it.'

Franz looked concerned. 'You must know. Without it I cannot proceed. You were given the ring; surely, you must have been given the number too.'

'The ring wasn't given to me under normal circumstances. There was no time for anything. I can assure you I don't have the account number. Nowhere. I wouldn't know where to start looking.'

Franz slipped the picture of the ring back into his pocket. 'This is tragic. I am sorry, but I can't proceed any further. If you don't have the number, I cannot engage with you.' He glanced towards Elaine and back to Helen. 'I am so sorry. I have known Elaine and John for many years. Since taking over from my father at the bank. And he, and his father before him, had the pleasure of serving your predecessors' needs. I know Elaine is genuine but the instructions are fixed. You must give me the number so I can respond.'

He sighed. 'I will leave you now. If you find the number then please get in touch. But a warning, don't guess, I can only accept one attempt at the number. You either know it or you don't.' Franz handed Helen a business card and then took a step backwards.

'Can't you give us a clue, how long is it? Does it have letters and numbers? How will we know if we find it?' Helen had never approved of the mysterious fund, but now it had appeared only to be snatched away she felt a sense of loss. Never mind the money. It was almost certainly part of the wider puzzle they had been grappling with.

Franz shook his head. 'I'm sorry, Helen, I may not discuss the account with you. I feel for you, but for me it is a sad day too. This account was one of the first ever opened at the bank. A founder deposit. For eight generations my family have managed it. Now it falls to me to see it end, our oldest and most esteemed account. I'm sorry, I must go now.' Without another word, Franz shook Helen's hand, stiffly, formally. He bowed his head just a fraction and she half thought she heard his heels click together. The man turned. Suddenly fading, he didn't seem quite so dapper. He paused beside Elaine, stepped closer and took her good hand. He gave it a gracious kiss: a last goodbye, an apology, an ending to a long story.

Helen and Elaine were equally stunned at the abrupt end to the visit. In silence, Helen watched a dejected Franz disappear round the side of the house as Elaine started to mutter and wave her good hand back and forth. Helen saw that she was making a stabbing motion with her good hand. The mumbling suddenly came to focus and Helen understood. Dagger. The numbers on John's dagger. It had to be that.

She ran round the side of the house, catching Franz just as he was getting into his hire car. 'Franz, wait! I've got the number,' she called.

Franz smiled genuine pleasure, relief. He stopped, closed the car door, and hurried back towards her. 'Are you sure? You only have one chance.'

'No bother,' said Helen, tapping her temple. 'It's right here, has been all along. I just didn't realise it.' She rattled off the number sequence from the blade. She had spent so long looking at it with Sam that she knew it as well as her own date of birth.

Franz also knew the number by heart. It had been with him throughout his career. The relief he felt that it would continue to be was clear across his face. Together they re-joined Elaine in the garden.

Xavier's story about the task and the ring bearers had already alerted Helen that the ring's role was to identify individuals. Clearly, the bank had come much later, so one of her predecessors must have thought it suitably symbolic, and secret, to use the ring as the identifier at the bank. Similarly, ascribing the blade's numbers to the account had created a secret code that would never be broken by guessing. It was clever, very clever and very simple. Perfect.

Sitting in the warm afternoon sun, Franz told her more about the trust. She was the beneficiary and could call on and direct funds as she saw fit. Helen suggested making no changes for the time being. St Bernard's would continue to receive the money. Franz noted her instructions, told her there would be papers to sign, things to inspect and check over. The bank's solicitors in Edinburgh would act as agent in the meantime and they would be in touch once things were ready. She could rely on the solicitors. They had dealt with matters for John and Archie and others before.

Franz had stressed that when the dust had settled and she was ready, it would be imperative for Helen to visit the bank in Switzerland. Essential. Of course, she wouldn't need to worry about the cost.

Finally, as Franz made ready to leave, Helen asked how much the trust was worth. Franz was coy as he hummed and hawed. After much qualifying about only having a modest amount of cash, cautioning over share prices fluctuating and property prices being difficult to fix at present, he muttered a number. Fifty-four million pounds Stirling, approximately.

The rest of the afternoon had vanished in a whirl. By the time Sam returned, Helen had scarcely started to absorb the scale of the trust fund. She was consumed alternately by glee and by guilt. There was a lot of thinking to do.

As the information had sunk in, Sam asked the question that had been hovering unframed in the corners of Helen's mind. If the parish's, no, if her trust fund was worth so much, how much would the actual Templars' treasure be worth? Enormous.

Chapter 32

MONDAY 1st JULY

Helen looked out from the study window. She could see Francis' parish minibus turning slowly into the driveway. She headed straight for the door, grabbing her overnight bag as she went. Sam followed, carrying her suitcase.

After the first relief at DCI Wallace's news of the killer's arrest, she had been overwhelmed with a desire just to go home. Not until the threat had been clearly removed did she realise just how much it had weighed on her. Then there was Herr Brenner's visit. On the one hand, such exciting news, on the other, just an extra layer of worry. Now she needed to unwind, spend time with her parents, catch up with family, see old friends, visit old haunts.

She had worried it might be seen as running away, abandoning her friends in Edinburgh; they would have none of it. She had to go. But as Elaine had stressed, she had to come back too. There was still a tussle to have with James Curry and they wanted her back for that. Back for good. She'd be back, no worries.

DCI Wallace had been happy to agree she could go away for a holiday on the understanding she would return when required by the investigation. The police were still holding the church as a crime scene, though Helen was relaxed about their searching - the dagger was not there any more.

With Grace's help, she had unearthed a cache of documents from a concealed compartment within the tunnel system. An initial inspection of the documents had revealed nothing that seemed relevant or might point them to the other daggers. But Sam had promised to start working through them in detail in her absence. Everyone was going to be busy while she was away and even as she hurried out of the manse, she could feel her friends exerting a pull; she knew it would not be a long trip.

A run of threat-free days and the warmth of summer had slowly raised everyone's spirits, everyone felt safer. Xavier's countrymen were gone. He had called them back to Sardinia once the man known as Innes had been apprehended. He had also reminded her of her promised visit. His door was open and he expected her soon.

The city council had acted remarkably quickly to promote security for the manse and the cemetery as a whole: sending in the stonemasons to block both the cemetery's pedestrian access gate from the main road and the private access gate into the cemetery from the manse's back garden. Everyone was pleased, but suspected it had been done more to enable the police to secure the environment than to give the congregation peace of mind.

• • •

Francis' minibus rolled into Edinburgh airport then forked off to the parking bays where it finally jerked to a halt. Everyone piled out. Helen, Sam, Grace supporting Elaine, and finally Francis, who paused to lock the minibus doors.

And then here they were, at the security check-in desk.

Grace squeezed up beside Helen and whispered theatrically. 'Next time I'm coming too, or you don't get to go.'

Helen laughed. 'You're on. It's a promise, right?'

'I'm holding you to that,' said Grace, giving her a hug and kiss, Helen reciprocated then stepped forward as the queue moved. Then her turn came. The group watched while Helen went through the check-in procedures.

After a few moments conversation, Helen opened her overnight bag and produced a small wooden carry case, opening it to show the check-in clerk a silver communion set: plate, cup and cross.

Helen explained the set was destined for her father's church at home. The clerk listened attentively and then made a phone call. Within moments, the security supervisor arrived and inspected the set carefully. She lifted the items out of the carry box in turn, inspected each one and then placed it on the counter. The set eventually formed a neat row beside the check-in clerk. The supervisor stood back from the counter, looked carefully at the set and then after a long and agonising moment she leant forward, placed her hand on the clerk's shoulder and whispered an instruction in his ear. The clerk listened intently and then began to type quickly on his keyboard.

Helen's stomach was knotted. Would it get through? The supervisor straightened up, took a further look at the communion set then smiled, admired the set and wished Helen a safe journey home. While unable to hear the words, Sam and the others were able to read the body language and everyone relaxed. They were going to get the dagger away, safe to a place where nobody would think to look. Helen relaxed, it would soon be out of sight, and hidden beyond anyone's reach, forever.

Turning to her friends, Helen smiled, signalling success, then she turned back to the counter. The security supervisor looked at Sam and the others. She smiled too; nice bunch, she thought.

Set high on the wall above the counter, a security camera's little red recording indicator glowed as the events below were captured. The camera caught the glistening high spots of reflected light as the polished plate, cup and cross all sat proudly on the counter. Framed behind them was Helen Johnson's smiling face, beyond her, just in the edge of the frame, were her friends. The stream of recorded images fired down the line into the airport's security drives.

Just for the record, a happy group of friends, an everyday airport *au revoir*.

The Temple Legacy

Thank you for reading *The Temple Legacy*. I do hope you enjoyed the story. If so, I would be most grateful if you would take a moment to give *The Temple Legacy* a rating and a sentence or two of review. Reader ratings are so important in supporting and enabling authors in today's digital reading world.

Thank you. D.C.

ABOUT D. C. MACEY

A first career saw Macey travelling around the globe for several years. It was an experience that provided a vivid insight into the exciting and confusing world we all share. In the process, it gave an introduction to the mad mix of beauty, kindness, cruelty and inequality that is the human experience everywhere.

There followed several years working in business, where it became apparent Macey's greatest commercial skill was the ability to convert tenners into fivers, effortlessly and unerringly. Unfortunately, it was a skill that ensured Macey had the unwelcome experience of encountering those darker aspects of life that lie beneath the veneer of our developed world. Thankfully, an experience restricted to just fleeting glimpses into the shadows where bad things lurk.

Eventually, life's turbulence, impending poverty and domestic tragedy demanded a change of course. As a result, the past decade or so has been spent lecturing, and a happy home and laughter have proven time and again to be the best protection against life's worries.

• • •

For more information:

contact@dcmacey.com

and visit:

www.dcmacey.com

BOOKS IN THE SERIES

The Temple Scroll

(The Temple - Book 2)

A lost treasure, an impenetrable puzzle and a psychopathic killer: a deadly combination.

The Temple Scroll is a rollercoaster ride of danger, mystery and murder. From New England to the islands of the Mediterranean, it follows the deadly hunt for the Templars' lost treasure.

Archaeology lecturer Sam Cameron and church minister Helen Johnson thought their old problems were done. They were wrong. Killers are set on finding the Templars' treasure and they believe Sam and Helen hold the key.

As the psychopathic Cassiter directs his team of killers towards their goal, the calm of summer vanishes in an explosive bout of blood and suffering.

Under pressure from every side, Sam and Helen must draw on all their instincts and professional skills to stay alive as they attempt to crack the puzzle that protects the Templars' treasure.

As the search for the Templar hoard moves inexorably to a conclusion, Sam and Helen must risk all in a frantic bid to save their friends, the treasure, and the priceless holy relics of the early Church. Now there is no mercy and no escape - there is only win or die.

The Temple Covenant

(The Temple - Book 3)

A quiet sabbatical spent visiting archaeological sites in the Great Rift Valley offers Helen Johnson and Sam Cameron the perfect opportunity to unwind and put the violent climax to their recent adventures behind them. But where they go trouble isn't far away. Disturbing alarm bells start to ring when Helen attracts the attentions of the mysterious Bishop Ignatius of the Ethiopian Orthodox Tewahedo Church. He is desperate to meet with her and will not take no for an answer.

Elsewhere, news breaks that senior British Intelligence Corps Colonel Bob Prentice is missing in Nairobi and security chiefs have cause for concern. Concern turns to panic when it's realised an operational prototype of the British Army's latest super-weapon has vanished too.

In a last gasp attempt to retrieve the situation the British Government turns to former Intelligence Corps officer Sam, hoping that his civilian status can keep him under the radar and his old skills might just be enough to turn the problem round.

Meanwhile, Helen is co-opted into a role that goes against her every belief - a role that her patriotism demands she fulfil even as she struggles to evade the determined attentions of Bishop Ignatius and his men.

Far from the cloudy skies of Edinburgh, a frightening and bloody hunt plays out beneath the burning sun of the East African bush. Racing against the clock, and with scant support, Sam and Helen must risk everything to resolve the challenge of the enigmatic Bishop Ignatius while fighting to preserve the West's place in a dangerous world.

The Temple Deliverance

(The Temple - Book 4)

Jolted out of their holiday season calm, Helen Johnson and Sam Cameron find they must play one last hand in a deadly game.

The final hunt is on to unpick an ancient code that hides the incredible nature of the Templars' greatest secret. From the depths of northern winter to the sun-kissed beaches of North Africa, Helen and Sam must hurry to piece together the final clues in a race against time to save themselves, their loyal friends and Christianity's greatest heritage.

Beset by danger, they must contend with the return of old foes who are hell bent on vengeance and determined to snatch the ultimate prize they have coveted for so long. As violence and death sweep across the continents, innocence is no protection; knowledge and grit are the only currencies of survival. Calling on trusted allies, Helen and Sam struggle against the odds, knowing that this time only one side can walk away.

Printed in Great Britain
by Amazon

16647911R00205